STOLEN INNOCENCE

Emberlyn Grace

Canoe Tree
Press

4697 Main Street
Manchester Center, VT 05255

Canoe Tree Press is a division of DartFrog Books

This book is dedicated to all sexual assault survivors.
You are not invisible or forgotten; your story and
your voice are powerful.

CHAPTER ONE

"It's okay, Dylan," I whispered to my son. "It's over now." His head was cradled against my shoulder as he cried, the sound breaking my heart into thousands of tiny pieces. I was doing my best to keep his eyes from seeing the gruesome scene surrounding us; and wished like hell I was able to do the same. I stroked his soft, fawn-colored hair to soothe him as the police and paramedics rushed about to do their respective jobs.

My eyes lifted from the bloody ground to meet the gentle gaze of Detective Nicholas Spencer, a man I had come to trust without question in the past seven years. He offered me a grim smile before reaching to help lift Dylan and me from the ground, his strong arms guiding us to the relative safety of his SUV. After I had climbed into the front seat with Dylan still firmly gripping my neck, I couldn't help but glance back at the bullet-riddled body one hundred yards away and wonder…how the hell did it come to this?

Seven Years Earlier…

"You need a lift?"

His voice had pulled me from the fog I had been in as I had stood by the front door of the library, trying desperately to avoid getting drenched by the rain. The window was cracked on his green Mustang, and he wore a smug smile on his face as he leaned across the passenger seat to talk to me. I had seen him around the library plenty; the joys of being a student worker there. Corey Foster was trouble on two legs…but damn if he wasn't sexy as hell and knew how to make a girl blush.

Being an undergrad while he was working toward his master's degree meant I found him intimidating. Add my social awkwardness and that my last boyfriend had been a complete ass together, and I was usually a stuttering fool when it came to Corey. But I had to admit, I really didn't feel like walking the ten minutes back to my dorm without an umbrella in the downpour or trying to wait for my roommate or another friend to come pick me up either.

I had glanced at my phone once more, wishing one of the guys had responded to say they could give me a ride, but so far, Corey was the only one offering. I'd sent a quick text to everyone saying I had found a ride and rushed down the stone steps of the library to his waiting car.

I slid into the seat and threw him a small, shy smile of gratitude before he pulled out from in front of the building. My clothes were clinging to my body, as was my hair, thanks to the rain, and I felt relieved I hadn't chosen to wear a white t-shirt that day. Corey seemed to have allowed his mind to venture to the same place, however.

"Maybe I should have left you in the rain a bit longer, Renee," he teased. "You could have taken first place at a wet t-shirt competition."

I rolled my eyes at his joke. Having been "blessed" with an ample bosom since puberty hit, I had been on the receiving end of jokes like these for years. They were nothing new, but I had hoped that college guys would be more mature than the high school idiots I had left behind. Typically, I didn't have to worry about Corey hitting on me too much; he usually opted for casual flirting. It seemed today he was bringing out the childish humor to help me lighten up since my mood clearly matched the dark clouds overhead.

"You're hilarious, Corey," I deadpanned, pulling my phone out of my pocket when it chirped.

Max was out of class now apparently, apologizing profusely that he hadn't been available to help and teasing me about getting a ride with Corey. No matter how many times I told him that there wasn't anything going on between the two of us, Max would just smile and shake his head. I really wished he would quit but I couldn't admit to him why I so desperately needed him to understand that simple fact.

Pulling the hood over my head to prepare to dash into my building, I turned to face my driver. "Thanks for giving me a ride."

"Not a problem," he answered easily. "Hey, before you go," he said, tugging on my sleeve, "how about we grab dinner tonight?"

I know my eyes widened in shock; I had felt it happen. I also knew I had a major test to finish studying for, so dinner was going to be microwave noodles in my room.

"I wish I could, but I can't tonight. I've got to cram for my biology midterm."

He shrugged his broad shoulders. "Another time then."

I smiled and nodded, grabbing my backpack and running to the door of my dormitory, quickly swiping my card to gain access. I waved as he drove off, furrowing my brow as I thought of his strange request, never knowing it was only the beginning.

At the time, I hadn't noticed the odd look in his brown eyes, or the way he raked his fingers through his light brown hair and licked his lips. Subconsciously, sure. Did I understand what those things meant for me? Not a chance in hell. If I had, maybe I would have been more cautious, more aware of the way he looked at me. It was the same way a lion eyes a gazelle…as prey.

CHAPTER TWO

"Please, Ren?" my roommate Miranda—Mira, for short—whined as she flopped on my bed. Her bright red curls bounced around her face, her hazel eyes doing their best puppy-dog impression as she pleaded with me to join her at some lame campus event.

I had calmly met her gaze, my finger keeping my place in my textbook as I set my mouth in a firm line. Mira knew I hated these types of events. I was the proverbial antisocial nobody who shied away from anything that even remotely resembled a party. The only reason she was even hounding me to go was we both had the night off from the library and it was a Friday.

"I think Max is going to be there, and so is Nick," she continued, like I hadn't been ignoring her request. "Who knows, maybe Corey will show up too!"

I blushed, thinking about the last interaction I had with Corey. After the car ride to save me from the rain, he had stopped by the library on one of my shifts. Since it was a quiet night, he had leaned over the counter to talk with me for longer than he probably should have, but I was bored and didn't stop him. Corey had a way of making an invisible girl feel like she was worth a million dollars. He also had a way of making her feel like a bug under a microscope…or a puzzle he needed to solve. Neither was very comforting.

Max and Nick however, those two were amazing. Only a year ahead of Mira and me, they were friendly, funny, sinfully attractive men who never flaunted that fact. They knew how to have a good time and make sure everyone else did too. Truth be told, I'd been enamored by them.

Nicholas Spencer was the more outspoken of the two. He was charming, flirty, and rocked his leather jacket and jeans. His dark blue eyes were enough to captivate anyone's attention and his laugh—good God his laugh—it rumbled through his chest and would reverberate through my own. He was also more of a ladies' man, although he never set out to be one. The girls just naturally flocked to his good looks.

Maxwell Harris was quieter, humbler, and definitely the sweeter of the two. I could sit and talk with Max for hours about everything and nothing. Those green eyes of his—every time he glanced my way I would melt. And of course, knowing that he was this amazing guy and was quickly becoming my best friend…Max was the guy Mira happened to like. Fuck my life.

"Earth to Renee!" Mira called, waving her hand in front of my face to snap me from my introspection.

I startled, causing my brown hair to cascade forward along my cheekbones. Frowning, I brushed my hair back behind my ears again, rolling my eyes at Mira's theatrics.

"Mira, I really just wanted to get ahead on my reading tonight," I told her, motioning to the book in my lap.

She let out a snicker before plucking the book from my hands.

"Hey!"

"Ren, you and I both know you are already passing your class and don't need to study for this," she chided. "Put the books down for one night and come hang out with me. Please."

I sighed before nodding miserably. She, of course, squealed like a little girl and jumped to start getting ready. I slowly dragged myself over to my closet to pick something other than my yoga pants and tank top, knowing she'd insist I change.

"Wear something hot, please," she called from her side of the room.

"What classifies as hot?" I asked, hands on my hips in frustration.

Mira and I were polar opposites. She was loud, I'm soft-spoken. She was flamboyant, I'm reserved. She was like fire and I'm ice. How the hell we ended up as roommates and friends is still something of a mystery to me.

She poked her head out of the bathroom where she was busy applying a heavy layer of eyeshadow. "Try on those cute jeans with the stitching on the pockets and your red and black tank top. Maybe throw on your leather jacket and boots with it. Then get your ass in here and I'll do your makeup."

I rolled my eyes. I was perfectly capable of doing my own damn makeup and not looking like a two-cent whore. I liked it natural-looking, not caked on my face. Mira thought otherwise, but I didn't care. I knew Max hated when girls wore tons of makeup; an opinion we shared. I secretly wanted to impress him tonight but knew I could never tell Mira the truth about that.

I glanced at my reflection and gave myself a small shake. I had to admit, the red tank top looked really good on me with the jeans, even if the plunging V-neck of the shirt made me a little uncomfortable. I sashayed into the bathroom to freshen up my eyeliner and lipstick, Mira giving me a funny look when I swatted her hands away from my makeup bag.

"I'm doing my own makeup, thank you very much, Miranda," I informed her. I only ever called her by her full name when I was being serious, so she knew I meant business. "You can give me input on what the hell to do with my hair, okay?"

Luckily for me, I had worn my hair in a braid all day before coming back to crash at the dorm. Cocking her head to the side, she grinned. "Leave it down, Ren. You've got that whole 'beach-waves' look going for you tonight."

Looking in the mirror, I realized she was right. But I wasn't prepared for what she said next.

"Wouldn't surprise me at all if Corey asks you if you want to have sex on the beach tonight."

Corey…right…because Mira was interested in Max. I plastered a smile on my face and half nodded at her, rushing out of our little bathroom to grab my jacket, phone, and keys. The last thing I needed that night was her becoming suspicious I had feelings for him when she was bound and determined to set me up with Corey and keep Max for herself. With a heavy heart, I let Mira lead me to the Student Center, unaware of how the night would progress.

CHAPTER THREE

"Hey, you made it!" Max said warmly, pulling me into a side hug. I was careful to keep my hands to myself, lest Mira get the wrong—albeit right—impression. Nick was leaning against the counter beside him, a couple girls standing there fawning over him. His easy smile and warm voice were clearly enchanting them, but I saw the spark of mischief in his eyes when he saw me. He was up to no good; I could tell I was going to be in for a night of teasing.

"Yeah, can you believe I had to drag this one away from a textbook?" Mira laughed, taking the soda Max handed her. Both of them were easily a foot taller than tiny little me, so they had to look down at me when they talked.

Max shyly smiled at me over her comment; he was just as much of a bookworm as I was. Mira was craning her neck to look around at the crowd as Max and I covertly made eyes at one another. I was just going to take a sip of my own drink when she nudged me with her elbow, causing me to choke.

"Told ya he would come," she teased, pointing across the room where Corey stood amongst his fellow grad student friends. Mira turned to Max and playfully ran her hand down his arm. "Max, tell Ren she looks great and should go talk to Corey. She's being a wuss when it comes to him."

By now, Nick had tuned into our conversation. I saw the quick look he and Max shared, probably best interpreted as a "what the fuck" look.

I didn't have to go anywhere though; Corey had noticed our little group and was sauntering in our direction. I felt my heart rate speed up and the bottom of my stomach fall out as I heard him approach.

Suddenly, I was engulfed by two muscular arms from behind, hugging me tightly. I could smell his spicy aftershave and the faint scent of beer on his breath. I bit my bottom lip and glanced apologetically at Max, who was looking as uncomfortable as I felt. Mira was still talking to him, and being the sweetheart that he was, he turned his attention to her, but his eyes kept darting my way every few moments.

"Look at you," Corey crooned, as he spun me around in his arms. "Looking good there, Miss Innocence."

Miss Innocence. It had started as a joke one night at the library because I was inexperienced in a lot of ways. I had walked in on a couple getting hot and heavy in the stacks, and when I had rushed away from the scene, I had run straight into Corey. He had taken one look at my flushed face and figured out the rest. The nickname came from that unfortunate event and he never let me live it down.

"Hi, Corey," I managed quietly.

His dark eyes were traveling up and down my body repeatedly, focusing on parts that I wished they wouldn't. I could feel myself squirm beneath his gaze; and while part of me was glad he was attracted to my body, the other part wanted to remind him where my eyes were. This had been the primary reason I had dumped my last boyfriend; he wanted sex and I wasn't ready.

"Want a drink?" he asked, jerking his head toward the table he'd just left.

"I have one," I answered. "Thanks."

"You have a soda, Ren. I can get you something else if you want," he urged.

I could feel Nick and Max bristling behind me. And then I heard Mira's whining voice, begging Max to go play a game of pool with her. Before he could protest, she was pulling him down the hall to the games room, intent on getting her way. Thankfully, Nick was still there, but the crowd of horny college girls was growing thicker by the minute.

"Really, Corey," I tried again, "I'm fine."

This time, I saw the brief flicker of anger in his eyes. I didn't register it as being dangerous toward me, just that he had had a couple of drinks and was annoyed. God, how wrong I was. Before I could even tell him to calm down, he flashed me a bright smile and nodded.

"Sure thing." He slung his arm over my shoulder and started to lead me away from Nick. "How about we go hang out over here and talk then?"

We were in a crowded place, I was still in the same room as one of my friends…surely, I was safe to sit on a couch and talk, right? I let Corey pull me onto his lap, something I was not at all pleased over, but his strong arms had me caged. His friends were there, talking, laughing, drinking. For the rest of the night, he didn't have a single drink, just intently watched as I slowly sipped my Coke.

I lost all concept of the passage of time. Corey had made it nearly impossible for me to get to my phone or to look around for Mira, Max, or Nick. My drink was gone, I was getting tired, and really wanting to head back to the dorms when I felt a presence beside the couch.

"Well…doesn't this look cozy," Mira snickered.

Max and Nick were waiting by the doors, a girl hanging off Nick's neck like an albatross. I disengaged myself from Corey's arms and pulled on the bottom of my shirt. Biting the corner of my lower lip, I risked a glance at Max, only to see him staring right back at me, arms crossed firmly across his chest and a worried expression on his face.

"I'm heading out and the guys were going to make sure I made it back," Mira continued. "Are you coming with us, or do you want to stay a bit longer?" she asked smugly.

"I'll come with you," I said, covering a yawn. "See you, Corey."

"Night, Ren," he answered, never taking his eyes off my face.

I felt like I practically ran to catch up with Max, with Mira chuckling behind me. Once he and I stepped out the door and were faced away from her, he leaned down to quietly ask, "Are you okay?"

I was glad it was dark so he couldn't see the blush painting my cheeks scarlet. The feeling of his breath feathering on my cheek when he asked had started a raging inferno inside of me, making me feel like a melted puddle of wax. I rubbed the back of my neck shyly. "Yeah, I'm fine."

He nodded and left it, but I could tell he wasn't quite sure he believed it. Truth be told, I wasn't sure I believed it myself.

CHAPTER FOUR

Acouple of weeks later, I was just collapsing on my bed after a grueling day of classes, a quick early dinner at the dining hall, and then work when my phone began ringing. Mira was working, so I knew it wasn't her. Secretly, I had hoped it was Max calling to check in on me. I'd felt my pulse quicken when Corey's name flashed on my screen.

"Hey," I answered, closing my eyes as my head found my pillow once more.

His chuckle rumbled through the phone. "You sound half-asleep there, Ren," he teased. "Don't tell me you were taking a nap at seven o'clock."

"I was thinking about it."

"Well, how about instead of a nap you meet me at my place, and we can go grab a pizza?"

I was sitting up by this point. I knew for a fact I had twenty bucks in my checking account and my truck was running on fumes. Corey didn't live that far from me, but it would still make things difficult for me to drive to his apartment and back again, plus him wanting me to eat out when I didn't get paid for another three days. I quietly groaned and rubbed my temples.

"Corey, I actually already ate at the dining hall—" I started.

"Then, you can just keep me company and we can talk. I feel like I haven't seen you in weeks," he pressed. "It'll be fun; I promise."

I sighed. "Um…what if you picked me up from the dorms?"

"I just got out of the shower, Ren, so unless you want me to come over there in a towel, that's not going to happen." He paused, and I could feel the tension radiating through the phone. "Just drive over here, that'll give me time to get dressed, I'll drive us over to dinner, and then you can leave from mine after we're done, okay?"

I felt trapped. It felt like he wasn't going to let me say no, despite my protests. And up to that point, I had felt relatively safe with Corey. I figured I could handle one lousy "dinner date." Sliding off my bed, I pulled my shoes on and grabbed my purse.

"Sure, Corey, I'll see you in ten," I begrudgingly told him, hanging up as I headed out the door.

When he opened the door those ten minutes later, I was anxiously shifting from one foot to the other and wondering what the hell I was doing. And truthfully? I had been just about ready to turn and run back to my truck before he answered, a smirk tugging at the corners of his mouth, like he knew he had me right where he wanted me.

He didn't even greet me, just nodded his head for me to follow him inside his apartment so he could pull on his shoes and grab his wallet. I stood around like an idiot while I waited, taking in the surprisingly spotless living room, everything almost fastidiously in place. I guess I was expecting his "bachelor pad" to be a little more lived in than it appeared, because he seemed amused by my expression.

"I do know how to clean, Ren," he teased, making my cheeks burn in embarrassment. He drew closer to tower over me, that same damn smirk still on his face. He brushed a loose strand of hair behind my ear and leaned down to whisper huskily, "I know how to do other things, too, so you know."

I gulped as he placed a large hand on the small of my back and steered me back to the door I had literally just walked through. Biting on my lower lip, I watched nervously as he locked his front door before heading to his Mustang. He unlocked the doors and we both slid inside, his engine roaring to life when he turned the ignition. Corey wasted no time gunning the car and speeding to the little pizza joint a few blocks from the campus.

As we'd sat in the dimly lit, greasy booth of the restaurant, I couldn't help but wonder again what I was doing. I was sipping slowly on a Coke; Corey was wolfing down his pizza and talking a mile a minute. It was practically a one-sided conversation since he didn't really need responses from me. And I was bored out of my fucking mind.

I was wishing I had found the backbone to turn him down and stay home. Even being at work would have been better than this awkward as hell pseudo-date. As I watched Corey start on his next slice of pizza, I found myself comparing him to Max. The green-eyed guy who would have never made me drive to him, and who would have been engaging me in conversation instead of simply talking at me. And more importantly, Max would have accepted it when I said I wanted to stay in my damn room for the night.

"I'm about done here; you?" I heard him ask.

I eyed him, a little dumbfounded. All I had was a drink, of course I was fucking done, as I had been for nearly an hour. But I kept my mouth shut and simply nodded, figuring it would be best to just stay on his good side and get home. Especially with the headache I could feel coming.

The drive back to his apartment was tense, and I felt nauseated the closer we got to his door. As soon as the engine died, he turned to me, his dark eyes glittering in the dim light, setting me even more on edge. His hand brushed the hair away from the back of my neck and then his thumb trailed down to my collarbone. It was becoming clearer what Corey wanted from me, but I had no intentions of giving it to him—that night, or any other.

"How about you come in for a while?" he whispered, leaning closer.

I shivered; it was nearly triple digits temperature-wise, and I shivered. Not from being cold, but from fear. Fear at realizing no one knew where I was; that Corey was so much stronger than me; that if he really wanted to, there wasn't a damn thing stopping him from taking exactly what he wanted. I had to get out of there, and I had to do it immediately.

"Maybe another time, Corey," I told him, rubbing the back of my neck, displacing his hand. "I feel a migraine starting and need to get back to take my meds for it. This was fun though. Thanks!"

I scrambled to get out of his car and hopped into my truck before he could stop me. Throwing it into drive, I slammed on the gas pedal and peeled away, never looking back. It wasn't until I reached my dorm and sat on the edge of my bed did I realize…I was still quaking with fear.

CHAPTER FIVE

"**D**amn him to hell!" Mira yelled as she stormed into our room. I sat up on my bed in a panic, arching a brow at her furious tone. "Who are you damning to hell and why?" I'd asked, setting my book aside.

Her hazel eyes burned like fiery coals as she glared at me, her red curls tamed into a fluffy ponytail that seemed to add to her wild look. "Maxwell fucking Harris, that's who, and because he turned me down!"

My nervous habit of biting my lower lip got the best of me and I nearly tasted blood from sinking my teeth in so deep as I met her gaze. Mira had mentioned she planned to ask Max out, but knowing him as I did, I knew he wouldn't agree. But there was no telling her that—not and keep her unaware of my own feelings for him.

"I'm sorry, Mira," I told her softly. And I was, truly, because no one likes being shot down when asking their crush out for a date. "Want me to roast him for you?"

Rolling her eyes, she tugged at the hair band keeping her curls at bay to release them in a red shower of tresses around her shoulders. She sighed before shrugging. "I guess if you want to, go for it. I'm going to go plug in my headphones and drown my sorrows in music and wish like hell I had a bottle of whiskey to drink."

Not waiting for a reply, she had stomped to her side of the room, leaving me alone with my thoughts. I pushed my hair behind my ears and quickly sat at my desk, turning my laptop on as I went, intent on finding Max online. Lucky for me, the guy practically lived on his computer, so always had his messenger app open. I clicked the button to start a conversation with him, feeling anxiousness fluttering in my stomach like hundreds of butterflies.

> renbabe327: Well…if your goal was to royally piss Mira off… congrats! You've just won first place in the idiot competition!

> maxthestud: Hello to you, too, Ren. For the record, wasn't trying to piss her off…just wasn't interested in dating her.

> renbabe327: *Sigh* Max…don't tell her I said this, but I knew that already. But for the love of all that's holy! Could you not have gone on one fucking date with her and then told her it wasn't going to work out between the two of you?

> maxthestud: That's going to be a hard pass from me. It would be too much like playing with her emotions to do something like that, and you know I'm not that type of guy.

And he really wasn't—he was right, I did know that. He was always acting like a gentleman, and I loved that about him. Unfortunately for both of us, that trait had put my roommate in the nastiest mood I had ever seen her in.

> renbabe327: Okay…fair enough. But still…she's in such a foul mood. Kill me now before it gets worse?

> maxthestud: Now why on earth would I want to kill one of my favorite people? I'll talk to her tomorrow and apologize if you think that will make any difference, okay?

> renbabe327: Thank you, Max. I think she would like that very much.

> maxthestud: Anytime, Miss Westhaven, anytime. So…?

renbabe327: What do you want?

maxthestud: How's the infamous Corey Foster? Is he still trying to get you to go out with him?

My heart dropped into my stomach at his words. I had been trying desperately to forget about Corey after the incident at the pizzeria and later at his apartment. I wanted so badly to confide in Max about what had happened that night, but the truth was, nothing of significance happened. I had managed to get out of there before it became too much of a dangerous situation. I assumed that following that rejection, Corey would want nothing more to do with me, and so far, I had been correct.

maxthestud: Ren? You still there?

renbabe327: Oh…yeah, sorry. Um, haven't talked to Corey in a few weeks actually. Just been really busy with homework and then work, you know?

maxthestud: Ah, well, that makes sense, I guess. I saw him in the hall a few weeks ago…he seemed a little…off?

renbabe327: Don't know what to tell you, Max. But listen…I'm really not interested in dating Corey, so please…drop it.

maxthestud: Uh, sure, sorry. Thought you were into him. Hmmm…anyone else you are interested in dating?

I had felt my cheeks begin to heat as I reread his last sentence. I was hoping he was referring to himself, but with the way my college experience was going, I was going to need him to say it explicitly.

renbabe327: Maybe…but that's all you're getting out of me tonight!

maxthestud: And here I thought we were friends, Renee. Gosh, won't even tell me who you want to date…such a shame. Especially if I know them and can help…hint hint.

renbabe327: Don't you have to go bother Nick now? I'm sure he's getting bored of studying his criminal justice books.

maxthestud: So now you're trying to get rid of me. I see how it is. You start this conversation to yell at me for rejecting Mira, then refuse to tell me who you like, and now you want me to leave and hang out with Nick. Make up your mind, tiny crazy woman!

I grinned at his comment. After a few more moments of playful banter, we signed off and I headed for bed. As my eyes stared sightlessly at the ceiling above me, my mind couldn't help but goad me with a single thought: now that Max had formally rejected Mira and I had rejected Corey, maybe—just maybe—Max and I could have a chance.

CHAPTER SIX

"That's the last of it," Max announced, setting down my final box in the new apartment Mira and I would be sharing just off-campus. She would be moving in from the dorms after she completed her summer school courses while I lived here alone during those two months. Nick and Mira would be coming over tomorrow evening for all four of us to hang out at the apartment pool together. Max had volunteered to help me move my things in, and in return, I had promised to cook him dinner. I struggled to keep things platonic between us, especially under such intimate settings as a private dinner, but so far, neither one of us had made a move on the other.

Max came and plopped down on the couch beside me to rest for a few minutes, both of us tired from moving things all day, even though our friend Roy from our Psych class had seen us by the mailboxes and offered to help as well. I had been so grateful for Max's help and couldn't help but chuckle to myself when I thought again of how he had responded to my request.

"Hey Max," I had said in a sing-song voice when he answered the phone.
"Uh-oh, that voice means trouble," he teased. "What do you need, Ren?"
"Well, you know how Mira and I are moving into that apartment?"
"Yeah?"

"I was wondering if you would be willing to come help me move some boxes and a little furniture into it in exchange for me making you dinner," I asked nervously.

"I don't mind helping you move anything," he started, "but did I miss something where I hit my head and forgot I had some amazing girlfriend who cooks for me? Because I have to admit, that sounds awesome!"

"Having amnesia sounds awesome?" I laughed.

His husky laugh rumbled through the phone. "No, I meant the meal sounded amazing. And if you're the one cooking it, the company should be pretty great too. Of course, this is assuming you can actually cook."

"Rest assured, Max, I can cook. I was thinking of chicken stir-fry."

"Sounds fantastic. Just tell me when you need me, and I'll be there."

"You're my hero!" I cheered. "Thanks, Max!"

I'd angled my body so I could see him better. I was in a pair of my favorite heather grey yoga pants and a baby blue tank top, my brown hair pulled away from my face by a clip. Max was looking rugged in his tight denim jeans and short-sleeved, green plaid button-up shirt that matched his eyes. He caught me staring at him and grinned. He was all lean muscle, and in seriously great shape. I definitely needed to think about hitting the gym with him and Nick sometime.

"I can't thank you enough for all your help today, Max," I told him sincerely, melting inside as I looked into his gorgeous green eyes. Blue had always been my favorite color, but if it were to ever be replaced it would be with the same green as Max Harris's eyes.

"Don't mention it, Renee," he assured me. "But I will admit I'm getting kind of hungry. Want me to help you make dinner?"

"You really don't have to help—"

He held up his hands to silence me, a smirk tugging on the corner of his mouth. "Have to help, no. Offering and willing to help, absolutely." He threw me a mischievous wink. "Besides, if I help you, we could maybe eat sooner."

I couldn't help but laugh at his logic, so we both hoisted our tired asses off the brown couch and walked over to the kitchen. Thankfully, grocery shopping was one of the things I did earlier in the day, so I had all my ingredients. Before long, Max and I were sitting at the island table, happily eating the stir-fry and talking about everything and nothing.

A feeling that I didn't want to acknowledge, but also didn't want to dismiss, was blossoming in my heart. I could tell that I was falling hopelessly and helplessly for Max. My problem was that I didn't know how he felt about me. Was I permanently in the friendzone? Or was there a chance for us to be something more?

We had literally just finished eating and were putting away the leftovers when my phone rang, signaling someone was at the gate calling to be admitted to the building. I shared an uneasy look with Max, confused as to who would be dropping by unannounced on my first night in the apartment. Answering, I discovered—much to my shock and dismay— that Mira had decided to randomly stop in.

The moment she walked into the apartment and saw Max helping me load the dishwasher with our plates and the pan I used to cook our dinner in, her mouth set in a thin line and her eyes narrowed to slits. At that moment, if I were to pick an animal to describe her, she would have been a cobra waiting to strike.

"So, what's going on here?" she asked, not even trying to keep the venom out of her voice.

"I promised Max I would feed him in exchange for him helping me move in," I replied.

The last thing I wanted was to get drawn into a game of tug-of-war between them. Max had apologized weeks ago and Mira had supposedly accepted said apology. The dinner we had just enjoyed had definitely been between friends only, so she had no cause to be upset. But Mira was livid.

Unfortunately for all of us, she kept that fact to herself, leading us to believe everything was fine. I wish I could say I was paying attention to the way she watched us or the tone she used, but I didn't. If I had, I would have realized it was merely the calm before the storm. A storm that would destroy so many lives.

CHAPTER SEVEN

My apartment was miserably hot in the West Texas heat since the builders had somehow managed to put a nail through a line to my air conditioner, causing the freon to leak. I'd tossed and turned in my bed, desperate for relief, not just from the sticky temperature in my room, but from the torturous thoughts running through my mind.

Being the overly analytical personality that I was, my lame self couldn't stop thinking about every conversation, every friendly hug, every tiny little gesture Max and I had ever shared. It was slowly driving me insane. If I had been in a field surrounded by daisies, they all would have had their petals plucked, with me being childish and saying, "he loves me, he loves me not," as each silken part fell to the ground.

I would have asked Nick for his opinion if I thought he wouldn't tease me for the rest of my life. Plus, he was at some training camp for prospective future law enforcement officers. Since his dad was a lawyer, he was torn between going into practicing law or being a cop. Max—being the good friend he was—had pushed him to sign up for the camp to see what his options were.

Annoyed, I'd thrown off my sheets and paced in my room, the moonlight seeping through my sheer blue curtains. The brand-new carpet was plush beneath my feet and sent momentary shivers up my spine. I knew at that rate I wouldn't be falling asleep anytime soon—just like I hadn't for the past three nights—and flipped on my bedroom light to pull out a book.

I'd frowned at my large collection of books, neatly organized on the shelves, as I attempted to decide what to read. *Screw it*, I finally thought, pulling a romance novel from the shelf. Curling up on my bed again, I lost myself in the pages of lust and heady scenes of romantic gestures and wished like hell I was the female on the receiving end of them.

While I was still a virgin, I had done enough web-browsing to know how to take care of my own needs. But I was starting to feel like my time of being an innocent girl was coming to an end. I had always planned on waiting to have sex until I was married, but admittedly, there were plenty of nights I would wake up still breathing heavily from the less-than-innocent actions Max and I were engaging in under the sheets in my dreams. Moments like those made me blush an unearthly shade of red and be grateful for the darkness of my room.

I paused my reading to think again about Max…the longing gripping my heart as I tortured myself for answers I couldn't give. Ever since the night I had run out on Corey, he had been avoiding me like the plague, which was fine by me. Nick had been casually dating some blonde bombshell, but none of us really saw it going anywhere long-term, so my fascination with him had dissipated. But Max—he still commanded my every thought, waking or otherwise.

Closing my eyes, I felt a few hot tears stream down my cheeks. I was miserable. This sense of not knowing what I meant to him, whether the flirting was intentional or just something he did to be cute, the piercing agony I could literally feel every time he walked away…all because I knew I had started falling in love with him. And I didn't know whether or not he gave a damn about me being in his life.

I tossed aside my book and buried my face in my hands as I cried. Eventually I fell asleep, slumped over on my bed, tears streaked down my face and soaking my pillow. When my alarm went off for class, I was dead to the world with so little sleep. I glowered at the bright sunshine streaming through my windows, seeming so cheery and oblivious to my heartache.

Getting through the day was pure hell. I was moving like I had been super-glued to the pavement. Eventually, I made it back home, after nearly falling asleep in every one of my four classes. I kicked off my shoes and sank down on my couch, still faintly smelling Max's cologne when I shifted on the cushions. As the scent hit my nose, the tears started anew.

Just as I was starting to get to the ugly-cry phase, my phone started ringing. I quickly wiped my eyes with the back of my hand and answered as best as I could.

"Hello?"

"Ren? Are you okay? You sound like you've been crying," Max's concerned voice came through the phone.

Shit, I thought. "Um…it's just been a long day, Max. And I haven't been sleeping well so I'm kind of tired."

He paused, and I could tell he was trying to tear apart my answer. I heard his keys jangle and then a door close. "Okay, I'm coming over," he informed me.

"You don't have to do that—" I protested.

"Like hell, I don't! Renee, you're clearly upset about something, so I'm going to come over, we'll eat, and then I want to take you somewhere, okay?"

I bit my lip. I hadn't even answered him before I heard his truck rumble to life. Chuckling, I replied, "I don't guess I have much say in this, huh?"

"Nope, you don't," he teased. "I'll see you in twenty minutes."

"Thanks, Max."

Hanging up, I hurried to set my makeup to rights. The last thing I needed was Max seeing my mascara dripping down my cheeks. I had just finished freshening myself up when he rang to be buzzed into the building. A few minutes later, his sure knock sounded on my door.

Opening it, I found him leaning against the frame, his signature smirk tugging at his mouth and a gentle expression in those gorgeous green eyes. He walked through my door and pulled me into a tight hug, letting the door close behind us as he stroked my hair. The soothing motion of his hand was enough to almost make me start bawling all over again, until he lifted my chin with his long fingers.

"None of that now, Ren," he whispered, looking deep into my tear-filled eyes. "Change of plans. We'll grab food on the way, but let's get out of here, okay?"

Smiling like an idiot, I nodded my head and let him lead me out into the night, intent on allowing him to chase away all my tears and insecurities.

CHAPTER EIGHT

"I can't get over how beautiful it is out here!" I sighed in contentment. Max had driven us out to his family's ranch and parked his red Dodge truck beside a tree, pulling a blanket from the backseat to spread in the bed. Grinning, he'd hauled me up beside him and snuggled me in his arms as we watched the stars overhead. Between the luminescent diamonds overhead and the intoxicating cologne of the man holding me close to his chest, I was in heaven.

He chuckled and I felt his lips brush against my temple for the briefest of moments. I was thanking each and every one of the stars above that they weren't brighter in that instant, so that Max wouldn't know how flushed my face became at that slight contact. I was doing my very best to not squirm since I was laying so close to him, but with his body so close to mine, it was proving difficult.

"You okay there?"

"Yeah," I answered, far more breathlessly than I anticipated. "Thank you for this, Max."

"You're very welcome, Ren." He was silent for a couple of minutes, just watching the night sky with me. "Now, do you want to tell me why you were really crying before I called you?"

I gulped. *How the hell did he know me so well,* I couldn't help but wonder.

"Did Corey do something to you?"

My body stiffened in his arms. Suddenly, he was leaning over me, his hand gently caressing the side of my face as he watched me. Despite the dark, I could see the concern plainly written in his eyes.

"Renee…please tell me he didn't do anything to you," he whispered.

"It's not about Corey," I whispered back.

Max sighed in relief, but then his head snapped up again. "If not him, then did someone else—"

"Max…" I said, forcing a soft smile on my face. "It had absolutely nothing to do with a guy hurting me, okay?"

He nodded, clearly pleased with my answer. His body relaxed onto the bed of the truck once more and he pulled me closer. I lay there, my head resting against his chest, just listening to the steady beating of his heart and the chirping of the crickets. It was a blessedly beautiful and peaceful night. The kind of night I wish I could have frozen, capturing it in a bottle to relive it whenever I wanted.

We talked for a few hours about our summer classes and our jobs, and he finally realized we should be heading back into town. I scooted to the end of the tailgate, where he gripped my waist to help me hop down from his truck. When my feet landed on the ground, his hands didn't immediately release me though.

One of his arms snaked around my back while the other found my right hand and without warning, he began dancing with me under the stars to absolutely no music. I giggled, but I was loving this romantic side of him.

"Typically, there's music for activities like this," I teased, my arms languidly clasping around his neck.

He smirked and began humming a Mark Wills song softly in my ear as we danced. Soon enough, the song ended with him bowing and saying, "Milady." I laughed as he opened my door and climbed inside. Little things like this were what made me fall for Max Harris without a second thought. And him insisting on walking me to my door when we arrived at my building, only added fuel to that fire.

"Thanks for tonight, Max," I told him, setting down my purse on the table. I turned to find his eyes trained on my face. "I really needed those few peaceful hours."

His hand reached out to brush my hair behind my ear as he smiled. "You are more than welcome, Ren. I'm glad I was able to cheer you up, although I still wish you would tell me what was bothering you."

I swallowed hard and walked away, sinking into one of the easy chairs in the living room while nibbling on my lower lip. I closed my eyes, but I could hear him coming closer, until he knelt before me.

"Although, I think I may already know…" he whispered huskily.

I couldn't look at him. I knew if I did, I would start crying or not be able to speak. "I've just had a question on my mind lately that I don't know the answer to, and it's been driving me insane," I quietly admit.

His hand reached up to cup my cheek, his thumb stroking my cheekbone with the gentlest of caresses. "You'll never get your answer though if you don't ask, Ren."

Sighing, I nervously opened my eyes and licked my lips. "Okay…I guess I've been wondering a lot about you and me lately." He smiled in encouragement and nodded. "Max, what are we?"

His other hand lost itself in my hair as he held my face, wiping away the stray tears that fell from my eyes. "Honestly, I don't know," he began, never breaking eye contact. "But I do know that I want to be more than your friend."

Fireworks seemed to be exploding in my heart when he answered me, and I found myself launching into his arms. He laughed and hugged me tight, stroking my hair. We sat like that for several minutes, just lost in the feeling of being that close to one another.

"I tell you what, Ren, how about we have our first date on Friday?"

"Really?"

"Absolutely," Max chuckled. "Unfortunately, I have to get going tonight though."

I pouted, gaining more laughter from him and another hug. "I'll see you tomorrow…girlfriend."

Girlfriend, I thought, watching him walk out my door. *I could get used to that.*

CHAPTER NINE

Iwoke up the next morning in a state of euphoria. For the first time in over a week I had actually slept through the night, without tossing and turning, worrying about whether or not Max and I could potentially be a couple. My cheeks were already beginning to hurt from smiling so broadly and the day had barely just begun—not that I cared one iota. My phone chirped on the nightstand, signaling the arrival of a text message, and my eyes lit with excitement when I saw Max's name on my screen.

> Morning, Sweetheart. Have a great day and I'll stop by and see
> you at work this afternoon. XO

I fell back onto my bed and shrieked with glee—until I saw I had another message. Mira had messaged me at the same time, wanting to know if we were still grabbing lunch together today. *Oh hell,* I thought. *How am I going to explain to her that Max and I are dating now?* My blissfulness seemed to implode as the thought hit me full force. I knew I couldn't keep this from her, I didn't want to hurt her, but I also didn't want to deny myself the chance to be happy.

Checking the time, I knew Max's class would be starting any minute, but sent him a quick affirmative reply back, mentioning I needed to talk to him about something later. Hurrying, I readied myself for my own classes, and rushed out the door with my backpack bouncing against my back.

I met Mira outside our class, noticing instantly the dark scowl she was wearing.

"Can't be bothered to reply to my texts?" she snapped.

Gulping, I sank into my seat beside her. "I was running late this morning, Mira. Sorry," I told her sheepishly. I pulled my notebook and pen from my bag as she eyed me with suspicion. "Lunch sounds great today though."

"Why are we talking about lunch at nine in the fucking morning?" came the sarcastic voice of our friend, Erin, as she dropped into her seat next to Mira. Wes was right beside her, practically attached at the hip, his longish dirty blonde hair falling rakishly into his blue eyes. Erin tossed her black ponytail over her shoulder and raised a brow, her chocolate brown eyes waiting for an answer.

"Ren and I are grabbing lunch at the hall later," Mira informed her. "Are you two joining us this time?"

Erin and Wes exchanged looks and shrugged. "Sure, why not," Wes answered for them both. Our conversation was cut short by the arrival of our professor, a stocky man with a long white handlebar mustache and dim grey eyes who loved to drone on and on about the reproductive cycles of cows and other farm animals.

Two hours later, class dismissed and the four of us headed to the dining hall to grab lunch. Despite the heat, we decided we would take our food outside, stealing one of the last tables under the shade of the awning. I had just taken a bite from my chicken sandwich when two of my other friends strolled by to say hello.

"Hey Munchkin," Eric teased, his country accent strong as he leaned down to hug me. He was like my big brother and loved to remind me I was a shrimp compared to his tall self.

"Hi Eric," I greeted. "Jen, I haven't seen you in weeks! Where have you been?" I asked another of our friends as she stole one of my fries.

"Had to run home to visit the folks," she said with a shrug. "I've got to get to class now, but give me a call this week, okay?"

I smiled easily at her. Jen had the biggest heart and never made me feel guilty if I missed texting her back by twenty minutes or twenty days—unlike some people. "Sure thing," I told her.

Jen waved and started walking away, Eric lingering a moment to eye the sandwich in my hand. I raised a brow and went to take another bite before he leaned down and quickly bit off a chunk of my sandwich and ran after her. Wes began laughing hysterically while Erin and Mira just rolled their eyes. And me? My jaw hit the ground.

"Eric! You owe me a sandwich, mister!" I yelled after him.

I could hear him chuckling as he followed Jen across the courtyard to the education building, a smirk pulling at my lips. I shook my head in mock frustration, eating the rest of my sandwich—minus the part where he stole the bite—and did my best to listen to the conversation being shared around the table. It proved a difficult task.

My thoughts kept jumping to the green-eyed man I now got the privilege of calling my boyfriend and the magical night we had shared. Normally I despised the long, boring hours at the library. That day, I couldn't wait to get to work since I knew I would get to see Max. Completely uncontrolled by my brain, my lips began to curl into a soft smile as I thought about him. Unfortunately, that got Wes's attention.

"What are you all smiley over?" he asked, causing me to jump in my seat.

Erin and Mira eyed me suspiciously as I blushed profusely. I ducked my head under the guise of taking a drink, but my roommate kept staring at me…hard. I still hadn't told anyone what had happened with Corey so I knew she was under the impression he and I could potentially start dating. Her next comments only served to make my heart sink further into my chest.

"Are you thinking about Corey?" Mira snickered. "When are you going to just jump his bones, Ren? He clearly wants you."

I choked, coughing and sputtering as I had been in the middle of sipping my drink. I knew that was exactly what Corey wanted from me and he sure as hell wasn't getting it. My so-called friends mistook my reaction for embarrassment, rather than the anger that was boiling within me.

"Do you really think she'd know what to even do with his dick once he got her into bed?" Erin asked Mira with a smug tone. Wes roared with laughter and I fought to tamp down the waves of nausea and rage threatening to overtake me. "Maybe we should sit her down with some porn to loosen her up and then send her over."

"And that's my cue to get out of here!" I huffed. I quickly threw away my trash and threw my backpack on my shoulder. "I'll talk to you three later," I grumbled, listening as they continued to laugh as I walked away.

CHAPTER TEN

"Any chance you could help me find this book?" a familiar voice said behind me.

I'd turned around with a smile to find Max leaning against the counter, a slip of paper with a few letters and numbers scribbled on it in his hand. He had a sly smile tugging on his mouth, and mischief glinting in his perfect green eyes. Helping him find a book was obviously a ruse to get me alone and it was thrilling me to my toes.

"Absolutely," I assured him sweetly, walking around the counter. I took the slip of paper from him and knew instantly it was a book on the third floor, far west side of the building. "Right this way."

Together we walked up the stairs, making idle conversation as we went. When we finally reached the proper shelf, I realized we were in one of the more isolated parts of the library. I raised my brow and smiled at him.

"Okay, I have to admit that was an ingenious plan, Mr. Harris," I teased, letting him pull me into his arms. I rested my hands on his chest and gazed up into his eyes, letting the anger I had been stuck with since lunch slowly drift away as I sighed in contentment.

"Glad you approve," Max said with a wink. "Did your class go okay this morning?"

"Class was…well, class," I answered with a shrug. "Nothing too special about it. How was yours?"

"They were fine." He studied me for a moment. "What's going on in that little brain of yours, Ren? You mentioned in your text this morning we needed to talk about something, and I could just tell when walking up to the counter you were upset."

I smiled softly. "How do you know me so well?"

"I like to think it's because we started off as friends," he chuckled. "But seriously, what is going on? You're not breaking up with me already, are you?"

He faked a gasp, pretending to be having a heart attack. I rolled my eyes and shook my head as I laughed quietly. "Not a chance," I whispered, meeting his eyes again.

"Whew," Max breathed dramatically. "Okay, if you're not breaking up with me, then what is bothering you, Renee?"

Taking a deep breath to steady myself, I launched into a brief recap of Mira's message and her snippy comments to me. I left out the part about them all teasing me about Corey wanting to sleep with me...for now. "It's just...she asked you out and you turned her down and then she got upset we were having dinner after you helped me move and now I don't know how to tell her we're dating without completely hurting her," I finished breathlessly.

Max stayed silent for a few minutes, and I worried I'd overwhelmed him. Hell, I was overwhelmed so how could I not expect him to be when I literally just dumped that much shit on him all at once. He suddenly pulled me tighter against his chest and stroked my hair.

"No wonder you were flipping out, babe," he breathed against my head. "Look, I'm the one who turned her down and caused her to get all pissed to begin with, so I will take the heat on that part for you."

"What?" I asked, not sure I was following.

Max sighed. "Renee, I'll talk to her and tell her about us, so you don't have to. It is the least I can do to make things easier for you. And it's one less thing for you to worry about."

Seriously, best boyfriend ever, I couldn't help myself from thinking. He continued to slowly brush his hand through my hair, the long brown strands tangling gently around his fingers with each sweep of his arm. I closed my eyes, wishing I could stay wrapped in this moment forever, but I knew I was going to have to get back downstairs soon before my boss came looking for me.

"Now," he breathed, "do you want to tell me what had you all riled up when I came in? Because I don't think it had anything to do with telling Mira that we're dating."

I sucked my bottom lip between my teeth as I felt my heart constrict. His left hand was firmly on the small of my back, holding me tightly to him, while his right gently angled my chin upward to force me to look him in the eyes. He had the most concerned look on his face and I found myself melting.

"Erin, Wes, and Mira were teasing me over lunch about Corey," I started, feeling his muscles tense around me. "Mira said I should jump him, and Erin said I wouldn't know what to do with him if I did. Not only do I not see him like that, it bothered me that they wouldn't leave me alone about—"

"About being a virgin," Max concluded. "Damn, I really want to hit them right about now. I can see why you would be upset about the teasing, but please know that it does not bother me one bit."

I smiled. "I know, Max. That's one of the things I really like and appreciate about you. You have never pressured me to do anything I wasn't comfortable with doing."

"And that is not going to change anytime soon," he told me as he brushed his thumb across my cheek. "I should probably let you get back to work, but I'll call you tonight, okay?"

"Yes, please," I whispered.

I headed back downstairs and finished my shift a few hours later. Once at the apartment, I quickly fell on my bed, kicking my shoes off as I closed my eyes and tried to relax. My stomach growled, forcing a frown to my face as I sat up, wondering what I would make for dinner. Before I could even head to my kitchen, my phone rang.

"Hello?"

"Hey, babe," Max greeted. "I'm downstairs. I've got dinner if you want to let me in. I think you are going to want to hear about how my talk with Mira went."

"Um, sure," I stammered. "Come on up."

CHAPTER ELEVEN

"I take it from the look on your face it did not go well," I asked while Max walked into my apartment and set down the bag of sandwiches.

He turned to face me and pulled me into his arms as he leaned against my table. His face nuzzled into my neck while he held me, and it felt like all the air got sucked from the room. Max sighed, his breath feathering against my skin and eliciting shivers down my spine before he spoke.

"It went better than I expected," he admitted. "She was a little angry at first, but I told her none of this was your idea or fault. And in the end, she said she was fine with the idea of us being together."

"She said what?" I choked, knowing the surprise was evident on my face.

He chuckled. "Mira wasn't thrilled but said she was okay with us dating since we bothered to be considerate enough to tell her before we officially began going out. Which brings me to my next point," he said, eyes sparkling, "what did you want to do on Friday?"

I could feel the heat rushing to my cheeks and nibbled on my lower lip. Max's eyes kept watching my every movement, making my body temperature seem to go even higher. I gulped, hoping I could figure out what to tell him.

"Well, there are always the standard first date options," I finally said.

"So, dinner and a movie?" he laughed. "I might have to take you back out to the ranch afterward though. Do some more stargazing?"

"That sounds like a marvelous first date to me."

Friday rolled around after a slightly awkward week with Mira. But at least she had been civil about the whole situation which lulled me into a false sense of security. God, I wish I was paying closer attention, but I was in my own little bubble with Max and deliriously happy. I didn't see the warning flags being waved.

I threw on my jeans and a cute white top along with my boots and had just finished touching up my makeup when there was a knock at my door. Answering, I found Max standing there with a dozen peachy-colored roses and a smirk on his handsome face. I absolutely loved roses, so this date was already off to a fabulous start.

"Why thank you, sir," I told him, carefully taking the flowers so I could quickly put them in a vase.

"You are quite welcome," he replied. When he's quiet for a minute, I glanced over at him, his eyes trailing up and down my body in respectful appreciation. "I have got to say, Ren, you look very pretty tonight."

"You don't look too bad yourself." His blue button-up shirt has the sleeves rolled to his elbows and tucked into his jeans, hugging the contours of his chest. Max was a great cross between an honest country boy and sophisticated future businessman. "So, where are we heading for dinner?"

"That is for me to know and you to find out when we get there," he told me, handing me my purse. I rolled my eyes at him but smiled, nonetheless.

Twenty minutes later we were talking over breadsticks at a cute Italian bistro in town, a little hole in the wall place called Napoli's. They had the best pasta in the area. We laughed and carried on over lasagna and manicotti, before heading out to catch a movie at the theater. While the restaurant had been a wonderful surprise, the movie choice was a bit odd at first.

Max had gone with a horror film, which I usually avoided since I scare easily. So, when I jumped the first time and he pulled me closer, I finally realized why the hell he had picked this movie. *Well played, Harris, well played,* I thought to myself as I snuggled in his arms. By the time the movie let out, the sun had set, and a chilly breeze had come through. I glanced at Max and asked if we could swing by my apartment to grab my jacket before heading to the ranch.

Ever the gentleman, he still walked me in, waiting in the living room while I grabbed my jean jacket from the closet. He was smiling at a picture on my coffee table when I came back in the room, one of his soft smiles that could warm you on the coldest day in winter. I unconsciously sucked my lip between my teeth again, just as Max looked up. His eyes were glittering like polished emeralds in the dim lighting as he drew nearer, his hands going to gently grip my waist.

"You keep doing that," he whispered huskily.

"Doing what?" I asked.

"I don't even think you realize you do it half the time, but whenever you get nervous or flustered, you pull that bottom lip of yours between your teeth," Max tells me, his nose brushing lightly against mine.

"Is that a problem?"

He chuckled. "No, but damn if I don't want to be the one doing it, Renee."

"And what exactly is stopping you?"

I felt like my heart was going to explode as he looked deep into my eyes as his hands slowly scaled up my body to softly cup my cheeks. "Is that a hint, Miss Westhaven?"

"It's a request," I whispered back.

My eyes fluttered closed as his mouth connected tenderly with my own, his fingers tangling in my hair. When I sighed into the kiss, Max took his opportunity to deepen it, running his tongue delicately along my bottom lip before gently nibbling on it like he wanted. My hands gripped his shirt and he slowly walked me back against the door, still passionately kissing me.

When we finally broke apart, he smirked at me, both of us breathless. *Well…that was one hell of a first kiss,* I told myself.

CHAPTER TWELVE

"**I** go away for two months and you two decide to hook up?" Nick asked, feigning shock as we sat down to drink our coffees.

The fall semester was a week away from starting and Max and I had been in a state of bliss for the past six weeks. After our first date and kiss, he had taken me out to the ranch where we had continued our make-out session beneath the stars. And since, we had enjoyed countless dates and hours together in my apartment, in addition to admitting we had quickly fallen in love with one another.

We still had not slept together, not because we didn't want to, but because we were waiting for the right time. Max was beyond respectful of my boundaries, but that didn't mean we didn't fool around in other ways. I worried Mira suspected he and I were already being intimate after she arrived home early one afternoon, and Max had been helping me choose an outfit for our date while I was in only my underwear. Once she had moved into the apartment, everything seemed to become twice as complicated.

"Seriously, this is great, you guys," Nick was telling us, forcing my mind back to the conversation at hand. "Hey, before I forget, I heard that the Saturday night before classes begin a couple of guys at your complex, Roy Miller being one of them, are having a party, Ren. Would you two be up for going?"

"What you're really asking is if I'll buzz you into the building so you can go," I teased. I shared a glance with Max who shrugged. "I don't have anything planned for that night, and Mira is supposed to be out of town that weekend, so it is fine by me."

"Sweet!" Nick cheered, earning a few stares from others in the coffee shop. "I mean, yeah, that uh, sounds good," he tried to recover.

I felt the laughter bubbling from my lips. Nick was like a little kid at times, but he was such a great friend. I knew that if I ever needed him, he would not hesitate to be there for me. Taking a sip of mocha, I arched my eyebrows.

"So, tell us how the training camp was, Nick. Did you decide if you want to be a cop yet, or are you still leaning toward being a lawyer?" I asked.

"I can already tell they whipped your ass in shape," Max snickered, eyeing his best friend over his mug. "Last time I saw you looking this beat was freshman year of high school."

Nick laughed. "Yeah, the first couple of weeks were brutal, but totally worth it. I definitely learned a lot while I was there, so thanks for pushing me to go, man. But to answer your question, Ren, I haven't quite made up my mind yet."

He paused, taking a deep breath and looking into the depths of his cup. Nick's a good-time guy, a high-energy, jokester. Watching him, I realized he was truly in a contemplative mood like I had never before seen him in.

"The plan is to keep thinking about it, and maybe something will give me the push I need to make a decision here soon," he answered seriously.

"Did they replace you with a cyborg or something while you were there?" Max asked, jokingly poking at Nick's chest. "Who are you, and what have you done with my best friend, because Nick Spencer is never this reserved."

Nick shrugged. "I know, I know. Crazy right? But you and I are starting our third-year studies, and this is getting more serious. And I know I need to make a choice within the next few months."

"You know Max and I will support you no matter what you choose, right?" I assured him, laying my hand lightly on his arm.

He shot me a smirk and laid his hand atop mine. Then his eyes turned impish as he gave my hand a little squeeze and looked over at Max. "You may need to hurry up and lock this one in or I'll steal her," he teases.

Max flipped him the bird and we all started laughing. "What happened to Sarah?" he teased his best friend.

Nick glanced at his cup. "Yeah, that didn't work out. She liked my dad's title and money more than me, so I cut her loose a couple weeks ago."

"That sucks," I murmured, sipping my own drink.

"It is what it is," he responded. "One day, I'll find a girl as nice as you, Ren."

He threw me a cheeky wink as we chuckled, and Max shook his head good-naturedly. After that, the conversation turned lighter until we went our separate ways, never knowing that Nick's push would come sooner than any of us imagined or in a way none of us expected.

The weekend before school started, Mira headed out—supposedly to go back home until Sunday—leaving me alone at the apartment. Max was busy helping his parents all day on Friday with something at the ranch, and rather than make him come to me or be the clingy girlfriend, I decided to suck it up and stay by myself for the first time in weeks. God…what a fucking stupid decision. Both Max and I had felt that something was off all day, but had chosen to ignore it, thinking it was all in our heads.

Neither of us could have ever imagined the hatred and jealousy that had been festering all these months that would come to a boil this weekend and would destroy so many lives. This would be the night that would change my life forever.

CHAPTER THIRTEEN

I will never know what actually woke me up—whether it was my covers moving, the presence of someone else in my room, or something else altogether—but I will never be able to erase the panic and fear that dominated my mind the instant my eyes flicked open. I remember going to push against the sudden weight atop my body when a hand gripped my face, the sickly sweet smell of some chemical—chloroform, as I would later discover—on a cloth clamped over my nose and mouth. Within moments, I was unconscious, waking only when his body pushed forcefully into my own.

"No!" I tried to scream, my voice barely more than a hoarse whisper as tears filled my eyes. The pain was overwhelming as his body hovered over mine in the darkness, and I could feel someone else at the foot of my bed, holding onto my ankles to keep my legs apart.

One of his hands wrapped around my neck and I heard the click of a knife being opened before I felt the cold steel blade against my throat. My eyes went wide in terror as his glittering eyes met mine, my breath being stolen by his brutal fingers on my windpipe, just as my innocence by his black and twisted soul.

"I would suggest you behave, baby," he growled, pressing the tip of the knife closer to my skin. "I would hate to leave you bloody and bruised, because fuck if this isn't going to be more than worth the wait."

The tears slipped from my eyes as I desperately attempted to place his familiar voice in my mind. I instinctively tried to move my legs, but the person at the end of the bed gripped me harder. The man above me began moving, pumping his body savagely into mine, eliciting more tears from me. His hand left my throat to grasp my wrists, pinning them above my head to control me.

"Please," I begged, "please just stop."

"Shut the fuck up!" he told me roughly, the knife inching ever nearer.

I wept, I bucked my body in a feeble attempt to get him off mine, I whispered Max's name over and over, pleading for this to end. Even in the dark and without my contacts in my eyes, I knew my attacker was wearing a look of primal satisfaction; I could feel it. And I realized I didn't stand a chance of ever seeing Max again if I continued trying to fight. My body sagged into the bed as the fight left me, the tears streaming down my face in a never-ending river of grief.

"Oh God Max, I'm so sorry," I whispered, my head tossing on the pillow to avoid looking at his monstrous face. I felt like I was failing my amazing boyfriend by not fighting against him more; a notion my attacker seemed only too happy to bombard me with.

He laughed, the sound of it chilling. "You think he'd want to have anything to do with a whore like you now? You're just a little slut, letting me fuck you. What happened to your fight, Ren? Your sense of innocence and virtue? Max won't want you now, but that's okay…I'll take it from here."

I gasped, choking on my sobs as he continued to move in and out of my body. He strained above me, and I felt a sudden rush of fiery liquid flood into me. *Oh God, no,* I thought, stricken. *He wasn't wearing a damn condom!* His evil grin confirmed my fears before I noticed his large hand coming toward my face, the same rag from before clutched in his palm.

"Time to take another nap," he sneered. "I'll wake you up for round two."

My eyes bulged in fear and I tried to push him away, but between everything he had just inflicted upon me, I was no match for him. I struggled against his hand but lost the battle within moments. Just as I lost every battle for the rest of the night.

I lost count of how many times my rapist forced himself on me. It became like a hazy dream, every time I would wake from the effects of the chloroform, to the pain of his body violating mine, to being knocked out once more. The fear, the anguish, the disgust, all washed over me until I feared I must be drowning, and there was no one around to save me.

From outside my door, a sharp feminine voice called to him, "Are you almost done in there?"

He snickered, pulling on his clothes while I lay in my bed, shivering from the cold, the fear, the shame. I could feel the eyes of his helper on my half-naked body.

"Are you really just going to leave her like this?" he asked, his voice a familiar baritone.

"I don't give a damn," my attacker replied, his fly zipping with a hiss as another knock sounded on my door. "Let's go; she's getting impatient for us to leave."

I felt gently fumbling hands pull my panties and shorts back up my legs before the covers were replaced over my shaking form. It could have been my imagination, but I swear I heard him whisper, "I am so sorry," just before he walked out of my bedroom.

The following morning, I awoke stiff and sore, my head feeling fuzzy. I stumbled into the bathroom to start my shower, knowing Max was coming over soon to spend the day before the party. I felt like I had had the strangest dream, but for the life of me, couldn't remember what it had been about. I attributed my soreness to the fooling around Max and I had done a couple days before, never thinking that my so-called nightmares had been real.

Without thinking, I tossed my pajamas into the closet and quickly showered, letting the hot water soothe my aching muscles and wash away the sticky feeling of what I presumed was sweat on my body. I had just thrown on a pair of shorts and a shirt when Max knocked on my door, sending me scurrying to answer. Something was nagging at the back of my mind, but I was oblivious to the signs as I greeted my boyfriend with a hug and a smile.

It wasn't until he was following me back to my room and I tripped over a shoe, sending myself into the corner of my bed that things took a frightening turn for us both. Max became concerned when I didn't get right back up, and gently flipped me over to find I'd hit my head on the corner of the bedframe. When my eyes fluttered open to him hovering over me, panic lanced through my entire body, widening my eyes as I tried in vain to back away from him in horror.

"Whoa, Renee, what's the matter?" he asked, worry lacing his tone.

"I—I don't know!" I cried, burying my head in my hands as my entire body shook with sobs.

CHAPTER FOURTEEN

Ilooked up at Max, mortified over my tears, the uncontrolled shaking my body was doing, and the overwhelming sense of fear gripping my mind. His beautiful green eyes held so much worry and compassion, they were my undoing. I melted into his gentle embrace and wept into the soft material of his shirt while he caressed my back in soothing circles.

Time ceased to exist as we huddled on the floor of my bedroom with Max enfolding my trembling body in his strong arms, offering me a sense of protection and fleeting tranquility. He rocked me slowly, his chin resting atop my brow, pressing gossamer kisses to my temple periodically as he whispered reassurances in my ear. I heard them, but my brain failed to comprehend them fully.

Instead, the fragmented images from the night flashed in my mind like lightning, adding to my sense of horror, shame, and utter confusion. Could the nightmares have been real? The faceless demon hovering over my prone body, the searing pain in my core, the sticky substance I had washed away when I awoke… Had I made a horrible mistake?

"Ren? What is it?" Max asked tenderly, his hand lightly stroking my cheek. "Your eyes are so wide, baby. I can't help you if you won't talk to me."

I swallowed hard against the bile rising in the back of my throat. The notion that last night hadn't been merely a dream straight out of the bowels of hell made me nauseous. As my eyes met his, fresh tears misted into my vision as I thought of the possibility Max would not be my first; that every aspect of our intimate life would now be tainted by the evil miasma that had permeated my room the night before. But I had no proof…because I had no true memories.

"I—I don't—oh, God, Max," I sobbed. "I'm scared," I whispered into his neck.

"Okay, why are you so scared?"

"I had the most terrifying nightmare last night," I began, my lower lip quivering as I spoke. I closed my eyes so I wouldn't see the expression change in his own emerald orbs. "Max—I'm not sure it was a dream though…"

I heard the breath rush out of his lungs and his arms tightened around me. "Sweetheart, look at me please," he begged. I shook my head miserably, sending the tears cascading down my cheeks once more. "Renee, please look at me," Max asked again, lifting my chin firmly with his fingertips.

When my brown eyes finally reopened, I had to bite down on my lip to keep from crying aloud. Max brought his forehead to rest against mine, his nose brushing the tip of my own as he stared lovingly into my tear-filled visage.

"Tell me about your dream…"

"No—I—" I gasped, the sound ragged and harsh. Max silenced me with the softest of kisses, stealing my breath away and reminding me that he loved me…no matter what. "What if it wasn't a dream?"

"What was it about, baby?"

"I'm not really sure," I admitted. I closed my eyes as I drew a shuddering breath. "It was dark, and I was asleep, but then I woke up and there was someone in my room—"

"Take your time," he murmured, stroking my arm.

"I don't know who it was, Max, but it wasn't you, and he," I paused, dreading putting a voice to the fear that had taken root in me. "In my dream he—he—"

"He raped you?" he breathed, finishing the statement when I had been unable.

"It was just a dream! It was a nightmare! That's it! It had to be just a nightmare, right?" I was practically screaming by this point, my hysteria growing with every word I uttered.

Max gently held my face in his hands, like I was a china cup that would shatter if he used too much or too little pressure. I could feel my stomach roiling, the nausea rising with the hysterics, and I knew I was going to be violently ill. Scrambling from his arms, I lurched into the bathroom and barely made it to the porcelain basin before I vomited, gripping the sides of the commode for support.

He rushed in behind me and grabbed my hair, twisting it back and securing it with my clip to keep it out of the way while I retched. As new tears spring to my eyes, Max dampened a washcloth and handed it to me to help cool my face.

"I'm a damn mess, huh?" I whispered, sitting back on my heels.

"Even if this wasn't anything more than a sick nightmare, you'd have every reason to be one, Ren," he assured me. "I'm not going anywhere, so don't worry. We'll figure this out together, okay?"

I nodded in a noncommittal way, unconvinced of anything in this moment but that our lives have been all but destroyed. Everything we had planned has suddenly been taken from us if this has in fact been more than a hellish lucid dream. Could I really expect Max to stay with me if it's true? Wouldn't that make me the most selfish person on the planet?

As my thoughts became a swirling vortex of inner turmoil intent on drowning what little sanity I had left, Max gently lifted me off the bathroom floor and carried me to the bed. Before I could control it, I began to hyperventilate as my heart raced, my eyes wide as I gasped for oxygen in my compressed lungs. He took my hands in his calloused ones, and slowly ran them up to my face to cradle my cheeks.

"Baby, breathe," came his soothing whisper. "I'm right here, and I'm not going to let anyone hurt you again. You're safe, Renee. It's going to be okay…just breathe."

He placed one of my hands on his chest over his heart and covered it with his own, encouraging me to match his steady breathing, all while never breaking eye contact. After several minutes, my vitals returned to normal, and the anxiety attack has been quelled…for now. My eyelids fluttered closed, and my chin drops as the pain etches into my face.

"This is going to be my new normal…isn't it, Max?" I asked quietly.

Leaning his forehead against mine, he sighed. "I wish I could say 'no,' but I have a sinking suspicion the answer is 'yes,' baby."

CHAPTER FIFTEEN

We spent the remainder of the day looking over my apartment for signs of forced entry, under my bed for anything they may have dropped, and throwing my pajamas and underwear in a plastic bag. Pulling the clothes from my hamper to place in the bag sent me into another panic attack that had me sobbing on the floor of my closet. It took Max nearly an hour to get me calmed down from that episode, and all I wanted to do was take another shower.

My phone began ringing as I was finally getting off the floor of the closet: my mother. The absolute last thing I wanted to do was tell my mom that I suspected I had been raped, but at the same time, I knew I needed to go get checked out at the hospital. Reluctantly, I answered.

"Hey mom."

"Renee, what's going on? You sound upset, honey," my mom said immediately.

I glanced at Max who gave me an encouraging nod. "Yeah, I kind of am, mom," I admitted. "Look, is there any way you could come down today to see me?"

My voice cracked as I spoke the last words, and Max gently pulled me into his arms. "I'm sure I could, but what's going on?" my mom asked again.

I let out a shaky breath. "Mom, I think…I think I may have been… um…" I paused, looking to Max for his support as new tears ran down my cheeks. "I think I was raped last night," I finally managed to whisper.

I heard her swift intake of air and the creak of her chair as she shifted in her seat. I could see her brown eyes, so much like my own, filled with worry as she absorbed this information. "Let me pack an overnight bag and I'll head right down, okay? Then you and I can go to the hospital if you haven't already."

"I haven't yet, so thanks, mom. I think it'll be best if you go with me."

"Of course, Renee." She paused. "It…it wasn't Max, right?"

"Oh, God, no, mom!" I exclaimed, quick to clear his name. "Trust me mom, I would much rather be telling you he and I jumped into bed together than to say I don't have a clue who may have done this to me."

"Okay, honey, I believe you," came her soft reply. "I'll be there as soon as I can. Do you have someone with you now?"

"Yeah, Max is here."

"That makes me feel a bit better. Hang in there, baby. I love you."

"I love you too, mom," I told her before hanging up the phone and leaning back into his arms. He squeezed me carefully, his hug speaking louder than any words. "Thank you," I whispered.

He kissed the top of my head as he sighed. "You don't have to thank me, Ren. I love you—more than I could ever say—and I am not leaving you to deal with this on your own. I'm staying until your mom gets here, and I'll be here when she leaves to go back home."

I nodded, unable to get the words out past the lump in my throat. Before either of us could break the silence again, his phone started vibrating in his back pocket, startling me. His green eyes apologetic, Max looks at the caller I.D. on the screen, then back at me with worry etched between his brows.

"Should I answer him?" he asked, showing me that it's Nick calling. I felt my pulse steady and sucked on my bottom lip as I shrugged in response. "Hello?"

"Hey, Max! I wanted to check to see if you and Ren wanted to grab dinner tonight before the party started. I was going to ask Roy too, since he was organizing the party, but I can't get him to take my call for some reason," Nick's exuberant voice rang through the phone.

My eyes widened as I remembered the party for the first time in hours and felt the tears welling once more. Max gave my cheek a gentle caress with one hand and covered the phone with the other. Looking deep into the frightened windows of my soul, he whispered, "I'll be right back, okay?"

Quickly, he walked to the living room to continue his conversation with Nick in hushed tones. At that particular point in time, all Max told him was that something had come up and we would not be attending the party. Knowing very well that Nick was well-liked by most of the student body, Max offered to give him the gate code so he could still enter the premises—with the hopes Nick might hear something that would be helpful.

Nick promised to stop by when he arrived since Max told him we would be staying in the apartment, and they soon hung up, allowing Max to return to my side. Even in my traumatized state I could tell he had something on his mind—and I was petrified I was not going to like it if he spoke of it aloud. Moments after he had sat on the floor beside me, his knees brought up close to his chest and his muscled arms lazily draped around his legs, his eyes met mine and he cleared his throat hesitantly.

"Ren, what would you think about asking Nick to listen for any gossip or rumors, and maybe looking for any evidence?" he asked delicately.

My mind was reeling. I had barely accepted the possibility of having been raped and was dreading the idea of being examined by hospital personnel, let alone telling my mother and my boyfriend, and now said boyfriend wanted to involve more people in this debacle? My mouth opened and closed a few times like a fish out of water and I felt my lip tremble as it dawned on me why he was asking.

Nick was in an intriguing position to gather information for us, without it having to be too personal for him since I wasn't his girlfriend, but he was also so popular that plenty of people would simply volunteer information without thinking about it when he was around. My eyelids fluttered closed as I allowed my troubled thoughts to continue to swirl mercilessly through my mind, a full-fledged debate raging within myself. Finally, I nodded my head.

"Okay," I breathed. "But, Max, do you mind talking to him about this when I'm not here? And please, tell him I don't want his pity."

"I'll tell him, baby," he assured me.

CHAPTER SIXTEEN

When my mother arrived at my apartment, I practically threw myself into her arms, sobbing into her comforting embrace. Max had been true to his word and not left my side while we waited for her to make the two-hour drive, and now was standing by the couch with a somber expression chiseled on his face. The three of us walked to the parking garage attached to the building, me trailing helplessly behind my mother while Max headed to his truck.

"I'll see you later, okay," he murmured, kissing the top of my head softly. He exchanged a rueful look with my mom, and waved farewell as we all drove away.

I fidgeted in my seat, my eyes downcast and unfocused on anything as we drove through Lubbock. To say I was nervous about the upcoming examination was an understatement. Petrified would be more accurate. Questions swirled in my mind like a vortex, threatening to uproot my fragile hold on my sanity in the blink of an eye. *Would the exam be painful, would the doctor believe me, would they find anything?* On and on they swarmed, like locusts, destroying everything in their path until my mom put a hand on my shoulder to pull me from my silent hell.

"Renee, we're here, honey," she said.

My head snapped up to see we had parked in front of the large emergency department of the hospital, causing my heart to begin racing once more. Her hand gave my shoulder a soft pat and together we exited her car. I bit my lower lip, wishing Max were with me to hold my hand, to protect me from whatever horrors I was inevitably about to face.

Entering the building, we were blasted with the icy feeling of the industrial air conditioning units designed to keep the building cool despite the suffocating west Texas heat. Goosebumps blossomed on my arms as a shiver went down my spine as we approached the check-in desk. Thankfully, a woman was running the desk that afternoon, her soft brown eyes looking up with mild concern as we stepped closer.

"Hello," she welcomed. "What seems to be the chief complaint this afternoon?"

I gulped, sinking into the chair she motioned to before her desk and reaching for the clipboard she handed me. Amazingly, there were hardly any people in the emergency room at the moment, so I was able to quietly meet her curious gaze and answered her in the shakiest voice ever.

"I think I may have been raped last night."

Her face became ashen at my words, the smile fading instantly as she realized the ramifications of my visit. Her lips set into a thin line of grim determination and she typed rapidly on her computer. When she faced me again to retrieve the clipboard, her brown eyes were filled with an emotion I despised…pity.

"I presume you would prefer a female doctor and nurse today, sweetie?" she asked, her voice syrupy.

I nodded, wishing I could run back to my mom's car and just forget this whole idea. The instant her demeanor went from mildly concerned to sickeningly sweet and full of pity, the panic had started to set back in for me. Would everyone from now on treat me like this? *I can't fucking stand people who pretend to give a damn about me or pity me,* my mind screamed.

We were instantly called back to the triage room for my vitals to be taken by a nurse, then shown to a private room where I was instructed to change into the pathetic excuse they call a hospital gown. I sat on the uncomfortable bed with the thin sheet tucked to my chin, my knees drawn up to my chest and my arms wrapped around my legs, doing my best to drown out the fear threatening to suffocate me. My mother reached for my hand, giving it a gentle squeeze and bringing me out of the shell I had erected around myself.

The doctor soon entered, a middle-aged woman with a world-weary expression on her face who asked a million questions that I had absolutely no answers for. Finally, she had me lay back for the physical side of the exam, snapping on her latex gloves as I slid to the edge of the bed.

"Have you been willingly intimate with anyone in the past twenty-four hours, Miss Westhaven?" she asked, looking at me as though she expected to catch me in a lie.

"Unless I really was raped last night, then no, I'm still a virgin," I replied, noting the surprise that lit her eyes.

I was accustomed to that look. In this day and age, most girls didn't make it to nineteen still proudly holding fast to their virginity. But at that moment, I was glad I could say that I had. It meant that I would know for certain if last night had been merely a horrific nightmare, or if I truly had been attacked based on what the doctor discovered during the exam.

"I see," the doctor answered, coming back over to the bed. "Okay, this may be a bit uncomfortable."

She lifted the sheet and I forced my eyes shut, unable to watch her. I bit my lower lip and squeezed my mother's hand tighter as the doctor's hand made its first contact with my body…and felt pain ripple upward. A tear slipped out as she continued the exam, not speaking a word as she probed and prodded the sensitive flesh of my womanhood.

After several moments, she finally sat back and draped the sheet back down over my legs. "Renee, I hate to be the one to say it, but it does look like you were correct," she said softly, regret lacing her voice. "You have severe bruising and vaginal tearing, consistent with sexual assault. I took swabs, but since you showered this morning, it's unlikely any of the samples will be useful to the police."

"Is there anything else we need to do?" my mom asked.

"I'll do bloodwork for a STD panel, but she'll have to wait to do a pregnancy test for a few weeks if she ends up late with her period," the doctor said, but her words were falling on deaf ears.

I truly had been raped. I was raped, I washed away the evidence this morning, and now there wasn't a damn thing anyone could do about it. I was probably going to lose my boyfriend over this too, because I couldn't expect him to stay. I had had my innocence stolen by another man, and I didn't have the first clue as to who had done it.

CHAPTER SEVENTEEN

An hour later my mom and I were parking once more at my building, and I was numb to the world. I felt as though someone had stripped my spirit from my body and simply attached it to a string—much like a balloon—leaving me to float insubstantially above myself. My limbs were leaden though, like every movement was being made through a thick gelatin that hindered my lifeless body.

I was a walking paradigm.

Since there wasn't much more we could do at this point, my mother had decided she would return home tonight. Max had called her while I was changing back into my clothes, telling her he and Nick would be heading back over to my place soon so she could leave at a reasonable hour. He had also checked in with his parents to ensure they were fine if I stayed in their guest room whenever I wanted, meaning I had a safe place to go, although he hadn't yet told them why I might need it.

I sank on the corner of my neatly made bed, eyeing my comforter with tears filling my eyes. The fear and sadness suddenly gave way to rage and I stood up, ripping the bedclothes away from my mattress, collapsing in the middle of them sobbing seconds later. My mother, who had been answering Max's knock on the door, came rushing into my room, finding me in a distraught heap on the floor.

Max's green eyes flashed with compassion as he wedged around her to kneel beside me and pull my quivering body into his arms. Nick stood back, rubbing the back of his neck, his keen blue eyes filled with an emotion I couldn't fathom at that moment. Above the sounds of my cries came the shrieks of intoxicated partygoers and the thumping bass of the blaring music down below, mocking me with their vitality while I felt my world crumbling around me.

"Ren," my mom said quietly, "are you sure you want me to leave? I can always stay for a few nights."

I took a deep breath to steady myself as I sat back from Max's comforting embrace. "No, I'll be okay, mom," I breathed, the tears still spilling down my cheeks as I looked up at her. "Thank you for coming though."

"Oh, honey, of course." She walked over and pulled me into a tight hug. "Call me as soon as you hear anything from the doctor, or if you just need to talk, okay?"

I nodded, unable to speak. She pulled away and stared into my eyes, a pained look etched into her gentle face. Looking quickly at Max, then Nick, then Max again, she said grimly, "You two will look out for her, right?"

"Yes, ma'am," Max answered solemnly, wrapping his arm protectively around my narrow waist.

Nick nodded in agreement as well as he leaned against my dresser, his arms folded over his chest. My mom sighed and pulled me in for another brief hug. It felt as though she were afraid to break me…which in that moment was a valid concern.

"Nicholas, would you be able to walk me out to my car?" she asked. "I am not keen on doing so alone with all those college boys doing God-only-knows-what thanks to their party."

"Sure thing, Mrs. Westhaven," he answered easily. "Ren, I'm going to borrow your keys for a few minutes so I can get back in, if that's okay."

"They're on the island, Nick," I told him absently.

I was looking again at the pile of bedding on my floor, the bile rising in the back of my throat as I thought of the nightmare that took place atop the very sheets I was standing upon. The clothes I was wearing last night had already been bagged, but I had not even thought about my sheets. My breath is coming in harsh gasps and my heart feels like I might explode as the panic escalates.

"Baby," Max whispered, slowly reaching out to grasp my shoulders. "Breathe. I know you're scared, and I know you're upset right now, but you have to try to calm your breathing. Deep breaths in and out."

He lightly ran his hands up and down my arms for several minutes, doing his best to calm my anxiety. Finally, my breathing shudders out and stabilizes into a normal rhythm once more, allowing me to open my eyes and sigh. I took a step forward and collapsed against his strong chest, letting him stroke my hair and back while I listened to the steady beating of his heart beneath my ear.

I heard my front door open and close, and we turned to find Nick had returned, a grim expression plastered on his face. He frowns at the sheets puddled around my feet; his blue eyes harder than I have ever seen them.

"Ren," Nick said quietly, drawing my tear-stained gaze, "do you want me to call my contact at the police department to come out and collect your clothes and bedding?"

I couldn't help but feel my lip tremble at his softly spoken words and gentle gaze. There is no pity in his deep blues though, for which I was immeasurably grateful; just the desire to help. Glancing at Max, I raised my brows in question, wondering what he thinks I should do.

"It can't hurt, baby," he said, "but it is your call. I will support you no matter what decision you make regarding the police."

"Do you remember anything from last night yet?" Nick asked.

"Broken images, a few flashes of dreamlike somethings," I replied, "but nothing that would help point the police in the direction of the person responsible for this nightmare. The doctor said the samples she took would probably be less than helpful since I had taken a shower this morning, but if he wore a condom, it doesn't matter anyway. I wouldn't have washed away his DNA."

A collective sigh fills the room. I felt a rogue tear trickle down my cheek as I sat back on my heels, contemplating my next move. I knew there was no way in hell I could stay here tonight—or ever sleep on these sheets again—and the doctor had said my memories may or may not ever return. I looked up at the guys, my decision made.

"Nick, will you go grab a garbage bag from the kitchen for the sheets please," I said as I stood. "I'll bag them for now and if I remember more, I can give them to the police then. But for now, I'm going to pack an overnight bag and go home with Max. I just know I can't stay in this apartment any longer tonight."

CHAPTER EIGHTEEN

Within ten minutes, we were heading out the door, the sheets bagged and in the back of my closet with the clothes from the night before, Max carrying my small duffle. Nick had elected to stick around the complex to see if he could glean any information from the residents and partygoers, all while promising to keep what had happened to me a secret. We said goodnight and soon Max and I were driving through the quiet streets of Lubbock toward his family's ranch.

Both of us were somber on the drive, not sure what to say to one another. His hand rested comfortingly on my knee the whole way through, the thumb brushing gently back and forth absently. That small, sweet caress kept me grounded the entire drive, reminding me yet again why I fell in love with Maxwell Harris.

Reaching his house, we walked in to find his parents had already gone to bed since they had an early start in the morning. Max set my bag down in the guest room and turned to me, cocking his head to one side and studying me with those gorgeous green eyes.

"Are you hungry, baby?"

"Not really," I answered, looking at my feet.

"I kind of expected that, but it would be great if you would eat at least a snack, okay?"

I sighed, knowing he was right and just trying to look out for me as he had promised my mother. I followed him to the kitchen where he pulled out my favorite crackers, a block of cheese, cured sausage, and strawberries. I smiled weakly at him as he began slicing the cheese and sausage, creating a little platter of munchies for me.

"Do you want to curl up in bed with these and watch a movie?" he asked lightly.

I could tell he was trying to carefully gauge my reactions and not overwhelm or frighten me. The thing about Max though, I trusted him—implicitly. And at that moment, nothing sounded better to get me prepared for the idea of sleep, than to curl up with him and watch a film.

"Sure, that would be nice."

The megawatt smile he rewarded me with had my heart bursting with pleasure, something I wasn't sure I could still feel after the bombshell I had had explode in my face earlier. We grabbed our plates and headed to my room, turning down the peaches-and-cream quilt on the bed and settling in against the pillows as he flipped on the television. I snuggled against him and popped a cube of cheese in my mouth as he scrolled through the movie selection on Netflix.

"I'm thinking something funny would probably be good for tonight, what are your thoughts, Ren?" he said, turning to face me while reaching for one of his crackers. I nodded in response, earning a small chuckle from him before he looked at the screen once more. "Panda 3?"

I couldn't help but laugh at this point. Max's suggestion of a kid's movie after everything that had happened in the past twenty-four hours was comical…but also oddly calming. He wiggled his eyebrows suggestively, and my laughter bubbled from my chest even more.

"There is that beautiful laugh and smile I love," he whispered, leaning over to kiss my cheek. Hitting play on the remote, he threw one arm around my shoulders and used the other to eat. I tried my best to focus on the movie, but I knew his eyes were darting to my face every few minutes, checking to make sure I was still okay. I nestled closer to his chest once we both had finished eating, content to stay wrapped in his arms until the movie was done.

"Sweetheart," he breathed against the top of my head, "do you want me to stay in here with you tonight, or will you be okay on your own? It's your call."

I gulped. Honestly, I wasn't sure I would ever be okay to go to sleep ever again. I squeezed my eyes shut and took a deep breath to steady my nerves before I tilted my head up to look into his eyes. "Maybe I'll try on my own. I just don't want to be clingy; you know?"

"Ren, you are not being clingy in the slightest, and I wouldn't blame you if you wanted me to stay."

"I know, I know. I've seriously got the best boyfriend in the world," I murmured.

"I'll be right next door if you need me, okay?"

I nodded, not trusting my voice as he eased off the bed. I sat still, watching as he walked out of the room and quietly closed my door, hearing his door close as well. Biting down on my lower lip to keep myself from crying, I slowly stand up to change for bed, my eyes darting to the door periodically. I stand by the light switch for probably ten minutes, trying to decide if I can handle being in the dark before I finally give myself a shake and turn out my light.

"Ren! Ren, wake up, baby!" Max was saying, gently shaking my shoulder.

I sat up suddenly, scrambling back from him in fear, my body quaking as sobs escaped my mouth. He turned on the bedside lamp, illuminating us both, his face pinched with concern as he sat on the edge of the bed. His hair was disheveled from sleep and his eyes looked a little dazed, like he was still not fully awake as he looked at me.

"Max?" I whispered, not sure what brought him into my room in the middle of the night.

"You scared the hell out of me, Ren," he murmured, reaching to brush the hair back from my face. "I woke up to hear you crying, and by the time I got in here you were thrashing and you—"

He broke off and looked uncomfortably at the floor. *Oh God, he's disgusted by this*, I thought in despair. When he looked back into my face, I gasped. His green eyes were luminous with unshed tears and he tenderly pulled me into his arms.

"Good God, baby, you kept crying about how sorry you were—to me—of all people, all while whispering the word 'no', over and over again," Max told me, his voice breaking. "It absolutely broke my heart and made me realize that if I ever find the fucking bastard that did this…I'm going to kill him."

CHAPTER NINETEEN

Max stayed with me the remainder of the night, holding me in his arms and waking me anytime it appeared I was straying into a nightmare. I felt so guilty because I knew he was going to be exhausted, but he just shook his head and kissed me softly on the lips. We took our time getting around that morning, leisurely lounging in the bed as the sunlight filtered in through the white curtains.

"Would you be up for going for a little walk?" he asked, stroking my arm. "Just here around the property, not anywhere crazy."

"Yeah, that would be okay, I guess."

Pulling on my tennis shoes, I followed him out into the blistering Texas heat, thankful I was only wearing shorts and a tank top. His parents had planted several trees around the five acres surrounding the house, a little wooden arch covered in ivy nestled between a small grove of them. A small bench seat rested beneath it—thankfully in the shade—and Max led me over to sit down.

"This is really pretty," I commented, my fingertips brushing against the trailing vines and ivy leaves. When Max remained silent, I glanced over at him to find his emerald eyes studying my face, a look of uncertainty awash within their depths. "What are you thinking about, Max?"

He sighed. "I know you probably don't want to discuss anything about yesterday, but I was wondering how it went at the hospital. Were you okay with the doctor? Did they tell you anything helpful?"

My eyes fell to my lap and I sucked my lip between my teeth. I could feel the tears beginning to build in my eyes and blinked, hoping they wouldn't begin to fall. Max gently tucked his fingers under my chin and lifted my face to meet his.

"Renee, I only ask because I don't want you to carry this alone. I want to be able to understand and help you through this. I won't be able to do so unless you talk to me." His eyes met mine as his hands cupped my cheeks. "Does that make sense, sweetheart?"

"Yes," I whispered, the tears dripping over his lean fingers. "What would you like to know?"

"Your mom mentioned test results, so why don't we start there. What type of tests did they do?"

I swallowed thickly. "They did an exam, of course, and ran tests for any STD's," I managed weakly. "The doctor called while you were in the shower this morning with those results though, and so far, everything is negative."

"Well, that's good to hear," he breathed, pushing back a rebellious lock of hair from my face. "Did the exam hurt, or make you uncomfortable, baby?"

"Yes, it did, but thankfully mom was there to hold my hand, and then it was over."

"What about a pregnancy test?"

I stilled at his words like I had been frozen solid. Max noticed my hesitation and brushed his thumb across my cheek before tangling his fingers in my hair.

"Sweetheart? Did they do one?" he asked again, with infinitely more patience than I would have been able to muster.

"No…she said it was too early to do one," I whispered. "Max, it was hard enough to accept that I had been raped, but to think that I could be pregnant too… I'm nineteen! It's too much, Max!"

He pulled me into his arms, stroking my back in soothing circles. "I know, I know. We'll keep our fingers crossed that he used a condom and it worked, so that you won't have to cross that bridge, okay? But, Ren," he said, tilting my face up to look deep into my eyes, "I'm not going anywhere—no matter what."

"But if I'm pregnant—"

"Then you and I can get married and I'll help you raise the baby as though it's mine."

I stared up at him in shock. He had said it all so calmly, like there was no second-guessing, no doubt in his mind he was prepared to marry me and raise a child with me…even if that child wasn't his. Maxwell Harris was twenty years old, to many, he would be considered a boy still yet. His actions, however, proclaimed him to be a man. Only a man would make such an offer.

"I could never ask you to—"

"You didn't ask me to, Renee," he interrupted. "I offered. And it's an offer I plan on standing by, and not just because it is the right thing to do. But because I love you. Nothing that anyone does to you will ever change that fact. Certainly not some cowardly bastard who thinks it's acceptable to force a woman to sleep with him. You are the one I love, and you are an incredible woman."

At this point, I lost the battle and broke down in tears. Between his sweet words, the overwhelming sense of loss I felt, the confusion and the turmoil plaguing my mind, I wept. There was no stopping the flood of tears that fell from my dark eyes, the sobs that shook my frame as he held me in his strong arms, or the fear from creeping into my mind as I worried that he would be put into a position he didn't deserve. Max refused to release me, holding me tight, comforting me, telling me over again how much he loved me as we sat under the wooden arch.

As the colors of early afternoon pearled into twilight, Max and I headed back to the apartment so I could grab a change of clothes and my books for my classes. I hadn't even needed to ask if I could stay with him another night before he had suggested it himself, seemingly unwilling to let me go. I fidgeted in the passenger seat as he drove, LeAnn Rimes playing softly on the radio. He threaded his fingers through mine as we walked to my door, my heart pounding against my ribcage with every step we took.

Walking inside, I was surprised to see the lights on in the kitchen, meaning Mira was back already. I had no desire to talk to her about any of this but knew I would be forced to do so. Max and I had just exchanged a look of unease when she emerged from her bedroom, shock written on her face.

"Where in the fucking hell have you been?" she growled.

CHAPTER TWENTY

Ibalked, retreating a step to be closer to Max's side, at the sharpness of her tone. His hand wrapped around my waist and tethered me to his body, offering me his strength as I faced my roommate. "Sorry…was I supposed to keep you updated on my whereabouts at all times?" I asked.

Mira rolled her eyes, annoyed by my surprisingly snotty response, and sauntered over to the fridge. After she grabbed out a beer—clearly, she had bribed someone to pick her up a case—she turned her attention to the both of us once more, her eyes narrowing on my face. I knew that look; after living together for a year now, I had seen it often enough to realize she was trying to figure something out.

In this case, it was me.

"I just expected you to be here when I got back, since you don't go out or have a fucking life," she sneered, plopping down on the couch.

I could feel Max bristle behind me, but I was in too much shock by her words to do much. Mira's eyes still had not left us, and it was beginning to make me insanely uncomfortable. I wanted nothing more than to grab my things and get the hell out of there, something Max thankfully picked up on.

"Ren, I'm going to borrow your bathroom, and then I'll meet you in your room to help you gather your stuff, okay?" he said quietly.

I nodded and he swiftly walked into my room, leaving me rubbing my arm as Mira continued to stare through me. "Going somewhere?"

"Um…yeah, I'm going to stay at Max's tonight," I told her softly, looking at the floor.

"Why? We have class in the morning."

"I just feel like it, okay!" I snapped, my eyes blazing. I could feel the tears threatening to fill my eyes, and I bit down on my lip as I dashed into my bedroom, shutting the door behind me. Leaning forward, my backside pressed against the wooden door, I struggled to stifle the sobs choking me. My hands clapped over my mouth to silence the sound with my elbows digging painfully into my thighs, the tears dripped hotly into the carpet as Max came into the room.

"Baby?" he whispered, gently pulling me into his arms. "Shh, it's going to be okay. Just sit down and tell me what you want or need packed and I'll grab it, alright?"

Emptying the dirty clothes from my duffle, Max and I quickly refilled it with enough clothes for the whole week, my makeup bag, and I filled my backpack with my textbooks and laptop. Noticing how heavy the latter is with all my science books, he threw that on his shoulder and then picked up my duffle as well, refusing to let me carry either one. Taking a deep breath, we headed back out to the living room, finding Mira still sipping her beer on the couch.

"I guess I'll see you for lunch tomorrow," I said, unable to meet her eye.

She snorts, setting the bottle on the coffee table in front of her, the tilt of her head telling me she knows something is off, and this conversation is far from over. "Fine then. Go have fun with Max."

At the mention of his name—and with the sour tone she said it in—Max shot her a withering look that pinned her to the couch, any further insults dying on her tongue. I nibbled on the corner of my lower lip as he took my hand and gave it a light tug, pulling me toward the door and away from her penetrating glare. I risked one final glance over my shoulder as we walked out the door, surprised to see a slight smirk tugging on her full lips as she reached for her beer once again.

By the time Friday rolled around, I hadn't slept at the apartment once all week, and Mira was becoming beyond suspicious. So, when I stopped by with Max to do my laundry and swap out my clothes for the weekend, she cornered us.

"Okay," she snapped, her hazel eyes blazing, "I think I have been more than patient with the two of you all week, but enough is fucking enough! What the hell is going on? Why have you not been staying here, Ren?"

At this point, she was practically yelling, her voice shrill and reverberating throughout the apartment. I took a deep breath and glanced at Max, sinking into the plush brown couch beside him as she stalked over to the armchair. Fixing us with a fiery stare, she arched her red brows as she waited for my explanation. Meanwhile, my entire body began to shake as fear of having to recount anything about the weekend before terrified me.

"I didn't want to say anything because I didn't want pity for starters, but I also didn't want things to be awkward between us," I began, dropping my gaze to the hands in my lap. Max reached over and laced his fingers with mine, giving me a gentle squeeze so I could continue.

"Oh, don't tell me," she broke in, "you two finally decided to fuck each other, and now you can't get enough of it. Is that it?"

My head shot up, and my eyes widened at her crass assumption. Beside me, Max bristled and practically growled in response. I knew the general notion would be that he and I had been intimate—and God, I wish like hell it had been him instead—but the truth was far more painful to admit.

"No, Mira, that is not it," Max snapped, his voice dangerously low.

"Well, you're sure acting protective of her, like you two have been jumping each other's bones all week, so what else am I supposed to assume here?"

I sighed. "Max and I did not sleep together, Mira. But unfortunately, I was raped last Friday night."

For a full minute, she was actually silent, just staring at us. Her eyes kept going between Max and then to my face, studying our weary expressions. I could feel Max nod his head, confirming my story, his hand rubbing soothingly along my back.

"Well, fuck," she breathed.

CHAPTER TWENTY-ONE

"So, you are telling me you were raped last Friday?" she asked, her brows still raised quizzically. "Do you know who the fuck did it?"

"Yes, I was. The doctor at the emergency room was able to confirm that on Saturday when I went with my mom," I answered. "As to the who… no, I don't remember much of anything."

"It's been too difficult for her to be here at the apartment, so I've been letting her stay with me," Max interjected.

"But neither of you thought to warn me that I could be in danger by staying in this damn apartment by myself?" she snapped.

Max and I glanced at each other. Mira was tall and voluptuously curvy…okay, actually she was more than curvy. She was really overweight. And she didn't have the personality of someone people really enjoyed being around. Sure, to some guys, sex is sex, and one girl's body is as good as another's, but in her case…most wouldn't bother.

"I have a feeling it was personal, Mira," I offered. "And you're better at defending yourself than I am, so you're safer."

Rolling her eyes, she blew out a heavy breath and sat back in the chair, continuing to eye me. "You really don't remember anything?"

"I guess I have been having nightmares about it, but other than that, not really. We think he may have drugged me so that contributed to why I don't, and the doctor said I probably have post-traumatic stress disorder now and that my brain is trying to protect itself by blocking out the memories."

We all fell silent for a few minutes, Max's hand running lightly up and down my back, distracting me from the anxiety threatening to flood my senses the longer I sat in the apartment. I began picking at the nail polish on my hand, glancing up to find Mira's eyes lingering on my stomach. I was about to ask where her mind had ventured when she asked the question I had been dreading for a week.

"Have you taken a pregnancy test?"

"No, not yet."

"They didn't do one at the hospital?" she asked skeptically.

"Why would they? It was far too early to detect a pregnancy then since it was the day after," I reminded her. With her major being art and mine biology, this was more my area of expertise than hers.

"Okay, fine," she huffed. "Why haven't you done one since?"

I swallowed hard. "It's not time yet. I still have just over a week before my period is due, and you can't really test until then."

Mira turned to Max, a wicked glint in her hazel eyes. "So, what is going to happen between the two of you if she ends up pregnant, Max?"

He frowned, clearly displeased by her tone. "What do you think is going to happen?"

"I know a lot of guys would drop a girl who got knocked up by someone else," Mira answered with a shrug.

"Those are boys, not men," he scoffed. "If Ren does end up pregnant, I have already told her that I'm going to help her raise the baby as though it's mine."

Her jaw dropped open an inch, and her eyes were filled with disbelief. Snapping her mouth closed, her eyes narrowed on my face once more. Suddenly, she snickered; a sickening laugh that made my mouth run dry instantly.

"You weren't really raped, were you? You and Max fucked, and now you're worried he knocked you up, so you had to come up with a cover story. That is why you weren't worried about someone coming back and raping me too," she mocked.

My lip trembled as the tears filled my eyes, blurring my vision. The anxiety bubbled to the surface, threatening to boil over and suffocate me if I did not get out there that very instant. I dashed blindly from the couch and ran to my closet, sobs wracking my body as I collapsed on the floor and curled into a tight ball. Even from two rooms away, I could hear Max screaming at Mira.

"You have got to be fucking kidding me, Miranda Lane! How dare you suggest she made that up! You have no idea what the hell she has been through during the past week, and if you even bothered to take one look at her, you would know she was telling the truth—just like she always does! She has been beyond terrified since that night, plagued by nightmares, struggling with severe anxiety at even the mention of this fucking apartment, and can barely eat or sleep!"

"It just seemed—"

"No! You don't get to talk," he said, cutting off her feeble excuse. "Ren is the sweetest person in the world and she certainly didn't deserve to have some lowlife bastard force himself on her and rob her of her virginity, but unfortunately, that is what happened. I am doing the best I can to help her heal and I will be damned if you tear her down or insult her one more time. Is that clear?"

I couldn't hear her response, but it obviously was not what Max wanted her to say.

"I said, is that fucking clear? It's a simple enough question, Mira," he sneered. "Surely even someone like you can handle answering a straightforward question like that with no problems."

"Fine, Max! I'll leave her alone!"

"Aces. Now, do us all a favor, and either go to your room until we leave, or get the hell out of here for an hour so she doesn't have to deal with you again today."

"You're a fucking prick, Harris!" I heard Mira shout, closely followed by the slamming of the front door.

A moment later, Max was kneeling on the floor beside me, scooping me into his arms and wiping away my tears. "Come on, sweetheart," he whispered tenderly, pressing gossamer kisses to my temple. "I've got you."

CHAPTER TWENTY-TWO

Sixteen Days Later...

I'd dragged myself out of the bed at Max's house, shuffling to get around for my classes. Since the rape, I had quit my job at the library. I was too much of a nervous wreck to work there without having a panic attack every five minutes, so instead I tried everything I could to focus on my homework. Even that was proving difficult. The closer to my period I got, the more my nerves escalated.

That morning my anxiety was at a fever pitch since I was three days late for my period—something that had never before happened. Prior to Max picking me up, I had skipped my last class the day before to rush to the on-campus drugstore to purchase a pregnancy test, shoving it to the bottom of my purse in the hopes he wouldn't see it. It had seemed like thousands of butterflies were trapped in my stomach as I had waited to buy the tests, praying no one would see me with them and start spreading rumors about me.

I had wanted to take the test at night upon arriving at the ranch house but reading the instructions I discovered I was supposed to get better results in the morning. I slipped the test package in between my clothes to conceal it as I walked quickly down the hall to the bathroom. Locking the door and flipping on the shower to muffle the noise of the wrapper, I unwrapped the plastic stick to use it, fear mounting in my stomach. Replacing the cap, I set the test on the counter, leaning against it while I did my best to not vomit in the sink as I waited for the results.

The test was meant to give me the answer within three minutes…I had it in under one. I blinked back the tears that pricked my eyes as I saw the word 'positive' in the window. Closing my eyes as the reality of that single word slammed into me, I choked back a sob, clamping a hand over my mouth to stifle the sound. I wrapped the test back in its packaging and then in my pajamas to keep it hidden, since so far, we had not explained to Max's parents about the rape.

Climbing into the shower, the hot spray mingled with my tears, and I came undone. I sank to my knees in the tub, the water washing over me but unable to wash away the anguish now gripping my heart. I could hear Max telling me he would stay by my side, that he would help me raise the baby, that he loved me…and I knew if I stayed with him I was being as selfish as the asshole who stole my innocence.

I slowly rose from my knees and washed my hair and body, knowing I needed to hurry for Max's sake. I had an appointment with one of the counselors on-campus this morning, and now I knew I had an even bigger reason to need to talk with her. I rushed to finish getting ready on time, hiding the pregnancy test at the bottom of my purse again so that no one would see it. I planned to throw it away in one of the campus bathrooms, meaning it couldn't be tied to me.

Sitting in the passenger seat of his truck as we drove to college, I felt ill. Max looked over at me repeatedly, obviously noting my green expression. He reached over to lightly clasp my hand, bringing a small smile to my face despite the trepidation I felt.

"I almost forgot to tell you," he said softly, his thumb brushing the top of my hand, "one of our classmates was found dead from an overdose the other day…in your apartment building too."

"Which classmate?"

"Remember Roy Miller from our psych class spring semester?"

"Yeah, sure," I say, surprised. "I saw him just over a week ago in fact, but didn't think to say anything to him because of everything that is going on with me, but gosh...that's a shame. Roy was always so nice and sincere. I never would have guessed he used drugs, and now his life is over far too soon."

"I know, right?" he responds. "Something so avoidable too, and now he's gone. Seems completely crazy...almost as crazy as you trying to hide that you went to the drugstore yesterday instead of class."

I gasp, turning to face him in shock. "How—how did you know that?"

"Nick called and said he saw you in there and that you looked insanely nervous. I put the dates together and realized it must have been time for you to take a pregnancy test." Max pulled the truck over briefly so he could look me in the eyes. "Did you take one?"

"Yes..."

"And what was the result, Renee?" he asked gently.

Again, my eyes filled with tears. His hands cupped my cheeks as he waited for me to give him the answer aloud. "I'm pregnant," I whisper, my eyes blinking closed, the tears spilling down my cheeks.

Max pulled me into his arms and held me while I wept. "I meant what I said Ren, I am more than willing to help you raise this baby, okay?"

"Max, I feel—I feel so selfish if I take you up on that offer though," I sob. "You're twenty years old and you still have college to finish; you don't need some broken girl for a girlfriend let alone some other guy's baby to look after."

"Sweetheart, I never want to hear you call yourself broken again," he chided. "You are not broken, age is just a number, I can and will finish my degree so don't worry about that, and I am more than happy and willing to raise your baby with you. Forget the part about this baby being some other guy's...this baby is part of you, Ren. And I love you."

He leaned forward to wipe away my tears and place a light kiss on the tip of my nose. I tried my best to smile at him in return, but his words... why did I feel like I was trapping him with this child? Like I was taking away everything from him? Max was the most generous man I knew, and I had no doubt he meant every word that he had just uttered, but could I allow him to do it?

Could I stay with him, save my reputation some of the tarnishing that was bound to come from this entire situation, raise a child with him… without it all becoming too much one day? Or would the illusion of happiness and contentment that he was working so hard to keep around us shatter—violently—leaving me in an even worse place farther down the road? I had some serious thinking to do, because decisions had to be made…and they had to be made fast.

CHAPTER TWENTY-THREE

"So, you just found out this morning that you think you're pregnant now?" Ms. Whitley, the guidance counselor asked, watching my face.

I nodded miserably. I had just concluded explaining my situation to her, the first person I had told as much of the story to as I remembered who didn't play a major part in my life. She had listened attentively, without interrupting, the entire time. Now, she looked at me with scrutiny, her eyebrows furrowed above her glasses.

"I would suggest double checking with a doctor on that to be certain, before you make any rash decisions regarding the baby, school, et cetera," she advised. "Furthermore, a good way to get over things of this nature is to get right back on the saddle, as it were."

"Wait, what?" I asked, confused.

"You mentioned you now fear sex in general, so a good way to combat that fear is to practice…a lot. Find someone, or several people, you are comfortable with in day-to-day life, and engage in sexual intercourse with them," Ms. Whitley suggested with a slight shrug. "Having sex regularly, and with multiple people, can help you overcome your fears and recover from your perceived trauma."

I was dumbfounded. Here it was, I had literally just told this woman I had been raped, didn't have a clue as to who had done it, according to a pregnancy test I took was pregnant, and she wanted me to go out and start sleeping with a slew of guys. Not a fucking chance in hell!

"What the hell kind of advice is that, Ms. Whitley? That sounds about as intelligent as suggesting someone should use a match to see how much gasoline is in their fuel tank. It is patently ridiculous, in case you couldn't tell," I snapped, rising from my seat. "I think we're done here."

I marched out of her office in a huff and headed downstairs from the health clinic. As I emerged from the building, I ran straight into Eric, his tall frame catching me before I tumbled down the five stone steps. His face lit with surprise and then concern as he noticed the tears blinding me, the rage burning in my cheeks as he steadied me.

"Ren?" he whispered. "What is going on with you?"

"I—I don't want to talk about it right now, Eric, sorry," I ground out. "I've got to get going."

Not waiting for a reply, I hurried away from him, ignoring the look of hurt and rejection that flared in his blue eyes as I walked away. Within five minutes, I had quickly walked to my apartment building, and soon was locked inside my bedroom. Mira was thankfully at class and planning to head home to her parents' directly afterward for the weekend, so the place was silent, but I still went and slumped to the floor of my closet—the new location I used for my meltdowns—and dialed my mom.

"Hi sweetie," she said when she answered.

"Hey."

"Renee, is everything going alright, all things considered?"

I closed my eyes and lightly banged my head against the wall behind me. "Not even close, mom," I whispered. "I was late, so I bought a test…"

"Since you're calling me and sound so upset about it, I assume it said you're pregnant," she concluded when my voice trailed away.

"Mom, what do I do? I'm already such a mess I've had to quit my job at the library thanks to the panic attacks, I can barely study or make it to classes, even eating and sleeping is difficult these days. How am I meant to keep up with all of this and have a baby?" I asked, my voice cracking by the end.

She sighed. "What did Max say about it? I hope you told him."

"He says he's willing to stay with me and help me raise the baby as his own, but mom," I pause, swallowing thickly, "I feel like I would be trapping him in the relationship if he stayed. That's not fair to him, me, or the baby."

She was silent on the other line for a moment, contemplating what I was saying. My mom had seen how devoted Max was to me just in the past few weeks, not to mention the months leading up to the attack. But even she must see the validity of my concerns.

"What do you want to do, Ren?"

"I don't think I can keep attending classes while I'm pregnant, and I especially don't think I can attend classes here any longer, mom," I told her softly, emphasizing the word 'here'. "I am constantly looking over my shoulder, wondering if the guy responsible is watching me, sitting next to me in a lecture, following me around the grocery store. It's exhausting. And now that I know I'm pregnant, I don't think I could handle the scrutiny that I would come under for being pregnant before I'm married."

"The circumstances were extenuating, Renee," she reminded me. "But I understand what you're getting at. Your dad mentioned the possibility of you withdrawing from classes when this first happened as well, so he's on board if you want to do that. We can come down and help you pack up everything, talk to the dean and your apartment manager to sort out your lease and tuition this weekend if you'd like."

It was all happening so fast. But I knew that everything from this point on was no longer just about me and would continue to come at break-neck speed. I bit back a sob as I thought about leaving Max, and even Nick, dreading the loneliness that would undoubtedly follow my departure. I closed my eyes and pictured him in my mind, leaning over the console of his truck this morning, telling me he loved me as he kissed my nose.

"I think that would be for the best, mom," I answered. "Thank you."

"You are going to get through this, sweetie," she said sweetly. "Your dad and I will be with you every step of the way…and we'll support you and the baby, even if you decide you don't want to be with Max any longer."

"God mom, of course I want to be with him," I sobbed, "but just because I had my innocence stolen so brutally, doesn't mean I'm comfortable with Max giving up his life…regardless of whether or not he says he's willing to do so."

CHAPTER TWENTY-FOUR

With shaking fingers, I dialed Max as I sat blindly on the edge of my bed. I had already begun packing up my room, and my parents were driving down to help with the rest. We even had an appointment scheduled for this afternoon to meet with the dean to sort out my withdrawal from the university and planned to speak with the apartment manager afterward. I felt my heart breaking with every ring of the phone, the pieces leaping to my throat when he answered.

"Hi sweetheart," he drawled. "Is everything okay?"

I blinked, causing a cascade of scalding tears to run down my cheeks as his concerned face and shining green eyes materialized in my mind. *I am so, so sorry, Max,* I thought in agony. The sobs choked my words, rendering me mute longer than I anticipated.

"Ren? What's going on, baby?" his voice was laced with panic. "Where are you—I'm coming, just hang on!"

"Max," I whispered, my voice a strangled mewl as I struggled to contain my emotions. "I'm not in danger, okay. Sorry, I was just overly emotional."

"Shit, you scared the hell out of me." I heard him slam the door to his truck. "I can meet you wherever you are in five minutes, you don't need to face this alone."

"You have class in half an hour," I pointed out.

"Fuck class, Ren, you are far more important to me," came his vehement reply.

Oh Max, my heart sobbed. "I was just checking in with you, letting you know my parents are coming for a quick visit so I'm staying in town this weekend," I fibbed, hating myself with every word that passed my lips.

"Oh." He sounded surprised. "Did you tell them about the baby?"

"Yeah…I did. Please, do me a favor and don't tell anyone else about that just yet okay? Not even Mira."

"If that's what you want, then sure, sweetheart," he acquiesced. "Do you want me to give you the weekend with your parents, or will I see you before I head out to the ranch tonight?"

I scrunched my eyes closed, his words like a knife to my heart. I knew if I saw him in person, my resolve to let him go would waiver. And as much as I loved him and wanted to keep him in my life, I knew I couldn't be selfish when it came to him. "I think we are going to be pretty busy the next couple of days, sorting out plans thanks to this new development. I'm sorry," I whispered, the last words having a double meaning he was yet to learn.

"Ren, it's okay. I'll see you on Monday. I love you."

"I love you too. Bye Max."

Hanging up the phone, I quickly clamped both hands over my mouth as the sobs ripped through my body. I let myself cry for a solid hour, torn between duty and my heart; wanting to protect Max, and protecting myself. I finally hauled myself off the bed and stumbled into the bathroom, the mirror catching my eyes. My eyes were red and puffy, my face blotchy from spending so long crying. I splashed some cold water on my face and was just drying it off with my blue towel when I heard the knock at my door.

Cautiously, I crept into the living room and tiptoed to the door, rising on my toes to peer through the peephole. Relief flooded through me to see my parents standing outside, and I hastily threw open the door to rush into my mother's arms. Her warm embrace cradled me briefly before we stepped inside my kitchen.

"Oh, Renee," she breathed, taking in my disheveled appearance. Even my dad looked horrified by the tears staining my cheeks and the dark purple bags under my eyes. Thanks to all my sobbing, the heavy concealer I had applied this morning to try and hide them had washed away, exposing my exhaustion to the world. "Let's get to work, shall we?"

For the next few hours, we packed my clothes, books, and random knick knacks I had at the apartment. When it was finally time to go meet with the dean, I was a bundle of nervous energy. Thankfully, he understood the situation and was willing to release me from my courses—meaning my parents would get back some of their tuition payment. As we stood to leave, he caught my attention.

"Miss Westhaven?"

"Yes, Dean Myers?" I asked softly.

"For the record, I believe you are making a very mature and wise decision," he stated. "I wish you nothing but the best and will be certain to put your name on the list of students we would be pleased to have return to us one day."

I smiled the tiniest ghost of a smile at the older man—whose lectures I had thoroughly enjoyed—thinking to myself that there might actually be some decent people in the world still yet. As we headed out of the building, we came face-to-face with a very surprised Nicholas Spencer, his blue eyes never leaving my face. *Shit,* I thought, knowing he could tell instantly when I was lying.

"Hi there," I said weakly, my eyes dropping back to the ground immediately.

"Hey," he answered, crossing his arms over his muscled chest. "Mr. and Mrs. Westhaven, nice to see you again."

"You as well, Nick," my mom said sincerely. "Ren, do you think we could borrow him to help us for a few minutes since you said Max was at the ranch tonight?"

My eyes widened, knowing I would be forced to explain things to him if came over. Nick's brows quirked above his eyes, his gaze penetrating mine and searching for answers. My mother was oblivious to this—or my absolute discomfort—as she and my father motioned for us to follow them back toward my apartment building.

"So," Nick started, looking sideways at me as we walked, "just what am I meant to be helping you with, Ren?"

CHAPTER TWENTY-FIVE

"**Y**ou are seriously moving out, and you don't think Max deserves to know?" Nick practically shouted, leaning against my counter while my parents had stopped to speak with my landlord. "After everything that has happened, everything that he's stood by you through these past few weeks, why—"

"I'm pregnant, Nick," I whisper.

I can see the emotions flicker across his face: anger, confusion, exhaustion, sadness, understanding. Sighing, he shakily runs his hands through his dark brown hair, leaning forward to prop his elbows on the island as he looks at me. "Okay, now I get why you don't want to stay here, but why are you not telling Max? Does he know about the baby?"

Nodding miserably, I sink on the couch, Nick following me to the living room and settling in the armchair. "He knows; I told him this morning after I found out," I answer. I bury my face in my hands, overcome with emotions. Nick hops over to the couch and carefully pulls me into his side.

"Ren, if he knows, then what is the problem? Why are you running away from him?"

"Because he doesn't deserve this, Nick. I know he said he would help me raise the baby, but I can't be selfish with Max. You know what he's like—he's far too good-natured to be shackled to a girl who is nothing but a broken, hollow shell of who she once was, and a baby that isn't his."

"What a load of crap," he stated.

My head snapped up, my eyes blazing. "Excuse me?"

"Renee, Max loves you—he is in love with you. What part of that do you not understand? You are not broken or hollow, and Max would be an idiot to ditch you because of a baby that he didn't father," Nick reprimanded. "But you know that already. No, he doesn't deserve this, but neither do you! Max was and is willing to be with you no matter what obstacles are in the way."

"I just feel like I'd be trapping him if I stayed with him because of the baby, Nick," I confess, looking at my hands.

He sits back from me, stunned. Sighing heavily, he pulls me into his arms once more, resting his forehead against mine. "Sometimes I forget just how big that heart of yours is, Renee."

"Does that mean you'll stop hounding me about this?"

Nick chuckles, the sound warming me. "Probably not, because I do not fully agree with it. But I promise I will help you and your parents pack and load things," he said, pausing to look me in the eyes. "But Ren, I really think you need to tell him."

"If I see him in person, I won't be able to say good-bye," I murmur. I sit quietly for a minute, listening to the pounding of my heart. "Nick, if I write him a letter, explaining all of this, will you promise to give it to him once I'm gone?"

"Ren—"

"I know it isn't fair of me to drag you into the middle of this, but I could really use your help," I plead. "Please, Nick?"

"Oh fuck, not those big brown puppy eyes," he moans, covering his eyes with his hand. "I can't resist them, and you know it! Besides, I guess it wouldn't be nice to deny a pregnant woman a request, huh?"

"Thank you," I say, giving him a fierce hug.

"Don't thank him yet," my dad jokes, "he hasn't helped me move your furniture!"

We all laugh, quickly setting to work. The guys move the things my mom and I have packed, while she and I continue loading things into the crates and boxes I had moved with them in. Around seven we paused to eat take-out, then got back to it. By nine o'clock we had loaded the last of my things into the cars, and I had written two letters—one for Mira to find when she returned, and one for Max.

Nick walked us to the vehicles, the letter tucked inside his leather jacket. He leaned casually against my sedan, his dark eyes shining like sapphires in the lighting of the parking garage. Offering me a grim smile, he pulled me into a gentle hug.

"Take care of yourself, okay?" he whispered in my hair.

"I promise."

"You can call me, for anything," he adds, pulling back to gaze into my eyes. "I mean it, Ren. Please keep in touch and if you need help—"

"I'll give you a call, Nick," I tell him with a smile. "Hey, please don't tell anyone about me being pregnant, okay?"

"It's no one's business but yours, so of course I won't."

"Renee," my mom quietly interrupts, "we need to get going, honey."

"Two seconds, mom," I call. "And please, Nick, please don't give Max that letter until Monday."

"Enough with the puppy-dog eyes, woman!" he cried. "I yield, I yield. I'll wait until Monday, but if he never wants to speak to me again, I am blaming you."

"Fair enough. Thank you, Nick, for everything." I climb into the passenger side of my car as my mom starts the engine. Throwing him a small wave, we drive off, following my dad's truck out of the parking garage and heading for my hometown. As the lights of Lubbock fade in the rearview mirror, I blink back the tears I've been holding in for the past few hours.

I wasn't certain if I was doing the right thing, but I did know it was too late to turn back. Everything had changed this summer, and the girl I had been was gone. I felt as though I had died, been dragged down into the bowels of hell to endure the flames and been reduced to a pile of ashes. Max was amazing, and probably the love of my life. And while I wanted nothing more than to remain by his side for the rest of my life and let him help me heal from this atrocity, I knew I had to take a stand on my own first. *Good-bye Max…I will never stop loving you.*

CHAPTER TWENTY-SIX

Four Days Later...

Knock, *knock.* I looked up from the book I had been curled up reading at the sound of someone knocking on our front door. Both my parents were at work, and I had been carefully avoiding Max's phone calls all weekend and yesterday. I was certain Nick had given him the letter by now, a fact that had caused me to cry myself to sleep last night. So, I had been slow getting around this bright and sunny Tuesday, only recently getting showered and dressed, choosing to read to pass the time.

The knocking continued, making me wonder who the hell was at my door. My brow furrowed as I padded down the hallway, catching a glimpse of my messy self in the mirror. My mousey brown hair was twisted into a messy bun atop my head, I had on loose-fitting yoga pants with a soft red cotton top hugging my curvy bust, and not a touch of makeup on my face. Whoever was on my front porch was about to get an eyeful.

I sighed with lament, wishing I had woken earlier or at least pulled on more than my sports bra, and unlocked the door. Upon opening it, I gasped in shock at the sight before me. Standing on my doorstep, a small suitcase on the ground beside him and a bouquet of stunning pink roses in one hand, was Max. Looking handsome as always in his blue jeans and a black polo, his boots firmly planted on the wooden porch where he stood.

"What are you—" I whispered, my eyes wide.

"I'm here to make you see sense, Ren," he stated, matter-of-factly, sweeping me into his arms.

I melted into his embrace, letting his lips place gentle kisses on my forehead and cheeks before he cupped my chin and slowly—sweetly—kissed my mouth. My arms seemed to move on their own accord, throwing themselves around his neck as his hands wrapped around my waist. Neither of us cared that the front door was still open, that my neighbors were sure to be catching quite a show, or that his suitcase was still resting on the porch. All that mattered in that moment was being in each other's arms.

"Max," I murmured breathlessly.

"I love you," he reminded me, cupping my cheeks and looking deep into my eyes. "I know you were scared and thinking I would feel trapped by this, but baby, nothing could be farther from the truth."

"It's a big decision…" I said, biting my lip.

"Yes, it is. There is no changing that fact. But choosing to stay with you, choosing to raise this baby with you, Ren, it's not a difficult one. Not for me." He kissed my forehead. "Now, am I allowed to come inside?"

Nodding, I backed up, allowing him to grab his suitcase and close the door behind us. Nervously, I reached for the flowers, knowing I needed to get them in some water, but also wondering how he ended up at my door. Jerking my head, I motioned for him to follow me to the kitchen.

"So…" I croaked, pulling down a vase to hide my embarrassment.

"So…" he teased. "If you're wondering what I did this weekend, I sat around waiting for my girlfriend to answer my calls. When she didn't, even though she had told me her parents were going to be in town, I started to get a little panicked."

He raised his fawn brows at me, and I turned scarlet. I had never meant to worry him so much. *I guess Nick was right after all,* I mused. *Damn it, he is never going to let me live that down.*

"Imagine my complete surprise when I show up at your apartment yesterday morning to find Mira in a rage, calling you every name under the sun because you supposedly packed up and left, only leaving her a note,"

Max continued, his green eyes never leaving mine as I trimmed the ends of the roses. "I told her there must be some sort of mistake, because you would not have left without saying good-bye to me."

"Max, I—I wanted to, I just…" I sighed, tears filling my eyes. "I knew if I saw you, I wouldn't be able to do what I thought was best for you."

"What is best for me is you to talk this through with me, Renee, and for us to decide together what we are going to do and where we're going to go," he said softly, resting his hand atop mine.

I tried my best to smile at him, but I'm fairly certain I failed miserably. He picked up the vase and filled it with water, setting it back on the counter in front of me to fill with the sweet-smelling roses he had brought me. "Thank you," I murmured. "What happened next?"

"What happened next was Mira threw me out of the apartment, and I went to find Nick. Mainly to commiserate. I needed him to knock some sense into me and tell me I wasn't utterly insane for the plan running around in my head. When I got to his place and he handed me your letter…"

Max closed his eyes briefly, the pain evident on his face. I realized in that moment that I had royally fucked up when I chose to walk—correction, run—away from him. The guilt ate at me, pushing me to pull him into my arms and run my hands through his hair.

"Nick handed me that letter, and do you want to know the first thing I did after I finished reading it?"

"What did you do, baby?"

"I punched him."

I gasped in shock, sitting back from him with my hands over my mouth and my eyes wide. "Max! You punched him? Why the hell did you punch your best friend?"

He chuckled, earning him a scowl from me. "That's why, sweetheart," he laughed, pulling me back into his embrace. "He is my best friend and instead of giving me a heads up or trying to stop you, he waited. And I was so afraid that him waiting to tell me was going to cost me the best thing in my life…you, Renee Westhaven, and I never want to lose you."

CHAPTER TWENTY-SEVEN

"**Y**ou still shouldn't have punched him, Max," I scolded.

"Water under the bridge, baby," he said, kissing my nose. "He forgave me, told me to get my fucking ass out here to you, and to make sure I told you 'I told you so,' whatever that means."

I laughed, thinking of Nick mocking me with that line. Sighing, I sank against his chest, listening to the steady rhythm of his heart beneath my ear, his hand tracing lazy circles on my back. The smell of his cologne, that intoxicating cedar and lime combination that drove my senses wild, invaded and wrapped around me, instantly putting me at ease.

"So, what are your plans for the day, sweetheart?"

I stilled, remembering what I was meant to do later this afternoon. Sucking my lip between my teeth, I angled my head to gaze into his eyes. "Oh, well...I actually have an appointment to go to," I confessed.

"Oh, well I can hang out here if that's okay—" he started, my fidgeting cutting off his words.

"Do you mind going with me?"

"What kind of appointment is it, Ren?"

"It's an...um...I'm seeing—" I stumbled over my words, causing him to raise his brows in question. *Shit just spit it out already.* "I have an appointment with an obstetrician."

"That's a doctor for pregnancy, right?" he asked cautiously.

I nodded. "Yeah."

"You really want me to go with you?" he asked, clearly dumbfounded by my sudden change of heart.

"I think if you are going to offer to stick with me through a pregnancy for a baby that isn't yours, the least I can do is have you go with me to my first appointment," I said. "You know, make sure you are truly okay with all of this."

"I would be honored to go with you, Ren," he answered, pulling me closer. "Just quit acting like you're going to get me to change my mind by throwing the fact the baby's not mine in my face every other sentence. It is not going to work."

Smiling softly, I wrapped my arms around his waist, hugging him tightly. "I'll do my best. But I probably should go change my clothes and do something with my hair before lunch and the appointment," I tell him. I cock my head to the side as a thought occurs to me. "Do my parents know you're here?"

"I may have called your mother on the way here," he laughed. "She was fine with me coming, so long as you didn't throw me out when I arrived."

"You are something else, Maxwell Harris," I chuckle. "Do you mind using my phone and texting her that you will be going with me this afternoon, so she doesn't have to ditch work?"

"Sure, sweetheart," he responds, kissing my temple as he reached for my phone.

I hurried back to my room, quickly throwing on a pair of jeans, a proper bra, and the red shirt before heading into the bathroom to set my hair to rights. I hear a creak of the doorframe and turn to find him leaning against it, arms crossed over his chest as he watches me. *Damn, he's quiet for such a tall person*, I think—and not for the first time either.

"What time do we need to leave for the appointment," he asks, his eyes on my hands as I quickly braid my hair.

"The appointment is at two o'clock, but they asked me to arrive half an hour early to do paperwork," I tell him. "I figure we can grab a quick lunch on the way."

"Whatever you want," he smiles. "I didn't want to press you when I first got here, but how have you been sleeping the past few nights? I know you've been having trouble with nightmares the last several weeks."

I take a deep breath, pulling my eyeliner from my makeup bag to avoid looking into his eyes. "I may have had some issues over the weekend," I admit softly. I set the black tube on the counter to face him. "And I really missed having you there to hold me during the night and tell me I'm going to be okay when I wake up crying."

"Oh Ren," he breathes.

"And thanks to my stupidity, I had the guilt of leaving you added into the mix, so I may have also cried myself to sleep a few times because I missed you."

"I'm here now, so no more feeling guilty. I'll let you finish your makeup but be thinking about what you want for lunch."

He headed back in the direction of the living room, leaving me to finish getting ready. Five minutes later I joined him, and we set out for the midday meal. All too soon we were sitting in the waiting area of the doctor's office, with me filling out a dozen forms on a clipboard that the receptionist handed me. Nervousness filled my stomach once I turned it back in and returned to my seat beside him, his hand threading with my own.

I knew he was battling his own anxiety when his knee began bouncing the longer we sat there waiting to be called back. The door opened and a ginger-haired nurse poked her head out, consulting the file in her hand.

"Renee Westhaven," she called.

Max offered me a small, yet confident smile as we rose from our seats, meeting her at the door. Following her down the hallway, our fingers still entwined, he leaned his head so that his lips brushed my ear and whispered, "Everything is going to be just fine, baby. I'm right here, and I'm not going anywhere."

And for the first time since this nightmare began, I felt the tiniest ray of hope.

CHAPTER TWENTY-EIGHT

"Hello, I'm Dr. Collins," a sweet blonde introduced herself ten minutes later upon entering the room. "Is it alright to call you Renee?"

"Yes, that's fine," I tell her, nodding nervously as I shake her hand.

"And you are?" she asks, holding out her hand to Max.

"Max Harris," he greets. "I'm Ren's boyfriend."

"Wonderful to meet you both," Dr. Collins says with a sincere smile. Sitting on her little stool, she looks up at me, her hands folded delicately in her lap. "Now, before we begin with anything else, I want to make certain that I understand the note in your file."

Her kind blue eyes meet mine, and for once, there is no trace of pity in someone's eyes when they first hear about what happened. "It says you were sexually assaulted last month, and that this pregnancy is a result of the attack, correct?"

"Yes, ma'am," I answer.

"And you've chosen to stay on with her and be supportive through this?" she asks, turning again to Max, a look of approval on her face.

"Of course. I just want what's best for her, and for the baby," he answers. "I may not have fathered the baby, but the baby is half of her, and she's pretty da—incredible."

"Good answer, Max," she smiles. "I can tell you two will be great parents."

"So, the pregnancy test I took was accurate?" I can't help but ask.

"That was the first thing we checked when you came back," Dr. Collins responds. "And the answer is 'yes', you are indeed pregnant, Renee. Now, here in a few minutes, I'll be doing a sonogram so we can get a clear picture of your little one, but before we do, I want to answer any questions you may have, and also get you prepared for the upcoming months, okay?"

All I can manage is a weak nod. Up until this point, a small—albeit, miniscule—part of me had been clinging to the hope that perhaps the test I had taken last Friday was wrong. Somehow, I knew that wasn't the case though. Hence why I was now sitting in an obstetrician's office in a gown that barely covered my ass and sans panties. Not exactly ideal.

"First things first, do you have any questions for me?"

I gulped. "Um, my mom said she had some pretty serious complications during her pregnancy with me. I know she had preterm labor, horrible morning sickness, things like that, and I was born about a month early," I stated, becoming more nervous with each second. "What are the chances I'll have similar complications?"

Dr. Collins studied me thoughtfully. "That depends on a lot of factors such as age, your overall health, stress can even be a contributor, just to name a few. Obviously, we will test you for gestational diabetes in your second trimester, monitor your weight, and other routine checks. How old was your mother when she was pregnant with you?"

"In her mid-thirties," I answer.

"And you're nineteen, correct?" When I nod, she continues. "Age may have played a large factor in it then for your mother, and you seem to be in relatively good overall health otherwise. I think the biggest thing we'll need to monitor in your case may be your stress levels. You being stressed or in distress after the trauma you went through is perfectly normal and understandable, and while you may not be fully ready to discuss it yet, it may be a good idea to start looking for a counselor or therapist who can help you when you're ready."

"The last counselor I spoke to recommended I go out and sleep with a bunch of guys to get over it," I say with an obvious bite to my voice.

Her eyes widen in shock and I can see Max stiffen in his seat. "Well, whoever that counselor was clearly needed to have their own head examined for attempting to give that type of advice," she stated. "I can give you the names of some top-notch trauma therapists in the area who will not be advising multiple sex partners as a method to combat your anxiety."

"Thank you," I reply, my voice soft.

"Of course. Any other questions for now?"

"Not that I can think of at the moment," I finally say. I glance over at Max. "Did you have any questions?"

"Does she need to have a special diet or any restrictions, aside from avoiding stress as much as possible, right now? When do we need to start worrying about morning sickness? And I know she loves to take hot baths to calm down, but are those still okay?"

I blinked, amazed at how invested and prepared he was for all of this. He had thought of, and asked, questions I had not even considered. Dr. Collins looked impressed and shared an easy smile with me.

"Great questions, Max," she praised. "Nothing too special for the diet, just don't overdo it on caffeine or fatty, greasy foods. Obviously, avoid alcohol if either of you sneak drinks from time to time. She may find she wants to rest more often, and that's perfectly fine, but other than not lifting ridiculously heavy items, she can more or less do what she would like activity-wise. Morning sickness tends to kick in around weeks eight to ten if a woman is going to get it, so having saltine crackers and ginger ale on hand then may be helpful. On the hot baths front however," she paused, looking over at me, "you'll have to switch to simply warm baths, because otherwise you'll get far too hot."

"Got it," we both say at the same time.

"Now, let's see if we can't get you a souvenir to take home with you," she says, a twinkle in her eyes. Directing me to lie back, she scans my womb and soon locates a tiny little peanut curled in a corner. Hitting a few buttons, she prints out the image, handing it to me with a smile. "Here's your baby, momma. I'll see you next month."

CHAPTER TWENTY-NINE

"**I** still can't get over this," Max gushed, holding the grainy black and white image in one hand while the other arm was draped over my shoulder, pulling me into his side. "This is the baby—your baby, Ren."

I couldn't help but smile as he said it. I know a lot of people—especially those my age in this very pro-choice era—would have been rallying for me to have an abortion. Here it was, this baby was not my boyfriend's, and would forever serve as a reminder of the horrors that I suffered. But like Max had said, this baby was half me. How could I end the life, the existence, of my child because of what his or her sperm donor had done to me? It was not this baby's fault they were created from a nightmare and ending my pregnancy wouldn't change anything that had happened to me.

"You really are amazing; do you realize that?" I ask him.

His emerald eyes lock onto mine, and he sets the sonogram picture on the table beside us. The hand that had been holding the printout captured my cheek, the thumb brushing tantalizingly across the arch of my cheekbone, slowly and seductively bringing my mouth closer to his. Max has been nothing but a gentleman our entire relationship, and that didn't change a bit when this happened. He took a huge step back, keeping our physical contact to a minimum just so I could be at peace. This kiss, though respectful of my boundaries, shot explosions of passion through my body.

"I love you, Ren," he whispered, his lips still brushing against mine.

"I love you too," I tell him, stealing another quick kiss before sitting back, a scarlet blush painting my cheeks. "As much as I was enjoying that, I suppose we should discuss what our next steps are going to be."

"Does that mean you're prepared to let me stick around?"

"Max, you know what this means, right? I don't have the choice to back out of being a parent to this baby, but you do," I say slowly. "I wouldn't blame you if you didn't want to be involved—"

"Hush," he says, laying his fingers on my lips, a smile on his own. "No, I don't have to be involved, but I want to be, Ren. This baby is not my responsibility, but I am more than happy and willing to raise him or her with you because I love you and I want to be with you. This child deserves to have two parents who love each other and who love them…regardless of how they were created."

"Oh Max," I breathe, throwing myself into his arms. His grip tightens around me as he lets out a low chuckle.

"I'm guessing you two worked things out then," my mom says from behind us. We jump apart, laughing nervously as my parents come fully into the living room. "I must say, I'm very happy about that and I—"

Her voice trails as she spots the sonogram on the table, her eyes growing wide and misting with tears. She reaches shakily for it, her free hand covering her mouth as she struggles to not cry. Her eyes meet mine and I feel Max lace his fingers through mine.

"Is this…"

"Yeah," I tell her, rubbing the back of my neck with the hand he hadn't claimed.

She thrusts the printout at my dad, her face lighting with a huge smile. "Patrick, look! This is our future grandchild! Oh, my goodness, I already love this little bean so much!" she gushed.

My dad was quiet for a full minute, staring at the picture in his hand, and I felt a pang of dread settle over me. We had never been very close— we acted far too similar for me to be a daddy's girl—but the thought that my dad was upset over the baby was unsettling for me. I watched his face, my teeth working my lower lip as the anxiety continued to build within me, until he finally looked up, his blue eyes filled with tears.

"Patrick Westhaven, are you crying?" my mom teased, clearly shocked at seeing him in this state.

"I don't know what you're referring to, Pam," he answered, quickly swiping at his eyes.

Max and I shared a conspiratorial look, and I released the breath I didn't realize I had been holding. *Well, at least my parents are on board with this whole baby thing, and so is Max,* I thought to myself. *Now we just have to tell his parents.* I knew his dad would be fine with everything once it was explained, it was his mother I was scared to death of telling. Since his last girlfriend had been a bit of a controlling and manipulative bitch—to say nothing of her psychotic inclinations—Brenda Harris was hardly my biggest fan.

"Ren, why don't you come help me with dinner," my mother suggested pointedly.

We left the guys seated in the living room, and I had my suspicions on what they would be discussing. On my way back to the kitchen after running to the restroom, I heard Max's low voice speaking to my dad, causing my heart to pound within my chest from where I stood in the hallway, seeing but not able to be seen.

"Mr. Westhaven—"

"I think we can dispense with the formalities at this point, Max," my dad laughed.

"Alright," he agreed, taking a deep breath. "I have no intention of leaving Ren to deal with this on her own and wanted to ask if you would have any objections to me asking her to marry me."

"Absolutely, I have objections," my dad answered, the look on his face serious–for once. "And so will you if you ever have a daughter of your own. But Max, you have stood by Ren through so many harrowing ordeals the past few months, and I could not be more grateful for your continued support of my daughter. She's my little girl, and all I want is for her to be cared for and loved. With that said, you have my blessing to ask her."

"Thank you, Patrick," Max smiled. "I will do my best to always support her and surround her with the love she deserves."

Heart in my throat—but in a good way—I crept back to the kitchen, unable to wipe the smile from my face for the remainder of the evening.

CHAPTER THIRTY

"**I** think we are going to head off to bed," my mom announced once our after-dinner movie ended. "Some of us have work in the morning."

"Night guys," I tell them, feeling overly fatigued myself.

Max turns to me from his place on the couch before pulling me into his secure embrace. "I presume I'm sleeping in the guest room, right?" he asks, pressing a kiss to the top of my head.

I angle my head so I can meet his gaze. The past four nights without him holding me had been hell. I had absolutely no intention of being away from him again now that he was here. "That would be a big 'no', Max," I tell him, a glint of mischief in my eyes.

"I didn't think your parents would appreciate us sharing a bed without us being married."

I chuckled. "If you think they don't know about you and I cuddling at night for the past month, think again. I was brutally honest that you were about the only way I had been surviving the nights lately. So, with that being said, I do not give a damn what tradition is at the present time, I don't plan to spend another night away from your arms if I can help it."

He leaned forward to brush a kiss on the tip of my nose and carefully scooped me up into his arms. Max carried me to my room, setting me gently on the edge of the bed, his green eyes never leaving my face.

"Fair enough, sweetheart," he whispered, brushing back my hair. "I'm going to grab my suitcase then and I'll be back in a minute."

For the first time in weeks, I felt something akin to giddiness bubbling inside of me, like someone had trapped hundreds of deranged butterflies within my stomach. Max was going to stay with me, he loved me, my parents were in support of our relationship, and I felt safer than I had in months. Despite the fact I had dropped out of college and was now expecting a baby at nineteen, it seemed like my life was finally looking up in ways I had never thought it could.

We readied ourselves for bed, crawling beneath my covers and snuggling close to one another in the dark. I fell asleep to the feeling of him stroking my hair and listening to the soothing melody of his heartbeat as the warmth of his body cocooned me with his intoxicating cologne. Hours later, my sense of security came crashing down around me as the nightmares began to plague my mind.

"Sweetheart, I'm right here," I hear Max saying through the haze of sleep. "Wake up, Ren."

His voice is filled with concern and it feels like someone has super-glued my eyelids closed as I attempt to open my eyes. My limbs ache, like I've been running a marathon in my sleep, my throat seems raw from the silent screams that ripped through my dreams. I'm drenched with sweat and shivering from the chill where the air conditioning is hitting my exposed skin, the blanket having been kicked to the floor due to my thrashing.

"Open your eyes, baby," he murmurs, his hands caressing the sides of my face.

Finally, I'm able to force my lids up, the bedside lamp he turned on illuminating his face as he hovers over me. We both had realized after the first few nights that if he attempted to wake me in the dark, it took him twice as long to calm me. Ever since, Max had made certain to flip on a lamp so I could see it was him in the bed with me, touching me, reaching out to rescue my drowning soul.

"That's it, Ren, it's going to be okay. I've got you," he assured me, letting me snuggle closer as I gasped and sobbed into his chest.

"Oh God, Max," I cry, swallowing hard against the bile rising in my throat. "I—I remember he had a knife."

He stills, his heart beginning to race when I utter the word 'knife'. Up until now, I hadn't remembered much of anything from my nightmares, let alone had any memories simply return to me. The only time Max has spoken about them was the first night when he had rushed into the guest room at his parents' house and said I had been telling him I was sorry.

"He had a knife?"

"Yes. He held it to my throat and told me to behave," I whisper. "Max…I know his voice, but I can't figure out who it is."

A heavy sigh rushes from his lungs as his hands resume their gentle caressing. "Someday you will, and this will all be behind us." He pauses, clearly torn on if he should ask me any further questions. "Do you remember anything else, Ren?"

"I think—I think there was someone else in the room," I confess. "Someone helping hold me down for him."

"Son of a bitch," his voice an angry hiss. "I am so sorry, baby."

I nestle closer to him, hiding my face in the crook of his shoulder. He leans over and pulls the blankets back onto the bed, covering me once more as he refuses to relinquish his hold on me. Brushing a kiss on my forehead, he reaches for the lamp, plunging my room into darkness once more. He holds me the rest of the night, and mercifully, the nightmares remain at bay.

By the time the morning light is streaming through my windows, Max is already sitting up in my bed, his laptop open in front of him. I gaze blearily up at him, smiling at the sight of him in my bed, the knowledge that one day this could be how I wake up every morning making me deliriously happy. I prop myself up on one arm, gaining his attention.

"Morning, sweetheart," he greets. "Sorry if I woke you."

"You didn't," I assure him. "What are you working on?"

"Trying to get my last two classes switched to online classes so I can focus on you." Seeing my surprised expression, he shrugs. "All but two of them were online already, and I contacted the Dean yesterday to get the ball rolling. Guess it is a good thing I'm an engineering major and can work on school from just about anywhere."

"Sounds great to me," I agreed, pulling him down for a kiss.

CHAPTER THIRTY-ONE

"**N**ot that it isn't great to see you, Ren, but what the hell are you doing back in Amarillo?" my best friend, Annie, asks as she walks into my house a few hours later, pulling me into a tight hug. She stands back, her golden eyes looking me over in curiosity, her flawless olive skin reflecting the sunlight streaming in through the windows and highlighting her dark brown hair.

I sigh, knowing I won't be able to get anything past her; she knows me far too well. I motion for her to follow me out to the sunroom at the back of the house, sitting down on the hanging swing nervously with her beside me. She wastes no time in turning her gaze back onto my face, waiting for her answers.

"I'm back for good," I tell her softly, ignoring her gasp of surprise. "Something happened last month, and I can't stay in Lubbock anymore."

"But—what about Max and becoming a biology teacher?" she stammers.

"Max is actually here too. He's working on a class right now, otherwise he'd be in here to say hello." I pause, collecting my thoughts. Annie is fiercely protective of me, even though I am the older of us. I have no doubt in my mind she is going to crave retribution far more than most when I tell her what transpired in my Lubbock apartment.

"Okay, so Max is here, and you say you can't stay in Lubbock now," she says slowly. "Ren…what happened?"

I look into her wide eyes, and see the fear dilating her pupils, much as I've seen in my own for the past month. Swallowing thickly, I brace myself for the onslaught of emotions this will undoubtedly cause. "Last month, the weekend before classes began, I was alone at the apartment," I begin, looking at my hands. "I still don't remember many details, which the doctor said was normal, but someone came into the apartment and—um…"

"Ren?" she breathes, her eyes wide as saucers.

"I was raped," I finally say. Her hands go to her mouth and tears fill her eyes. "Unfortunately, it gets worse."

"What is worse than being raped?" Annie asks.

"I'm pregnant," I whisper.

Her jaw falls open and the tears she had been holding at bay abandon her eyes. I can see the anger lurking just beneath the surface of her concern for me, waiting to burst like a dam. She pulls me into her arms and we both completely come undone, tears soaking each other's shirts. I lose track of how long we sit there, slowly swinging sideways as we cry, until someone clears his throat from the doorway.

"You two alright?" Max asks gently.

"That is a fucking idiotic thing to ask, Max," Annie scoffs.

"Annie," I warn. "Max has stood by me through all of this, okay. And he's even offered to help me raise the baby, so chill."

Wiping her eyes, she turns to consider him. Annie rises from the swing and walks confidently to stand in front of him, which is an amusing sight since she's not much taller than me, so he still towers over her. She crosses her arms over her slim chest and glares up at him, causing Max to look at me, concern written plainly on his handsome face.

"You didn't have anything to do with what happened to her, right?" Annie snapped, her eyes blazing.

Hands in front of him in surrender, Max hurriedly denies it. "No, absolutely not! Annie, you know I would never do anything to hurt Ren. I love her. Believe me, if I knew it was going to happen, I never would have let her stay at the apartment that night."

Finally, she nods. "Very well, then you may assist me in castrating the bastard that did this."

Max grins sardonically. "How very generous of you, Annie, but I assure you, castration is far too simple and gentle for what this fucker did to her. And if I ever find out who it was and get my hands on him, his balls may be the only part of him they ever find."

I can't help but gape at the violent insinuation my boyfriend just made, but at the same time, I feel incredibly safe. Annie smiles in satisfaction, clearly agreeing that Max has things well in hand, and comes to sit back by me again. Max sinks into one of the chairs opposite the swing, a look of contentment in his eyes.

"So, what is the plan for you two then?" Annie asks, looking between us.

"I've switched all my classes to online so I can do them from anywhere and be with Ren," Max informs her. "At some point, I will have to go home and tell my parents about this, since all they knew was this visit was for me to check on you," he adds, smiling at me.

"I know," I agree. "As for me, I'm taking a break from school right now because of my anxiety issues from this and to prepare for the baby."

"I still can't believe you're going to be a mom," she says, shaking her head in disbelief. "I mean, I can, I just never imagined it would happen like this."

"That makes two of us," I reply.

"Do you mind if I tell Zane about this?" she asks, referring to her longtime boyfriend.

"I suppose that's fine; I just don't want a lot of people knowing."

Annie smiles, gripping my hand comfortingly. The three of us sit and talk for another hour or so before she heads out, leaving Max and I to plan a quick trip back to see his mom and dad. We decide we'll head back on Friday morning, only staying for the weekend. Max has some things to do around town, so plans for me to stay out at the ranch while he's occupied. To say I was nervous about the prospect of going back was an understatement…I was scared as hell.

CHAPTER THIRTY-TWO

"Hey Ren! It's good to see you," Max's father, Jerome, greets as we walk in the door. He envelops me in a warm hug, his green-blue eyes twinkling in the light. "We have missed having you around the past week."

I chuckle nervously, but I am glad at least one of his parents has missed me. Brenda didn't even bother to stand from her chair when we entered, and so far, has only spoken to Max. Her indifference toward me varies daily between downright pettiness, snide remarks, or the classic Antarctic freeze-out (which I personally think is her favorite when it comes to me). It sucks, because I honestly would like to have a good relationship with her, but I don't even know where to start getting it back on track—let alone how the hell it derailed to begin with.

"Hi Jerome," I respond. I walk over to the couch where Max is patting the seat beside him and sit down, letting him pull me into his side. I don't miss the way Brenda's eyes narrow at me and start fiddling with my fingers in my lap.

"So, we kind of wanted to talk to you guys about something," Max starts, looking over at his parents. "You might want to sit down for it though."

"Don't tell me she's pregnant," Brenda says with a hiss.

My eyes fill with tears instantly and I try to stand up to run off, but Max just wraps his arms around me, pulling my face into his neck. I don't have to look at his face to know he's scowling at his mother right now.

"Mom, first off, if that is the way you would react to your first grandchild, damn," he snarls. "Second, I don't know what your problem with Ren is, but get over yourself! I am totally and madly in love with her, and I do not appreciate how you treat her. So, knock it off because we have way more important shit to deal with than your fucking attitude!"

"Maxwell," his dad warns.

"Look, I'm sorry, I know I should be more respectful, but Ren has been through enough lately without dealing with this too."

I peek out from the safety of his arms to see Jerome looking intently at us—me, in particular—while Brenda is sitting there with her arms crossed over her chest and a frown on her face. I bite my lip and glance up at Max who gives me a little squeeze to reassure me.

"Okay, son, why don't you start over," Jerome says quietly.

Max sighs. "Ren has left the university and returned home to Amarillo, and as you know I have transferred all my classes to online, which is so I can be mobile to be near her."

"We were hoping for an explanation for that," his dad chirps.

"I know you were, which is why we're here. You also know that last month, Ren began staying here nightly—"

"Even though she had her own apartment in town," his mom interrupts.

"Yes, mother, she did." Max glares at her while taking my hand. "There was a valid reason Ren didn't stay at her place, which we are getting to."

I sigh, knowing I need to speak up and not leave Max to do all the talking. "The weekend before classes resumed for the fall semester, I was at the apartment alone," I said softly, drawing their attention. "I still don't remember much, which the doctor thought may be thanks to them drugging me, but..." I take a deep breath, trying to steady my nerves. "I was—I was assaulted."

I can see Jerome's eyes harden in anger, and even Brenda gasps a little at my revelation. I can feel the tears pricking my eyes, blurring my vision.

"Ren hasn't been having the easiest time dealing with this, as you can probably imagine," Max continued. "It came out of left field for both of us when we realized what happened to her, but I've been trying my best to be there for her. School became too much for her, so she went back home."

"Oh, Ren," Jerome whispered.

"I had already told her that even if by some chance she ended up pregnant because of this I wasn't going to leave her. I would help her raise the baby," Max said, leading up to the next bombshell. "She found out last week."

"She really is pregnant then?" his mother said.

"Ye—yes," I murmur, pulling out the sonogram picture and offering it to them.

Jerome takes the image and stares at it, a small, teary smile on his face. Showing it to Brenda, her façade finally cracks, and the tears fill her eyes. Max lets his thumb stroke the back of my hand gently, soothing my very soul as we sit there.

"I am going to be there for Ren and for this baby," he states calmly. "I felt—we both felt—you two should know before things got more serious."

"I'm proud of you, son," Jerome said with a broad smile.

Max smiled in turn and looked at his mother, whose eyes hadn't left the grainy photo once. We all waited with bated breath for her to speak, to say something encouraging about the situation. I don't think any of us were quite expecting the venom-laced words that flowed from her mouth next.

"I just want to know how you did it."

"How I did what?" I ask, confused as hell.

"How did you convince my son that you were raped so that he would be compelled to help you raise some bastard child you are now carrying?" she snapped, eyes blazing. "I will be damned, Renee Westhaven, if I allow my son to pay for your choices to be a slut who went out and slept with some random guy instead of being faithful to her boyfriend, and is now pregnant. You want to keep Max? Have an abortion! You want to keep your bastard child? Leave Max!"

CHAPTER THIRTY-THREE

Three loud gasps went up around the living room at her words before I leapt from the couch and ran to the guest room in tears. Throwing myself atop the bed, I curled into a ball and sobbed. I lost track of the time, but I could hear Max and Jerome yelling at Brenda, and her yelling right back at them. The door creaked open, and the bed dipped behind me, Max tenderly taking me into his arms.

"Oh God, sweetheart, I am so sorry she said that to you," he whispered, holding me tight.

I shuddered in his arms, leading him to quickly pull the blankets over me. His fingers brushed through my hair, slowly calming my sobs.

"Why does she hate me so much?" I whisper in between hiccups.

"Beats me to hell but try not to let it get to you. Both my dad and I stood up against her for saying what she did. We are going to get through this, Ren."

There is nothing for me to say in response to that, so I lay silently in his arms, listening to the chirping of the crickets outside the window. Eventually, I fall into a restless sleep, dreaming of faceless monsters chasing me through the night, grabbing at my ankles and my neck. Gasping for air when I wake, I struggle against the feeling of Max's arm as it lays across my body.

"What's wrong?" he asks suddenly, eyes flashing open beside me.

One look at my face tells him everything he needs to know, and he gently pulls me back into his arms. My muscles are rigid at first, denying me the peace and relaxation I so desperately crave, but his patient caresses slowly loosen the knots that have formed, allowing me to melt into his embrace.

Despite everything—all the horror, all the fear, all the pain and exhaustion, to say nothing of the self-loathing I'm experiencing—Max has been my tether in this storm, and one of the only remaining links to my sanity. Without him, I would truly be lost. I know he won't hurt me, and that he will do anything in his power to protect me. Trusting Max is easy. Showing him that is another matter at times.

"I should have slammed the damn door in your face, huh?" I murmur, my eyes closed tightly to avoid seeing his reaction.

"What? When?"

"On Tuesday when you came to my house. I shouldn't have let you in. Then you wouldn't be in this situation with your mom now."

His fingers curl under my chin, angling my face upward. "Ren, look at me please." I crack my eyes open to gaze up at him in the darkened room. "I would not change a damn thing other than you never having to go through the harrowing experience you did. I love you, and my mom is going to have to get on board with that fact."

Though whispered, his words are full of passion, and I know he means each one. "I know you do," I reply, reaching my hand up to tangle my fingers in his hair, "I just hate that you are suffering because of this too."

Shaking his head, Max leans down and brushes the lightest of kisses over my lips. "How is it that you have been through absolute hell the past month, and yet you're still more concerned with how this is affecting everyone else than how it hurts you?" I smile up into his emerald eyes. "You are incredible, Ren, never forget that."

His nose bumps mine, earning him another grin, and he pushes tendrils of my brown hair off my forehead with his fingertips. I relax into his touch, letting my eyelids flutter down to veil my eyes once more, and sigh in contentment.

When I awaken next, sunlight is streaming in through the blinds, filling the room with golden warmth. I roll over in the bed to find Max gone, a frown creasing between my brows as I take in the place where he had laid all night and wondering when he left. I flip back to my nightstand to check the time on my phone, surprised to find that it is nearly ten in the morning.

A quiet knock on the bedroom door startles me, but I'm relieved to hear Jerome's voice through it. I throw back the covers, noting that I never bothered to change out of my clothes from yesterday, so I was at least decent enough to answer the door.

"Morning, Ren," he says with a small smile when I prop the door open.

"Morning. I am so sorry I slept so late—"

He holds up his hand to cut off my comment. "Don't even worry about that. Max mentioned you had a rough night before he left." Jerome must have noticed the shock that lit in my eyes because he immediately explained himself. "He ran over to see Nick this morning but said to tell you he would be back early this afternoon. I've got some breakfast things if you're hungry."

After the events of last night, I had completely forgotten Max had planned to go visit Nick this weekend. I bit my lip, thinking about having to deal with Brenda without Max around. I knew Jerome would stick up for me but hated to think of him being pitted against his wife on my behalf.

"I may take a quick shower if that's alright, and then I will gladly take you up on breakfast," I said, smiling.

"Whatever is most comfortable for you is perfectly fine. If I'm not in the kitchen when you get done, feel free to help yourself."

Tossing me another grin and a wave, Jerome heads back down the hall toward the kitchen, disappearing around the corner. I scurry to gather my things, wanting to hurry and get around so I can be ready when Max gets back from seeing Nick. The heat from the shower does wonders at helping to wake me fully, in addition to massaging the knots in my aching muscles.

By the time I step out and onto the terry cloth rug to dry off, I feel charged and ready to take on whatever challenges are going to be thrown my way. All that changes once I dress and dry my hair, heading to the kitchen for breakfast—well, brunch by this point—to find Brenda sitting at the table, her face a glowering scowl as she waits impatiently for my arrival, and unfortunately, Jerome is nowhere to be seen.

Well…this can't be good…shit.

CHAPTER THIRTY-FOUR

I shift nervously as I take in her thick arms, crossed firmly over her chest, the hard look in her eyes, and the unwavering aura of malice hovering around her. My stomach flips, causing me to fear I'm going to vomit, and I swallow painfully, doing my best to stand my ground. She doesn't even bother to stand up to greet me, just continues to sit at the table…glaring at me.

Sighing, I realize she and I need to have it out if we're going to have any sort of relationship in the future—especially knowing that Max plans to ask me to marry him—and slowly resume my approach. Her eyes narrow further as I step forward, and it takes every ounce of courage I possess to not shrink back in fear. The only thought that makes me put one foot in front of the other in this moment is Max. He is the source of my bravado. My rapist stole much of my bravery—my sense of empowerment.

"You've got some nerve, coming in here this morning," she snaps, halting me with her venomous words.

My eyes widen in anger. "And you've got some nerve giving me hell after I know both Jerome and Max told you to back off last night," I rebutted.

She had the good sense to at least look ashamed when I said that… even if only for a moment.

I sink into one of the chairs at the table, opposite her, and let my hands drop into my lap. "Look, Brenda, I know you don't like me for whatever reason, but we need to figure this out now."

"Yes, because Max is bound and determined to keep you and your bas—"

"Don't you dare even finish that word!" I fume, feeling the heat rising in my cheeks. "If you think I went out and slept with some random guy, you're insane. And if you think I asked to be—to be raped, you have got another thing coming. This entire situation has been hell for me. Trust me, the last thing I wanted was to find out I was pregnant. And you can ask Max. I tried to push him away so he wouldn't be caught up in this and he could move on. He refused because he is such an incredible man, he's willing to help me raise a baby that he didn't get to father."

I pause, taking a deep breath to steady myself, watching as she does the same. "You and Jerome raised him to be a gentleman, for which I have been so thankful. He never pressured me to do anything I wasn't ready to do," I whispered. My eyes fill with tears as I look back at her. "It kills me that I can't say Max was my first. I know it would have been special with him and he would have treated me right. Instead, all I know about my first time is that it was forced with one guy holding me down while another held a knife to my throat."

I saw the shock register in her eyes when I said those words and her mouth went slack as the truth hit her. She knew I was being honest; there was no escaping that realization with what I had just said. The proud lift of her shoulders faltered, and she slumped in her chair, defeated.

"Oh God, Ren, I—" she looked up at me, regret carved into her stony face. She sighed heavily. "I am so sorry for what I said. After Max's last girlfriend, and everything she tried to pull on him, I was worried he would end up with another girl who would try similar stunts. It didn't matter how different you acted compared to her, as his mother I still worried."

"I get that, truly I do," I reassured her, "and trust me, I have asked him more times than I can count if he's positive he wants to stick around and be a part of this baby's life since he's not the father. I didn't want him to feel trapped by a child that wasn't his, no matter what he had said. He hasn't relented once, and he has actually started to get rather annoyed with me for asking."

"Sounds about right," she laughed. "So…do you think we can start over?"

I smile tentatively at her. "I know it would make Max beyond happy if we did and I personally would like nothing better."

"Thank you, Renee," Brenda murmured. "Are you hungry at all? I can warm up something for you if you'd like."

"Believe it or not, but I'm famished."

A few minutes later, I was nibbling on a biscuit and a slice of bacon when the front door opened, allowing Max, Nick, and Jerome to enter the house. Since Brenda and I had been conversely pleasantly as I ate, the three of them had stopped in wide-eyed wonder at the spectacle.

"Am I hallucinating?" Max asked them, hands held in front of him in denial.

"If you are, then I am too," Nick replied, quirking one of his dark brown brows upward. "Nice to see you again, Renee."

"Hi, Nick."

The five of us chatted over the next few hours and on into the evening, enjoying our time together. It seemed like the first real conversations I had been a part of in weeks, with the fear ebbing away from my mind as we talked about the ranch, the classes Max and Nick were taking, and everything else but the trauma that I had been dealt. It was a blessed reprieve from the vortex of turmoil that controlled my mind.

For the duration of the weekend, I remained at the Harris's house, outside of town. Max periodically went within city limits to meet Nick, but I was content to stay hidden away and out of sight. My parents had agreed to allow Max to live with us, so he and I kept busy packing some of his belongings so he would feel more at home there.

We both promised Brenda and Jerome we would visit again soon and encouraged them to drive up to Amarillo when they were able. I knew returning to Lubbock often was not ideal for the sake of my own sanity, but felt I was being horribly unfair to Max if I didn't accompany him on his trips back home when he was willing to sacrifice so much to be with me. I knew he understood the panic that gripped my heart at the mere notion of being in Lubbock, but there was no persuading him to consider leaving me behind.

I truly had lucked out with having Max Harris in my life.

CHAPTER THIRTY-FIVE

Acouple weeks after we broke the news to his parents, Max surprised me by flopping down on our bed after his classes one day, grinning at me from where his head rested on his arms. I had been propped up against the pillows, reading a new thriller by my favorite author while he worked, and tucked my finger inside the book as I smiled back at him.

"You do realize you completely messed up the comforter, right?"

His green eyes looked down his long, lean body to observe the rumpled blue spread, wrinkled under him as he lay sprawled on the bed. Eyes still twinkling mischievously, he met my gaze once more.

"I think the comforter will forgive me if I take the beautiful girl sitting on it out for a date tonight."

"You want to go on a date tonight?"

"Pretty sure that's what I just said," he teased, uncurling one of his arms to reach over and gently squeeze my knee. "What do you say, Ren? Can I take you out?"

"I suppose that would be okay," I replied, leaning over to kiss his forehead.

He shifted at the last minute, pulling me into his arms and crashing our lips together. I was slightly stunned at how quickly and easily he had maneuvered me under him, but the warmth of his embrace was making me deliriously happy. Max had a way of ensuring I was never frightened of him, never worried that he would hurt me, never in fear of history repeating itself.

He handled me delicately—as though I was a priceless porcelain figure he treasured.

"I may have pulled out a cute little dress for you before I came in here," he admitted, letting his nose brush against mine gently. "I'll go change in the guest room and let you get ready in here, okay?"

I nodded, smiling, my heart racing inside my chest as he left. After having accidentally eavesdropped on the conversation between him and my father, I was suspicious of his intent for the evening…but in the best possible way. Knowing he wanted to marry me, to stick with me and the baby, was such a blessing. I wasn't convinced he had found the time to come up with a ring by then though, so assumed it truly was going to just be a date. Max had other plans.

Slipping into the soft blue sundress that fell to my knees, I pulled on the matching sandals and left my brown hair swishing in satiny waves around my face. I kept my makeup simple and threw on my silver spiral earrings and the silver butterfly necklace Max had given me as a belated birthday gift this year. I spritzed on my favorite perfume—the only one I could still tolerate with my pregnancy nose—and declared myself ready.

Heading into the living room, I found Max talking with my mom, his fawn hair perfectly combed and his jeans hugging his muscular hips. And that didn't even begin to cover the black dress shirt he wore, tucked in at his waist and showing off his strong arms. I bit my lip to keep myself from drooling on the spot, reminding myself that nothing was going to be simple from here on out.

"Oh, Ren, you look lovely!" my mother crooned, her eyes alight.

Max turned to face me, and I saw the desire flare in his eyes. For the first time since the rape, I was reminded of where our relationship had been, and how close to breaking down our intimate barriers we had been before the attack. I gulped when I saw his emerald orbs slowly trace up and down my form and sucked my lip further between my teeth. Meeting his gaze, my heart nearly stopped when he threw me a cheeky wink.

"Lovely indeed," Max murmured. "Are you ready to go?"

I nodded, not trusting my voice to come out as anything but a squeak, and together we headed out the door. Opening my door, he helped me into the car and kissed my fingers before shutting the door. Climbing in beside me, he revved the engine and off we drove, the brilliant Texas sun high overhead.

"So, where are we heading?" I asked since he had not been forthcoming.

"That's a surprise, sweetheart."

"Max," I whined. I was not a patient person, and he knew it.

He chuckled. "I promise it will be worth the wait and the suspense, Ren. Trust me."

I sighed heavily and sat back in the seat, watching the golden light flooding the town I had grown up in set the windows of stores aflame, before slowly beginning to mute to a dusky orange glow. Max pulled up outside of a small Italian bistro, a place similar to where we had gone for our first date, and I offered him a radiant smile. Taking my hand, he leads me inside for a delicious dinner, reminding me yet again of why I fell for him.

By the time we got done with dinner, darkness had settled over Amarillo, the stars coming out to play like flickering fireflies. Max drives toward a little garden Annie and I used to hang out at after school, complete with a pond and gazebo in the center. Together, we stroll leisurely through the heady scent of the rose bushes, small lights in the rocky beds illuminating them from below. In the distance, I can see the gazebo beside the pond, decorated with hundreds of twinkling fairy lights.

"I don't remember these lights ever being here before," I say quietly, admiring them and their reflection in the water.

"That's because Annie helped put them up today," Max replies from behind me.

"Why would Annie—" I start to ask, turning around to find him down on one knee in the center of the gazebo, the lights causing his emerald eyes to sparkle.

In his outstretched hand is a black velvet box, with a shimmering diamond set in a white gold band.

"Renee Olivia Westhaven," he says, in an even tone, "I love you so much more than I can ever hope to say. Will you please do me the honor of marrying me?

CHAPTER THIRTY-SIX

My hand clapped over my gaping mouth as tears sprang in my eyes. Max's face was filled with hope and love as he gazed longingly up at me from his knee. Overcome with emotion, I slowly sank to my knees in front of him, unable to keep my smile—or my tears—at bay any longer.

"Yes!" I whispered excitedly. "Yes, I will marry you, Max!"

I didn't think it was possible for him to smile wider than before, but he proved me wrong as he gently took my hand in his and slid the ring on my finger. Tossing the velvet box over his shoulder, he pulled us to our feet amidst my giggling, crashing his lips hungrily against my own. His hands tangled in my hair as he held me close.

Before I knew it, those hands were drifting down my body to my waist, and he gripped me in his arms and spun me around. Laughter bubbled from my chest, and I felt lighter than I had in ages…all thanks to Max. My feet finally touched the ground once more, but my heart was still in the clouds. My eyes were closed as I allowed him to dance and sway with me like we had at the ranch the night we had admitted we wanted to be more than friends.

I could have stayed in that moment forever.

"You two are adorable," came the unmistakable voice of my best friend from behind us.

I turned, startled by Annie's sudden appearance, Max's hands never straying from around my waist. The cocky grin plastered on her face as she leaned against the side of the gazebo holding a camera had me narrowing my eyes playfully at her.

"And just what are you doing here, missy?" I snipped. "And why the hell do you have a camera?"

Annie burst out laughing and I felt my stomach drop. "Oh, someone asked me to hang up some twinkly lights and then hide out to wait for him to show up with my best friend so I could take some photos of your memorable moment," she teased.

"I'm just glad the two of you didn't decide to go at it after he popped the question," came a deep male voice to her left.

"Zane!" I squealed, hurrying to give him a hug. Then his words sank into my addled brain. "Oh my God! Why the fuck would you think we would do something like that?" I asked, punching him in the arm.

He laughed. "Because I fully expect Annie to rip my clothes off me the second I put a ring on her finger, whether we're in public or not."

I could feel the blood rushing to my cheeks, causing them to burn in embarrassment. Annie smirked, taking note of my red face.

"While that may be true of us, babe, Ren here is not one to get slapped with a public indecency charge."

I groaned, Zane shrugged, and Max and Annie laughed. But I was thankful, nonetheless, that Max had been thoughtful enough to have her come take the pictures, to document the start of our life together. This had been a magical, memorable moment, and now I would have the photos for the rest of my life to remember it by.

"Why don't you take her home, since I'm sure *Madre and Padre* Westhaven are dying to hear her answer, and Zane and I will take care of the lights," Annie suggested, calling my parents by her favorite nicknames for them.

"Thanks, Annie," Max told her. "I appreciate it. You too, Zane," he said, shaking his hand.

"Not a problem. You're practically going to be my brother-in-law, so I was happy to help."

I smiled, thrilled that they got along so well and looking forward to "family" get-togethers in the future with them. Max bent down to retrieve the ring box before taking my hand and leading me back to the car. My new engagement ring glistened in the light of the streetlamps as we drove, and I couldn't hold back the happy tears that trickled down my face.

"Ren, are you okay?" he asked, clearly worried.

"Damn pregnancy hormones," I muttered. "I'm fine, just so fucking happy, Max. And the ring is gorgeous! When on earth did you have time to get it?"

He linked his fingers through mine, toying with the item in question as he grinned. "When we went back to Lubbock to break the news to my parents, the next morning I went to see Nick, remember?" I nodded, and he continued. "I conned him into going to the jewelry store with me and he helped me pick it out for you."

"You're kidding."

"Nope; why?"

"You managed to get Nicholas Spencer into a jewelry store? I'm going to have so much fun with that," I chuckled.

"I figured you would get a kick out of knowing about that," he said lightly. After a moment's pause, he glanced at me, giving my hand a gentle squeeze. "Sweetheart, I know things are moving rather quickly right now, but what are your thoughts on going ahead and getting married sooner rather than later? That way the baby would have my last name on the birth certificate."

I squirmed in my seat, unsure of how to respond. On the one hand, it was a good idea to go ahead and move forward with the wedding as soon as possible and prior to the birth—and before I became a small elephant—but on the other, I was terrified of moving too fast. I chewed on my lower lip as we sat at the stoplight, turning his question over in my mind. My eyes caught on the glittering diamond resting on my finger as the light turned green, and I suddenly knew my answer.

"I think I can't wait to become Mrs. Harris," I confidently stated. "Think we can get everything planned in less than a month?"

CHAPTER THIRTY-SEVEN

Walking into the house, half the lights were on, meaning my parents were up and waiting for us. What I was not expecting—or more accurately, who I was not expecting—was Brenda and Jerome to be standing in the living room along with them. My mom had the biggest smile on her face, and I could feel the anxious energy radiating off her from across the room.

"Hi?" I asked, more than said, a puzzled smile tugging on my lips.

"Hi sweetie! How was your date night?" my mom gushed.

I rolled my eyes, but I was pleased they were so excited. Glancing up into Max's green eyes, I offered him a sly smile and a wink.

"It was fine," I answered in a bored tone.

"Just 'fine'?" my mother teased.

"Yeah. He took me to dinner and for a walk."

All four of them were practically on the balls of their feet, ready to spring forward at the news, but I was totally grand-standing. And Max was letting me. It was taking every ounce of restraint in me to not burst out laughing.

"Dinner and a walk…" Jerome trailed, encouraging me to finish the sentence.

I shrugged, still managing to keep my left hand partially hidden behind Max's back. "It was nice; rather reminiscent of our first date to be honest."

I could see my mom's shoulders beginning to sag and heard Max choke back a laugh. *Okay, I guess I've screwed with them long enough*, I thought. "Oh, and he gave me this," I said, holding up my hand so that the diamond sparkled in the light.

"You little—" my mom hissed. Her eyes were bright with unshed tears, and a broad smile lit her face. Pulling me in for a hug, she lightly swatted my ass. "That was a very dirty trick, Renee."

"Couldn't help it, mom," I chuckled.

Brenda came nearer, a pleased smile on her face, causing hope to swell within my heart—perhaps there was hope for our relationship yet. I held out my hand so both she and my mother could get a better look at my ring, hearing them swiftly inhale as they looked it over in awe.

"It looks beautiful," Brenda sighed. "Max did a marvelous job selecting the ring."

"Indeed, he did!" my mother agreed heartily.

The guys were talking quietly together by the couch, but Max shot me a warm smile and a wink, causing my heart to race and my temperature to rise. I turned back to our mothers, knowing I should probably drop the bombshell that we wanted to get married in the next month or so, but figured they may want to sit down first.

"Um," I started, clearing my throat. "How about we all sit down for a minute?"

Eyebrows arched around us, and I could practically feel the speculation that was running through their minds. I settled in next to Max and took a deep breath.

"So, we were talking on the way back here about when we would want to get married, what with the baby and everything," I said nervously. "Hopefully, you guys will be on board with us on this, but we want to try to plan the wedding for next month."

All four of them had their jaws hit the floor when I said that, causing my anxiety to skyrocket. Max laced his fingers through mine, his thumb sweeping across the back of my hand to calm my nerves. His green eyes steadily met the stunned expressions of our parents as they slowly closed their mouths, and he took over the explanation.

"One of the reasons we were thinking of pushing ahead like this is for the sake of the baby. It will make things much simpler when filling out the birth certificate and all if she and I are already married, plus, I don't want her to be under any extra scrutiny than she may already be facing due to this," Max announced.

"I also don't want to look like a whale on my wedding day, and if we wait too long, it will be very evident in photos that I'm pregnant," I continue. "I don't necessarily need or want anything big and fancy. Personally, I always wanted something kind of small and in a garden—like where he proposed."

"That sounds like you," my mother interjected, giving me an encouraging grin. "If you aren't after a large affair, a month or so is a doable timeframe, and I think your reasoning is logical."

"I have to agree," Jerome said, nodding. "Just let us know what you need us to do to help, and consider it done."

Max and I smiled broadly at our family. Rocky though it may have been, it was a nice start to our life together knowing that we had their support moving forward. My dad grabbed a notebook and pen and began jotting down notes as we all talked and tossed about ideas and plans, labeling the different things we each would end up being responsible for overseeing. Eventually, the clock in the hall chimed eleven, and we were all stifling yawns.

Breaking off to our separate rooms—my parents to the master, Jerome and Brenda to the guest room, and Max and me to mine—we collapsed into our beds, anxious for sleep to claim us. Pulling me into his muscled arms and kissing me deeply, Max sighed in contentment.

"I didn't think it was possible to be this happy, Ren."

"That makes two of us," I whispered back. "Especially after everything that's happened in the past month. But damn, I am so fucking happy, Max."

He chuckled, brushing a kiss on the tip of my nose. "I'm very glad, sweetheart. I can't wait to make you my wife. I can't wait to wake up to you every morning, sleep next to you every night, experience all the firsts we can together. And I promise, *our first time* will be the magical experience you deserved."

Oh shit.

CHAPTER THIRTY-EIGHT

I shouldn't be this freaked out over what he said, I chided myself as I brushed my hair the next morning. His words had played on an endless loop all night long. Did I want to have sex with Max? Sure. I was very attracted to him physically, and emotionally he made me feel safe. The idea of it however, made me a blubbering mess and I was terrified I would puke at any given moment.

I loved Max; so much that I was more than willing to marry him and spend my life with him. But thanks to the rape, I trembled at the mere thought of intimacy. How was I meant to get over my trepidation in only a month's time? He had never forced me to do anything I wasn't ready for in our relationship, and I knew that hadn't changed now, but once we were married, he deserved to sleep with his wife. And not just in the same bed, but in the intimate, clothing-optional manner.

If not for the fact I knew both our mothers would be tagging along all of today, I would have pulled Annie aside to ask for her advice on this at some point during our errands. Even though she was younger than me, she was far more experienced in that arena than I was and would undoubtedly have some tips for me. As it was, finding a wedding dress, maid of honor dress for her, choosing flowers and the venue kept me hopping all day long.

Annie was easy to dress, choosing a halter-style cornflower blue gown that fell to the ground in simple, yet elegant Grecian layers of taffeta. The high empire waist was accentuated with navy beading and gems that glittered in the lighting, and her olive skin was shining where exposed—like the entirety of her back. She looked stunning in the gown, and effortlessly strutted around the little catwalk of the shop in the paired blue stiletto heels.

"Ren, thoughts?" she asked, doing another turn and causing the skirt to flare.

"You look marvelous," I told her sincerely. "It's perfect."

"Great! I'll get out of this then and we can find you your dream dress!"

I chuckled from my place on the couch, but I was insanely nervous. What type of dress would I need to get since I wouldn't really have time to get it altered but I also didn't know how quickly my waist would expand with the pregnancy? As if reading my mind, my mom rested her hand on my knee.

"I would recommend we look for a dress that has the laces in the back. That way we can let it out more if we need to on the actual day."

"Great minds think alike," Brenda laughed. "I was just thinking the same thing."

I sighed. "Thanks. I was honestly having a mild freak-out worrying about what type of dress to look for, so now I know."

Annie skipped out of the changing area, ready to march into the racks of wedding gowns in search of "the one." She and I looked on one side of the aisle, while Brenda and my mom looked on the other. A couple caught my eye, but nothing really stood out about them. And then, Annie and I reached for the same dress at the same time.

Our eyes met after a quick moment, my teeth sinking into my lower lip as I tried to hide my smile. She helped me pull it out of the sea of white satin to inspect closer. Just then, a cry of excitement sounded from behind us, and we turned to find my mom and Brenda holding the exact same gown.

"Oh Renee, you must look at this—" my mom began to gush, her words dying when her eyes finally landed on the material in our hands. "What are the odds?" she laughed.

"I say it's fate," Annie declared. "It clearly means this is the dress you are supposed to go try on, and I will bet it's the one you're meant to wear when you say those two little words."

At this point, I couldn't keep the smile off my face. The saleswoman, a severe-looking woman named Trudy, bustled over to take the gown from Annie, and escorted me to the changing room. She fussed over me, helping me into a corset—which I had to insist she loosen due to the strain it put on my tender breasts and womb—then a slip, and finally the dress itself. Turning to face the mirror, I gasped as I caught sight of my reflection.

I'll be damned, I thought to myself, tears beginning to prick in my eyes. *Annie was right.*

I walked slowly out to reveal the dress to them, knowing they would love it. The sweetheart neckline was flattering without showing too much of my cleavage, the off-the-shoulder cap sleeves seemed to shimmer thanks to the organza over the satin. The dress tapered at my waist, ruching adding a dynamic aspect to the side and would help to hide my bump if I had started to show, before cascading down in delicate layers of satin and organza, all shimmering with opalescent beading. It laced comfortably in the back, meaning I would be able to loosen it next month should I need to, just as my mother had suggested.

Stepping out onto the little catwalk in the white heels, the saleswoman helped arrange the skirt on the platform to show off the small train before heading to a nearby rack to fetch a veil. I smiled as I saw my mom's eyes fill with tears of joy, followed closely by Brenda and Annie, and did my best to not begin jumping up and down as the veil was carefully placed on my head.

"Oh Ren," my mother breathed, her hand at her heart. "You look beautiful, honey."

"You really do," Brenda agreed, surreptitiously wiping away the tears in her eyes.

Annie grinned. "Called it! This is the dress, isn't it?"

Chuckling, I rotate so that I can see myself in the mirrors surrounding me. The dress was perfect. It was everything I had ever wanted in a wedding gown, and I knew Max would find me beautiful in it as well. I nodded happily.

"This is definitely my dress."

Both my mom and Brenda cheered, happy that the dress experience had been blessedly simple, while Annie snuck up behind me to whisper in my ear. "You look incredible, and believe me, Max is going to think you look sexy as fuck in this thing. He may have the hardest time focusing on saying his vows because all he'll be wanting to do is get you out of your dress, Ren," she teased.

She sat back down, pleased, but I was suddenly back to where I had begun my day—in hell dealing with my worst fears.

CHAPTER THIRTY-NINE

I swallowed down my nerves and carefully tucked my insecurities away over the next few weeks. The absolute last thing I wanted was for Max to think I was having second thoughts about marrying him—which was not even remotely close to the truth. Wedding plans were progressing like clockwork despite pushing the date back an extra two weeks, Max was charging ahead with his online studies, and we had even found a little apartment in town about twenty minutes from my parent's house that we would move into once we were wed. On the surface, everything seemed perfect.

As I sat in the waiting room for my check-up, alone this time since Max had to run home for an emergency at the ranch, I could feel the nausea bubbling up again in my stomach. Morning sickness had hit me full-force a couple weeks ago, and I was miserable. Saltine crackers and ginger ale were my only salvation in the mornings (short of puking my guts up for almost an hour straight), and all I wanted to do was sleep.

"Renee," the nurse called from the doorway.

I collected my purse and windbreaker, following her down the hallway for the routine weight and vitals check. There was no little gown to change into this time, so I simply perched on the end of the exam table, my legs dangling over the edge as I waited for Dr. Collins to come in. I studied the posters on the walls depicting the stages of childbirth, the sight causing my stomach to clench and churn more than it already was. Thankfully, the door swung open before my mind could start racing, and I was met with the kind blue eyes of my physician.

"Hello, Renee," she greeted. "How are you this month?"

"Queasy."

She chuckled. "I take that to mean you've been dealing with morning sickness?"

I nodded miserably, running my hand through my hair. "I've been keeping crackers and ginger ale by the side of the bed to have first thing when I wake up, but there are still some days I spend an hour or so worshipping the porcelain god."

"I can't say I've ever heard it described that way," Dr. Collins grinned. "I'll have to remember that for next time. Have the crackers and ginger ale seemed to help most of the time though? Your weight hasn't fluctuated too drastically, so I'm not overly concerned just yet."

"Most days they seem to do alright," I admit. "Is there anything else I can do to help make sure I'm okay?"

"I can always prescribe some medicine designed to help stave off nausea, such as Zofran, and you taking your prenatal vitamins and a vitamin B-six in the evenings may help as well." She paused to look at me, questions in her eyes. "I notice you're alone this time. Is everything okay on that front?"

"Oh, yes, Max had an emergency to go help his parents with, so he had to miss today. But we're actually getting married in two weeks."

Dr. Collins smiled broadly. "That's wonderful news. He seems like a very nice young man. Has the planning been overly stressful for you?"

"Actually, it hasn't, but…"

"Something else has been weighing on your mind."

"Yeah." I sighed. "It's the concept of being…intimate. I mean, I get that I'm already pregnant, but I was a virgin when I was raped. And now, just the thought of having sex with him, even though I love him, is honestly scaring me half to death."

Looking like she was carefully weighing her words before she spoke, Dr. Collins shifted on her stool. "Renee, I can understand how that would be frightening for you. And I know this isn't really my business or part of my job, but have you spoken to Max regarding your concerns?"

"I've been too worried he would think I was having second thoughts about marrying him," I confess. "And it's not like I don't want to be intimate with him, it's just…" I sighed heavily again. "As his wife, that is one of my responsibilities too, and I don't want to cheat him of that."

"I don't think Max will see it that way. I saw the way he looked at you last time you were in here, and I got the distinct impression he would do anything for you. My personal recommendation is to speak to him about it, preferably before you get married, to ease your stress. Have you given any further consideration on speaking to a trauma therapist?"

I hung my head. Being so caught up in the whirlwind of wedding preparations and morning sickness, plus dealing with the fatigue that came from combining pregnancy and night terrors, therapy had been the farthest thing from my mind. I shook my head, my brown hair swishing around my shoulders.

"I tell you what," Dr. Collins said, "why don't I give you the list of the therapists I personally would vouch for, that way you have it for whenever you are ready to talk. You don't have to call any of them today, tomorrow, or even this month, but you'll have the numbers if you need them."

Offering her the smallest ghost of a smile, I met her kind gaze. "I would appreciate that. Thanks, Dr. Collins."

"Not a problem at all. Now, any other concerns before we wrap up here?"

"This may seem like a dumb question, but would sex be something to avoid right now?"

"If you're looking for an excuse to get out of talking to him about this, I'm not helping you," she chided. "But no, under most circumstances, sexual intercourse during pregnancy is perfectly safe. You don't appear to be a high-risk patient, and everything else looks normal, so intimacy shouldn't be an issue if you two decide to proceed." I nodded and she continued. "But remember this, Renee, whether it's between a husband and wife, or just two random individuals, intimacy should be consensual and if you try to force yourself into doing it just because you think Max wants it, you'll only make things worse for yourself in the end. Just something to keep in mind."

"I'll remember. Thank you."

"Good. See you in a month, hopefully as a happily married woman."

CHAPTER FORTY

The morning of our wedding dawned clear and beautiful, and I actually felt halfway human when my feet hit the plush carpet of my room. The nausea was finally settling down as I was nearing the end of my first trimester, and the Zofran helped keep the rest of it at bay. My previously flat stomach now had the slightest bump, signifying the new life growing within me. I swallowed hard as I stared at my reflection in the mirror, the sight of where my baby was almost paralyzing me with overwhelming emotions.

I placed my hand over the tiny swell, blocking my eyes from seeing how my body was changing because of one man's cruel actions. This was not fair. It was not how things were meant to play out for me. I was supposed to date Max, continue to fall more in love with him, then the natural order of things would have happened to allow us to get engaged and married, and *then* I would have gotten pregnant with *his* child. But instead, another man's child was growing inside of me, and even though Max and I were getting married, I couldn't shake the feeling that I was still somehow cheating him…all because of the tiny little person hiding within my body.

I bit back a sob, I sank to my knees, feeling like such a failure. I was blaming things on the baby—my baby—when none of it was his or her fault. I knew I would love this child because they were a part of me, but I could hear the questions echo in my mind daily: would this baby be better off away from me? Would I ever be able to look at this child and not be reminded of how they came into existence? Would Max?

Ever since I was a little girl, I had dreamed of being a mother. I loved children. But I couldn't get the thoughts out of my head that this wasn't right.

A knock on my bedroom door broke through the trance I was in, and Annie stepped inside. Her eyes went wide as she took in my puffy eyes and the tears raining down my cheeks, and she tossed her dress onto my bed and rushed to my side, pulling me into her arms.

"Hey, shhh," she soothed, stroking my hair. "What's going on?"

"Am I a horrible person if I'm wondering if this baby would be better off without me?" I whispered.

"Oh Ren. No, you are not. You are in the world's shittiest position right now and you are doing your best to be strong and carry on in spite of everything. It is going to be okay. You've got your parents, and his, plus me and Zane, and best of all, Max. That man loves you so damn much, and he's going to take care of you both."

I wiped my eyes with the back of my hands and nodded.

"Now, come on. We've got to get you ready to marry your knight in shining armor!"

For the next couple of hours, Annie helped me with my hair and make-up, and then carefully aided me in slipping into my dress after she had pulled on her own. When my mom entered to check on us, my best friend was just finishing setting the veil in my curled and pinned brown locks.

"Oh Renee!" my mother gasped, her eyes becoming suspiciously bright with unshed tears. "You look so beautiful sweetie."

I smiled back at her. "Thanks, mom."

She came closer, Annie stepping to the side to give us a moment. "I have something for you," my mom said. "Grandma left this for you, and I think you should wear it today."

From behind her back, she produced a gorgeous diamond heart pendant, and quickly fastened it around my neck. I had admired the necklace when I was younger, and my grandmother had promised to leave it to me when she passed away. I had completely forgotten about it until now.

"It looks perfect," I whisper. "Thank you."

I gently hugged her, doing my best to not wrinkle her blue dress and she did her best to not wrinkle my gown and veil. I heard the click of a camera, and turned to find Annie snapping away, catching us in some candid shots for the photo album.

"Alright you two, let's get this show on the road!" she exclaimed, causing us both to smile.

We headed to the gardens where Max had proposed, ready for the small intimate wedding we had planned. Tucking my hand into the crook of his arm, my dad walked me down the path that comprised our "aisle," leading us to the gazebo where my dashing fiancé waited for me. I thought he looked good in jeans and a dress shirt…merciful heavens he looked downright delectable in his tuxedo.

He winked, sending hundreds of deranged butterflies clamoring against the walls of my stomach, and soon I was taking his hand to stand before the priest. I felt like I was in a haze of euphoria, the words being spoken like the droning of bees, as the gentle breeze drifted through the garden, catching my veil slightly. My name being spoken was the only thing that broke the spell Max's emerald orbs had placed on me, and soon I found myself repeating the vows to bind myself to him.

"I, Renee, take thee, Max, to be my lawfully wedded husband, to have and to hold from this day forward, for better, for worse, for richer, for poorer, in sickness and in health, to love and to cherish, until death do us part," I spoke confidently.

"I, Max, take thee, Renee, to be my lawfully wedded wife, to have and to hold from this day forward, for better, for worse, for richer, for poorer, in sickness and in health, to love and to cherish, until death do us part," Max repeated.

Behind him, Nick grinned at us, and I could feel Annie's smile on my back. We slid the wedding bands onto each other's hands, and then were finally given permission for Max to kiss his bride. What started out as a simple and sweet kiss soon evolved into him—carefully—dipping me, his tongue deepening the kiss and setting my body ablaze. Cheers went up from all around us, and he pulled me upright once more.

"May I present Mr. and Mrs. Maxwell Harris!" the priest said excitedly.

"Shall we, wife?"

"We shall, husband."

CHAPTER FORTY-ONE

On the other side of the gardens was a small, indoor hall, perfect for receptions. Greenery and twinkling lights filled the space, creating a storybook-like setting for our special day. Walking through the twisting branched archway, I felt like a fairy entering her mystical realm.

Tables draped in baby blue cloths were placed around the room, ready to seat our limited guests for a small dinner, and another with the small three-tiered cake and punch stood across the room, small blue stones shimmering atop the table cover whenever the lights hit them. Max led me over to the head table and held my chair for me, helping me with my skirts as I sat down. The others filtered into the hall as he sat beside me, linking his hand with mine under the table.

Annie and Zane sat on our left, along with my parents, while Nick, his date, and Max's parents were on our right. Soft, lilting music played over hidden speakers, just loud enough to be heard, as the dinners were quickly brought out and served.

"Yum!" Annie moaned, thoroughly enjoying her first bite of the marinated chicken we had selected.

I couldn't help but chuckle as she dug into her plate with relish, polishing off her garlic red-skinned mashed potatoes and steamed broccoli in between morsels of the poultry and rolls. Everyone else around the room seemed to be finding the meal to their satisfaction as well, and I smiled as I slowly chewed my own meal.

Max's hand was soon resting on my thigh, scorching me through the material of my dress, as we listened to a few toasts. Annie's was heartfelt yet humorous, and I was thankful I had asked her to be my maid of honor. As Nick stood nervously, he shot me a look that nearly stopped my heart.

"For those of you who don't know me, I'm Nick, and I've had the privilege of knowing Max since we were boys," he began. "We played football together, raced cars together, did most things together growing up, and one of those things included going off to the same university. That's where, our second year there, we met this girl."

I smiled, thinking back to quite literally bumping into the two of them as they left the library one day, and how that had been the foundation of our entire relationship.

"Ren is this amazing person who can make you laugh when you're upset, supports you when you need it, and always seems to know what to say to put things in perspective. It wasn't hard to see that she was an angel, and Max fell for her hard and fast." He paused to look at me with a smile. "You two are so lucky to have each other, and I feel honored to have been a part of your special day. I—"

He cut himself off, swallowing hard before meeting my eyes. Giving himself a little shake, he raised his glass and looked at the people around us. "To Max and Renee!"

"To Max and Renee!" came the echoed din.

As he sat back down, I couldn't help but wonder what he had wanted to say but held back, and why. I had little time to think on the matter however, as my new husband was tugging at my hand to lead me to the center of the room to dance. A few songs in, after being contentedly in his arms and full of bliss, Nick stepped up and tapped Max on the shoulder.

"Mind if I cut in for one?"

"Go ahead, but I get her back," Max teased, before walking away to dance with his mother.

Nick carefully pulled me into his arms, like he was doing his best to not be overly close, but not looking like he was uncomfortable dancing with me either. I found it an odd balancing act for him. Gazing up into his dark blue eyes, I found their stormy depths focused entirely on my face.

"I didn't get to tell you earlier, but you look beautiful, Ren."

I felt my eyes widen slightly at his compliment. Nick had never really seemed to pay much attention to my appearance, so I was taken aback by his words—pleased, but shocked. I offered him a grin once the surprise wore away.

"Thank you, Nick. And thanks for not only being our best man, but for everything you've done for both of us over the past few months."

"You don't have to thank me, Ren. Max and you are my friends. I was happy to help in any way I could," he admitted. "Although, I have to confess that I don't feel as though I've done much good here lately with regard to that one issue."

I knew exactly what he was referring to without him having to explicitly name it: the rape.

"Nick," I whispered. "You know there was nothing you could have done that night."

"I didn't quite mean it like that," came his reply as we continued to sway, "although I do wish Max and I could have prevented it. I'm more referring to the aftermath. I hate that you don't have answers, Ren. And I hate that it's tearing you apart. But I wanted you to be the first to know. I made my decision on the future."

"Oh? Why me?"

"Because you are part of my motivation, Renee," he murmured, coming to a halt. His cobalt eyes locked onto my hazel ones as his hands firmly gripped my shoulders. "I couldn't help you this time around, but I will be damned if I stand by and allow anyone else to hurt you, Max, or this baby in the future. I'm going to be a cop, and if it takes me the rest of my life, I will find a way to get you justice for what happened, Ren."

I gasped, moved by the ardent fervor of his words. He leaned forward and lightly kissed my forehead before walking briskly away, leaving me standing alone in the middle of the dance floor. Max hurried to my side when he noticed my expression, his light brows arched in curiosity. I shook my head and tried to give him a smile, walking into his embrace. Nick's words refused to leave me for the rest of the afternoon though…until Max and I departed for the hotel that is. At that point, the only thing running through my mind was if I would be capable of allowing my husband to have his hands on my body, or if I would end up in a torrent of tears.

CHAPTER FORTY-TWO

The hotel room was lovely and came with chocolate covered strawberries and non-alcoholic champagne (since Max had been thinking ahead and told the concierge no alcohol for his pregnant wife). The huge king size bed was made with satiny sheets in whites and red, plush downy pillows lined the top of the bed just begging to have our heads resting against them, and a pair of swans made from towels surrounded by rose petals perched on the end. And as I stared at the bed, I could feel my palms becoming clammy, my mouth going dry, my heart beginning to race, and my breathing becoming shallow gasps.

Max had left his charger in the car and had run back to grab it, meaning I was alone with my torturous thoughts. I was so wrapped up in the terror surrounding me, I never heard him re-enter the room behind me. So, when his hands gripped my waist, I shrieked.

"God! Ren, what's wrong?"

I slowly backed away and sank onto the edge of the bed, knocking over the swans in the process. My eyes had to have been wide as saucers as I panted, attempting to draw oxygen into my brutally compressed lungs. Max's face was filled with concern as he edged closer, kneeling before me, the pain flashing in his emerald eyes when I flinched as his hand reached for me.

"Ren, sweetheart, it's okay," he whispered, trying again.

I drew a ragged breath and then the tears began to fall. I threw my hands over my mouth to muffle my sobs, hiccupping as the panic attack raged on within me. I could feel Max's hands, infinitely tender, cupping my cheeks as he tried to wipe away the never-ending river of tears.

"I—I'm so—sorry, Max," I sobbed. "Tonight was—supposed to be—perfect, but I—I ruined it, didn't—didn't I?"

"You didn't ruin a damn thing," he said, pulling me into his arms and stroking my hair. "Why would you think it's ruined, baby?"

"Because I don't—think I can do it."

"Do what?"

"Have—have—"

Realization dawned in his eyes and he sat back from me. Shame and fear washed over me like a tidal wave, threatening to drown me. *Dr. Collins was right…I should have talked about this with him before*, I thought miserably.

"Oh God, sweetheart, is that what you're worried about?" Max asked in shock. "Renee, look at me," he tilted my chin to force my eyes to look into his. "Yes, we got married today, and yes, most couples have sex on their wedding nights. But I was never going to force it or push for it to be tonight. It must be on *your* terms to be right. And if you are not comfortable with it being tonight, then we will wait until you are ready. Simple as that."

"You don't feel like I'm cheating you of your wedding night if we don't—"

"No," he interrupted, laying a finger across my lips. "When you are ready, we'll be intimate and it will be an amazing experience, but we're not doing it one minute before that and certainly not because it's considered customary for tonight. Now, how about I help you out of the dress, you can change into something comfy, and we can snuggle and watch a movie?"

A shuddering sigh wheezed past my lips and I threw myself into his arms. "Thank you," I whispered. "You truly are the best husband I could ever hope to have."

He chuckled. "Damn straight," Max joked. "No more tears, now."

Soon, we were changed and curled up in the bed with the lights off, strawberries devoured, and a movie playing on the television. My eyelids began feeling heavy—it had been a long day, after all—and I nestled closer to his chest. Sleep claimed me…for a while at least.

Suddenly, I was bolting upright in the bed, screaming and crying, clutching at the covers as Max quickly flipped on the lamp. My heart was still pounding, and I could feel the terror rushing through my veins like a toxic drug. He delicately pulled me into his arms, tangling his fingers through my hair as my hands gripped the material of his shirt.

"Oh God, Max! I could feel their hands on me; holding my ankles and keeping my legs down on the bed even when I tried to kick at them to get them to let go. And his hands on my neck—it hurt," I sobbed. "I was so afraid he would slit my throat with his knife, so when he told me to behave, what choice did I have? He said you would leave me; that you would only ever see me as a whore after what he did to me that night. He kept putting a rag over my face, saying I needed to sleep. Max…I knew their voices…"

His arms stiffen around me, the first indication of emotion he's shown since I began my tortured monologue. His eyes close in agony and I can hear him grind his teeth together. After what must be a count of at least fifty, he opens his eyes again and looks down at me.

"Whose voices are they, baby?"

"I—I can't remember!" I cry, melting against his chest once more. "Why can't I remember, Max? Why won't these nightmares stop? I hate this!"

"I know, I know," he soothes. "I hate it too, Ren. First of all, I'm not going anywhere, as I think you know thanks to us saying 'I do' less than twelve hours ago. Secondly, I really think we need to reevaluate the idea of you seeing a therapist. Maybe they would have a good idea on how to help you with the nightmares, okay?"

I sigh. I had put this off for over two months now after the last counselor and her idiotic suggestion, but this had to come to an end. I thought back to the list Dr. Collins had given me a couple weeks earlier and slowly nodded in affirmation.

"Deal. I'll do some research and make the call on Monday."

CHAPTER FORTY-THREE

"Hello Renee, I'm Niyah Prajesh," the therapist greeted me warmly, extending her cinnamon colored hand for me to take. Her dark chocolate eyes and black hair complemented her appearance perfectly, and her lightly accented English bespoke her intelligence and compassionate nature.

I felt instantly at ease with this woman.

"Hi," I returned, shaking her hand and waiting until she sat in the chair opposite the couch I had been shown to moments earlier.

"So, I understand you're here because of a trauma you experienced several months ago, correct?"

Nodding, I shifted in my seat. I knew I needed to talk about it, but I wasn't sure if I should just blurt out everything all at once or dribble little bits of information at a time. Seeming to understand exactly where my mind had wandered, Dr. Prajesh smiled.

"We'll start slowly. Trying to heal from trauma is a long process, and not one that you rush. If you attempt to push yourself to talk about it all at one time, your psyche will not be able to handle the overload. So, we're going to start with something away from the trauma first," she explained.

I felt the relief wash over me. While I knew I was coming to see her to come to terms with what had happened to me, working my way up to discussing it sounded like a far better option. I offered her a small smile in return.

"I understand you were married this past weekend, is that right?"

"Yes, although that is partially connected to what happened," I answered.

"Well, why don't you tell me a little about your wedding and the preparations leading up to it. In particular, how did the planning of the wedding make you feel."

Blinking, I sat back to ponder her words. "We decided to get married sooner rather than later after we got engaged, because I'm pregnant due to the…incident," I finally said. She nodded in encouragement for me to continue. "My husband has been so supportive of me since the beginning and has promised to be the father, so we wanted to be married before I delivered, and I wanted to not look huge in the photos. So, we accelerated our plans and got married seven weeks after he proposed."

In my head, I pictured the notebooks spread across the bed as we selected various aspects for the wedding together, and the way Max had done everything in his power to keep the stress away from me. "Max ensured I didn't stress over things, and thankfully neither of us wanted a lavish wedding so it was pretty simple to plan it in the timeframe we had. And it turned out beautiful. We got married at the same garden where he proposed to me, so I enjoyed the symmetry of that, and the reception hall at the garden looked like fairies should live there."

"It sounds absolutely lovely," Dr. Prajesh interjected. "Were you keen on getting married to Max in the first place? Or did his proposal come as a shock to you?"

"I've been in love with him for months, and I actually overheard him ask my dad for permission to ask me after we found out I was pregnant."

"That's not really an answer."

"I guess it's not," I sighed. "Did I want to marry Max and spend my life with him? Absolutely. Did our wedding look like I had always dreamed it would, regardless of the circumstances? Of course. Do I wish the reasoning for the hasty proposal and marriage wasn't a factor? Without a doubt."

"That makes sense. I want to ask about your hobbies now. What are some things you enjoy doing or that give you peace?"

"My hobbies?" I repeated, puzzled by where she could possibly be going with this.

Dr. Prajesh nodded. "I have a reason for it, I promise."

"Okay, um, I like to read, watch movies, I do jigsaw puzzles often, and I do yoga four times a week."

"Good. Now, have you ever kept a diary or a journal?"

"Sure, when I was younger."

She stood and walked over to a bookcase by her desk. From a lower shelf she pulled a blue notebook out and came to sit once more. I eyed the soft leatherbound book in her lap, curiosity getting the best of me.

"I would like for you to begin keeping a journal. It will help when you have times of overwhelming emotions, nightmares, things like that," she said, handing me the book. "You can bring it in whenever you'd like if you have things you want to discuss that you've written down in between sessions but consider this an additional form of therapy. Sometimes just writing down your thoughts, even if you're not telling anyone in particular about what you've written, can help you deal with the trauma that you're facing just as much as sitting in therapy for an hour."

"Okay," I said slowly. "I think I can do that."

"Great. Try to think of the journal as a silent best friend if that helps you. Someone you would tell all your deepest fears, hopes, concerns, things of that nature to," Dr. Prajesh explained. "You may find that if you wake from a nightmare and begin to write about it, you will calm quicker, and the subject of the nightmare may not affect you as much after some time as it did in the beginning."

"I was meaning to ask you about nightmares and the like. I've been dealing with them on an almost nightly basis, where I wake screaming and crying. Up until recently, I haven't remembered much of what happens while I'm asleep, but on our wedding night I felt as though I was back in my apartment where it happened." I paused, looking deep into her brown eyes. "I could feel and hear them, and halfway see them, although it was like looking at them through a hazy window."

"I need to warn you, Renee, night terrors in trauma situations are very common, and often...only the beginning."

CHAPTER FORTY-FOUR

"What do you mean, 'only the beginning'?" I asked, feeling the fear seeping into my body like lead.

"With trauma, oftentimes the mind struggles to comprehend what's happened to the body and will go into self-preservation mode. In essence, your mind is trying to keep you from experiencing further pain and suffering by blocking out the memories of what occurred. The only problem is, those memories are still within your mind and will tend to resurface—most commonly when you're asleep as nightmares, night terrors, or flashbacks—which can then cause more harm because you are unprepared to cope with them.

"During the episodes, your mind is actually capable of tricking your body into reliving the entire experience," she continued. "You can feel things, hear, see, smell, and sometimes even taste things that you suffered during the original trauma. This causes you to awaken disoriented, in a highly elevated state of fear, and can even lead to physical damage if you struggle in your sleep."

"So, you're telling me that one night of terror wasn't enough?" I whispered. "That I'm doomed to always be tormented by visions of what happened to me at night, but never fully knowing or comprehending who was responsible or why."

Her dark brown eyes met mine sadly and she offered me a hopeful expression. "It may feel that way in the beginning, Renee, but there will hopefully come a day when you have become empowered and overcome the fears that seek to cripple you. It is also possible that with time, or even another form of therapy in addition to our sessions and journaling, that you may regain additional knowledge of your trauma and find the answers you seek."

I sat silently for several moments, turning her words over in my head.

"This is going to sound patently ridiculous but try to remember these things take time and you must be patient. It isn't fair in the slightest, but patience—especially where trauma is related—can be a virtue."

Be patient? She was right; it sounded ludicrous. I had already suffered so much, and I was only nineteen years old. But I remembered what my grandmother used to tell me when I was a little girl, waiting for our cookies to finish baking.

The best things in life will come when you least expect them, Renee. And sometimes, we have to wait longer for them than we think we ought to, but they will always be worth the delay.

Okay, Grandma…I'll try to be patient like you told me, I thought, letting my fingers lightly caress the pendant she had left me that I still wore around my neck. I nodded to Dr. Prajesh.

"I think I understand. I can't say that I particularly like that advice, since apparently I've been impatient since before I was born," I said, causing her to smile, "but I will do my best to try."

"Good. Well, we've got about ten minutes left, and I want to ask you one question that is somewhat related to your trauma, if you think you're up to it."

"Okay…"

"You mentioned you were now expecting a baby due to the…'incident', I believe is the term you used," she said, carefully watching my face. "And you said that your husband has agreed to become the child's father. How are you feeling about the pregnancy, just in general?"

A shuddering breath blew past my lips and I took a deep breath to calm my nerves. "I've always loved kids and wanted to be a mom, but I will admit that this development threw me. I think the hardest part of this whole situation is knowing that the baby isn't Max's. Yes, he's promised to stick with me and help me raise the baby—and he actually promised that before I even knew I was pregnant—but a part of me is still very discouraged and concerned over the simple fact that he isn't this baby's biological father, and I have no idea who is.

"Up until I went to the doctor the first time and she did a sonogram, I was holding onto the hope that perhaps the pregnancy test was wrong," I confessed. "I felt I would be trapping Max—despite his vow—with a child that he hadn't fathered, and I hated that feeling."

"That's perfectly understandable," she stated. "Has your pregnancy been relatively easy so far?"

"Other than some morning sickness, yes. I think I'm still a little in shock though. Our next appointment is when we're due to find out the gender, if we want to of course, and I'm a little apprehensive about that honestly."

"Why do you think that is?"

I considered her question. "I'm not really sure just yet, but something about it sets me on edge. Does that make sense?"

She nodded. "You may discover the answer by the time your appointment rolls around, but don't be surprised if it never fully reveals itself to you either. So, now that our time is just about over, how are you feeling? Do you think seeing me will be helpful to you?"

I smiled in spite of myself; she simply inspired that much relief for me.

"I was nervous to come, if I'm honest, after what the counselor at the university said to me, but you have managed to put me so at ease during this hour, and you've offered me some valuable guidance to help me cope with everything I'm dealing with due to this whole situation," I told her. "And your approach to not dive into the deep end of my trauma first, is clearly the better option for handling it, and I think I'll be leaving here feeling the tiniest bit lighter than when I first walked in."

"That's the goal!" she said enthusiastically. "I'm glad this has been a positive experience for you today, and hopefully, we will be able to keep all our sessions along those lines in the future."

Dr. Prajesh rose from her seat and I followed suit, grabbing my purse as I stood.

"I'll see you again soon, Renee," she told me, shaking my hand once more.

"Thanks Doctor." I tossed her a wave and headed out the door, a renewed sense of calm overtaking my heart, soul, and mind in the midst of the storm.

CHAPTER FORTY-FIVE

"Okay, everything is looking good," Dr. Collins announced with a smile. "Are you ready to start the ultrasound?"

I glanced at Max, worrying my lower lip as he reached for my hand. At nearly eighteen weeks pregnant now, my morning sickness had finally dissipated, my energy levels had begun to return to normal, and my tiny bump had slowly expanded to the size of a small melon. It was now apparent I was pregnant, especially since I was so petite and had nowhere for the baby to grow except outward. I was also almost halfway through this pregnancy and today was when we were supposed to find out the gender…if we wanted to.

Nodding to my doctor, she squirted the warm gel on my exposed midriff and slowly ran the wand over my stomach. Whooshing sounds filled the air and I turned my attention to the monitor, watching the grainy image resolve to show the squirming child within me.

"Here's the head, and you can see someone has the cutest little button nose already," Dr. Collins said. "And they've got their thumb in their mouth."

"Ren…" Max breathed, and I could hear the awe in his voice.

My eyes were locked on the screen, hypnotized by the sight before me.

"Spine looks perfect, and this little one is going to have some long legs," she continued, turning the probe as she spoke and changing the angle of the view. "Here's the heart, nice steady rhythm."

I watched as the tiny valves fluttered, pulsing as they pumped the blood throughout my baby's body, and felt tears fill my eyes. The heartbeat echoed in my head as I continued to stare, caught up in the emotional entanglement I felt knowing I was responsible for this child—for their well-being, their emotional and physical development, for their safety...

What would happen to my baby if the man who attacked me ever attempted to come back into my life? Would I know who he was? Would he come to the realization that this child was his and would he try to inflict more pain and suffering on me or the baby at that time? *How can I keep my baby safe when I don't know from whom I'm meant to safeguard him or her?*

"Sweetheart?" Max said, gently shaking my shoulder and bringing me out of my troubled thoughts.

I looked up at him, and then realized Dr. Collins had been asking me a question. "I'm sorry," I murmured, blinking back tears. "What?"

"I was just asking if you two wanted to know the gender," she said softly, her blue eyes offering me a sad smile.

Max and I had gone back and forth about this very subject for the past two weeks, and we had never been able to come to a consensus.

"It's up to you, Ren," he told me.

I knew, deep down, that he really wanted to know. And part of me did too. So, I found myself slowly nodding my head. "Sure. If you can tell us, it might be nice to know."

Max squeezed my hand lightly, and I knew he was silently communicating his thanks to me. I returned the gesture but could sense my anxiety rising within me as my doctor moved the wand over my stomach again, angling to get a better view. Could I handle knowing the truth about this baby?

If it were a girl, I think I could, just because Max would be a wonderfully doting father. But then I thought back to how I had ended up pregnant in the first place, and I knew I would forever be terrified of someone doing the same thing to my daughter, should I have one. The notion of my child being hurt like I had been caused my heart to clench painfully, and as much as I wanted a little girl, the fear killed any excitement over that potential outcome.

But what if the baby's a boy? With Max as his father, he would undoubtedly be raised to respect women—and more importantly, their boundaries—but would he take after his biological father in looks or personality? Would I be forced to look everyday at a miniature copy of the man who stole my innocence at knifepoint, who threatened me, who left me afraid of my own shadow and with so few memories of what truly happened? Somehow, that option seemed ten times worse.

"Ah! There we are," Dr. Collins said finally, breaking through my rambling thought processes. She hit a few keys on the keyboard, causing the printer below the monitor to whir to life, spitting out a roll of sonogram pictures for us to take home with us. "Someone was being a little shy and keeping their legs crossed, but I was able to get a good look at last. I hope you're ready to be kept on your toes, you two, because you are having a baby boy. Congratulations."

She grinned as she handed Max the pictures and me a towel to clean the gel from my stomach. I felt as though I was on a rollercoaster that had just descended suddenly from a great height—the bottom of my stomach seemed to have dropped out—leaving me queasy. Swallowing hard against the lump in my throat, I wiped the cooled gel from my body, feeling frantic when it didn't seem to be coming off with the towel. My husband, always attentive, set the pictures down on the seat and came to help me get cleaned up.

"Could you give us a minute?" he asked Dr. Collins quietly. She nodded and quickly departed, leaving Max to gently grasp my shoulders. "Ren, sweetheart, it's going to be okay. I promise," came his whisper as his hands slipped into my hair.

"Max, what if—"

I couldn't bring myself to voice the concern aloud. How could I? Max would think I was going to be a horrible mother if I did. Hell, *I* thought I was going to be a horrible mother for thinking it at this stage, and the baby wasn't even here yet.

"Whatever is on your mind, we will get through it together," was his ardent reply. "And when you're ready to talk to me about it, you know I'll listen. I love you, Ren. You, and this little guy."

He gently caressed my stomach and kissed my forehead, and I leaned into his chest, breathing out heavily as I closed my eyes, choosing my next words with care.

"We love you too, Max."

CHAPTER FORTY-SIX

"You look rather pensive today," Dr. Prajesh said as she sat down. "Does this have something to do with your ultrasound yesterday?"

After seeing her a minimum of once a week for the past month and a half, Dr. Prajesh and I had developed a sort of comradery. Other than my mom, Max, and Annie, I felt I could be myself and tell her anything without fear of judgment. She knew how anxious I had been regarding the ultrasound, so it was no surprise to me that she picked up on my unease when she walked in the door.

"Pensive is a good word for my mood, I suppose."

"Care to elaborate?" she asked when I fell silent.

I sighed. "We went ahead and found out the gender yesterday. It's a boy. But I can't help but feel like having a boy may cause me more strife than I originally thought it might."

"How so?"

"What if this baby looks like the man who raped me? Or acts like him? I realize Max is going to be raising this baby as his own, but if he takes after his biological dad any, won't that only cause me additional trauma every single time I look at him? And how is that fair to have such insane realizations thrust upon an innocent child just because of the crime committed by his sperm donor?"

"Okay, okay," Dr. Prajesh cut in, holding up a hand to quiet me. "I see where you're coming from, and I understand your concerns. They are absolutely valid and not something you can sweep under the rug, Renee. I could always make the nature versus nurture argument to you, and since you were a biology major, you should understand that one quite well. But I'm going to point something else out to you instead.

"Should this child favor his biological father in any regard, you may find yourself at an interesting crossroad. Thus far, you have been unable to recall the identity of your attacker, and though we have not discussed your attack in depth as of yet, I do know how much that haunts you. This baby may provide you with the answers you have been seeking, and you may discover those answers help bring you peace."

I paused to consider what she said. While it was undeniably true that I had been unsuccessful in my attempts to discern the identities of those responsible for my trauma, I still couldn't imagine being forced to look upon the face of my attacker daily in the form of a child. I was certain that knowledge alone would drive me over the edge and sever my tenuous grip on my sanity.

"Take it one day at a time, Renee. This child is still half you, after all, and from what I've learned about you in the past month is how resilient you are." She smiled at me.

"Thanks. I'll keep that in mind."

"Anything else on your mind today?"

"Well…"

Her black brows rose in delicate arches on her forehead as she waited for me to speak. I squirmed, unsure of how to begin to address the proverbial elephant that I dealt with every night upon entering my bedroom.

"Okay, so the thing is," I stammered, looking up nervously, "I was a virgin when the rape occurred, and even though Max and I got married we still haven't… I mean, I wanted to try to on our wedding night but I ended up having a massive panic attack, which led to him telling me we were not doing anything until I was ready, but I still feel like I'm cheating him out of part of a typical relationship all because I'm scared of being intimate."

"I see."

"Max and I had fooled around to a degree before I was raped, but we hadn't had sex at that point yet, and now I just feel like I'm letting him down."

"Let me ask you this: are you afraid of Max?"

My eyes widened and my hands fell away from where they had been brushing my hair behind my ears. "No; of course, not."

"Alright, keep in mind that everyone recovers from this type of trauma differently, and you cannot rush it," she reminded me. "You and Max need to sit down and discuss this when both of you are in a relaxed state of mind. Don't put any pressure on either of you to do anything at that time but just talk. Explore your level of trust in him—make sure he understands that you aren't afraid of him if he doesn't—so that you're both on the same page and move on from there.

"Once you've established your comfort level with him, you can attempt to experiment with levels of foreplay, so long as he keeps in mind that you may need to stop if things become too overwhelming. If you can handle that, you may be able to progress to mutual masturbation," my cheeks flamed as she said this, "and continue until intimacy is not something you fear, but something you look forward to. Does that make sense?"

I nodded. "Yeah, I think so."

We continued our discussion for the remainder of my session with her, until finally, it was time for me to head home. Her words turning over in my head on a constant loop as I drove, I resolved to have a heart-to-heart with Max that evening. He deserved that much from me after all the consideration he had always given me.

I trusted him implicitly, and tonight, I would show him that—even if it was only by talking things out with him. I sat on our tan couch and pondered how to begin the conversation with him, lost in an endless cycle of doubt chasing desire. So lost, in fact, that I didn't even hear when he came in.

"Hi, baby," his deep voice tickled my ear as he leaned over me from behind. He gave my cheek a quick kiss and came to sit beside me, a puzzled expression flickering in his green eyes. "Everything okay?"

"I think we need to talk, Max."

CHAPTER FORTY-SEVEN

A frown made its way between his eyebrows, furrowing them as my words sank into his mind. I could instantly tell he was expecting something horrible and considering how fucked up our last six months had been, I could not blame him for thinking the worst. I tried to offer him a small, shy smile, hoping that would put him—and more importantly, myself—at ease.

"Okay…what's on your mind, Ren?"

"I was talking with Dr. Prajesh today about a couple of things, and I realized I needed to address something with you that we've both kind of brushed off for some time now," I started, locking my fingers together in my lap. "She gave me a good idea on how to finally do that, so I figured I wouldn't put it off any longer, because if I did, I would only end up hurting us both more than I already had."

"You're not making a lot of sense—"

"I want to talk to you about intimacy," I interrupted.

His eyes went wide. "I told you on our wedding night that I'm not going to put any pressure on you in that department, Renee. As horrible as it may sound, I am more than capable of taking care of that for myself if the need arises, but I don't want you to feel obligated to entertain those thoughts if you're not ready."

Brushing a stray lock of my hair behind my ear, I met his soft gaze. "And I have more than appreciated your patience with me. I'm not certain if I'm ready to experience sex yet, but I need you to understand something Max," I said, making sure our eyes were locked on one another. "I *trust* you. More than I trust anyone other than maybe my parents. I know you won't hurt me.

"But I miss how we were before this all happened too. While you were always respectful of my boundaries and my body, we weren't afraid to be affectionate or engage in foreplay," I managed. "I was thinking, what if we started there as a means to build up to being intimate?"

Max smiled. That slow, heart-stopping smile that always made me turn into a puddle of melted wax, and gently cupped my face in his hands. He pulled me closer, our noses touching, and my eyelids fluttered closed as he kissed the corner of my mouth. My hands, seemingly uncontrolled by my mind, found their way to his thighs, resting atop the muscles of his legs.

"Tell me when you want me to stop, okay?" he whispered, before kissing the side of my neck.

"Should we maybe move to the bedroom?" I giggled.

"That can be arranged."

Before I was able to stand on my own, his arms snaked around me and he swung me off the couch and carried me to our room. I could not keep the smile off my face as he sat me on the edge of the bed, tilting my face upward to capture my lips once more with his own. I tugged on his shirt, pulling him into the bed beside me, sending us both into gales of laughter. Catching his breath, he leaned over me to caress my cheek, his eyes filled with a tender look.

"You are so amazingly beautiful, Renee Harris. I hope you know that."

"And suddenly, my clothes are too hot for my body," I teased. I saw the lust flare in his eyes and risked a glance down to notice his pants were straining. I bit my lip suddenly, worried I would not be able to please him. "I am hot but would you rather I stay in my clothes right now?"

"This is about what you are comfortable with," he reminded me. "How about I help you off with your jeans and top for now and we can go from there?"

"Only if you do the same."

He nodded, and helped me sit up, carefully pulling on the hem of my shirt to lift it over my head. His shirt followed mine to the floor, and my eyes traced his sculpted stomach appreciatively. I stood and slipped my jeans to my ankles, kicking them away and leaving me in my underwear, my stomach churning at the thought he wouldn't find me near as beautiful now. He smirked, leaning down to kiss me—more to distract me than anything else—while he removed his own pants.

Max picked me up again and carefully laid me back on the bed, his eyes shining as he looked at me. My hand stroked the side of his face before tangling in his hair, and that seemed to be all the encouragement he needed. His lips came down to kiss, nibble, and suck on my neck, while his hands slid softly down my curves. A moan I could not suppress slipped from my mouth, earning me a chuckle from him.

"I take it that feels good?"

"Yes…" I whispered breathlessly.

"What would you like for me to do now, Ren?"

I bit my lip, meeting his enquiring gaze. My heart was pounding, but in a good way this time. I was not afraid…I was aroused. I licked my lips and took a deep breath.

"Would you—would you maybe…touch me?"

He leaned closer and moved his mouth to claim mine, causing my eyes to close in rapture. Just as I had gotten accustomed to the sensations his lips and tongue were eliciting, I felt his fingertips brush against the outside of my panties, sending shockwaves of pleasure through my sensitive core. I lazily drifted my hands down his back and his arm as he continued to kiss me and lightly stroke me through my panties, a decision made.

I gripped his hand and slightly redirected it so that his fingers caressed me directly…skin on skin, rather than through a piece of cotton. Max groaned into our kiss as he slipped the tip of his finger between my folds, feeling how wet he had managed to get me. His erection pressed into my thigh and, despite the boxers holding it back, sent a powerful yearning through my entire body.

I wanted to touch him, to give him pleasure in turn. As his kisses persisted passionately and his fingers deftly massaged my oversensitive clit, I trailed my hands between us and eased down his boxers.

"Ren? What are you doing?" he rasped.

CHAPTER FORTY-EIGHT

As his erection sprang free, I swallowed down any hesitation I felt, knowing this was right and I wanted him. I smiled up at him as he stared worriedly into my eyes, his body stilled from the moment my hands had tugged on the fabric of his boxers.

"I'm okay, Max," I assure him. "Please; kiss me?"

He looked like he was about to protest, but I wrapped my small hands around his throbbing cock, feeling him pulse under my touch. His eyes glazed slightly, but soon he slammed his lips back onto mine and his fingers once again nimbly worked my body. I stroked his long shaft, carefully circling the head with my thumb and causing him to moan into my mouth.

"God, Ren," he groaned, burying his head into my neck. "Is it okay for me to take off your panties now?"

I giggled. "I suppose—"

I didn't even finish my sentence before he yanked them off my hips, hunger written in the depths of his emerald eyes. He looked at me, seeking permission, and I slowly nodded, knowing exactly what he was insinuating. Gently, he pushed my legs apart and brought his lips to the inside of my thighs, kissing up my left leg while he stroked the right with his hand.

His eyes met mine for a brief moment, and then his kiss landed on my clit. I moaned, my head thrashing against the pillow and he laced his fingers through mine. His tongue slid up my folds before swirling lightly over that magic spot that had me seeing stars.

"Max…" I cried softly, my body filling with ecstasy.

Releasing one of my hands, he gently inserted two of his long fingers inside of me, curling them and stroking my inner walls while his tongue flicked and played above. The hand he'd released gripped the comforter as I felt myself nearing my climax. I was panting, moaning, writhing as he pleasured me…

"Fuck!" I hissed as my orgasm ripped through me.

I trembled beneath him as he continued to stroke and kiss my lower body, allowing me to slowly drift down from the high he had just helped me achieve. A radiant smile lit his face as he crawled up my body, kissing me as he went, until he was staring directly into my eyes again.

"Now, that was definitely worth the wait," he said, kissing my lips. "Did that feel as amazing as it seemed?"

"Oh, hell to the yes, baby," I assured him with an equally large smile.

"I'm very glad, Ren."

"And now, it's your turn."

His brows quirked upward. "Oh yeah?"

"Yeah," I stated matter-of-factly.

"Ren, you don't have to—"

"Have to, no," I say, pushing him onto his back. "But I *want* to do this. I just hope you're not disappointed with me only giving you a blowjob tonight."

He chuckled. "How could I possibly be disappointed by that?"

"Because it's not going all the way?" I asked timidly.

"We'll get there, Ren. Tonight has been a huge step."

He was right. And I could not have been more thankful that I had Max in my life. Straddling his legs, I grinned at him. *I think now is a good time to show him that gratitude*, I thought to myself. He had been patient with me and then gave me a mind-blowing orgasm to kick-start my intimacy rehabilitation tonight, and now, I was going to return the favor.

Licking my lips, I swallowed in preparation for having him in my mouth again—something I had not done in months. But like riding a bike, once you learn, you never forget. My tongue ran softly down the long, hard length of his shaft and back up to swirl around his sensitive head before I popped just the very tip of his cock in my mouth. My hand gripped the base of him to hold him steady until I was ready to use it to pump him as I sucked.

I slipped him a tiny bit farther into my mouth, letting my tongue dance along the underside of his shaft, sending his eyelids fluttering closed. After a couple more moments of those shallow licks, I swallowed his entire length, slightly gagging as he hit the back of my throat.

"Fuck, Ren," he moaned.

I pumped his cock with my hand as my mouth and tongue stroked him. I hummed as I sucked, the vibrations causing his fingers to tangle in my hair as he panted with exertion. I could tell Max was getting close and moved my mouth over him in quick, fluid motions. Combined with my hand working at the base of his shaft, he suddenly grunted, and I felt the hot release in the back of my throat. I struggled to breathe as I swallowed his thick cum, sitting back and wiping my mouth as we both came down from our high.

He pulled me into his arms and kissed the top of my head. "That was… wow!"

I giggled. "I agree. I'm glad I decided to talk this out with you, Max."

Wiggling his eyebrows, a mischievous look twinkling in his eyes, he said, "That was talking?"

Rolling my eyes at him we collapsed in each other's arms once more. Contentment washed over me, and I knew we would get through this crazy ordeal…one way or another. While I may not have been ready to have sex in that moment, I knew when we did it would as perfect as what we just experienced. Armed with that thought made thinking about intimacy not nearly as scary and intimidating as it had been since the night my life went to hell.

CHAPTER FORTY-NINE

Over the next couple of months, Max and I slowly rebuilt a firm foundation for our physical intimacy to stand on. We kept to things we had already experimented with and knew we both found enjoyable for the first month, until finally, the anticipation outweighed the anxiety for me, and I surrendered myself to my desire. And despite my new-found carnal need, the first time still had me quaking until Max carefully pointed out the differences for me.

He left the lights of our bedroom on, meaning I was able to see his face the entire time. He went slowly, making certain I was practically dripping before even attempting to enter me, meaning I didn't experience near as much pain as I sensed I had the night I had been raped. And for the duration of our lovemaking, he tenderly held me, kissed me, and whispered over and over again how much he loved me. Max was mindful to keep his hands away from my neck and didn't hold my hands or wrists down against the bed to control me either.

When tears unconsciously slipped from my eyes, he paused his thrusting to wipe them away and verify I was okay before he continued. By the time he allowed himself to climax, I had finally felt the fear melt away from my body and my mind and was thoroughly enjoying the feeling of him filling me. The night Max and I first consummated our marriage, he showed me the difference between sex and love…and it was a beautiful miracle.

The new semester for Max had begun in January, as had his paid internship at a local engineering firm. He was learning online and in-person with his new job and was nearly finished with his third year of his mechanical engineering degree. With the way he was mapping out his coursework, he was expecting to graduate by the end of the year.

I was beginning my Lamaze classes soon since my due date was in May and it was now the first part of March. Around the New Year, I had begun to feel the baby kick and move. By the end of January, Max was able to as well, which thrilled him to no end. He seemed to kick more whenever I would eat chips and salsa—which I craved at least four times a week—and slept when I would eat chocolate. It still amazed me every time he moved, but there were plenty of times when I wished he would let me get some sleep rather than playing soccer with my kidneys in the middle of the night.

Since I had withdrawn from school, I needed a way to stay productive while Max was at work, without having to worry about a traditional job or education. Fortunately, I was able to obtain a part-time position working from the comfort of our apartment where I typed reports for a local doctor's office from transcripts I picked up on Mondays. On Friday, I would drop the finished reports back off to the secretary. It was easy to do and I found I actually enjoyed it, making me wonder if I should have considered a career in journalism or English literature instead of biology.

But today we were heading to my parent's house where Annie and our mothers had thrown together a baby shower for us. Truth be told, I was nervous even having one, but the three of them insisted. So, dressed in pale hues of blue—a cute maternity tunic top over jeggings for me, and khakis with a baby blue polo for Max—as per the instructions we were given by a very excited Annie, we prepared ourselves for a couple hours' worth of craziness and cake.

Adorable safari animals comprised the theme for the shower since our moms had decided that would be cute for the nursery. And the guests who had shown up were wholly supportive of us and ready to help us welcome "our" baby boy. A table was crammed with cake and punch, along with other little snacks on one wall of the kitchen, and in the sunroom was a comfy-looking rocking chair waiting for my pregnant ass to collapse into it. Surrounding the chair were all manners of baby gifts, to the point they were overflowing from the bassinet we were gifted.

I could not have held back my smile if I tried.

"Ren and I are so thankful each of you were able to come over today to help us prepare for our little guy's arrival," Max said with his hand on my shoulder as the party wound down. "They say it takes a village to raise a child, and I believe it. We're glad we have our village of all of you—great friends and family who care about us and our baby before he even gets here. Thanks again!"

We thanked and bid our guests farewell, until finally, it was just us, our parents, Annie, and Nick. I continued to rock in my new chair, content to stay put rather than move since a certain little someone was digging his toes into my ribcage. I poked at my stomach, trying to get him to turn over.

"I can hear you now," Nick teased, handing me a cup of punch.

"What?"

"I'm not touching you!" he said in a sing-song voice, his deep blue eyes twinkling.

I rolled my brown eyes at his theatrics but chuckled, nonetheless. "I'd like to see you handle a tiny little person constantly putting their toes in between your ribs, Nicholas," I scoffed.

"Okay, well, what about this one: don't make me come in there!"

"I suggest you stop before the steam comes out of her ears, man," Max laughed, noting my aggravated face. "Ren, your mom wants to know if pizza is okay for dinner."

Nodding sweetly, I smile. "Sure. Thanks, Max."

Flicking his fingers at Nick—meaning he had his eyes on his friend— Max headed back to the kitchen to help. Nick plopped down on a nearby chair, watching the sun set behind the house with me. For several moments, neither of us spoke, we merely enjoyed the tranquility of the evening.

"Alright, being serious now," Nick softly said, drawing my eyes, "is everything going okay for the three of you? And I still haven't heard what you're naming my godson."

"For the most part, yes, things are going as well as expected for us," I answer. "I'm a little antsy since we're getting so close to the due date, but otherwise, okay. As for the name…we still haven't decided on one."

He tossed me a lopsided grin. "I know whatever you choose will be great. The kid is going to be my godson after all, so he'll be incredible."

"You're too much sometimes, Nick," I sass. "But thank you for that."

CHAPTER FIFTY

It was three days before my due date, and I had been at home on bedrest for the past month thanks to preterm labor complications. I was expecting Max home at any moment and had been flipping through a new cookbook to figure out what to cook for dinner when it hit me—the first true pain of labor. I had to bite down on my lip to keep from crying aloud as the contraction rippled through my body, and slowly rose from the couch to head for the bathroom. I barely made it to the tile before I felt the first trickle run down my leg.

Shit, I thought, panic rushing over me. *I think my water just broke.* I managed to change my dampened bottoms, adding a thick pad to my underwear to hopefully help prevent further embarrassment, and was pondering what the hell I was supposed to do next.

Thankfully, Max walked in the front door at that moment, calling for me. I carefully walked to the door of our bedroom, peering out to find him peeking into the refrigerator, oblivious of what was happening behind him.

"Max…"

"Hey sweetheart," he greeted, still facing away. "What do you want for—Ren? What's wrong?" his expression changed to wide-eyed concern as he turned to face me.

"I think my water just broke," I answered slowly.

"Oh," was his stoic reply. A second later, his eyes widened further, and his jaw dropped open. "Oh! Okay, well, let's grab your hospital bag and we can give Dr. Collins a call on the way."

I nodded, unable to form any words with my addled brain. Between the intense cramping from the contractions and the anxiety that was flooding my body, my mind had effectively been rendered useless. I could feel the hot tears filling my eyes and a strangled sob slipped past my lips. Max, who had run into the bedroom to get my bag, dropped it to run to me when he saw my expression.

"It's going to be okay," he whispered, pulling me carefully into his arms. "I know you're scared and probably in pain, but I'm going to be right beside you the entire time."

He lifted my chin so that my eyes met his, warm sincerity radiating from their emerald depths. "I promise you, Ren. I'm not going anywhere."

His lips pressed a gossamer kiss to my forehead and then he gently placed his hand on the small of my back, leading me over to the door. My bag in one of his hands, he gripped my waist with his other, maneuvering me into my car outside. Within two minutes, we were out of our parking space and heading for the hospital, Max calling to let our doctor know we were on the way. Sitting in the passenger seat trying to distract myself from my nerves, I sent a group text to our parents, Annie, and Nick, informing them that it was show time.

The twenty-minute drive to the hospital felt like an hour, with the contractions ripping through my lower body like a machete blade to bamboo. It occurred to me that I had been experiencing mild cramps for the past day or so and had chosen to ignore them. There was no ignoring them now.

Once at the hospital, we were quickly settled into our room in the labor and delivery wing, my clothes swapped for the indecent hospital gowns that barely cover your ass, and an absorbent pad was on the bed under me since they took away my underwear. I was mortified, and having nurses coming in to lift the sheets periodically to check me only served to ramp up my already sky-high anxiety. After three hours like this, my heart rate went through the roof, as did my blood pressure, and Dr. Collins came rushing into the room since alarms were going off by my bed.

She took one look at my face and seemed to connect the dots instantly. I had barely gotten over having her checking me during my appointments, but all these random other people—women or not—were freaking me the hell out.

"Jackie, I'll take it from here," she stated with authority.

The nurse looked puzzled, but Dr. Collins's face left no room for argument, and she quickly left the room. "Alright Renee, I need you to do your best to breathe through this right now and calm yourself down," Dr. Collins urged. "Your vitals being so high puts more risk on you and the baby, and that is the last thing we want today."

Max gripped my hand with one hand while the other gently stroked my hair. "Come on, babe, deep breaths. Do you want me to put on your relaxation music?"

Focusing on carefully controlling my inhales and exhales, I simply nodded to him, biting on my lip as another contraction began. Dr. Collins checked the monitors, her face pinched with worry as she continued to watch mine and the baby's vitals wildly fluctuated. A second alarm sounded, drawing our attention, and she turned to us.

"I think at this point, it may be a safer option for both of them if we do an emergency c-section," she stated. "Her blood pressure is still through the roof, and unfortunately, the baby's heart rate is decelerating. We need to deliver him now."

"Won't her blood pressure being so high be a problem in the operating room?" Max asked, his face pale.

"The stress is what's causing her blood pressure to spike. We can't give her high doses of sedatives to calm her down without affecting the baby too much, unless we go ahead and do the surgery. It's truly the safer option."

"Max…" I whispered, gripping his hand as the fear closed in around me.

"Ren, it's going to be fine. You both are," he encouraged.

"Max, if you want to be in with her, I'll need you to go with the nurse to get scrubbed up properly, and I've got to get prepped myself," Dr. Collins announced, stepping over to push a button behind the bed, calling for the nurses. "Everything is going to be okay, Renee, just breathe."

Before I could fully process what was happening, I was being wheeled down the hall to the operating theatre where sterile blue curtains were hung and draped around my body. Sedatives were pushed through my I.V., making me drowsy, but calming my anxiety. Max was back at my side, holding my hand the entire time. Then, all at once, my world expanded more than I knew it could.

CHAPTER FIFTY-ONE

I heard the first cries, soft whimpers, and then a small body was brought closer so I could see him. Thanks to the medications in my system, I was essentially paralyzed, but I swear my heart fucking stopped the moment I laid my bleary eyes on him. Sobs began to choke me, the nurses mistaking them for tears of happiness, when in fact…I was about to become hysterical.

Fortunately, Dr. Collins noticed my distress and immediately pushed another syringe of sedatives, causing me to lapse into unconsciousness.

When I awoke, my body ached, but I was back in my original room, the sun having set below the horizon hours earlier from the depth of the darkness. I guess I groaned or made enough noise to alert Max that I was awake, because he jumped from his place on the hideously uncomfortable hospital couch to come to the side of my bed. His green eyes were bloodshot, but still gazing at me with such tenderness, it brought the tiniest smile to my face.

"Hi gorgeous," he smiled, brushing my hair away from my face. "How do you feel?"

"Like I got caught in a damn barbed wire fence," I said, wincing as I angled my bed upright some more.

"Dr. Collins said you would be pretty sore for the first couple of weeks, but thankfully everything went really well during the surgery, and our little guy is doing well."

"That's—that's good."

A soft knock landed on my door just then, and the nurse came bustling in, a small rolling bassinet with her. "Oh, good, mommy's awake," she said with a wide smile. "Someone wanted to come meet you, honey, and I need to do a quick check on your incision to make sure it looks okay."

She came closer in her light pink scrubs, which made her raven black hair and chocolate skin almost glow. I didn't recognize her, so figured she must have come in with the shift change while I was asleep. She snapped on a pair of gloves and gently lifted the sheets to glance at my stomach.

"Everything looks good so far," she announced, tossing her gloves in the trash. "Now, someone is about ready for a bottle, since Dr. Collins said nursing would be out of the question for the next day or so. Mommy, you up for holding him?"

She scooped him up in her arms, bringing him and a tiny bottle over to me. As she extended her arms to hand him to me, I felt my panic flare, my chest constricting painfully as I looked at him.

"No!" I cried, burying my face in my hands as I sobbed.

Max pulled me into his arms and stroked my back as I began to hyperventilate, my cries causing me to hiccup as they continued. I'm sure the poor nurse was completely aghast at my outburst and didn't have the faintest clue as to how to react to my tears.

"Would it be possible to give her the night to rest?" Max asked softly, cradling my body against his chest as I heard my baby begin to wail as well.

"I—of course," the nurse responded, and soon was heading back out the door.

"Oh, Ren," he murmured into my hair. "Just close your eyes and sleep for now, okay? It'll be better in the morning."

I wasn't sure I believed him, but I obediently closed my eyes, letting him continue to rock me gently until I fell into a tortured sleep. Hours later, I woke covered in a cold sweat, my breathing coming in ragged gasps as I recovered from yet another nightmare.

This hadn't been a flashback; no, this was like a prophecy for the future. One where a cloaked madman stalked me, stalked my child, hunting us like a wolf hunts for lambs. And though it was now the middle of May, it had ended with my son and I lost in the woods, surrounded by trees and glistening white snow…until the madman appeared and the purity of the snow was destroyed with crimson spray.

I looked over at Max, curled up asleep on the couch-bed, just as the nurse entered.

"You alright, honey?" she asked softly.

"Just had a nightmare," I admitted.

She offered me a sad look. "Is there anything I can do to help?"

I motioned to the cabinet where my bag was located. "Do you mind getting something out for me?"

"Not at all," she whispered. "What am I looking for?"

"It's a blue journal."

She quickly found it and brought it to me, along with the pen I always kept hooked to the cover. I thanked her, let her quietly take my vitals, and then she slipped back out of the room, leaving Max snoring softly. I opened the book Dr. Prajesh had given me months ago, slowly flipping through the pages until I came to the next blank one.

A small light was constantly on over the bed, so I had no need for additional light, although it did make it a little difficult to read at times. I knew that for the morning to be better as Max believed it would, I needed to deal with my emotions and anxiety right then. Uncapping my pen, I took a deep breath and began to write my entry.

I gave birth today. I haven't even held him because I've been such an emotional mess, the very thought of touching him makes me physically sick. Some maternal instinct, huh? I was so full of anxiety that I was actually endangering his life…to the point Dr. Collins insisted we do a c-section. Another scar to add to my repertoire. At least this scar is visible and had a purpose.

More purpose than my fucking nightmares. One would think with all the medication they gave me I wouldn't dream tonight. Sadly, I did, and in it, my child and I are being pursued by a menacing man (who I can only presume is his biological father). And even though Max's name will be on the birth certificate where it says "father," I have to come to grips with the realization that this child is my rapist's son...

CHAPTER FIFTY-TWO

One Week Later...

"How are you feeling today, Renee?" Dr. Prajesh asked as I slowly sank into her couch, her dark brown eyes lingering on my waist. "I would imagine your body is still quite sore between the labor, the surgery, and sleep deprivation, am I right?"

I offered her a weak smile before nodding. Folding my hands in my lap, I bit my lip and thought about how to best answer her questions... because I knew she was not simply asking about the state of my physical well-being.

"You would be very correct in assuming my body is ridiculously sore still yet, but thankfully, the incision seems to be healing nicely. I also have been blessed to have plenty of help the past week in caring for Dylan, so that has made things better."

I hesitated, disappointed in myself as I thought back over the past eight days since I had given birth to my son, and the cries and hysterics I had broken into so frequently when I attempted to hold him. I hated to bring it up with her, but knew I needed to be honest about this regrettable development.

"What seems to be on your mind, Renee?"

"I'm embarrassed to admit to this, even though I have gotten better about it in the past couple of days, but when he was first born I—I could not hold him without bursting into tears or becoming violently ill due to my hysterics," I tell her, feeling ashamed. "What kind of mother can't hold her own child?"

Dr. Prajesh had the most sympathetic look on her face. Not one of pity; but one of understanding and compassion.

"You said that you have been able to do better with that the past couple of days though, right?" she confirmed.

I nodded, earning me a small smile in return. "Renee, I think the fact that you have chosen to not only keep Dylan, but to be his mother, love him, and cherish him, despite his method of conception, is beyond admirable. The fact that you are struggling with holding him now is completely understandable due to your trauma. Don't try to rush yourself on any of this, and do not feel less of yourself as a mother because of it.

"Does he look like you, or does he remind you of anyone?" she asked cautiously.

"It's kind of funny," I start, giggling a bit, "one of the nurses had absolutely no idea about the situation so truly believed Max was his father. And she was pointing out how much Dylan looks like him. She was saying he got Max's ears, his fawn-colored hair, his mouth, and eye shape."

Dr. Prajesh smiled. "He sounds adorable. Did he get any of your features?"

"He ended up with my nose and that is about it," I chuckle. "But yes, he is pretty cute, and you can see him when we're done since I still am not allowed to drive. Max drove me so he and Dylan are in the waiting room."

"Oh, I cannot wait!" she exclaimed. "I love babies; if you couldn't tell. I know things have been a whirlwind for you, Ren, and I know you are probably going to doubt yourself and your mothering skills in the months and years to come due to your PTSD, but I want you to understand something. You have a phenomenal support system in place and that means you can make this work. You just need to give yourself some time to get there, okay?

"And you can always make extra appointments with me if you need them, and we can talk through whatever may be troubling you. I promise that if you will take this one step at a time, you will get the hang of this soon. I want you to be confident in yourself, but I do need you to promise me that you will watch for signs of postpartum depression, just in case."

"I understand," I reply. "Is that something that Max should be in here to listen to the warning signs for as well?"

Rising from her seat, Dr. Prejesh nodded. "Good thinking, Ren. I'll poke my head out and call him in here."

Within moments, my husband was seated on the couch next to me, Dylan's car seat was on the floor with his diaper bag tucked inside of it, and Dr. Prajesh was gushing over the tiny baby in my arms. Her enthusiasm was enough to coax a broad and sincere smile to my tired face as Max casually draped his arm around my shoulder.

"It is so nice to finally meet you in person, Max," Dr. Prajesh finally said, turning her attention back to the adults in the room. "Ren has told me so many wonderful things about you over the past several months."

"Likewise," he returned easily. "I cannot thank you enough for all that you've done to help her."

My therapist waved her cinnamon hand dismissively, but her smile told me she appreciated the compliment. "So, we called you in to join us so I could make sure you were aware of warning signs of postpartum depression. Since Ren already has PTSD she is at a higher risk for developing PPD, and I know we would all like to see her healthy and thriving instead. Ideally, catching PPD early is the best way to help the mother cope, and since you have been so attentive thus far…"

"Understood," Max agreed. "That sounds like a plan. I would like to keep my wife happy as much as possible," he finished, kissing my temple.

"If you notice Ren is having more trouble sleeping than usual, appetite changes, severe fatigue, frequent mood swings, trouble bonding with Dylan or maybe acting like she isn't interested in him suddenly, a drastic increase in crying—especially for no apparent reason—or trouble concentrating, just to name a few," she listed as her eyes went between the two of us, "please do not hesitate to contact either her OB GYN or myself immediately."

"I know she struggled this first week with holding him, but I don't think that counts in any of this," he said slowly. "And besides, she has managed to overcome that and she seems to be doing much better now."

"She mentioned that to me," Dr. Prajesh agreed. "But good job on being observant. If you have any questions or concerns, please feel free to call."

"Absolutely," my husband said with a firm nod.

"Now," she began, turning her beaming face to me, "may I beg your indulgence to hold this cutie for a minute?"

CHAPTER FIFTY-THREE

"**I** come bearing gifts!" Annie's voice chirped through our front door. "Let me in!"

Carefully easing myself up from the rocking chair, I made my way to let her in, my eyes going wide when I saw just how many bags she had with her. Dylan cradled in my arm, I held the door open so she could sweep within my living room to begin setting down her many packages. Just as I went to close it, Zane cleared his throat lightly, causing me to jump.

"Sorry, Ren," he said quietly.

Shaking my head, I offered him a grin and allowed him to follow Annie inside, noticing the additional bags he had been carrying for her. I shut the door softly, doing my best to not wake the baby in my arms since it had taken me nearly an hour to get him to sleep after Max had left for work.

"So, do you want to tell me what the hell all this is?" I asked in a hiss as I reclaimed my seat in the rocking chair. "And I thought you were coming over on Friday, not Wednesday."

Annie stopped digging through the bags to turn and face me, cocking her head to one side to give me a smirk. "Ren, sweetie, it *is* Friday."

"No it isn't," I started to argue. "I had therapy with Dr. Prajesh yesterday, and I have therapy...on Thursdays. Damn it. I think I may be a little tired."

Annie giggled. "I know you are. Which is why Zane and I are here. Max won't be home until late tonight, and I know you need to get some extra rest, so we are going to stick around here to help you today."

"Annie is going to be on babysitting duty, and I'll be helping around the apartment since I know Max has been busy since he took off work for a week and now has to make up for that," Zane continued. "I'll be your bonus house-husband of sorts."

I chuckled, making my incision from the c-section ripple with pain, but thankfully it was short-lived now that I was past the one-week mark.

"Thank you so much, guys. I appreciate it."

Annie blew me a wink and a kiss while Zane shook his head in embarrassment. Dylan squirmed in my arms, our conversation disturbing him. I bounced him lightly in my arms, hoping I could keep him from waking, but his dark blue eyes blinked open and he looked up at me as his little fingers gripped my shirt.

"Oops, sorry Ren," Annie whispered, taking in his movements. "Never fear, Aunt Annie has just the thing!"

She turned back to her plethora of bags and once again began rifling through them until she found what she had been looking for apparently. A plush brown puppy with drooping ears and his little pink tongue peeking from his mouth rested in her arms. I had to admit, the toy was adorable, even if it was bigger than my son currently.

"His name is Dodger," Annie exclaimed in excitement. "Isn't that cute? It'll be Dylan and Dodger against the world!"

"Babe, you do realize that thing is bigger than the baby is, right?" Zane asked, his brows arched.

Annie's golden eyes widened as she looked between the toy and Dylan, her face falling a bit when she realized he was correct. I couldn't help but smile; she had been so excited about the stuffed animal, and I could tell she had put so much thought into it.

"It is such a sweet plushy, Annie," I assured her. "Dylan may just have to grow into it a bit first."

Satisfied with my response, Annie sat Dodger on the floor beside her and began rummaging through the remaining bags, soon finding a rattling lovey blanket with a bear head at the top instead. She came over and gently took Dylan from my arms and shook the little bear for him, making his little eyes go wide as his hands tried to reach for it.

"I've got him if you want to go take a nap or a long, hot shower," she told me. "I know neither have been luxuries you have had time for really the past few days, so have fun. Zane and I will make some lunch in a few hours."

I bit my lower lip, unsure if I should be okay with leaving Dylan like this, even if they were my best friends and I did trust them. But I knew I would be useless to him, to Max, and to myself if I did not indulge in a little self-care every now and then. One fifteen minute shower and maybe a little nap wouldn't hurt. Nodding gratefully, I headed for my room.

Nearly three hours later I finally emerged, showered, changed, and rested from my nap—that was admittedly far longer than I intended it to be—to find Annie sitting in the rocking chair with Dylan. He was hungrily drinking his bottle while she smiled down at him, telling him stories of our high school days.

"Your mommy was the nicest person at our school. And boy, could she sing. I'm sure you'll figure this out as you get older, Dylan, but your momma is wicked talented when it comes to music. And smart to boot. She is one of the strongest people you will ever know, and your daddy is pretty great too," she told him.

"Aunt Annie is pretty incredible in my book," I added, causing her head to snap up.

"I second that," Zane spoke up from the kitchen. "Of course, I also think she's sexy as—"

"Zane, I don't need to hear that!" I screech, interrupting him. "And I am fairly certain my week-old son does not need to hear that either!"

Annie and Zane both laughed while I shook my head.

"Lunch will be ready in about half an hour, Ren," Zane announced, turning back to his cooking as I went to sit on the couch.

"Thanks. So...is this making you want one?" I tease, eying my best friend with a smirk.

Annie looked up at me in mock horror. "Hell no! Well...not yet at least. I love kids and I am happy to babysit and play Auntie, but let's not go giving me two-point-five kids and the white picket fence just yet, okay?"

"Fine. But for the record, I get to buy your first kid an obnoxiously large stuffed animal when they are first born too," I tell her with a wink.

"Love you too," she muttered before turning Dylan over her shoulder to burp him loudly.

CHAPTER FIFTY-FOUR

Three Weeks Later…

After nearly a month of being a new mother, I thought I was slowly getting the hang of the sleepless nights, two a.m. feedings, and learning to rock the messy-bun-with-leggings look. I was getting Dylan onto a schedule for his feedings and attempting to get him on one for sleeping, and Max and I had found a good rhythm for alternating tasks. And then disaster struck.

It was late one Tuesday night, amazingly Dylan had not yet woken up for his bottle, but it was nearing two a.m. when I jerked upright in our bed, screaming. As the harsh sounds ripped from my chest, Max sprung into action beside me, throwing on the lamp and reaching desperately for me as I panted and gripped at the quilt on our bed. Then we heard it; Dylan's wails through the monitor.

My screaming had startled him and woken him.

Max was torn, unsure if he could leave me in that moment as panicked as I was, but knowing he needed to attend our son. Giving me an extra hug, he began easing off the bed, but in my terrified state I tried to keep him with me instead.

"Sweetheart," he whispered patiently, leaning back to brush my sweat-dampened hair back from my face, "I will be right back. But I need to go get Dylan. I will bring him and all his things in here, okay, that way you are not alone. But Dylan needs us."

I drew in a ragged breath and tried to comprehend what Max was saying to me, but all I could hear was a raspy voice telling me to behave. The tears continued to drip down my face as he forcibly pulled away from my grasp, letting my hands fall back onto the mattress as he walked out to the kitchen. Dylan's cries mixed with my own, forming a never-ending cycle of sorrow and pain I wondered if I would ever escape.

"Look, Dylan," I heard Max say softly, breaking through the trance I had been in since he left, "there's mommy. See, she's okay, little man; just very sad. Maybe you can help cheer her up."

He settled onto the bed beside me again with Dylan in his arms, and a hopeful expression on his face as he popped the bottle into our baby's mouth. Dylan's dark blue eyes were trying to focus on me because of how Max had carefully angled his little body, and I could tell he was hoping I would reach out and take him. But I couldn't.

I felt fresh tears begin to course down my cheeks as I looked at my son, and hung my head in shame. Why was this so easy for Max, especially when he wasn't Dylan's biological father? Was this what having postpartum depression looked like? Was I failing my child because of my PTSD?

"Ren," Max murmured, his free hand coming up to stroke my cheek. "Sweetheart, please talk to me."

"You'll hate me," I whispered, eyes squeezed shut because I could not bear to look at the hurt in his emerald eyes.

"I could never hate you," he said adamantly. "Now please, tell me what your dream was about."

I shook my head, making my tears fall harder than before, but cracked open my eyes to stare at Dylan's fuzzy little head. I nibbled on my lower lip as I prayed for the strength to ask the love of my life a sinister question.

"If I ask you to say something, will you say it?" I blurt out, refusing to look at them both.

"Um, yes?"

Taking a deep breath, I forced myself to raise my head and look at Max, who was clearly confused since his brows were furrowed. "Tell me to behave and that it's going to be worth it."

His eyes went wide; first with shock, then anger.

"Why the fuck would you ask me to say that, Ren?"

"Please, just...just say it," I plead.

"Do you really think I had anything to do with what happened to you?"

At this point, Max was seething. He had been nothing but patient with me and all my tears and panic attacks from day one, and now I was asking him to essentially clear his name. Fuck; I was being a damn fool.

"No, I really don't but...I can't explain it, Max!" I cried. "I keep hearing it in my dreams! I keep hearing him tell me that over and over and I know his damn voice but I can't remember who the hell he is! It's driving me fucking insane! I'm sorry; I'm so sorry! Please don't hate me!"

I dissolved in tears once more, my anger and frustration exhausted, leaving me a blubbering mess. Max pulled me into his arms, sandwiching Dylan in between us gently, and stroked my back soothingly.

"Ren, I swear to you I had nothing to do with this and that I do not hate you or ever could, but one day, you will see that something good will come of this. And that good will be worth all the bad. I believe Dylan will be a big part of that for you."

Max lifted my chin to look deep into my eyes, his anger dissipated and replaced with his love for me. He wiped away my tears and leaned in for a slow, sweet kiss that stole my breath completely. Dylan took that moment to kick and coo, drawing our attention back to him with plenty of laughter as I reached for his tiny body.

"Come here, sweet boy," I murmured, pulling him close to my chest. He snuggled against me at once with a small sigh and yawn, bringing a smile to my face before I leaned down to brush a kiss atop his downy head. "No matter the circumstances, I will always be thankful for you and love you with all my heart, Dylan."

CHAPTER FIFTY-FIVE

"Look at this sweet boy! Nana loves you! Yes she does!" Brenda cooed at Dylan as she sat in the rocking chair in her living room with him.

Jerome was helping Max bring in the rest of our things so I could make Dylan's bottle. It was our first real trip with him since he had been born, and even though going to Lubbock wasn't very far from where we lived in Amarillo, it still felt like we had over-packed for the short weekend trip to visit his parents and Nick. I could not keep the grin off my face as I re-entered the living room and watched my husband's mother interact with my son...the child she had told me to abort. Dylan was such a precious soul, Brenda could not help but fall in love with him instantly.

"Here we go, buddy," I announce, shaking his bottle vigorously to finish mixing it. Since I had to be on antidepressants for my PTSD, I was not allowed to breastfeed him. Fortunately, he took his formula well and was gaining weight nicely.

"Ren, do you mind if I feed him?" Brenda asked as she cradled him.

I didn't bother answering her, but handed her the bottle and burp rag with a smile, sinking into the chair beside her. I hadn't been seated but a minute before Max and Jerome came back inside the house, done bringing in our bags. Max came and slid onto the floor in front of me, leaning his head against my knee, while Jerome took a seat in his recliner.

"What do you guys have planned while you're here?" Jerome asked, smiling at Dylan before turning his attention to us.

"We were going to visit Nick and his folks tomorrow afternoon," Max stated with a small shrug, "but other than that, I think we had planned to more or less be here with you two."

"I did get that email from Jen saying she and Eric were in town and that she would love to see us if we had time," I reminded him timidly. "I'm just not sure how excited I am to be in Lubbock proper. It's one thing to be here at the ranch or to go to Nick's parent's house, but to be somewhere in town? To be frank, it scares the absolute hell out of me."

Jerome offered me a sympathetic look. "I think that's to be expected, honey, but don't forget, Max will be there and he won't let anything happen to you. But if it would help you feel better, you know you are more than welcome to invite those friends to meet you out here. We will be out working in the fields during the days so the house will be empty, and Dylan doesn't need to be out there with that noise or dust."

"He's right, Ren," Brenda chimed. "You can have them come here if that would work better and if your friends can manage the drive. We just want you to feel safe and besides, then Dylan can take a nap if he needs to."

Max tilted his head so those emerald eyes I loved so much could look up into my face, his upside-down smile making me giggle amidst my mild anxiety. His gentle hands snaked around my waist as he smirked at me, and I could feel the blush rising into my cheeks as he stared into my eyes.

"Is that something you would want, sweetheart?" he asked, lightly stroking my hips and thighs.

I gulped as his hands continued to move slowly along the tops of my legs, distracting me from the question he had asked. Biting my lower lip painfully hard to bring myself back into the moment, I narrowed my brown eyes at him before nodding slightly.

"I think that could work. Thank you for suggesting it, guys," I answered sweetly, looking up at my in-laws.

I forcibly removed Max's hands from my legs and stood, side-stepping him to head toward our room. Shaking my head to dispel the impure thoughts racing through my mind as I walked quickly into the bedroom, I threw myself back onto the bed in mock frustration. I still had a minimum of two weeks before my doctor would clear me to consider engaging in intercourse, and here was Max, riling me up in front of his parents of all people. My body may not have been physically ready for sex but my mind was saying 'hell yes' as he had been caressing my thighs and sending me into overdrive.

The door to our room suddenly creaked open, and in walked my rather confused-looking husband. He softly closed the door behind him and came to sit beside me on the bed with concern still plainly written on his handsome face.

"Did I do something wrong, baby?"

I felt my eyes widen in shock at his words and then sighed in defeat.

"No," I chuckled. "You absolutely did not. In fact, you were doing something I found far too amazing and enticing, hence why I needed to walk away before it became apparent that I wanted you to do unholy things to me."

"Oh…" Max whistled. "So, you're telling me that my sweet, beautiful little wife was getting all hot and bothered just by me stroking her sexy legs?"

I rolled my eyes. "There is no need to be sarcastic and tease me about it, Mr. Harris."

His fingers landed on my lips, silencing my words as he leaned closer. "I am not being sarcastic in the slightest, Ren. You are the sweetest woman I know, and I happen to find your body beautiful and think your legs are sexy. And if you roll your eyes at me again, I may have to spank you, Mrs. Harris."

"Is that so?" I whisper, leaning into him, lightly gripping his t-shirt.

He brushed my hair behind my ear and cradled my cheeks in his hands. "Absolutely. Now, I know I can't ravish your body just yet, but I can savor these lips. Just," he paused to gently suck my lower lip between his teeth like he did the night of our first date, "like this."

And for the next several moments, Max proceeded to tenderly kiss me, making love to my mouth in lieu of my body. It reminded me yet again of how this man chose to cherish me day after day, for which I was immeasurably thankful.

CHAPTER FIFTY-SIX

"Max, get in here, honey!" Nick's mother, Sheila Spencer, cried with happiness when we arrived the following afternoon.

Her face was beaming with a wide smile as she held the door open to allow the three of us to enter her home, making me feel right at ease. I had only met her once before, but Sheila was as sweet as they come, welcoming and maternal to the core. Her husband, David, fortunately left his cold lawyer persona at the office and in the courtroom, making him a jovial companion to his wife. Nick looked exactly like his father, same dark hair and olive complexion, but he had his mom's dark blue eyes.

"Sheila, it is so good to see you again," my husband was telling her, embracing her warmly.

"Max, you know we are always happy to see you!" she replied, tucking her dark blonde hair behind her ears. Her eyes swiveled to me where I stood holding Dylan, and her smile grew even broader. "Renee, it is so lovely to have you here and just look at this precious little baby! Oh, he is just too cute!"

"Thank you; I know I am," Nick snickered, sneaking up behind his mother.

Sheila turned to lightly smack his arm, earning a grin from Max and a giggle from me.

"Well, come on into the living room you guys, and get comfortable. We've got some time before dinner and I would love to spend it playing with this precious little boy."

I grinned and held Dylan toward her, causing Sheila to cheer with excitement. She carefully scooped him into her arms and swayed with him as she walked into her rosy living room, complete with its beige leather couches and recliners, hardwood floors and peach-colored rug in the center of the room. Nick shook his head in mock dismay as we followed her, listening to her calling for David as she went.

By the time we made it to the couch, Sheila was gently bouncing Dylan in her lap and cooing at him and David was entering the room from the direction of the back deck, the scent of grilling meat floating in behind him. With all the commotion, Nick's younger sister, Allison, finally emerged from her bedroom to come see what the fuss was about.

"Max, good to see you, son," David greeted, clapping him heartily on the back. "And you as well, Renee."

"Hello, Mr. Spencer," I replied softly.

"Oh, none of this Mr. and Mrs. Spencer nonsense, sweetheart," Sheila interrupted. "Max may as well be a second son to us with as much time as he spent here growing up, and we will happily claim you too. Please call us by our names."

"Ren, do you mind if I have a turn holding him?" Allison asked me timidly, softly stroking Dylan's downy head as she sat beside her mom.

"Of course you can," I answered her with a smile. "That is, if your mom will give him up."

We all chuckled as Sheila pretended to pull Dylan closer and away from Allison briefly before she finally handed him over to her daughter. David conned the guys into going outside to help him finish up with the grilling, so the three of us girls stayed inside and chatted for the next half hour in the coolness of the air conditioning.

"Thank you so much for dinner," I said, my stomach sated after we had finished eating an hour later. "It was absolutely delicious."

"Not a problem," Sheila answered, carefully burping Dylan. "Thank you for bringing this little cutie to see us."

She tossed a sly look to her son before looking back down at my now-sleeping infant. "Nicholas, I think I would like one of these from you one day soon. Think you could find a nice young woman to settle down with to give us one?"

Nick groaned, dropping his head into his hands. "Jeez, mom. What the hell? I'm twenty-one; give me a fucking break, will you?"

"Language," his father warned lightly. "But your mother is right, a grandchild at some point would be nice, son."

Nick looked up at me with a pitiful glint in his deep blues. "Ren, can my mother please claim Dylan as her adoptive grandson for now? Because let's be real, between the police academy and my continued online criminal justice classes, I don't exactly have the time to go out and find a wife. I mean, I could just randomly make a baby with someone, but I don't think that's what they want me to do."

Sheila sent him a death glare over his last statement, the look causing me to hide my face behind my napkin as I fought back my giggles. Allison did not even bother to try and erupted with laughter beside me, as did Max.

"Oh, for the love of God, Nick," David moaned, the sound of his chair scooting away from the table following his words.

"Nick, I think if you randomly knocked some girl up, your mom might just kill you and raise the baby on your behalf," Max teased, still laughing.

Across the table, Sheila gasped at his choice of words. "Maxwell, that was a horribly crude way of phrasing that, young man!" she scolded. "Girls, I am so sorry for the manners they are presenting tonight."

"Trust me, Sheila, my best friend and her boyfriend can be much worse when they want to be," I assured her. "Max is just teasing and Nick, I'm certain you will find the right girl someday. Then you can give your mom those adorable grandchildren she wants. But until then, yes, she absolutely can claim Dylan as hers if she would like."

CHAPTER FIFTY-SEVEN

"So, what is it like being married and a mother by twenty?" Allison asked me later when we were out by the pool.

At sixteen, she was inquisitive, brimming with vitality, joie de vie, and *innocence*. With Nick as her big brother, she was not completely naïve, but I also knew he guarded his little sister passionately. While he might have been a bit of a playboy in school, there is no way in hell Allison was hooking up with random guys...especially at her age. Nick was making sure of that.

And I envied her.

She still got to experience her first time the way it was meant to be truly experienced—as something special and meaningful, not as a nightmare—she could still enjoy the remainder of her teenage years without fear dominating her every moment. Allison would enter her twenties without being married or a parent—unless that was her choice—and live her life according to how she chose to plan it.

I loved my husband and son more than I could explain, but the path that got me to where I was at was not one I would have chosen. I don't think anyone in my shoes would have either...

"Ren?"

"Sorry," I reply, shaking my head to bring myself back into the moment. "I got lost in thought for a minute. It's obviously not where I thought I would be at this stage in my life, but I truly love Max, and Dylan is my world," I told her with a small smile.

"You know," she started, brushing her blonde hair behind her ears and looking up at me shyly, "the first time Nick showed me your picture I thought you two would end up together. You and Nick, I mean, not you and Max. But you and Max are great together too."

I looked at her, a puzzled expression on my face. "When did Nick show you a picture of me?"

"Oh, this was back when the two of you, well, I guess technically the three of you, first met," Allison went on to say.

I wasn't even aware he had one of me back then, I thought as my mind drifted back to that fateful day.

I was a freshman in college and I was rushing from the science building to the library. I needed to get some books for a new research project, plus I had heard from Mira that the library was hiring for student workers. I wanted to get my application in before all the spots had been filled. I desperately needed a job on campus, and this seemed like the perfect one for me.

It was my second semester at the university and my feeling of being homesick was fading. I was making friends, and thought I was finally figuring out where I belonged at that damn school. I had just finished sending Mira a text to let her know I might be back at the dorms late, and was about to shove my phone back into my pocket, when my shoe caught on an uneven brick in the sidewalk, pitching me forward toward the library steps.

I remember a squeaking sound whistling past my lips as I closed my eyes, threw out my arms, and braced myself for impact with the hard stone of the stairs. But that was not what I felt next. Two pairs of arms had halted my fall, doing their best to not grab at inappropriate places on my body—although one of them had their hand very close to my boobs. I took a couple shuddering breaths to calm myself, wondering if I was imagining things, but then I heard them speak.

"Are you okay?"

I slowly opened my eyes to find two shockingly good-looking guys holding onto me, their eyes studying me. I heaved a sigh of relief when I realized I was unharmed, then began looking for my phone.

"I'm okay, but my phone…"

"Right here," the hottie with dark blue eyes had stated proudly, holding out my phone. "Managed to catch it right before it hit the ground. Looks like all those years of football training paid off, Max!"

The green-eyed hunk rolled his eyes but smiled nonetheless at his friend. "Whatever you say, man. I'm Max, by the way, and this is my friend Nick."

"I'm Renee, but most people just call me Ren," I replied weakly. "I cannot thank you both enough for catching my clumsy ass and for saving my phone."

They chuckled. "Our pleasure," Max assured me. "We couldn't have a pretty girl like you covered in cuts and bruises, now could we?"

My mind had been racing…this guy had just called me pretty. Was I dreaming? If I was, I did not want to wake up.

"Are you heading inside?" Nick asked, jerking his head at the library behind us, his hands gripping the straps on his backpack.

"Yeah, I need some books for a research project and was hoping to get hired on as a student worker here," I confessed. "And wow, that was probably way too much information considering we just met. I am so sorry."

"No need to apologize," Max reassured me with a smile. "If you don't mind a couple of guys hanging out with you, we can share a study room or table."

I grinned. "I would really like that. Thanks."

That had been the beginning of our friendship. I literally had fallen into both of their arms. I had no clue though that Nick had a photo of me from back then, though I guess I shouldn't have been surprised. Hearing that Allison thought he and I would have ended up together though, did surprise me. Not because I had never thought of it myself, but because I didn't think anyone else had.

"Huh, I don't guess I knew he had a picture of me," I tell her aloud, staring into my empty cup. "I'll be right back; I'm going to get some more tea."

"Sure thing, Ren. I'm going to see if mom will let me cuddle with Dylan!" she said with a wink.

I headed to the kitchen, still lost in thought and old memories. After pouring myself a drink, I was leaning against the counter to take a sip when I heard the guys' voices coming from down the hall. Curiosity got the best of me and I tiptoed closer.

"Why did you never tell me about that, Nick?" I hear Max huff.

"Because I wasn't sure if it had anything to do with that night or not."

"And now? Do you think that's connected to her rape?"

CHAPTER FIFTY-EIGHT

I felt frozen on the spot, unsure of what I was listening to.

"You asked me to listen and ask around at the party that night," Nick said, the sound of someone sinking onto the bed punctuating his words. "Roy was supposed to be throwing the party, but I couldn't find him anywhere that night. I figured since he knew Ren, and lived in the building, maybe he could help me ask around discreetly."

"But Roy Miller?" Max asked, the skepticism ringing through his voice clear as day. "Nick, I get that you two were closer than he and I, but do you really think involving him would have been a good idea?"

"I was not about to tell him what the fuck happened to her, Max!" Nick hissed. "Ren asked that we not tell anyone, and I respected her privacy—not that it was anyone else's business. All I wanted to know was if Roy had seen anyone or anything suspicious since he lived there. But like I said, I could not find him anywhere that night.

"Then, the next few days, he seemed to be avoiding me, but I figured later it was because of stress. When he was found dead from the overdose, I felt bad for even thinking of asking him anything because it clearly would have made things worse for him," Nick concluded.

I heard Max groan in frustration. "Fine. I guess the big question now is, do we tell her about this?"

"You're thinking of not telling her?"

"Nick, let's be real, what is there to tell her?"

I pushed open the door, my eyebrows raised. Both men looked at me in shock, eyes wide. "There may not be much to tell me, Max, but I would still have appreciated the honesty," I snapped at him. His mouth opened but I cut him off. "Save it! I don't care what excuses you are going to try and spit out right now, just…save it. You're right that there is not much there to go on, so let's move on, okay?"

I turn to walk out the door, pausing long enough to call over my shoulder, "Nick?"

"Um…yes?" he replied warily.

"Thank you for looking into this and looking out for me. Now let's get back outside before your parents come looking for us."

"So, tell us how the police academy has been going for you," I direct to Nick once we return to the seats surrounding the pool.

He fixes me with his steady cobalt gaze and gives me a small nod, knowing exactly what I'm doing. This is my way of forgiving him for keeping me in the dark for months, and for thinking he could get away with not telling me now.

"Well, as you know I'm doing my training with Lubbock while taking criminal justice courses online for my master's degree. I am ten weeks into the basic training program, and still have twenty-six left to go for it, plus patrol training, followed by my exams since I said I wanted to go for detective." He paused to look me in the eye. "I told them point-blank I didn't want to remain a beat-cop for long; that I wanted to be going after the sick fuckers who thought they could get away with committing heinous crimes against others."

"While I do not approve of the language," David interjected, "I approve of the path. You can arrest the creeps and I can prosecute them."

"Meanwhile, I can teach the next generation to be nicer to each other," Sheila said, her blonde brows raised. "And to use better vocabulary terms."

"Mom, last time I checked, there isn't a blackboard—oh, excuse me, you use white boards now, don't you—out here," Allison teased. "Chill out with the teacher-speak, woman!"

"Ren, have you given any thought on returning to school when Dylan gets a bit older, honey?" Sheila asked, carefully reaching for her iced tea while balancing my son with her other arm.

I smiled. "I have, actually. And here lately, I've given more thought to pursuing a career involving writing over my initial thought of becoming a biology or science teacher. I know the world needs more teachers, but part of me is thinking that writing has become such a huge and pivotal aspect of my life recently, and I think it could be something that is useful. And not just for me, but for others as well."

Max draped his arm around my shoulders and gave me a gentle squeeze, knowing exactly what I was referring to with my writing. I felt a blush creep into my cheeks and ducked my head to take a sip of my own tea, lifting my chin at last to see an odd expression etched on Nick's face. It was almost one of...longing? And then it vanished, replaced by his signature smirk.

"Max, how is your internship going? You're still all set to graduate in a couple of months, right?" David asked.

"Yes, sir," he replied, a proud look on his face. "I've got another two months of the internship left, but I have already been offered a full position for when it ends because they have been so pleased with my work. They were tempted to end the internship early but since it was connected to my college credits, they realized they couldn't without jeopardizing my graduation."

"Didn't you say that they were talking about having you move to the hydrology and hydraulics engineering department for a month?" Nick asked, his brows furrowed.

"That was one possibility, yes, but they decided to go with their engineering investigations department instead based on my background," Max informed him. "They are trying to get me as well-rounded in the engineering field as they can, and they want me to be able to work with the structural engineers and investigators later on."

"Look at you boys," Sheila gushed, "out to change the world. I just knew you two would grow up and do amazing things. And look at you now! Max is married to an angel and has this precious little boy, and my baby boy is working his ass off to become a police officer."

Nick and Allison exchanged wide-eyed looks. "Doth my ears deceive me, or did our mother just refer to my posterior as an 'ass'?" he teased.

"Keep that attitude up, Nicholas, and see if I don't kick your ass into the Grand Canyon," Sheila sassed back.

"Yes ma'am," he replied, hands up in surrender while the rest of us laughed 'our asses off'.

CHAPTER FIFTY-NINE

Two Months Later...

"I could have sworn I left you on your tummy, my little man," I said to my three-month old baby when I leaned over him on his mat.

I had run to the restroom, leaving him to have some tummy-time on his playmat while watching an episode of Sesame Street, and when I returned, Dylan was no longer on his stomach on the mat. Instead, he was rolled over on his back, kicking at and reaching for the hanging toys above him. Kissing his cheek, I gently turned him back onto his stomach and sat beside him on the floor, pulling my laptop over so I could get some work done before Max got home.

Dylan kicked his chubby little legs in excitement, cooing at the bright colors on the television screen. I looked up from my computer just as he managed to flip himself onto his back once more, looking very proud of himself. I set my computer aside and crawled over him, letting my hair brush his face and tickle him.

"Well, would you look at that! Three months old and rolling over! Is mommy more interesting than the TV, baby?" I asked, attacking his little face with kisses.

Dylan let out a loud squeal and then...the cutest little giggle ever escaped his mouth. I sat back from him in surprise, causing him to reach for me. I picked him up off his mat and into my arms, unable to hide the smile tugging on my lips. I brought our foreheads together and rubbed my nose against his, eliciting another tiny giggle from the tiny human I held.

"Did he just laugh?" Max asked from the doorway, his green eyes wide.

I had been so focused on Dylan, I had not even noticed my husband entering the apartment. Face beaming with a bright smile, I nodded quickly and motioned for him to join us in the living room.

"Dylan, you have to show daddy what else you learned today!" I cheered, placing him back on his mat.

Max arched his brows but I held up a finger, indicating he should be patient.

"Dylan, where's mommy?" I called, causing my son to kick his legs and begin to turn his little head in search of me.

When he managed to flip himself over just a moment later, I gave Max a triumphant smile. My husband just looked amazed. His eyes were like saucers and kept bouncing between Dylan and me, before he finally reached down to carefully scoop our baby into his arms.

"Great job, buddy!" he praised, stroking Dylan's soft hair and then his back. His hand reached for me to pull me into his embrace as well. "Not that I'm complaining, but isn't he a bit young to be rolling over already?"

"Not really," I tell him with a shrug, my arms loosely wrapped around his waist. "It usually happens between months three and six."

Max gave me a quick kiss. "Well, I still think it's great. Did you want me to order some dinner tonight?"

"I threw a lasagna in the oven twenty minutes ago, babe," I tell him with a wink. "Dinner will be ready in half an hour."

Later that night, I could not rid myself of the uneasy feeling that had settled over me. I had been moodier than usual all week, felt more on edge, had more trouble sleeping, et cetera. All the excitement that had filled me earlier from Dylan rolling over and giggling for the first time seemed to have evaporated, leaving me a taut bundle of nerves.

I had just finished getting Dylan to sleep and was entering our bedroom and caught sight of Max looking at the calendar in the lamplight with a frown disturbing his handsome features. Closing the door, even as softly as I did, drew his attention, and he hastily threw the calendar away from him. Eyes narrowing on his face, I crossed my arms over my chest and steeled myself for a fight.

"Max, what the hell is going on?"

"What do you mean?"

"Please don't insult my intelligence," I practically growl as I march closer to him, pausing just long enough to pluck the calendar from the floor. "Would you care to explain why you were studying the calendar so furiously before I came in? Or maybe you can enlighten me on some of the strange things I've noticed between us this past week. With everything that we have been through together, I really never thought you would push me away—"

He held up his hands to stop me. "Whoa, whoa; hold up, Ren! I was not trying to push you away at all, sweetheart, but I was hoping that we could make it through this week with as few hiccups as possible. I was actually hoping you wouldn't even realize what this week was with how tired and busy you've been with Dylan."

"What the fuck are you—" I paused mid-sentence as I suddenly realized what he meant. My eyes dropped to the calendar in my hand, but by now it was shaking so badly I could barely read it. It was now August, meaning it had been a year since the night I had my life destroyed.

I felt the strength abandon me as the calendar slipped from my hand, Max rushing forward to catch me in his muscular arms. I could feel, but not hear, the sobs as they ripped from my mouth, the agony of the moment crushing down upon me. Max's hands gently cradled my body against his chest and he stroked my hair and back as he tried to calm me.

"I am so sorry, sweetheart," I heard him murmur into my hair. "I didn't want you to remember if you didn't already. You didn't deserve to remember it again, to live through the pain of what that bastard did to you again." He paused, letting out a heavy sigh that spoke of his own personal torment and hell. "And...I am also sorry that I haven't kept my promise."

"What promise?" I sniffed.

"It isn't important right now."

I sat back, rubbing my eyes with the back of my hands. "Please, Max. Tell me?"

He sighed again, then brushed my hair behind my ears. "I promised I would find the son of a bitch that did this to you. I haven't been able to do that yet."

"I don't blame you for that at all," I whispered. "You have to know that I don't."

Pulling me closer as we huddled in the dim room, his emerald eyes met mine with a dark sincerity shining in them. "You may not, but Ren...I do."

CHAPTER SIXTY

"You're sure you have everything?" I asked my mom for what felt like the hundredth time.

"Renee," she huffed, the exasperation evident in her voice, "I have everything and I do know how to care for an infant. I managed to raise you, did I not?"

I sighed, hugging Dylan closer to me. It was now October, meaning Max and I were celebrating our first wedding anniversary. Both of our parents had convinced us to take a short trip to get away and be...well, young people. Jerome and Brenda had plans to come up later this evening to spend the weekend with my parents and Dylan while we were in Dallas. But since it would be my first time away from my son since he was born, I was a wreck.

Max came back into the living room from my old room where Dylan's crib was set up, his brows raised when he saw my worried expression. He didn't bother to say anything, but walked briskly to us, wrapping his arms around me and kissing my brow.

"He's going to be fine, sweetheart," he gently reminded me. "He will have two sets of grandparents watching him nonstop, making certain he is perfectly safe, and probably spoiled rotten."

"I won't bother to deny it," my mother called over her shoulder as she headed for the kitchen.

I rolled my eyes and fought back a chuckle and my tears. "I think—no, I *know*—he will be okay, Max, it's just…" I sighed heavily as I let my words hang in the air.

"You haven't been away from him since he's been born, I know," he finished. "I get it, Ren. I am going to miss this little guy too, but I have to admit, I am really looking forward to having some alone time with his momma," he finished suggestively.

"I do not want to hear that, Maxwell," my dad chimed, coming in from the garage and causing Max's hands to drop away from my body suddenly. "Shouldn't you two be on the road already? You've got more than five hours of a drive ahead of you."

Nodding miserably, I give Dylan another series of kisses, making him squeal in delight. My mom sneaks back into the living room at the sound, letting my dad give her a quick kiss on the cheek while I pass Dylan over to Max for his good-byes. I nibble on my lower lip as I grab my purse from the couch, determined I will not cry today. I watch through misty eyes as my husband carefully hands my son to my mother before sliding his arm around my waist.

"Let me know if you need me for anything or if he does something new please," I remind my mom softly.

"I promise, Ren. Now, go and enjoy yourselves this weekend," she tells us with a broad smile. She takes Dylan's chubby little arm and helps him wave. "Say 'see ya later, gators'!"

Max turns me toward the door and quickly walks me to our car—probably afraid that if we don't get out of there immediately I will grow roots and refuse to leave. Soon, we are sailing down the highway jamming to a crazy mixture of music from rock to country and even some R&B thrown in. Since Dylan is not in the car with us, the volume is cranked up to an unhealthy level, but between the beats pounding in my ears and chest, the company resting his hand on my thigh as he drives, and the scenery zipping past my window, this may be the freest and youngest I have felt in nearly a year.

When we finally arrive in Dallas that afternoon, we quickly get checked into our hotel and set out to choose a place for dinner. I had thrown my hair up in a bun that morning, so I took the hair tie and bobby pins out, letting my brown hair tumble past my shoulders in big, loose curls. After freshening up my mascara and lipstick, I declared myself ready to go since I had worn a comfy black maxi dress and blue jacket for the drive. The look on Max's face when I stepped out to meet him was priceless.

"Holy…" he paused to take a deep breath. "Are you trying to kill me, Ren?"

I giggled. "No. I take it you like what you see though?" I asked him as I casually draped my arms around his neck, his hands automatically going to my hips.

"Damn straight I do. We better get out here before we don't leave this room at all tonight," he groaned, reaching between us to adjust himself. "I may need a minute though."

"Are those jeans not providing enough room for you?" I teased.

"Renee," he warned, a mischievous glint in his green eyes. "I will spank you, young lady."

"'Young lady'? You are only one fucking year older than me," I scoff.

He leaned closer, causing me to get a tantalizing whiff of his citrusy cologne as his lips brushed the shell of my ear. "And don't you forget it, baby," he said, punctuating the final word with a swift but light smack on my ass.

Throwing me a sexy wink, he turned on his heels and headed for the door, leaving me to watch the jeans clinging to his well-defined posterior and the white dress shirt that molded along his muscular back. I felt my mouth slightly hanging open in shock, surprised that Max actually followed through on his threat to spank me—but also somewhat turned on by the action as well. He paused at the doorway, a smirk on his lovable face when he turned back to face me.

"Are you coming, sweetheart?"

Dinner ended up being rather reminiscent of our first date and the night he proposed, which I guess I should have expected since we both loved Italian food. The restaurant was gorgeous and had the most romantic ambiance as we snuggled together in the booth enjoying our pastas, sharing bites every now and then. When it came time for dessert, we opted to share a slice of their strawberry cheesecake, letting the creamy goodness melt in our mouths.

"Mercy, I wish I could learn to make one of these damn things," I moaned, scooping another sinfully silky bite onto my tongue.

Max chuckled into the crook of my neck, knowing my frustration with attempting to bake cheesecakes over the past six months. With my eyes closed to savor the taste of my dessert, I was caught off-guard when his lips brushed the faintest of kisses below my ear, sending a shiver down my spine.

"Max," I whined quietly. "We're in public."

"And it's our anniversary," he reminded me. "I think that means I am allowed to kiss my wife."

I playfully narrowed my eyes at him and bit on the corner of my lip. Sliding my small hand from his knee up his thigh, I watched his pupils widen with lust and eyes darken. "Then perhaps you should take me back to the hotel, Mr. Harris," I whisper. "Because there is no way in hell you're getting me all riled up here."

With that, I swiftly sat back from him, completely removing my hand from his leg and took another bite of the cheesecake like I hadn't just teased him. I struggled to maintain my poker face though as he began frantically looking for our waiter, finally waving for the man to come to our table.

"Ready for the check, sir?"

"Oh, hell yes!" Max exclaimed.

CHAPTER SIXTY-ONE

Back at the hotel, Max wasted no time in pushing my back against the door and trailing passionate kisses along my jaw and down my neck. His hand fisted in my thick curls, causing my head to tilt further to the side and offered him more room to paint the skin of my neck with gentle red love bites, a soft moan escaping my lips. My own hands were clutching desperately to the front of his dress shirt, the nails digging into his muscled chest in an effort to hold myself upright as he sent wave after wave of pleasure coursing through my body.

"God, I have missed this," he growled, his voice choked with desire as his hands roamed my body.

"Missed what exactly?" I had to ask, biting my lower lip.

"Having you all to myself. Don't get me wrong, I love Dylan and would not trade having him for the world, but having some uninterrupted time with my gorgeous wife…this is heaven, baby. And I know that it'll be even more difficult to get time like this the older he gets or when we have another baby down the road," Max whispered, pulling me closer. "Now, shall I show you just what all I have missed?"

A twinkle in his green eyes, he gently led me to the bed and carefully laid me back, my dress sliding up my legs in the process. I blushed profusely and went to push the slinky material back down, only to have his lean fingers halt my movements, a tsking sound on his tongue.

"Why the hell would you try to cover these sexy legs, Ren? I'm trying to get you naked here."

"Max!" I shrieked, thrown by his blatant comment, but found myself smiling nonetheless.

Smirking into my face, his hands cupped my cheeks, stroking the hair away from my face as he leaned in to tenderly kiss my lips. "I don't know why that surprises you. Now...why don't you let your husband show you how much he loves you. I think you deserve to experience some bliss tonight, wouldn't you agree?"

I felt my pulse begin to race as I met his desire-filled eyes. His hands slid down my body sensually until he got to the hem of my dress, his eyes never once leaving mine. I gulped as he pulled the dress up and over my head, removing it and my jacket from my body, leaving me in only my red and black lace lingerie set. It was easy to see from the expression on his face that Max was loving the flimsy material covering the most intimate parts of me, making me glad I had listened to Annie and splurged on the set.

"Hot damn, my wife is fucking sexy," he groaned. "When did you get this?"

I chuckled. "Annie insisted I needed some new lingerie when she found out we were going on a trip without Dylan for our anniversary so she took me shopping last week," I informed him, reaching forward to tease the bulge in his jeans. "I'm assuming you like it?"

"Hell yes I like it. You may have to be the one to take it off though, Ren, because it looks expensive and I don't want to rip the lace," he sighed, his head sinking onto my breast.

Lust speared through me at his words, causing my body to tremble beneath him. His hands moved and began kneading my breasts lightly through the material of my bra, setting my nerves afire with each brush of the lace against my sensitive nipples. I could feel the molten heat settling in my stomach and in my core, reaching out for Max to satisfy me as only he could.

Soon, my bra and thong were being tossed aside—thankfully still in one piece—leaving my body open to his skillful fingers and tongue to manipulate. My hands fought to find a grip on the sheets of the bed beneath me as Max worshipped my body until I was a quivering, mewling mess. He brought me to bliss, had me seeing not just stars, but entire galaxies in the blink of an eye as his tongue stroked over me.

"Oh *God*," I moaned, my eyes fluttering closed while I caught my breath.

"Pretty sure my name is Max, sweetheart," he teased, hopping off the bed to begin stripping.

I cracked an eye to toss him an unamused stare, raising a brow in defiance of his ego. My husband simply sent me a cocky wink and dropped his boxers, allowing his manhood to jut proudly, hard and ready. He pulled out the condom, rolling it onto his throbbing length before climbing back onto the bed and nudging my knees apart.

As he plunged into me, his lips found my neck while his fingers laced themselves with mine against the mattress. His hips began rocking into my own, the waves of pleasure rolling through my entire essence with each powerful stroke he made as he kept our bodies joined. Throughout the past few months since Dylan had been born—and I had been cleared to enjoy intercourse once more—Max and I had been experimenting with various aspects of foreplay and different techniques in the bedroom. I knew that tonight, I was in for a wild roll in the hay.

"I'm not hurting you, right?" he murmured into my hair.

I pulled his lips to mine for a passionate kiss, desperate to reassure him. "Not at all, my love."

Max raised up quickly and pulled out, gripping my hips to help flip me over onto my stomach. He wasted little time in pulling my ass toward him and lining himself back up with my core before he slammed back into me, hitting a new spot with a staggering force that had me seeing little black spots dancing in my sight.

"Mmmmmm," I moaned, doing my best to muffle my cries of delight with the pillows on the bed. "Max...I'm gonna..."

"That's right, Ren," he whispered, his hands still clutching my waist to tether me to him.

Just when I thought I could not take any more from him, we both hit our climaxes at the same time, backs arching as low moans ripped from us. His thrusts became sloppy and finally slowed before stopping altogether while his fingers danced along my back gently. My breathing was coming in ragged gasps like my husband's and I collapsed onto my stomach on the bed. Max slowly pulled out again, a sudden groan drawing my attention.

"Something wrong?" I asked him, peering over my shoulder.

He looked stricken, like I had kicked him in the stomach, with his eyes wide. Max rubbed a hand down his face and tentatively met my gaze, swallowing hard.

"Well, I guess I was a bit too rough with you after all," he said softly.

"What makes you say that? I'm not too sore, and really enjoyed that position," I rushed to tell him.

He chuckled, rubbing the back of his neck. "I'm glad you said that, but not what I meant. I meant too rough as in the condom broke."

I jerked upright in the bed, my eyes wide as saucers. "What?"

CHAPTER SIXTY-TWO

"**O**h fuck, are you serious right now?" I cried, jumping off the bed to stare at him.

Max had a hurt expression on his face as he sat back on his heels. "Ren, calm down—"

"Calm down? Calm is the last thing I am feeling right now!" I said as my fingers dug into my hair. "This is not happening…"

"Okay, I get that the timing sucks, but why is this such a big deal? It's not like we're unmarried or unable to handle having a baby."

I whirled on my heels to face him, mouth agape. His hands, raised in surrender, dropped back onto the bed when he saw the flash of angst in my eyes. Suddenly, I felt a wave of panic and nausea sweep over me, sending bolting for the bathroom. Dropping to my knees by the commode, I blew slow, steady breaths in an attempt to quell the roiling in my stomach, praying I wouldn't lose the dinner we enjoyed an hour earlier.

"Here," he said softly, draping a cool washcloth over the back of my neck. "I'll be right back."

He tossed the broken condom in the trashcan on his way out the door, leaving me to my troubled thoughts again. A few minutes later, he re-entered the bath with his boxers securely on his waist and my phone in his hand.

"Thanks," I hear him say to whoever is on the other line. "Here, Ren; talk to her and I'll be outside when you're ready."

Nervously, I took the phone and watched him walk away from me, guilt eating me alive. I glanced at the screen, somewhat surprised to find he called Annie, but slowly put the phone to my ear.

"Hi," I murmured.

"Hi yourself," she chirped. "What the hell is going on, Ren? Max called and said you were having a panic attack and thought you could use a quick chat with me."

I sighed, pinching the bridge of my nose as I sat on the edge of the tub. "Uh, yeah. So, you know how we're in Dallas this weekend?"

"Yep. You had better be putting that lingerie to good use too. Oh shit, you aren't having your period this weekend are you?"

Chuckling, I feel my eyes fill with tears. "No, the lingerie got worn today, and before you ask, yes, he absolutely loved it," I told her. "But, sexy lingerie tends to lead to certain things, Annie."

"Ren...that is kinda the point of sexy lingerie. That is why I kicked your ass until you agreed to buy the damn set, remember?"

"Yeah, but sex can turn sour awfully quick when the damn condom breaks," I moaned.

"Oh…" she said, elongating the word for longer than she should. "Okay, so you are freaking out because the condom broke and you aren't ready for another baby? You are married now, so it isn't like *Madre and Padre* are going to pitch a fit, but then again, Dylan is only five months old so that would make another one really close in age. But is that the only reason you're having issues?"

I took a deep breath. Annie could always read me like a book. "Those are the primary ones, but Annie, I barely survived being pregnant with Dylan because of the emotional onslaught that I dealt with on a daily basis. I don't know if I could handle that again just yet, even if it was for a child with Max."

"Then tell Max that, Ren," she encouraged me gently. "You and I both know that man loves you more than anything and will do anything for you.

He has been beyond understanding with this entire process and I don't see that changing anytime soon. Talk to him, not me."

"Thanks Annie," I sighed. "I appreciate you calming me and helping me rationalize what I need to say to him."

"What are best friends for, bitch?" she giggled. "Now, go make up with your man and I am going to get back to mine. I love you, Ren."

"Love you too."

I disconnect the call and exhale slowly, steeling myself and working up the courage to go back to the bedroom. I tugged a towel around my body and made my way into the quiet hotel suite, finding my husband slumped on the edge of the bed. His fawn-colored hair is falling over his fingers since his head is clutched in his hands, making him appear so weary...and so much older than his twenty-one years.

"Max?"

"I'm not saying I'm ready either, but sweetheart, you know that I am not going anywhere, right?" he said without looking up. "I didn't when you found out you were pregnant with Dylan, and I certainly wouldn't if you were to become pregnant with my child now."

His emerald eyes slowly rose to meet my gaze. "Let's take it one step at a time, just like we did then, okay? Tonight was truly an accident, but if we end up gaining the blessing of another child because of it, then we will get another blessing."

He rose from the bed to draw me tenderly into his arms. "Renee, I love you. End of story. Okay?"

I gave him the smallest of smiles and nodded. "Okay. I love you too. So much, Max. And...I am so sorry I jumped down your throat and freaked out the way I did. I'll work on it. I promise."

He brushed a kiss on my nose. "How about we do that together? You are not alone."

My arms tightened around his waist. "Deal. So...now that I've had my weekly dose of crazy, what else is on the agenda for this weekend?"

"Well, Mrs. Harris," he teased, trailing his hands up and down my sides, "tomorrow we will be going to the Dallas Arboretum, followed by a gondola ride complete with dinner in Irving. Sunday we will be hanging out at the NorthPark Center for some shopping, food, and a fun experience called Dreamscape Immersive, before we head home."

"Sounds like you have thought of everything," I purred. "And it sounds incredible, baby."

CHAPTER SIXTY-THREE

"Look at you, sitting up by the tree," my mother crooned at Dylan. "You look so handsome, little man."

He giggled and bubbled happily in response as he chewed on his teething ring, his eyes focused on the colorful lights of the tree. Since it was his first Christmas, both sets of grandparents, David and Sheila Spencer, Annie and Zane, along with Nick, went slightly overboard with the decorations and presents for him. An enormous pile of gifts waited for him by the wall, all beautifully wrapped.

I was curled up on the couch with Max, snuggled into his side happy and content as I watched my mother play with my son. Thankfully, it was still just the three of us—our little mishap during our anniversary trip didn't come to anything—and we were excited to be celebrating Christmas with our little boy, especially now that Max was done with his internship and officially graduated.

"Merry Christmas!" came some shouts from the front door, and in burst my best friend, Zane hot on her heels.

Dylan squealed loudly when he saw his Aunt Annie, earning him a bright smile from her. He raised his chubby little arms, indicating he wanted her to pick him up and cuddle with him, with which she was only too glad to comply.

"Hi there, baby boy," she said, hugging him close. "Are you so excited to open all your presents, Dylan?"

"More like, ready to play with all the paper and boxes, Annie," Max chuckled.

My mom nodded in agreement. "Yep, that is typically what little ones this age do. They don't know what to do with the gifts themselves but they find the packaging fascinating. Ren did the same thing her first Christmas. Her first birthday was the same."

"Thanks for that, mom," I grumbled, feeling like she was tattling on me.

Soon enough, everyone had joined us in the living room so we surrounded Dylan with his presents, watching his eyes go wide as he took in the multitude of shiny colors of the wrappings. His little fingers reached out to pull at a red string, giggling when it bounced back to its original position when he released it. Smiles were on all our faces—this joy was something we clearly all needed after the hellish year we had been forced to endure.

Max and I sat beside him on the floor and helped him pull at the paper on his gifts, amused when he finally seemed to connect the dots that when he yanked on the slippery stuff, his toys were revealed with a big ripping sound. I think the sound was what he enjoyed the most of those moments though since it made him laugh so much. He passed the wadded paper from one little hand to the other until I attempted to take it from him to hand him a little infant-safe truck. Needless to say, Dylan was not happy with me.

"Hey, buddy, it's okay," Max consoled, picking him up as Dylan wailed. "Mommy is trying to show you your cool new toy. See? Vroom, Vroom, Dylan."

While he spoke, I gently ran the soft tires of the truck over Dylan's arm, mimicking his words. Finally, my son ceased his crying and turned his attention to the toy in my hands, making noises like he was trying to talk with us and ask for it. Max turned him around and sat him in front of his lap so I could "drive" the little truck over to Dylan, making a screeching noise as I got to his legs.

"Do you want to try, baby?" I asked, letting go of the toy.

His little hands reached clumsily for the toy, but his eyes went wide with delight when he grasped it, pulling it close. Max and I continued to unwrap his gifts for him, but Dylan was focused solely on the truck at this point. A while later, our parents all left to golf, leaving just the twenty-somethings to hang out together. Nick snuck over and scooped him up and set him and his truck inside a large box, then proceeded to push the box around the living room floor.

"Dylan Express, coming through!" he cheered. He crashed the box into my legs, making himself and Dylan chuckle. "Say, 'hi, mommy'. Here's your present, Ren."

I rolled my eyes at his antics, but I was smiling regardless. Dylan was having fun and that was the important part. "You are just a big kid, you know that?"

"Yeah, but you love me," Nick teased.

Max rolled his green eyes this time, right along with me. "Surprisingly, yes, we do. But there are times when I wonder if you will ever grow the hell up."

"Maybe someday," he replied with a shrug. "But until then, I get to be the fun uncle that Dylan knows will let him get away with anything!"

"Hey!" Zane complained. "What about me?"

"Okay, I'll share the title," Nick said with some reluctance. "And that is only because you have proven to be a kickass partner in crime these past few months."

Zane smirked and the two high-fived each other. Annie and I exchanged looks. "Do we want to know what you two idiots are talking about?" she asked, her brows raised.

"Trust me, Annie," Max chimed, "the answer to that question is a resounding 'no'. And I only know that because I was present for a few such escapades. These two are considered a menace when together, but hilarious to watch. I should have recorded it for blackmail purposes."

"Blackmailing a police officer is a felony, ya know," Nick quipped.

"Hmmm," Max hummed, stroking his chin. "Last time I checked, you aren't one yet."

"Jackass."

"What was that?" Max teased since Nick had muttered the word.

"You heard me," Nick replied, leveling his cobalt gaze on my husband. "Now, let's not turn this into a British or Canadian thing and have a brawl, okay? I'm sure the girls don't want to see our version of 'boxing day.'"

"Damn straight, we don't," I growled. "And I do not want Dylan to be raised with a bunch of brutes, so straighten up."

"Oooo, Ren's momma voice," Annie chirped. "I'd be careful if I were you boys, or she just may put you both in time-out."

CHAPTER SIXTY-FOUR

"Okay Dylan, blow out the candle!" I encouraged him, holding his little cupcake close—but not too close—for him.

It's his first birthday, and I was admittedly a bit of an emotional mess. He had been crawling all over the apartment since he was a little more than nine months old, and had started pulling himself up on things to stand and trying to creep around the furniture while holding onto it. He hadn't taken his first solo steps yet, but I knew that they were not long off at that rate. He had two adorable little teeth on the bottom, and would proudly say "dada," "mama," and "uh-oh," which happened to be his first word.

A couple of little friends from our Mommy and Me class are there, along with our family and close friends. Since it was the seventeenth of May, we had little baby pools set up in my parent's backyard for the kids to splash in, helping to keep everyone cool in the West Texas heat. We had chosen to do a super cute little book-themed party, so we asked people to bring a book for his library, and made him a storybook cake, and cupcake with little books and worms on them. Overall, the party was great.

I was in turmoil. My baby was a year old. Thankfully he looked so much like me—and strangely enough, a little like Max—so I couldn't tell anything about who his "real" father was. But everytime Dylan would say "dada," my heart would lurch within my chest. I was so glad and beyond grateful that Max had stepped in and was raising Dylan as his own, but a part of me still had that sense of terror when I thought about the man who had actually given my son life. Would he ever try to take Dylan away from me?

Drawn from my introspection by the cheering as the tiny flame went out, I quickly yanked the candle from his little cake and pulled away the baking paper, setting his cupcake on his tray. His little fingers immediately went for the vanilla frosting, digging greedily into the creaminess before shoving them into his mouth. His eyes—now shifting to a more brown color—widened with surprise and delight as the sugar hit his taste buds and he instantly went back for more. Max and I laughed and shook our heads, knowing he was going to be a sticky mess by the time he was done.

My mom had been busy slicing the other cake and passing out slices to our guests, so there wasn't much for me to do at the moment except enjoy the happiness on my child's face as he inhaled his cupcake.

"Here," Annie's voice cut through the fog in my mind as she waved a plate with a slice of cake on it under my nose. "Eat this, Ren."

Chuckling, I took the plate from her and dug the fork in with pleasure, savoring the tender chocolate cake and creamy frosting. Annie grinned and tossed me a wink before heading back over to the dessert table to continue assisting my mother. Max came closer and snaked his hands around my waist, his nose brushing along my neck.

"Can I have a bite? I would ask Dylan, but…" he chuckled as he let the sentence hang.

I loaded up the fork and let him steal a bite of my cake, a twinkle forming in his eyes. I repeated the motion, making him think he was going to get a second one, but at the last second popped the bite into my own mouth instead.

"Dylan, did you see that? Mommy was mean," Max whined to our son. "She didn't share it with daddy."

"Dada! Dada! Dada!" Dylan shouted with increasing volume.

With each of his cries, my heart raced faster than before, and I felt my lip begin to tremble. Max met my panicked gaze with worried eyes, but I held up my hands to keep him at bay. I quickly let my eyes dart around the yard as my breathing became harsh gasps.

"Max, stay with Dylan," I whispered. "I'll be back out once I compose myself, okay?"

I didn't give my husband a chance to respond, but turned on my heel and rushed into the house, heading straight for my old room. Once inside with the door closed, I sank onto the edge of my bed, resting my hands on my knees as I struggled to breathe. My eyes were squeezed shut while I choked back the sobs, desperately trying to figure out why I was so upset, but I kept coming up clueless. The door opened quietly, and a figure knelt before me and gently clasped my hands in his; his woody cologne invading my senses.

"Ren," Nick murmured, brushing my hair away from my face. "Come on, I need you to listen to me. Tell me five things that you can hear right now."

My eyes slowly blinked open to stare into his dark blues as I thought about his question. Focusing on the sounds floating around me, I began to list them aloud. "Um, the speakers outside playing music, the fan overhead, the kids shrieking, my heart beating, and I guess your breathing."

"Good," he praised. "Now, four things you can see."

"The mirror on my dresser, the curtains, my blue comforter, and," I paused, taking a deep breath, "um, your eyes."

He smirked at me before nodding his head. "Okay, let's keep going. Three things that you can touch, Ren."

"My hair," I said, running my fingers through the thick length, "my teeth into my lower lip—"

"Not sure that counts, but whatever," Nick interrupted with a slight shake of his head. "One more."

"Um, your hands holding mine," I whispered sheepishly.

"Good. Do you feel better?"

I blinked. Surprisingly, I did feel better. "Yeah, actually I do. How the hell did you do that?"

Nick chuckled. "It's called a grounding exercise. Allison had panic attacks often several years ago because of medical drama so we learned to guide her through those steps if she was having one. I noticed you ran inside and Max said you were upset, so volunteered to come and help."

"Well, thank you, Nick. I will definitely be using that in the future," I told him with a small smile.

He gently squeezed my hands. "You are more than welcome, Ren. I think you know by this point I would do just about anything for you. I'll always be there for you; that is a promise. Now, do you want to tell me what made you so upset?"

"Honestly, I'm not really sure what it was, so maybe it's best to just move on since I seem fine for now, but thanks."

"If you change your mind, you know where to find me."

CHAPTER SIXTY-FIVE

"Ren!" Max yelled, practically bursting through the door of our apartment. His eyes were bright and his face was glowing with happiness as he rushed to where Dylan and I were seated in the rocker. The excitement he's exuding is palpable, even from across the room. "You are never going to believe what happened today!"

"I can tell it's something important, just by how you are acting, so why don't you come tell me," I responded with a smile.

He dropped his bag on the table and hurried to drop a kiss on Dylan's head and then my waiting lips before he kneels in front of us. "So, you know how I have been working with the company since December, and it's only now August?" I paused, nodding along with his frantic words. "Well, my supervisor came in today, praising me up and down for my work ethic and how the higher-ups are so pleased with my work, especially on that last big project I helped consult on. They have decided to promote me to a management position."

"Max, that's amazing! I am so proud of you, sweetheart!" I told him sincerely, leaning forward to embrace him.

He had worked so hard for this over the past several months, and I knew it was just a matter of time before his bosses realized he deserved his own team. So, I was expecting that news from him. But I was wholly unprepared for what he said next.

"Do you know what this means though, Ren?"

"That you will get to lead your own team, just like you've wanted and deserved to do from day one?"

"Well, that too," he agreed, "but no. We can finally look at moving out of this apartment, getting a house together, and then think about having another baby. Dylan's over a year old now, I will be getting a raise, and I think it would be an ideal time to be getting started with that process, don't you?"

I sat back in shock, unable to even process the words that my husband was saying. The hopeful expression on his face was slowly withering the longer I sat speechless. My brows were furrowed and my teeth grinding together as I struggled to control the emotions pressing down upon me.

"Ren...you're starting to worry me, sweetheart," he said lightly. His hand reached for my knee, but I jerked my leg out of his reach just before he could take hold. "What the—"

"Do not touch me right now," I snapped, my voice a raspy hiss.

"Renee, I don't understand—"

"How the fucking hell could you even think about suggesting we start trying for another baby right now, Max?" I shrieked. "You know I'm not ready! I told you that in October!"

"Yes; in October, Ren! It's August now!" he yelled back, his emerald eyes flashing with hurt.

I jumped from my seat and began pacing around the room, the frenetic energy forcing me to move my shaky legs. My hands tore through my hair at random, causing my brown locks to become tangled and disheveled with each pass of my fingers, but I didn't give a damn.

"This is still not something I want to consider just yet. I am still not ready for another child and I need you to respect that!"

He groaned in frustration, his eyes narrowed on my face. "So, let me get this straight. You won't even think about having a child you and I create together, but you are willing to carry and give birth to the child of the son of a bitch who raped you?"

As soon as he said it, I could tell he regretted the words that left his mouth, but it was too late. The tears sprang to my eyes and I rushed from the living room, slamming our bedroom door behind me. I hit the lock, keeping him out as I sank onto the floor and leaned my back against the door and sobbed.

He knocked on the door, pleading with me to let him in, but I ignored him. His apology seemed hollow, obligatory. I covered my ears with my hands, desperate to block out his voice, but his words kept seeping in despite my best efforts.

"Leave me alone, Maxwell!" I screamed through my tears, feeling as though my heart was being torn to shreds.

I heard his head bang slightly on the door, but he finally conceded. Lifting my eyes from the floor, I knew I could not stay in the apartment. Forcing myself off the ground, I moved to grab my duffle bag and began throwing random clothes inside along with my toiletries. I heard our front door open and close, followed by the sound of his car starting, and bit back a fresh wave of tears.

Hurrying, I grabbed the rest of my things and then packed a bag for Dylan, who was playing in his crib. I tossed the bags into my trunk and ran back into the apartment to grab my son, noticing the note Max had left for me on the table.

Going to the store. Be back soon. I'm sorry.
—Max

"I'm sorry too, but we won't be here," I muttered, crumpling his note in my hand. "Come on, buddy."

I marched out to the car and strapped Dylan into his carseat, then backed out of my parking space to hit the highway before Max could return. A part of me felt guilty for not leaving him a note, but I knew I needed the space just then. I bit my lower lip as I tried to control my breathing and keep the tears at bay, knowing I needed to be as safe as possible while I drove since Dylan was in the car with me.

About two hours later, I was pulling up outside another apartment building with my emotions all over the map. I had turned my phone off as soon as I had gotten into the car, ensuring I wouldn't receive any calls from Max, because honestly, I had no interest in speaking with him. But I had not warned the person whose place I was randomly showing up at that I was coming either.

I could just hope they wouldn't turn me away.

Sighing, I unbuckled Dylan from his seat and walked up to the door and knocked, shifting nervously while I waited. My son was tugging at the hem of my shirtsleeve when the door suddenly opened, the lights from inside spilling out into the dusky evening and illuminating the only person I believed would help me.

His cobalt eyes widened in surprise as he took in my appearance, his lips forming a thin line a second later. "What are you doing here, Ren?"

CHAPTER SIXTY-SIX

"Nick," I greeted, shifting nervously from one foot to the other, "could we come in?"

Running his hand down his face, he finally nodded and stepped aside, allowing me—Dylan still in my arms—to enter his apartment. The door shut behind us as I made my way over to his dark brown couch and sat down, setting my purse and Dylan's diaper bag on the floor beside my feet. I bit my lip as I met his gaze once more, seeing him standing with his muscled arms crossed over his chest as he stared at me, hard.

"I like what you've done with the place," I told him, gesturing vaguely to his decor.

His eyes narrowed on me again, something unreadable in their stormy depths. "You didn't drive all this way to comment on my apartment and the sad lack of skill I have when it comes to decorating, Renee," he stated, sauntering closer. "What are you doing here and why is Max not with you?"

I sighed and hung my head, knowing I cannot look him in the eye. Taking a deep breath, I forced myself to raise my chin, but still my brown eyes darted everywhere but his face.

"Has he called you?" I asked softly.

"No, not yet. So, do you want to answer my question now?"

Unbidden, the tears filled my eyes again, and I blinked rapidly in hopes to keep them at bay. But when the first one coursed down my cheek, Nick's face softened and he sat beside me on the couch and wrapped his arm around my shoulder.

"Ren," he murmured, "what the hell happened?"

"We had a fight, Nick," I sobbed, turning my head to bury my face in his shoulder. Dylan was now caught in between us and couldn't understand why his mommy was crying. "God, it was awful, and some of the things he said…"

Nick sat back so he could cradle my face in his hand, tilting my chin so he could look into my eyes. "You two don't fight often, so it was obviously something major if you came to see me about it. And what do you mean by things he said? What the fuck did he say to you?"

Knowing that Nick and Max have been friends their entire lives, I was hesitant to tell the man before me what my husband said to me mere hours earlier. I had little doubt in my mind that Nick would be outraged with Max considering everything that has happened, but I hated to be the one to cause that rift to form. Before I could continue that line of thinking though, Nick interrupted my reverie with a gentle reminder.

"Hey, just because he and I have been friends for years, does not mean I won't kick his ass if he was being a douche or just plain disrespectful, and you know that," he said emphatically. "I also cannot help you if you refuse to tell me what the hell is going on with you."

"Fair point," I sighed. "Max came home today all excited because he is receiving a promotion. And don't get me wrong, Nick, I am so proud of him for that, and that is not the issue at all. The issue came when he suggested we move out of the apartment, get a house, and start trying for another baby."

"O-kay," he said slowly, trying to follow along. "And I get the feeling you aren't ready for another one just yet?"

"No, which we had discussed last year on our anniversary trip," I confessed. I closed my eyes, dreading the next part of the conversation. "Then he snapped at me, saying that I was fine to carry and give birth to my rapist's baby but I wouldn't have one that he and I created."

Nick's cobalt eyes went wide then darkened with anger. "Oh...hell no!" He jumped up from the couch to pace around his living room—much as I had done in my own apartment earlier—his face a glowering mask of rage. "Fucking hell, Max! He should have known better than to say something like that!"

"I thought so too," I managed weakly. "I locked myself in our bedroom for a bit, refused to talk to him, and eventually he gave up and left. I decided there was no way I wanted to be around him for the foreseeable future, so I packed a couple bags for myself and Dylan then high-tailed it out of Amarillo before he had a chance to return."

He turned to face me, his hands pausing their rubbing motion on his temples to drag down to his jaw. "You asked if he had called me, so I'm guessing you left him a note saying you were coming here, right?" I merely squirmed in response. "Ren, you did leave him a note saying where you were going, didn't you?"

"No."

"What the hell do you mean, 'no'? You took Dylan and just ran?"

"Pretty much," came my meek whisper, my eyes scrunched tight so I couldn't see the look of disapproval I knew was on his face. "Look, I know it was a shitty thing to do, but I had to get out of there. I figured I would talk to him once I was calmer and his apology was sincere."

"Oh my God..." he groaned, dropping down into his recliner.

His phone suddenly began ringing from its place on the coffee table, the screen lighting up with Max's name. My heart was racing as Nick reached for it, terror building up and choking me as I wondered whose side he would end up being on in the end.

"Please don't answer it," I begged.

"He needs to know that you two are safe," Nick argued logically. "And he also needs to know that I may be coming up there to kick his ass for his asinine comment to you, but that is another matter."

His phone stopped ringing while he spoke, the guilt, shame, and anger battling within me as I stared at the device in his hand. Nick lightly gripped my knee and offered me a grim smile.

"You do not have to talk to him tonight, Ren, but you will need to at some point. I'm going to call him back now though," he said, hitting redial. I could hear Max's frantic voice coming through the phone when he answered, and Dylan perked up at the sound. "Max, is there something you want to tell me?" Nick asked, his tone rough.

"Besides the fact that I was a fucking moron and now my wife hates my guts?" Max snapped. "Judging from your tone, I'm guessing that somehow you know this already though, so please tell me you know where she is."

Nick sighed. "Yes, I do know about what you said, which by the way, you are way past the designation of moron. And yes, I do know where she is, but," he said, cutting off Max's outbursts, "she is not ready to talk to you tonight. You can try again tomorrow."

"Nick, I understand that I royally fucked up, but that is my wife and son you're talking about. I have the right to know where they are! Are they there with you? She turned off her damn phone so I can't see where she is. She didn't leave me a fucking note, which I did for her when I left by the way, so when I got back I was panicking because she wasn't here.

"I have been calling her parents, her phone, Annie and Zane, my own parents, and even the hospitals," he listed, his voice haggard, "for the past two hours, just trying to figure out where she could have possibly gone. I just...I need to know that they are safe."

"They're safe, Max. I promise you that, okay? Give her tonight to settle her emotions and collect herself, and talk to her tomorrow. I will drive her back myself if I have to and mediate if necessary, but...let her be for one evening. It won't kill you to let someone else take care of her for a night."

CHAPTER SIXTY-SEVEN

The following morning, Nick made certain I loaded Dylan and myself into the car and headed straight for Amarillo. Since it was the weekend, he hopped in his truck and kept to his word, following us all the way back to my apartment. I gulped nervously when I pulled into my parking space, dreading seeing Max after what he said the night before, but I knew Nick was right and we needed to talk this through.

I had barely exited the car when the door to our apartment flew open and Max came running out, hair disheveled, dark circles under his bloodshot eyes, and still in the same clothes from yesterday. It was obvious he had not gotten much sleep—even after Nick had reassured him that Dylan and I were fine—and I once again felt the pang of guilt stab at my heart.

"Ren!" he shouted, voice raspy as he rushed to me. His arms engulfed my body, pulling me into his chest with a crushing force that would have knocked me over had he not been holding me upright. "God, I am so sorry, sweetheart. I...you have to know that," he pleaded, pulling back just far enough so his tear-filled eyes could meet mine.

I sighed, my lip trembling as I fought back the tears that threatened to pour down my cheeks. His hands stroked my neck and tangled in my hair as he kept me pinned against the side of my car, almost as if he were afraid I would run again if he let me go. Dylan let out a shriek from his seat, drawing all our attention, but Nick motioned us to head inside.

"I'll get the little guy," he told us. "You two go sit and talk."

Hesitantly, I allowed Max to lead me inside our apartment and to set me down on the couch, my teeth digging painfully into my lower lip the entire time. Nick soon followed us into the apartment, Dylan in his arms, and headed straight for the nursery to give us a modicum of privacy. Max, sitting a couple spaces over from me, opened and closed his mouth half a dozen times like he was trying to figure out how to start the conversation with me, but did not know where the best place truly was.

"First and foremost, Ren, I need you to know how sorry I am for that one comment I made," he finally said. "It was beyond out-of-line and I should never have said it. I never meant to hurt you, but I managed to do so and could not be more sorry for that fact. I can only hope that you will be able to forgive me."

My head was bowed as I listened to his words. This is the man I married, not the accusatory brute from yesterday. This is the gentle and caring individual who always valued my well-being and being honest with me above all else. This was the man I fell in love with as he held me under the stars and wiped away my tears.

"I won't lie to you and say that your words didn't hurt me, Max," I told him softly, knowing I had to be honest with him, "because they did. I never thought you would hurt me like that, which I think is why it made it feel so much worse than it was. You have been my rock through all of this, and I know I would never have survived if not for you—"

"Ren…"

"No, let me finish, please," I cut him off. "I know it is not fair of me to deny you a child of our own when I did choose to carry Dylan. You and I both know that having an abortion would not have changed what happened to me, and as you pointed out so often, he is half me. I couldn't get rid of him. And I am so thankful that he has you as his father.

"And while I admit that a part of me would love to have a child with you, Max, emotionally I am not ready. But not for the reasons that you think. You remember how difficult my pregnancy and then delivery with

Dylan was for me, partially because of the rape, and partially because of the fact that Dylan was not technically yours. I am not physically ready to go through that again just yet—"

"Baby, that is understandable, but I wish you would have just told me," he moaned.

Sighing, I continued. "That isn't the only reason though. While I understand that any child we create together would have the most loving father ever, there is a part of me that is still hung up on the notion that I don't know who Dylan's biological father is. Do you remember me having that panic attack at his birthday party?"

Max nodded in agreement, his green eyes filled with puzzlement. "Yeah, sure. I sent Nick in to help you calm down since I knew he had some good tips for those and I was busy with Dylan."

"At the time, I couldn't figure out what was triggering it. I later put the pieces together while talking it out in therapy. Dylan kept yelling 'dada', and while I know we tell everyone that he is your son, and for intents and purposes, he is, but..."

"It made you think about his biological dad," he said, realization dawning on his face. "Oh God, Ren. I am so sorry. Why didn't you tell me?"

I locked my hands around my knees as I sat there, doing my best to steady my breathing so I could keep talking. "Because when I realized that, you were working on that really big project—ironically, the one that got you the promotion—and I did not want to split your focus. Look, Max, I truly would love to have a baby with you sometime in the future, but...I'm just not ready yet. I still need to work on so much of myself in order to be a halfway decent mom to Dylan and an okay wife for you. Adding another baby to the mix right now seems to be asking for trouble.

"Give me some time, okay? I promise, when I'm feeling like the timing is right, I will let you know and we can go from there," I told him, slowly reaching over to grasp his hand.

"I already think you are a terrific wife and mother," he consoled, a smile on his face, "but I can respect that. I love you, Renee."

"I love you too."

"Awww, and I love you guys too!" Nick said in a syrupy voice from the nursery door. "Now that you two seem to have worked things out, Ren, little man is all yours again."

I arched a brow in his direction before shaking my head. "I take it Dylan needs his diaper changed?" I asked.

Nick shot me a cheeky grin. "How did you guess? When he gets older I can teach him to pee behind the trees at the ranch like Max and I used to do."

Rolling my eyes, I took my squirming child from him. "You are vile."

"Not as vile as your son's pants, Ren," he called. "That smell alone is enough to make me not want kids for a few years."

Max and I each gave him a death glare while he collapsed on the couch, a huge grin on his face. "What? Too soon?" he asked innocently with a wink and a chuckle.

I headed into the nursery to change Dylan and heard Max smack the backside of Nick's head, followed by him saying, "You're an even bigger idiot than I am."

CHAPTER SIXTY-EIGHT

"I don't know who the bigger child is in this situation, Zane or Dylan," Annie muttered as she shook her head good-humoredly.

We were hanging out at the park with Dylan, who was now two-years old and a very active toddler, and the boys were running around the playground while Annie and I sat on a bench together. Max was busy at work with an emergency project, so he had sadly been forced to beg out of the afternoon of summer fun. All of us were clad in shorts due to the heat, the boys were in light-colored t-shirts, Annie wore a pink crop top, and I had on a baby blue tank. And with Annie's gorgeous legs on display, she was getting plenty of ogling looks as she sat beside me.

"Those guys had better get their damn eyes back in their heads before Zane sees them, or else he is going to permanently remove their eyes," she growled, catching yet another leering pervert checking us out.

"I hope Dylan learns to have more respect for women when he gets older," I sighed, shivering in disgust as the eyes of the men in the park rove over our bodies again.

Annie's golden gaze met mine with sympathy etched on her face. "Ren, between you and Max, to say nothing of all his grandparents, Zane, Nick, and myself, that little boy will likely grow up to be willing to lay down his life for any woman with no questions asked. Respecting women will come as easy to him as breathing."

"While I appreciate your optimism, I can't rule out the fact that his biological father was hardly respectful," I slowly stated. "Something that Niyah and I have been discussing randomly in therapy is how sadistic the attack was, like it was personal. Annie, there is a very real chance that his father was, or is, a sociopath. That shit is genetic."

Her hand came to rest atop mine. "I know, babe. You gotta have faith."

We both looked up to see Zane barreling toward us with Dylan giggling in his arms, both of the boys sweaty but happy-looking. Easy smiles came to our faces as they approached, my son's infectious laughter brightening the already blinding day.

"Someone says he's thirsty momma," Zane said with a wink. "And I am too, sexy," he added to Annie.

"We are in a place filled with children, Zane," I groaned. "For the love of God, keep it in your pants until you two get home please."

He chuckled as Dylan launched himself into Annie's arms, grabbing his water bottle that she was watching while I'm rifling through Dylan's bag, looking for his sippy cup. A frown furrows my brows when I can't find it, and I realized I must have left it in the car. Annoyed, I snatch my car keys from the bag and stand from the bench, bopping Dylan's nose with the tip of my finger.

"I guess his drink is in the car. I'll go grab it real quick," I told them, then started walking across the park.

It was the middle of the day, the sun was shining overhead, and my friends were directly behind me keeping watch over me and my son, and yet, I felt a sliver of fear skate through me. Doing my best to brush it aside, I picked up my pace and hurried to my car, with my keys clutched tightly in my hand. I had just unlocked the door and was leaning in to get his cup when I heard the footsteps behind me, forcing me to whirl around.

"Love that ass, cutie," the creep smirked, eyeing the hem of my shorts.

I gulped audibly and realized I was trapped between my car door and him. He reeked of stale cigarettes, sweat, and old beer, a nauseating combination that made my stomach roll with each breath that I took.

Looking up, I met his muddy-brown eyes and an involuntary shudder went down my spine.

"Please leave," I managed to say, but my voice was weak thanks to my uneven breathing.

He chuckled at my cowardice and advanced another step toward me. "Now, that isn't very nice. I just gave you a compliment."

"And I didn't want it, so back off," I hissed, my voice going up a couple octaves.

His body was suddenly completely blocking my path, his look menacing as he stared down at me with the car door pressing into my back. My entire body was trembling as I was wildly attempting to find Zane, knowing he is the only one I trust to help me just then. Just as his hand made a move toward my throat, I heard a shout behind us, and my heart sent up a quick prayer of thanks.

"Hey! Get the fuck away from her!" Zane roared, pulling the guy back by his collar by the end of his sentence.

"Is there a problem here?" a new voice asked, drawing all our attention.

To my left were two officers with the Amarillo Police Department, concern written blatantly on their faces. Their gazes go from me to Zane to the man sprawled on the ground between us before settling back on my face.

"Ma'am, are you alright?" the second officer asked.

Tears choking off my words, I shook my head 'no', sinking back against the car as my strength began to evaporate. Zane hauls the slimy creep over to their squad car and quickly, quietly explains what happened. In a matter of minutes, the man was cuffed and sitting in the back of their car, as he apparently had several warrants pending for his arrest.

"Mrs. Harris," the first officer said gently, "when you're up for it, we will need to get your statement about what happened today, but you can come by later."

I nodded in agreement, my eyes falling on Annie's approaching form, Dylan in her arms.

"Ren? What the h-e-double hockey sticks happened?" she asked, spelling the word so that maybe Dylan would not repeat it.

"He wouldn't back up," I whispered.

As the tears started anew, Annie handed my son over to Zane, and came to wrap her arms around me. "Oh, sweetie. You are safe now, okay. I promise." When I don't respond, I feel her look over my shoulder at Zane. "Maybe it would be best if we get you home."

"Yes please," I cried, still trembling.

It took both of them to get me in the car, because my panic spiked again as soon as I stepped near the door the man had pinned me against. Thankfully, Annie had talked with Max and Nick though, and learned the grounding technique Nick had taught me the year before, and she slowly began guiding me through the exercise once we were in the car heading for the apartment.

By the time we reached my front door I was calmer, but still shaken. Max was home and surprised to see us, then livid when he heard what had happened. He pulled me into his lap and held me, asking me over and over if I was okay while gently kissing my temple. The entire incident made one thing stand out to me though…

My battle with my mental health was far from over.

CHAPTER SIXTY-NINE

Two Years Later...

"**D**addy!" Dylan cried happily as Max walked through the door, abandoning his blocks on the floor.

I glanced up from my book just as he launched himself into Max's arms, smiles on all our faces as my husband held him close. Dylan was wiggling in his grasp, desperate to get down so he could drag Max over to show him the tower he had been busy building all afternoon with the new wooden block set Jerome and Brenda had given for Christmas.

"Hang on, buddy," Max chuckled, stopping by the couch to drop a kiss on my lips. "Hi sweetheart. I missed you today."

"I missed you too," I answered him, tucking my bookmark inside my book. "Did you have a good day at the office though?"

He collapsed next to me on the couch and pulled me into his side. His green eyes bounced between our happily playing son and my face, twinkling with contentment as he took in the scene before him.

"Business as usual," he said with a small shrug. "However, I have been approved for a conference next week, and the boss said I can take the two of you so we can make it a working vacation. I will attend the lectures during the day that I'm assigned to, and we get to go to dinner in the evenings. Plus, I will have a couple of extra days so we can explore and just have some fun as a family."

My eyes widened in surprise. We had not taken a family vacation since Dylan was two and a half, so this was long overdue. Even if Max would have to work part of the time, I knew it would still be a fun memory for us to cherish in the future.

"That sounds amazing, Max," I tell him. "Where are we going?"

"I wish I could say someplace more interesting, but Abilene," he said, rubbing the back of his neck. "I already looked up some of the local attractions, so we can take Dylan to the Abilene Zoo, the Storybook Garden, the National Center for Children's Illustrated Literature, and even the Discovery Center. They also have some really nice parks there too."

While a part of me was impressed that Max had already researched things to do in the area—and found so many that Dylan would more than likely love—another part of me felt as though my heart was in my stomach at the mere mention of where we would be heading. I had not spoken to her since my hasty departure from school, but after the way she treated me in the wake of my assault, I had no desire to run into my former roommate, Mira.

Abilene was her hometown.

"Ren, are you okay?" Max asked, breaking through my thoughts.

Sighing, I motioned for him to follow me to the bedroom, not wanting to worry Dylan with our conversation. I gently closed the door behind us, leaning against it as Max sat on the edge of the bed, his arms open and waiting for me. I walked into them, snuggling into his chest as I took a deep breath.

"Do you not want to go?" he asked softly.

"It isn't that. Mira was from Abilene, and I have not said one word to her since I left college after the rape." I paused, looking up into his eyes. "I guess I'm just worried that we could run into her there and she would give us hell about Dylan. You know she had no filter back then, and I would be shocked if she had one now. What if she started spouting off about him not being your son?"

Max pulled me closer and lightly stroked my back, his touch soothing me. "Easy there, baby. First of all, if Mira tried to come within one hundred feet of you, she would discover I am still just as protective of you as I was back then. She would not be able to say anything to you because of that. Secondly, if she somehow managed to say anything remotely similar to what you just suggested, we would counter it with the truth—Dylan is my son. It says so on his birth certificate.

"I may not have given him life, but I am his father. End of story. And finally, if Mira tried to cause any other trouble for you, I happen to know a fantastic lawyer who would be more than happy to help us press charges against her, plus a cop who can help us get a restraining order against her," he concluded with a wide grin.

I giggled at his vehemence, but he had made me feel much better about the trip. Kissing his cheek, I nodded in agreement.

"Fair enough, babe," I say, wrapping my arms around his neck. "I'm sure we will have a great time...even if we are just going to Abilene."

"Damn straight, Mrs. Harris," he teased. "I am just bummed we can't have two rooms up there because I would love to be able to ravish my sexy little wife. I guess there is always the shower if we time it right." He brought his lips right up to my ear, gently nipping at the lobe. "And assuming of course that you can keep your voice down."

I playfully slapped his chest, squealing as his lips connected with the sensitive spot on my neck. "Max!"

Dylan came running into our room a moment later, having heard my shriek. His eyes went wide as he saw us sitting together on the bed, with Max kissing my neck and cheek as he held me close.

"Mommy?"

"Hey buddy," I stammered, pushing away from Max a bit, feeling breathless. "You alright?"

"I heard you yell," came his little voice.

"Daddy just tickled me; that's all," I assured him. "Guess what!"

"What mommy?"

"We get to go on a family trip next week because daddy has a work conference," Max told him, a big smile on his face. "We will get to go to some fun parks and museums, and even the zoo!"

Dylan's eyes lit up with excitement. "The zoo? Will we get to see tigers?"

Max and I chuckled at his enthusiasm. "We'll see when we get there, sweetheart," I told him.

He went running from our room to his own, yelling about all the things he needed to pack for the trip, leaving my husband and me laughing and shaking our heads.

CHAPTER SEVENTY

"Mommy, look at that!" Dylan cried, dragging me to the fountain in the park.

We were exploring by ourselves while Max was finishing attending a lecture at the conference and then he would join us for dinner. It was our final day in Abilene and overall we had been having a blast with no hiccups to speak of. The zoo had been the highlight for Dylan; seeing all the animals had made him light up like a firework.

Thankfully we had not yet run into Mira during our stay, but as my son barreled toward the water, a woman on the other side of the park caught my eye. I felt my heart drop into my stomach as I realized she greatly resembled my former roommate, but no sooner had the notion registered in my mind before she turned and briskly walked away. I furrowed my brows at her odd behavior, certain she had seen me and that was the reason for her hasty departure.

"Mommy, there are fishies in here!"

Dylan's voice cut through the fog that clouded my mind, pulling me back into the present. I gave myself a little shake, and peered into the water with him, watching as the koi swam back and forth.

"Those are called koi fish, Dylan," I told him. "They are kind of like really big goldfish."

"Goldfish are yummy," he said with a giggle, referring to one of his favorite snacks.

"Yes, well, these fish would love it if you would not eat them," I laughed.

"Are we eating fish for dinner?" a deep voice said behind us.

Dylan and I turned to find Max standing there, his hands in his jean pockets and a grin on his face. His work polo with the company logo was fitted against his muscled chest and made him look great. I was glad I had worn a sundress since I was now feeling feverishly hot standing in his presence, and brushed my hair behind my ears to subtly hide my embarrassment at checking out my own husband.

"Daddy! Are you done with work?" Dylan asked, launching himself into Max's arms.

Max had knelt down just in time to catch his little body as he catapulted himself into his grasp, standing upright again once Dylan was secure in his arms. He laughed, pushing Dylan's fly-away fawn hair off his forehead and walked over to brush a light kiss on my cheek before he answered him.

"Yep, I am all done, buddy. You and mommy get the rest of my time."

"Does that mean we can take mommy for dinner now? She said she was crazy hungry," Dylan explained, waving his arms around dramatically.

Max arched a brow at me, no doubt wondering if there was something I needed to tell him, but I simply shook my head and gave him a small smile. His lips in a firm line, he held Dylan with one arm and draped the other around my shoulders, turning us in the direction of the car while our son kept talking animatedly. I knew we were due for another baby talk just from the look on his face, but honestly...was dreading it.

After dinner that night, we tucked a very tired Dylan in at the hotel and sat on the balcony of our room, just staring at the moon for several minutes. Max was the one to finally break the silence.

"Do you want to say it, or shall I?"

"Max..."

"I'm not pushing, I'm just asking, Ren," he said with a sigh.

I glanced over at him to see his eyes were closed and his facial features were slightly pinched, almost as though this conversation were the last thing he wanted to do. "I was going to tell you when we got back but..."

His green eyes snapped open and they fell to my face. I didn't know how to tell him because I knew he would be crushed. Hell, I had been and I was torn over the entire concept to begin with. I felt my eyes begin to water and I looked at my lap.

"Ren, are you…?"

His question hung in the air…like a knife to my heart. And the first tear rolled down my cheek.

"Sweetheart, this is—"

"I lost the baby, Max," I whispered, closing my eyes in pain.

The previous week, I had noticed I was not feeling well and went to my doctor. There I discovered the unthinkable: I managed to conceive while on birth control. I had immediately stopped taking the pills, but she had warned me there was still a high chance of miscarriage—which was why I had waited to tell Max. I did not want to get his hopes up until I knew I was out-of-the-woods.

Three days ago I had begun bleeding—heavily. After calling Dr. Collins, relaying all my current symptoms, and taking a home pregnancy test, I was able to confirm that I had lost the baby. She had called in a favor at a local women's clinic and got them to run my bloodwork for her. They had called with the results this morning to verify that the child Max and I had wanted was gone.

"I am so sorry," I murmured. "I didn't want to tell you until I knew for sure one way or another. I was hoping I could surprise you and tell you I was moving into my second trimester in a few weeks when I passed the danger zone, but…"

He came to kneel in front of me, gently wrapping his arms around my midsection. His eyes shone with unshed tears when he looked up into my face. "I don't understand. Did you forget to take your pills, or did you go off them?"

"No, I didn't go off of them, but I guess I must have forgotten just enough of them, or maybe it was when I was on the antibiotics last month for that ear infection," I answered weakly. "I stopped taking them as soon as I found out, but Dr. Collins had warned me there was a chance I would miscarry because of them. I...I'm sorry. I'm so sorry."

He pulled me into his arms as I sobbed, stroking my back and telling me how much he loved me. I let the worries that had been bombarding me all week fade into oblivion as his gentle hands held me: the guilt I felt over losing the baby, the fear I had felt at seeing the woman that looked like Mira, the questions that swam through my mind of where did we go from here. I knew that with Max by my side, I could get through anything that life threw at me...or so I thought.

CHAPTER SEVENTY-ONE

One Year Later...

"Renee, I want to read this one part that you wrote and get your thoughts on it briefly," Dr. Prajesh said, looking up from my journal.

I persisted in seeing her at least twice a month, and thanks to her guidance, I was a better wife to Max and a better mother to Dylan.

"Sure," I answered easily, crossing my legs.

"You wrote, 'I need to find an escape, an outlet, a retreat from the torment of my mind. Unfortunately, it's near impossible to extricate oneself from a prison composed of your own memories. Like the heaviest steel chains, they shackle you to yourself, forcing you to acknowledge their existence with every suffocating breath you draw.'"

She set my journal down on the table between us and met my gaze. "In the past five years, you've come a long way with your recovery and in reclaiming your memories of the night of the rape. The only major thing you've not been able to remember is the identities of your attackers. Before I ask you my questions, I would like to know what prompted you to write these words."

"It was after a particularly bad week of night terrors," I began. "It truly feels like torture to be able to go back into those moments, to feel their hands on me, to hear them speak, but to not be able to remember who they are. It's like being locked in a room playing the worst horror film of all time on screens built into every wall, and you can't escape it, no matter what you try.

"And Max is great, he's patient, he's loving…but he doesn't always understand that even all these years later, when I have a flashback or a night terror, I may as well have just experienced the trauma of the rape all over again. It's so vivid for me—despite the missing pieces. That's where the torture aspect comes in. I know that I know their voices, but for the life of me, I can't remember who they are."

I think back to all the conversations she and I had in the past few years discussing both my attacker and his accomplice—and the possibility that there was a female involved somehow based on the broken memories I have of a woman's voice in the background that night. I have told Niyah repeatedly how I cannot think of my rapist without feeling fear, disgust, hatred even, but when it comes to his accomplice, ironically those emotions don't cross my mind. I remember hearing him say he was sorry and feeling him cover me. He showed a modicum of remorse, even if he did not turn himself or anyone else into the police like he should have done.

"Okay, that's a great explanation for it, and very informative for anyone who hasn't dealt with this manner of trauma themselves, in my opinion," she said. "Do you feel like your memories, even though they may be fragmented, are suffocating you?"

I ran my hand through my hair. "There are times when I find it insanely difficult to breathe, and there's really no reason for it other than I'm having issues with my anxiety, or someone says something that reminds me of what they said that night. So, there's an actual, physical aspect to it, but I also meant figuratively. This type of trauma, this nightmare that never seems to end no matter how much therapy you do and how well you think you're doing, it can zap the proverbial air out of anything in your life if left unchecked."

"Very insightful, Renee," Dr. Prajesh nodded. "And I have to say, you seem to be doing a marvelous job at recognizing these things here lately.

You've grown significantly in the five years I've known you and are starting to show signs of empowerment in the way that you talk about your trauma. Have you felt like you've reached that stage?"

"Maybe to a certain degree," I concede. "I think I'm still struggling with things that hold me back too much for me to lay claim to being empowered just yet, but I will say I feel I'm on my way to being there."

She smiled warmly. "I'm glad to hear it. I haven't ever brought this up before, but would you ever consider hypnosis to help you regain those missing parts of your memories?"

"Do you think it would work?"

"It's difficult to say, but there are many who have success with it. Just keep it in mind, okay?"

I nodded in response. I didn't honestly know what else to say at that point. At this stage in my life, I had more or less come to terms with never knowing who was responsible for the rape. Sure, I had my suspicions, but no proof, and I could not exactly go around throwing accusations at the guys who had been in my life at the time. And Dylan looked like me, just with lighter brown hair that was almost the same soft shade as Max's, so I couldn't even base my theories on his appearance.

As far as Dylan knew, Max was his father in every sense; we had never told him anything different. We figured at five years old, he was too young to understand that his biological father was a sadistic bastard who had forced his mother to allow him to steal her innocence. And Max was great with Dylan. He's so loving and so involved, he may as well have fathered my son.

The only wrinkle to any of this was Max and I were continually hounded by others as to when we were having "another" baby. He was not shy about the fact that he wanted to have children with me, and how much he wished Dylan would have a younger brother or sister to play with as he grew up. I was still the roadblock in the equation. Despite my longing to fill a home with children, after my traumatic pregnancy with Dylan, and my miscarriage the year before, I was hesitant to become pregnant again.

I comforted myself that the last few "discussions" Max and I had had regarding more children at least had not been as bad as the time I had packed up Dylan and ran to Nick's with no warning. They had all been civil conversations, but nothing had been resolved.

Noting the time on Dr. Prajesh's wall clock, I realized I would have to bring that topic up during our next session since it would undoubtedly take longer than the remaining three minutes we had. Instead, we chatted companionably for those few moments about the weather, and how we were glad the heat of summer had finally broken, allowing for the cooler fall temperatures to roll in. What I didn't know, as I bid her farewell, was that something else was rolling in as well.

Something sinister, dark…and wholly bent on my family's destruction.

CHAPTER SEVENTY-TWO

"Mommy!" Dylan cheered, running to jump in my arms as I exited Dr. Prajesh's office. His little arms wrapped around my neck as he clung to me, hugging me tightly.

"Hi buddy," I greeted, squeezing his warm little body. "Have you been good for daddy?"

I peered over my son's ruffled hair to see Max's green eyes glisten with mischief, a smirk tugging on the corners of his mouth as he leaned against the trunk of the car. They had dropped me off for my session this afternoon and then headed across the street to play in the park while I was inside. That way, Dylan could run off some of his extraneous energy before we met up with Nick for dinner.

"He's always good," Max assured me. "Nick called and said he was about two minutes away."

"Perfect. Should we walk over to the restaurant then?" I ask, setting Dylan back on the ground.

At five, he has grown so much that he comes to my bust line since I am so petite. I can't carry him indefinitely, no matter how much we both might wish I could. He slips his little hand into mine, and we all set out for the little Mexican joint across the square, excited to see Nick for a few days.

We are halfway through the park when I first feel the sensation. The hairs on the back of my neck stand on end, and fear slates through me. *Someone is watching us,* I think, my eyes darting all around. Dylan has caught his first glimpse of Nick, waiting at the far end of the park for us, and releases my hand to go running to meet him. Max continues walking casually, chuckling at our son's antics.

I'm frozen in place.

It reminded me of the IMAX films I once saw as a little girl, where the camera panned in a circling loop around its subject, my world spinning wildly around me as I tried desperately to focus on the people passing by, looking for anyone who may have been paying too much attention to us. Nobody stuck out to my critical gaze, but still my eyes searched for anything—anyone—out of the ordinary.

"Ren?"

I swung my panicked face back in the direction of the boys in response to Max calling my name. His emerald gaze held mine, questions arching his fawn brows as he waited for me, hand extended, to join them. Nick had Dylan in his arms and the two of them were talking animatedly, my son clearly thrilled to have him back in town.

Giving myself a mental shake, I hurry to catch up with them, offering Max a small smile when I take his hand. His fingers gently squeeze mine as they lace with my own and I'm quick to return the gesture. *Surely my imagination is getting the best of me*, I think to myself. *Right?*

As we enter the restaurant, I cast one final look furtively over my shoulder, frowning as I see a familiar green Mustang pulling away from the opposite side of the square. I blink and look again, but the car is gone, leaving me to mull over my preposterous thoughts, a shiver running down my spine. The notion that someone was watching me settles like a lead balloon in my stomach, making me horribly uneasy.

All throughout dinner, the prickling sensation refuses to abandon me, and I get lost inside my own head as I attempt to unravel the minimal clues I had been handed. *Could I have imagined it? Or was someone truly watching us? And that car…why did it feel like I knew it?*

"Yoo-hoo! Earth to Renee!" Nick teased loudly, disturbing my thought process.

Dylan giggled as I tossed a chip at Nick's chest in annoyance. I had been oblivious to the conversation at the table, content to let the boys talk and carry on without me while I sat in silence. But I suppose that was too much of a difference for them to not notice.

"Okay, what's up with you?" he asked, crossing his arms over his chest. "For as long as Max and I have known you, you've never been this quiet during a meal. What gives?"

Max's green eyes travelled the same journey as Nick's cobalt ones, concern flashing within their sparkling depths. Dylan continued to color on his menu but paused briefly to look up and nod at me as well. *It must be serious if my son picked up on my silence.*

"Don't mind me guys," I say with a wave of my hand. "I'm just a little tired this evening; that's all."

"Ren…" Max drawled, rubbing a hand down his face.

"Seriously, I'm okay. I'm sorry I am not better company tonight."

"We're just a little worried about you," Nick countered, meeting my eyes steadily. "That's all. You didn't seem like yourself."

I try to offer them what I hope is a reassuring smile, but I'm honestly not feeling very optimistic. After a few more seconds of them studying me, they both reluctantly nod, dropping the subject. I breathe a silent sigh of relief.

"So, one of the things I wanted to talk to you guys about is my job," Nick said, changing the topic. "I've accepted a new position with the Amarillo Police Department."

"Really?" Max enthused. "Nick, that's fantastic!"

"It really is, Nick," I quickly agreed, proud of him. "Does this mean you're getting the promotion?"

He smiles. "Yes ma'am. You're now looking at Detective Nicholas Spencer."

"Congratulations, man!" my husband tells him, slapping his best friend on the back. "It'll be great to have you closer on a permanent basis."

"We can get back to watching the football games together on Sunday," Nick jokes, earning big smiles from Max and Dylan.

As great as the news was that Nick was moving to Amarillo and had gotten his dream job, I couldn't help but be apprehensive the remainder of the evening. Even as I readied myself for bed, I felt like I was being hunted—haunted, even—stalked by an unknown predator intent on my demise.

CHAPTER SEVENTY-THREE

Two Weeks Later...

Dylan ran ahead of me into our apartment, a grocery bag with sliced bread and potato chips in one hand and another with deli meat and cheese in the other while I stopped to check our mailbox on the way inside. I had nearly forgotten about the incident as we had headed into dinner with Nick a couple of weeks earlier, but something was about to throw it back into sharp focus. I set my own bags of groceries on the counter, along with the stack of mail, and returned to gather the remaining bags from the trunk of the car.

Ten minutes later, all the food had been put away, Dylan was curled up on the couch with a little book he was learning to read, and I was finally flipping through the letters we had received. *Bill, bill, junk mail, bill,* I thought to myself as I leafed through each piece, sorting them into neat piles. At the very bottom of the stack was one addressed to me, and right away it struck me as odd.

There was no return address in the upper left-hand corner, and my name and address had been printed neatly—almost too neatly—in the center. Stranger still was the fact that there was no stamp on the white envelope. I frowned, turning it over in my hand to look at the back, but nothing else about it stood out. I grabbed my letter opener and slid it along the top, my frown deepening when I saw what was inside.

A regular sheet of white paper—the kind one would find in a printer—had been meticulously folded in thirds and carefully stuffed inside the envelope. Smoothing out the creases, I was even more puzzled when I realized there was absolutely nothing written on it. I went as far as holding it up to the light, looking for a watermark on the paper, but nothing was visible.

No return address, no stamp, nothing written, no watermark, I thought to myself. *What the hell is this?*

Dylan noticed my expression and set down his book, coming over to where I stood in the kitchen. "Mommy, are you okay?"

"Huh?" I asked, looking down at him. "Oh…yeah, honey, just a little confused, that's all."

His brown eyes followed my gaze to the envelope and paper resting atop our table. Looking back up at me, he shrugged. "I found that when I came inside."

Panic thundered in my mind and made my heart skip a beat. "What do you mean, Dylan?"

"When I came into the apartment," he said again. "It was on the floor like someone slipped it under the front door."

I felt my mouth run dry at his words. *That note was dropped off by hand! Shit!*

"Mommy?"

"I'm okay," I whisper.

I quickly fall to my knees and pull Dylan into my arms, resting my chin on his slim shoulders. His arms encircle my neck as I close my eyes and do my best to steady my breathing. Maybe I'm overreacting and this is something from our landlord, and they simply forgot to print the page. Hell, I've done that plenty of times before. This does not have to mean anything sinister.

"Just…don't worry about this, okay, sweetie?" I say, motioning to the letter on the table.

Dylan gives me a funny look, but soon nods his head and trots back to his spot on the couch to read. Slowly, I rise from the floor, placing the blank sheet of paper back inside the envelope before I walk into my bedroom. I go straight to my dresser and tuck the envelope at the back of one of my drawers, propping clothes in front of the offending paper to keep it from being too noticeable.

I take five minutes to finish composing myself, sitting on the edge of my bed and breathing deeply while I try to picture myself beside a crystal-clear lake in the shadow of timeless mountains capped with pearly snow—my peaceful guided imagery location. I can hear the front door open and close, Dylan's excited voice greeting him, and I know Max has gotten home from work. The last thing I want to do is worry him. Swallowing down what is left of my anxiety, I force a smile onto my face and slip into the living room to welcome him home.

"There's my beautiful wife," he greets, pulling me close to capture my lips with his own.

"Eww!" Dylan cries, covering his eyes.

We both chuckle; smooching a little longer than necessary because of his dramatics. I slip my fingers under the knot of Max's tie, loosening it with a little wink while his hands come to rest on the sides of my hips. His eyes sparkle with desire, chasing away the panic that had plagued me moments before with lust…hot, unadulterated lust.

"I need to get started on dinner, Mr. Harris," I tease, still holding his tie.

His lips brush against my ear, sending shivers throughout my body. "Are you on the menu? Because I could definitely eat you tonight."

"Max…" I moan, feeling my panties dampen at his words.

Despite my hesitation over having another baby with him, and how our intimate lives began, there was no denying the sexual chemistry he and I had developed through the years. Thankfully, his words incinerated the darkness that had encroached upon me, setting me ablaze as only my husband could do. The letter was forgotten for the evening, safely out of the way while we ate our dinner as a family, got Dylan ready and into bed, and then as Max and I reveled in our alone time in our own bed.

That reprieve would be short-lived, as I was soon to discover. And no amount of lovemaking with Max, cooking, journaling, or running was going to save us from what was coming next. That blank note was merely the calm before the storm; the sign that I had never been forgotten by the demon who haunted my nightmares. He had found me…and he was coming for me.

CHAPTER SEVENTY-FOUR

Three Days Later...

I had just completed my usual Friday errands: dropping Dylan off at school, stopping by the office to deliver the reports for the entire week, grabbing Max's dry cleaning, my weekly lunch date with Annie, and finally, taking coffee to Nick at the precinct, arriving back at the apartment exhausted. Parking my car and killing the ignition, I grabbed my purse and keys, heading for my front door. I still had a couple of hours before Dylan would be done with school, so figured I would curl up with a good book for a bit.

Fate, it would seem, had different plans for me that day. Staring up at me from the floor of my entryway was an envelope, identical to the one hidden in my dresser. I gulped, reaching a shaking hand to pick up the seemingly innocuous letter, fearing that its appearance was deceiving. Upon opening it, I find yet another meticulously folded sheet of white paper...although this time, there's a message.

Looking good, Ren.

The blood drains from my face as I read and then reread those three little words written neatly in the center of the page. They make it abundantly clear that my intuition two weeks earlier was dead on the money—someone *was* watching me. And not just anyone.

I'm horrified by the letter in my hand and yet, I cannot seem to put it down. It's like a train wreck…you have to keep on looking. There is no signature, no clue as to who sent it, and yet, I know it must be from my attacker. *If only I knew who he was,* I groaned.

I nearly hit the ceiling when my cell phone began to ring inside my back pocket, where I tucked it upon exiting my car. The sudden noise in the void-like silence set my heartrate to a staccato. I pull it from my pocket, not even looking at the caller I.D. before I answer.

"Hello?"

I am met with silence on the other end of the line. For a brief moment, I wonder if perhaps the caller didn't hear me the first time.

"Hello?" I tried again.

Once more silence reigns. *No…that isn't exactly true,* I realize. There, so softly I can hardly hear it, is the sound of someone breathing. A shiver runs down my spine.

"Can I help you with anything?" I ask breathlessly.

A few more seconds pass with nothing but the creepy sound of breathing coming through the phone before the call ends abruptly. I stare at the phone in my hand, and then my gaze shifts to the letter in the other. I slam them both on the table and hurry to double check the locks on all my doors and windows. Once satisfied they are secure, I pull up my call history, only to discover the call had come from an unknown number.

Fuck, this is not good.

I know if I tell Max anything about this, he will completely come unglued. Swallowing hard, I pick up my phone and scroll down to Nick's number, figuring he might be able to help me in some small way or another. I bite my lower lip while I wait for him to answer, my leg bouncing uncontrollably with my anxiety.

"Hey Ren! Miss me already?" he teases when he answers.

"Nick…" I whisper, trailing off as the tears begin to pool in my eyes.

"Whoa, what's wrong?"

"I think he's found me."

"You think who's found you?"

"The guy who…"

I don't have to finish my sentence; he knows exactly who I mean now. I hear his swift intake of air and his desk chair squeak, and I can imagine he's sitting up straighter now.

"What makes you say that Ren?"

"That night we went for dinner, I thought someone was watching me then—"

"That's why you were acting weird?"

"Yeah," I admit. "And a couple days ago, Dylan found a letter that had been slipped under our door addressed to me. No return address, no stamp, and the paper inside had nothing written on it. I just got home about fifteen minutes ago to find another envelope on the floor addressed to me, only this time it had a message written on the paper."

"What did it say?"

"It said, 'Looking good, Ren,'" I said with a shudder. "And then someone called my cell phone from an unlisted number and just sat there breathing for a few seconds before hanging up. Nick…what the hell do I do?"

I hear a string of soft expletives leave his mouth. "Do you still have the first letter?"

"Yes…"

"Okay, good. I'm going to come pick them up and I'll see if I can get one of the IT guys to pull your phone records. Maybe we'll get lucky and the phone company can tell us who the bastard is, okay? In the meantime, I want you to stay vigilant, Ren. I will do my best to help you get to the bottom of this and keep you all safe. I promise."

"Thank you, Nick."

"Thank me when that fucker is six feet under," he sighed. "I'll talk to you soon."

CHAPTER SEVENTY-FIVE

It had been a week since the second letter arrived, and needless to say I had been completely on edge the entire time. So far, no new mysterious letters had been delivered or ominous phone calls had occurred, but I had noticed smudges on the outside of our back-patio window…like someone had been trying to peer inside. After that incident, I began keeping all the blinds and curtains tightly closed, garnering my husband's attention. As expected, he hit the roof when he saw the notes, and immediately began working with a realtor to find us a new place to live.

I had just finished dropping Dylan off with my parents for the weekend after running to all my other Friday stops, pulling up in front of the apartment later than usual since my mom had wanted to talk. Having scheduled an emergency session with Dr. Prajesh for this afternoon, I assumed I would be all talked out, but my mother conned me into a cup of coffee anyway, and I was surprised we conversed for nearly two hours in the sunroom.

Now, I knew I was barely beating Max home. Coming up the walkway, I noticed a long box propped on my stoop, a local florist shop's name proudly emblazoned on the cardboard in scrolling purple ink. A small smile tugged on my lips as I thought my loving husband had bought me flowers. Unlocking the door, I carefully picked up the box and carried it inside, relocking the door immediately after I set the box upright on the table.

I tossed my purse and jacket onto the chair before hanging my keys on the hook by the door and went to grab the scissors from the drawer. I slit the tape keeping the box together and set them down, opening the box to reveal the most beautiful white lilies and roses bouquet in a black glass vase. The vase seemed odd to me, but Max knew how much I loved lilies and roses, so I was prepared to overlook the monochromatic theme.

Then I reached for the card at the bottom of the box.

Suddenly, it was as though my breath had been completely stolen away. I wanted to scream, but no sound escaped my lips as I stared at the card—at the seemingly innocent flower arrangement—like I was looking at a deadly viper. And honestly, that is what they were. Beauty and elegance on one side, pain and torment on the other.

I know he's my kid, Ren.

The world around me began spinning and growing darker. I lunged forward, desperate to find something to hold onto. In the process, I knocked the vase from the table, sending it crashing to a million pieces on the floor.

My heart was thudding painfully inside my chest and my breaths were ragged gasps—like a fish out of water. Black spots danced on my sight, making everything seem hazy. From my constricted throat came a strangled cry before everything went black.

"Ren! Please wake up!"

I painfully lolled my head to the left, toward where I heard my name. Everywhere on my body felt like a giant bruise was forming, making me dread opening my eyes.

"Ren, please sweetheart, I need you to wake up," I heard him plead.

Max?

Even in my disoriented state, I could hear the tears in his voice. *Why does he sound so upset? And why does everything hurt? Fuck, this bed is hard*— My eyelids fluttered open, but damn did it take more effort than I thought it should. Finally, my vision cleared, allowing me to realize I was on the floor of my kitchen.

"Oh, thank God!" Max whispered fervently. "You scared me to death!"

With his help I slowly sat up, feeling woozy all over again. I risked a glance at the floor around me, seeing the carnage of the shattered vase and flowers strewn across my floor. I must have cut myself at some point, because the previously stark white flowers were now peppered with blood. I clutched Max's shirt frantically, feeling the panic rise once more.

"Max, we have to get out of here!"

"I've already called Nick, babe," he soothed. "We have to stay here until the police come to take statements and all that. Afterward, if you want to go, absolutely, we will head to a hotel for the weekend, okay?"

A shuddering breath hissed past my lips, but I nodded in reluctance. I heard a car screeching to a stop outside and the slam of a door seconds later and knew Nick had arrived on the scene. He bounded through our front door as Max was carefully helping me up off the floor, his eyes wide.

"Shit, Ren! Are you alright?"

"I don't know, Nick, how do I look?" I ask sardonically.

My eyes landed on the card that had come with the flowers, and my knees threatened to give out on me all over again. I looked up at them in terror, wondering if this madman knew where Dylan was tonight.

"Dylan," I whisper. "We have to get to Dylan."

"What on earth are you talking about, sweetheart?" Max asked.

I gestured to the card, hoping they would understand better once they saw it for themselves. In those simple, yet terrifying words, my attacker had lit a fire under me. They say hell hath no fury like a woman scorned, but they clearly have never seen a mother fighting for her child either…let alone a Texan mother.

"I will be damned if that son of a bitch lays so much as a finger on my son," I say with a hiss. "I'm done hiding and I don't give a rat's ass who he is, if he touches Dylan, I'll kill him myself."

CHAPTER SEVENTY-SIX

Nick clamped his hand over my mouth and dragged me toward my bedroom, Max hot on our heels. Glancing behind him nervously, Nick's cobalt eyes met mine with such intensity, I could have been knocked over with a feather.

"Would you keep that kind of talk down?" he whispered loudly. "Max and I completely get where you're coming from with that, Ren, but for the love of God, you cannot say something like that with other officers on their way. What if one of them had heard you?"

"I'm sorry, okay, I didn't think of it like that," I retorted. "But I meant every word, Nick."

"I know you did," he sighed, running his hand down his face. "Max, do me a favor and call her parents; tell them to pack up and get Dylan out of town for the weekend, okay?"

Max nodded, already dialing my mother's number as he walked into the living room, leaving me alone with Nick. His hard gaze shifted from the wreckage that was the black vase to my disheveled form, his eyes widening as his brows furrowed in concern.

"Shit, Ren, you're bleeding."

He reached behind me and grabbed a handful of tissues from the box on my bookshelf, gently pressing them to my temple to stem the flow. His hand stayed in place for several minutes, checking periodically to see if the bleeding had stopped before heading into our bathroom to throw away the tissues and wash his hands. He beckoned me to follow, reaching under the sink for the first aid kit he knew we kept there.

"What are we going to do with you?"

"I've been asking that question since the day we ran into her outside the library, Nick," Max chimed from where he leaned against the doorframe. "I still don't have a fucking clue to be honest."

Nick chuckled as he helped clean the cut and bandaged it, offering me a cheeky wink to help ease my anxiety. I peered over his broad shoulder at Max, who knew instantly what my inquiring eyes were asking.

"Dylan is fine. Your parents are going to take him to Dallas for the weekend. They thought he might enjoy going to the zoo and a museum. They're going to call us when they get there to check in, and they know to be on the lookout for anything suspicious, and to not let Dylan out of their sight."

I breathed a small sigh of relief. My baby—for now, at least—was safely out of the clutches of the monster who had done his best to destroy my life. Just then, a knock sounded on our door, causing my bravado to crumble. Five minutes ago, I was ready to rip out the heart of whoever was stalking me, and now I was cowering in my bathroom against the sink. Nick motioned for Max to move to my side while he went to the door, his hand resting on the gun at his hip.

Thankfully, it was his fellow officers, coming to take my statement, and check out the flower box. I was grateful to have both Max and Nick with me as I sat and recounted everything in detail to the officers, feeling their strength flowing into me as we sat on the couch. Soon, they were done, and encouraged Max to take me somewhere else for the night at least. Since the flowers had been delivered via the florist shop and not the actual person targeting me, our apartment was not classified as a crime scene, but I still didn't want to stay there another moment.

We packed our overnight bags and made reservations at a nearby hotel, locking up as we left. Nick followed us over after stopping to pick us all up some Chinese take-out since we were starving. Checked-in to our room for the weekend, I collapsed on the bed as the last of the adrenaline that had been coursing through my body abandoned me, leaving me weak as a mewling kitten.

"Okay, so what's the next step?" Max asked Nick, while shoveling in a mouthful of noodles.

Nick set down his carton and sighed heavily, looking far older than his twenty-six years. He leaned back in the chair, Max mimicking the action from across the small table where they both sat.

"As fucked up as this is going to sound," he said wearily, "we almost need him to make another move."

"Wait…what?" I exploded.

"I said it was going to sound absolutely fucked up, Ren. But right now, we do not have much to go on. Your insistence that you were being watched a couple of weeks ago, then the two letters, one phone call from an unknown number that did not last long enough for the cell company to be able to give us much, and now these damn flowers. It's a bunch of little, disconnected things that we can't tie to anyone," he finished.

"I *know* there was someone watching us that night, Nick," I whisper.

"And I believe you. I know you've got great instincts."

"Maybe start with that," Max suddenly chimed.

"How so?" Nick questioned.

"Ren," Max said, turning fully toward me, "can you remember anything else about that night that stood out to you?"

I closed my eyes and thought back to the restaurant, to the park beforehand, the hairs standing on end on the back of my neck. *What am I forgetting? I didn't see anyone in particular that stood out as suspicious, so—* My eyes flew open and I could feel my lip tremble.

"The car!"

"What car, baby?" Max coaxed.

"The green Mustang! I knew it seemed familiar, and I obviously can't be certain it was the same one, but it seems too much of a coincidence all this is happening at the same time, and then with all of his advances on me—oh God…I know who it was," I sob.

"You remember who raped you?" Nick asked quietly.

"Corey Foster…it had to be Corey," I whisper, my heart feeling like it had been impaled.

CHAPTER SEVENTY-SEVEN

"Corey Foster?" Nick tested the name, like he was attempting to conjure an image of the man by just saying it. He glanced at Max, whose hands were balled into fists, his face contorted with barely concealed rage. "Wait a second…that was the grad student who had a thing for Ren her first year, right?"

"Ren, what makes you so sure it was him?" Max asks through clenched teeth.

I bite nervously on my lip and rub my arm like I'm cold, realizing I never had opened up to either of them about what Corey had tried that night in his car. I knew that after the start of the second year—about a week after the rape in fact—Corey had tried to convince Max that I was nothing more than a tease and that he would be better off if he walked away from me. None of it made sense at the time, but now…

"Max, do you remember when Mira asked you out?"

"What the hell does Mira asking me out have to do with Corey fucking Foster?"

Shit…he is beyond pissed, I realized.

"Just answer her question, Max."

I saw Max roll those green eyes I loved so much at Nick's comment, but he turned his attention back to me and nodded. Taking a deep breath to collect my thoughts, I continued.

"I had messaged you because she was upset and then you asked me how Corey was because you had seen him in the hall of the business building and he seemed off to you. I made the comment I wasn't interested in him and asked you to drop it."

"I vaguely remember this conversation," he agrees. "Are you telling me he did something around that time to make you think him capable of raping you a few months later?"

"Yes…"

"Damn it, Ren!" Nick practically yells. "Why didn't you tell us this before?"

"Because I hadn't seen him in months so I thought maybe… Look, I clearly misjudged him and all, but I didn't think he would go that far!" I fire back, tears running down my face.

"What happened, Ren?" Max asked, his voice somber.

My eyes squeezed shut, sending another cascade of scalding tears down my cheeks as I think back to that night, and the fear that had gripped me as I sat in the passenger seat of his damn Mustang.

"He called me one evening, insisting that I go out to dinner with him," I start with a sigh. "I had already eaten and didn't want to because I was broke, and my truck barely had any gas, but he wouldn't let up, so I finally agreed to drive over to his apartment—"

"Why the fuck would you drive to his apartment?" Nick interrupted.

"Because he claimed he had just gotten out of the shower and he needed time to get dressed. He said that he would be ready to go by the time I got there, then we could take his car to go eat. Then, when I was ready to go home, I would have my truck available. It was dumb, but I could not think of any way to get out of it, and believe me, I tried several times to tell him I wanted to stay in my room. He was not having it that night.

"So, I ended up driving to his apartment, then we went to the pizza place a couple blocks over. He ate, I drank a Coke, and I was miserable the entire time. He had already made some creepy sexual innuendo before we left his apartment, and then, when we pulled up to it afterward, he started touching—"

"What the hell? He touched you and you didn't think I should know?" Max fumed.

"He was touching my neck, Maxwell, but I got the gist of what he wanted," I snapped. "I had absolutely no intention of going back inside his apartment with him, even though he was inviting me in and doing his best to be persuasive. I knew if I did, there was a good chance he would do everything in his power to get me to sleep with him. I had zero desire for that outcome to happen, so I faked a migraine and got the hell out of there."

We all sat silently for a few minutes, the guys absorbing the informational bomb I had just dumped on them. Max had begun lightly banging his head against the table, clearly frustrated over what I had told him. Not that I could blame him. Even Nick looked taken aback by what I had shared.

Max's eyes slowly rose to meet mine, and within their glimmering depths I saw so much regret. The dreaded two words were clearly circling inside his mind as they had been in mine for years… "if only." If only we had known Corey was a danger to me. If only we had listened to our instincts that night and not stayed apart. If only…I had told Max and Nick about what had happened between Corey and me months earlier.

How much of the pain and torment could have been prevented if I had just spoken up about the way he scared me? Would I have been raped at all? *But then, I might not have Dylan*, I thought. And while I would never choose to willingly allow a man to use—or rather, abuse— my body the way that Corey had that night, I would not trade my son for the world.

Dylan was the silver lining to the blackest rain cloud imaginable. And he was beautiful. I could see his little face in my mind, and while most of him reflected me—my big, brown eyes, upturned nose, fair skin, even my dimples—I now could see his father in him. *Correction, his sire. Max is his father.*

Nick and Max were talking now, discussing what we should do next, but my thoughts were elsewhere. If Corey truly was the one who had raped me, I knew it was only a matter of time now that he had found me before he finished what he began that night. The memories of his hand on my neck and the sound of the blade clicking open played on an endless loop, and I felt a certainty in my heart that these little stalking stunts…were only the beginning of whatever twisted and evil plan he had in store for me and my family.

CHAPTER SEVENTY-EIGHT

The next evening as Max and I were finishing up dinner at the restaurant in the hotel lobby, my phone began ringing. Looking at the screen, my face paled when I read the name UNKNOWN. I quickly rejected the call, only to have my phone start its incessant ringing two minutes later. I could feel the panic rise in me as I stared helplessly at the phone in my hand. Max rushed me back to our room upstairs, where I rejected the fourth call that had come through in ten minutes.

He dialed Nick, his face a mask of fury. My phone pinged, signaling the arrival of a text message. Since my mother had been sending me photos of Dylan all day, I was hoping it was her. I felt like I had been punched in the stomach when I saw that it was not.

I suggest you answer the next call, Ren. Or else...

I began shaking a leaf as I reread the text. And then, my phone rang.

Closing my eyes and releasing a shuddering breath, I answered. "Hello?"

Max's entire body turned my way at my voice, shock written in his eyes. I shook my head as I cried, trying to convey to him that I did not have a choice in answering the phone. Before he could comfort me, the sinister sound of breathing morphed into a voice...*the voice* that haunted my dreams and very soul.

"Good girl, Ren. I knew you would behave."

"What—what do you want?"

"I would have thought that would be simple," came the voice. "I want to pick up where we left off. But for now, I'll settle for telling you I left you a little gift on your bed at home. You should really think about getting better locks by the way. Night Ren."

And suddenly, he was gone. Leaving me a quivering mess of anxiety. I tossed my phone aside, collapsing on the bed as I sobbed hysterically into the pillows. Max carefully sat beside me, pulling me into his arms and gently stroked my hair and back in his attempt to calm me.

"He—he said—he left something on our bed," I stammered.

Max stilled at my words. "On our bed?"

I could only nod at this point, the emotions had overtaken me once more. Max picked up his cell phone and called Nick back, asking him to head over to our apartment with another officer if needed, but that he suspected someone had broken in and left something on our bed. I heard Nick promise to come by as soon as he was able with a report on what they found.

It was almost two hours later when he knocked on our hotel door. The look on his face was grim. He had a folder tucked under his arm, a cup of steaming coffee in his hand. Sitting at the table where he had been the night before, Nick glanced warily at me and pinched the bridge of his nose.

"I couldn't bring it here obviously, since it's evidence, but I brought photos," he started. "You were right, someone had been in your apartment. The back door was unlocked when we arrived—the lock had clearly been busted—and we know it was locked when we left last night."

He paused, looking at me with more worry. "Ren, you may not want to see these photos," he warned.

I knew he was trying to spare me, but at this point, I had to know what I was up against. Slowly, I eased off the bed to come and sit on the corner by the table, doing my best to steady my nerves with each step I took.

"Are you sure?" he asked.

I nodded, and he opened the folder. "We found a small box sitting on top of your bed, just like you said," Nick stated, pointing to the first picture. "It's what was inside the box that makes this highly unsettling. God, there is no easy way to say this, but it was a pair of panties."

Max stiffened. "What do you mean a pair of panties?" he growled.

Nick eyed me apologetically and flipped to the next picture, where the box had been opened and a pair of black, lacy underwear lay on the evidence table. I gulped, recognizing them almost instantly. They had been my favorite pair of panties in college, but I had thought I had lost them in the communal laundry room before I returned home when I suddenly couldn't find them anymore.

"Those were mine," I whispered.

"Then his note is right," Nick sighed, turning to the last photo, revealing a card that had been tucked inside the box as well.

Thought you might like these back…

She said these were your favorites, and now I'm wishing I could have seen you in them…

"I think I'm going to be sick," I say, rushing from the bed into the bathroom.

I barely make it to the porcelain basin before I heave the contents of my stomach in painful retches. *He's kept my underwear for over five years? I do not even want to think about what he's done with them in those years… they ought to be doused in holy water and then set on fire. Even then I doubt very seriously if that would destroy the evil he's sure to have imprinted on them in that amount of time,* I think to myself as I lean my head back against the cool rim of the tub.

It's only then that I realize what the second line of the note implied. There was a female involved in my attack; someone who knew intimate details about me. The nausea is back as another puzzle piece clicks into place.

Mira…my fucking roommate. She's the only one who knew that those panties were my favorites and who could have let anyone into the apartment. *Oh, dear God…she helped those bastards rape me.*

CHAPTER SEVENTY-NINE

Istagger back into the room, the guys cutting off their conversation as I enter. Max jumps to come wrap his arm around my waist and helps me sit back on the bed. Nick's eyes dart to the floor as my husband brushes a strand of hair off my forehead.

"Ren, are you going to be okay?" Max whispers.

I shake my head. "Mira…"

"Mira?" Nick asks.

His eyes lock onto mine and I can see the moment the piece clicks for him. I have never seen Nick look as pale as he does in this instant. Risking a glance into Max's eyes, I find he's still turning her name over in his mind, trying to figure out why I brought her up after all these years.

"Mira is the only one who knew those were my favorite pair of underwear," I said softly, unable to meet the gaze of either man. "She is the only one who could have told anyone that little tidbit of information. She also had a key to get into the apartment and was conveniently away that weekend. Mira let Corey into the apartment and let him—"

"Don't say it," Max breathed, his eyes closed.

I knew this would be difficult, when the pieces finally started coming together, but this? This is brutal. The pain—both mental and physical—is so intense, and not just for me. Sure, I was the one they attacked physically, but I know for a fact Max and Nick would have kicked their asses if they had been there. They have spent the past five and a half years with the regret of not being able to prevent the attack in the first place…to not keep me safe.

"Ren, Max mentioned that you remember a second guy in the room, and that it was someone whose voice you knew, right?" Nick asks slowly.

"Yeah, that is unfortunately correct. Why?"

"I was looking through a box the other night when I was unpacking, and I found something that struck me as odd," he said, folding his hands in his lap. "What do either of you remember about Roy Miller?"

"He was in our psychology class the spring semester before she and I even got together," Max states. "Then…wait. Didn't he die of an overdose close to the time this all happened?"

"Officially, yes."

"What do you mean by 'officially', Nick?" I ask warily.

"Roy never did drugs. He was from a good, middle-class family, had solid grades, I could go on. I happened to have several classes with the guy, and since our dads were friends, I went to his memorial. Seeing a picture of him the other night reminded me of his death—which I always found slightly questionable—so I decided to do some digging.

"Lubbock PD was not particularly thrilled I was looking into the case, but I managed to pull a few strings and got a copy of his autopsy records. And wouldn't you know, there were bruises on his body the coroner could not explain, but thought they looked like Roy had been tied with a rope or something. Add to that fact he was given an extremely lethal dose of heroin, and the site where he was injected was severely bruised as well, and I call that suspicious circumstances."

"I'm not following, Nick," I interrupt. "What has Roy's unusual death got to do with me?"

"Because Roy was in classes with Corey as well," Max finished. "Are you thinking he had something to do with her rape?"

"You said the second guy seemed somewhat remorseful, right? That he bothered to give you back your shorts after Corey—or we're assuming Corey—was done," Nick continued.

"Yes…"

"Roy was a good guy, but he still had his own demons. I happen to know he was struggling to find a way to tell his parents that he was gay. I also know he had a tendency to meet up with his boyfriend at the library in the west stacks," he said, looking meaningfully at me.

"Mira and I worked there," I breathed. "You think she caught him, or maybe Corey did, with his boyfriend and threatened to out him if he didn't help them?"

"That is exactly what I'm thinking happened. Ren, the timing lines up. I ran into him a couple of days after you were raped, and I knew something was wrong with him then, I just did not press him for more information. After that one encounter, Roy stopped coming to our classes, kind of like he was avoiding me. Since I was friends with you, that makes perfect sense because he knew he would not be able to keep that from me," Nick concluded.

"And you said he was supposed to help host the party at the apartments the night after and never showed," Max recalled suddenly, causing Nick to nod his head in agreement.

I sat back against the pillows in shock. I had trusted and liked Roy during our class together. He would often study with Max and me for the exams. The notion he had been involved made me sick all over again. Swallowing thickly, I looked up at my husband.

"Max…do you think Roy could have been it?" knowing he would understand.

His eyes flickered sadly. "At this point, I think anything is possible. Nick, do me a favor and don't be a cop for the next thing I say. If Roy was involved, he better be damn glad he's already dead because I would have killed him myself for hurting my girl."

"I had the same thoughts, Max," Nick murmured. "The only problem I see is this: we did not know who was involved at the time, meaning we had nothing to do with Roy's demise. I find his death highly suspect, and I would be willing to bet my badge he was murdered, or at the very least forced to take the drugs. So, the question is, who did kill him?"

None of us said it aloud. We didn't have to. It was painfully evident we all believed the same person, or maybe people, were responsible for Roy's death. And while a part of me was thankful he had given me back a shred of my dignity that night by returning my clothes, that did not mean I was okay with the concept of Corey killing him to keep him silent. Because I knew if Corey had murdered Roy, it was only a matter of time before he killed someone else that I loved.

CHAPTER EIGHTY

Max and I had both taken off work for the week after the break-in, staying in the hotel most of the time twiddling our thumbs or working with Nick on the case. It was now late Wednesday, and my parents had finally returned with Dylan, unable to remain in Dallas any longer due to their own jobs. Nick had volunteered to go meet them to pick him up for us, giving Max and I time to figure out how to break it to our son we would have to move.

Nick had my car while we drove in Max's SUV, with the plan to meet at the park down from my therapist's office in half an hour. Although it made me insanely antsy, I soon realized sitting in the vehicle was not going to work for me, and I needed to get out. Yet another of my fucking brilliant ideas.

Holding my hand as we casually strolled through the spacious park, Max was uncharacteristically quiet and so was I. He gave my fingers a gentle squeeze, pausing under a giant oak tree to tenderly stare into my eyes. I did my best to smile at him, leaning into his palm as he caressed my cheek.

"How the hell are we going to tell Dylan we have to leave Amarillo?" I ask.

"He will be fine. He's a tough kid and so long as he has you and me, nothing will happen to him."

"You always seem to know exactly what to say, don't you?"

He smiled softly. "I know things have been terrifying lately, Ren, but I want you to know how much I love you," he said, never breaking eye contact.

"I love you too. So very much, Max."

He closed the distance between us, wrapping his arms around my body and placing the sweetest of kisses on my forehead before moving down to claim my lips. I clung to his shirt, pulling him closer, even though there was barely a hairsbreadth between our bodies as it was. Max was my anchor—he had been for years.

We broke apart, slowly, both clearly dissatisfied with being in public and not able to rip one another's clothes off. I laid my head against his chest, listening to the steady rhythm of his heartbeat, and secretly wishing we were back at the hotel. While I had missed Dylan, this weekend had hardly been conducive to a romantic getaway for us, and we were long overdue. If I had realized what was about to occur, I never would have gotten out of bed that morning.

I would have nestled my head against his shoulder while he stroked my hair. I would have insisted we order in and watch movies in bed for hours. I would have happily made love to him the entire day through.

Instead, my world came crashing down around me for the second time in my twenty-five years.

Neither of us saw it coming, although I think we both expected it. One minute, the birds were chirping in the trees overhead while children played on the playground behind us, the next…people screamed, bringing our heads up to see the unmistakable silhouette of a gun being aimed in our direction.

Fear slated through me, freezing me to the spot. That's the thing about post-traumatic stress disorder they never tell you: instead of the typical fight or flight response, you get thrown another one. Frozen. I'm certain I looked like a deer in the headlights for the few seconds we stared down the barrel of the handgun, and I'm more than thankful Max had grown up hunting.

As shots rang through the park, echoing off the neighboring buildings and sending the birds to the sky, Max lunged sideways, knocking me off my feet. I impacted with the hard ground, a root from the oak tree smashing against my temple as I fell. Max landed beside me, face down, which I only knew because I could feel his warm body next to mine. I was so dizzy from hitting my head I could not move for several minutes, closing my eyes in hopes it would ease.

All around me I can hear the screams of women and children, filling me with horror as the seconds tick by agonizingly slow. The squeal of tires fills the air, followed by the sound of sirens approaching, and I begin to feel hopeful.

Slowly, I open my eyes, willing the world to not spin around me. I peer to my right, noticing Max is still just lying there, so close to the same root I had hit my head upon. *Shit, he must have knocked himself out when we fell,* I think, looking at his motionless body.

"Max…"

His name is a groan from my lips, soft and full of pain. I reach my arm out to stroke his shoulder, my fingers barely reaching, but I gently make contact.

"Max, baby, can you hear me?"

I can hear the voices of people drawing nearer as I struggle to sit upright. The second I do, the dizziness returns, forcing me to close my eyes again as I take deep breaths to force down the nausea. I crack my eyes open and peek at his prone body, unease beginning to fill me.

"Max?"

I reach my hand out again to gently shake his shoulder. *Why isn't he responding?*

"Max!"

I crawl closer, feeling the tears fill my eyes. I check his forehead for the place I assumed he must have hit it on the root, terror gripping me when I find nothing. No cut, no knot forming, nothing.

"Maxwell!" I scream, my voice sounding foreign to me.

Carefully, I push him to lay on his back, gasping in horror when I look down at him. The tears are pouring from my eyes now, scalding as they descend to water the ground below us. I want to scream, but this time the sound will not escape my lips.

His eyes, his beautiful green eyes, are closed. His body is still. Dirt and bits of grass and leaves cling to the front side of his jeans and even his light grey sweatshirt. But the shirtfront is barely recognizable now.

A giant hole is torn in the center of his chest and blood is coating the entirety of it.

CHAPTER EIGHTY-ONE

Istare at the blood covering his chest and the ground where he had lain, and I know it instantly…Max is gone. My hands reach for him, shaking uncontrollably.

"Max," I sob. "Please, no!"

I grip onto his bloodstained shirt frantically, my teeth chattering with each shuddering breath I take. My tears mingle with the crimson flooding his sweatshirt, but I know that nothing is going to bring him back. My husband, my best friend, my lover, my anchor…with one little piece of lead he was taken from me.

"Max!" I cry again, my forehead coming to rest against his as I hold his face in my hands. "I—I can't—I can't do this—without you! Please! Please don't—don't leave me," I whisper, my tears choking my voice.

Someone tries to pull me away from his body, forcing my eyes to snap open. I struggle against the arms, but soon realize I cannot fight against their strength, sagging as they hold up my body. When a paramedic and another police officer kneel beside Max's motionless body, checking for his pulse and sadly shaking their heads, I lose it completely.

My screams and cries become hysterical as I reach for him, desperate to hold him again. I hear the blood pounding in my ears, drowning out the sound of everyone else's voices. The officer holding me back is attempting to pull me farther away from Max, but my feet are flailing as he nearly picks me up to move.

Suddenly, I hear a shout break through the sound barrier my mind erected, and the officer holding me stops moving. My eyes are still fixated on my husband, unable to look away from the macabre scene no matter how much I wish I could. Until someone else pulls me roughly into his powerful arms, pushing my face into his chest to block out the view.

His woodsy scent gives away his identity. *Nick.*

I sob harder into his shirt as he cradles my body against his, his hand stroking my hair. My fists grip the material, afraid that if I let go, I will fly apart. It isn't until a drop lands on my hand that I realize he's crying with me.

"Nick…" I whisper.

"Shhh, I've got you Ren," he murmurs into my hair. "I've got you."

It is only then I remember that he was bringing Dylan to us. My eyes snap up to meet his as a new fear freezes the blood in my veins. I try to look around us, but Nick quickly takes hold of my face, refusing to allow my eyes to roam from his.

"Nick," I wheeze, "where is Dylan?"

"He's okay, I promise," he assures me, staring straight into my eyes. "When we pulled up and saw the police cars and ambulance, I insisted he remain in the car and left two officers with him."

I sag against him once more, relieved that my son was safe. I can hear someone approaching us, but again, Nick refuses to allow my eyes to leave the sanctuary and shelter his body is providing.

"Detective Spencer, we need to get her statement," the officer says behind us, his voice filled with sympathy.

"She can do it tomorrow, Thompson, she is in no state to give it now," Nick snaps.

"Spencer—"

"I said tomorrow!" he growls.

Officer Thompson walks away and Nick hugs me a little tighter. The sun has begun to set at this point, painting the sky as red as the blood soaked into Max's shirt. My trembling has returned, and Nick quickly looks down at me.

"Ren, I want you to close your eyes."

"What?" I stammer.

"Close your eyes and put your arms around my neck. I need to get you out of here, but I do not want you looking at what is going on around us. Easiest way to ensure that is to carry you out while you promise not to open your eyes until we reach the car," he explains, wrapping a lightweight jacket around me.

"Put this on, please, I don't want you scaring Dylan just yet with the blood on your clothes."

I slipped my arms through the sleeves as he pulled on one as well, zipping my jacket first to hide the crimson stains. My eyes drifted to his own shirt, once a solid white dress shirt, now smeared with Max's blood that had been on my hands.

"Alright, arms around my neck and close your eyes, please."

Nodding as I bite my lip, I followed his instructions. One of his muscular arms slipped around my lower back and the other my knees, and suddenly I was hoisted into his embrace. Obediently, I kept my eyes closed tight as he walked, feeling the hot tears slipping from under my lashes the farther away from Max we went. I didn't reopen them until he carefully set me down, his hands holding fast to my waist.

His cobalt eyes shone with the tears he was holding back, and I knew he was hurting as much as I. After all, they had been best friends since they were children, and now—thanks to Corey and maybe thanks to me—Max was gone. I swallowed thickly, wishing like hell I knew what to say to him.

Behind us, a car door opened, and tiny footsteps slowly approached. I launched myself at Dylan, holding him close and blocking his view as Nick had done for me. I felt the tears begin anew as I held him, Nick's hand resting on my shoulder. From his place in my arms, Dylan's little voice asked the question I did not want to answer…

"Mommy…where's daddy?"

CHAPTER EIGHTY-TWO

Nick settled us into the SUV, seeming more like our chauffeur than a cop from where we sat in the back seat. Dylan's eyes were wide, but so far, he had not cried. I was not convinced he understood what I meant when I told him Max was gone. How do you explain to a five-year-old child that the only man he has ever seen as his father is suddenly never coming home again?

We drove in silence, my heart pounding with every revolution of the tires. I felt so broken, so inadequate, so empty without him, and he had barely been gone half an hour. Pulling up outside his new apartment, Nick marched us inside, eager to get us to safety.

But would I ever feel safe again now that Max was dead? Would Dylan ever be safe until Corey had met his end as well?

I was not a violent person, but Corey Foster had ignited a powder-keg within me, and I was ready to detonate. He had taken my virginity—my innocence—my courage, and now, my husband. I would be damned if he took anything else from me.

Nick pulled out some spare clothes for me, gently pushing me toward the bathroom to shower and get out of my bloodied clothes. And, as I had the morning I had discovered I was pregnant, I fell to my knees in the shower, my tears mingling with the hot spray washing over me. I came undone, sobbing bitterly in the bottom of the tub.

It was several hours later when I finally managed to exit his bedroom, the gym shorts and sweatshirt he had given me to wear hanging loosely on my small frame. Dylan was tucked under a red chenille blanket on the couch, watching cartoons with Nick while they finished eating bowls of mac 'n' cheese together. The sight was comforting; bittersweet but comforting.

"Feel any better?"

I slowly met his gaze, his blue eyes filled with compassion and pain, emotions I knew were reflected in my own. Offering him a sad smile, I shook my head. Nick set his bowl on the coffee table to come and carefully pull me into his arms, my own locking instantly around his neck as I felt the tears beginning to pool in my eyes again.

"I called both of your parents," he whispered. "I didn't want you to have to worry about doing it tonight."

Tilting my head back, I let out a shuddering breath as I looked into his face. "Thank you, Nick."

His arms tightened around me. "You do not have to thank me for anything, Ren."

Dylan's show came to an end and he began to yawn where he sat. I disengaged myself from Nick's embrace, moving to kneel before my son's small body. Nick took their bowls to the sink, giving Dylan and I a moment alone.

"Mommy," his brown eyes filled with tired confusion, "why isn't daddy coming home?"

I brushed his light brown hair back from his face, doing my best to smile with reassurance at him. Biting down on my lip hard enough to have the coppery taste of blood fill my mouth, I felt the tears slip from my eyes as I continued to look at my son's innocent expression.

"Daddy won't be coming home, Dylan," I said slowly. "Not again, I'm afraid."

"Uncle Nick said he was hurt."

"He was, baby. He was hurt so much that he went to sleep, and he won't be waking up again."

Dylan looked at me, his brown eyes locked onto mine. "Is daddy with the angels now?"

I hung my head as my eyelids fell closed, the tears abandoning the space they had occupied. We were not overly religious—especially after everything that had happened to me—but we did try to make it to mass when we could. Dylan suggesting Max was with the angels brought about a new wave of agony in me, but also provided a soothing explanation.

"Yes, Dylan," I whispered. "Daddy is with the angels now."

His little arms went around my neck, holding fast to me as I stroked his soft hair. Nick walked over, a cup of steaming coffee in his hand for me. The mug was carefully set on the table beside us, and Nick rested his hand on top of Dylan's head.

"Hey buddy, how about I help get you tucked in tonight?" Nick asked quietly.

My son nodded, giving me another quick hug before taking Nick's outstretched hand and walking with him to the bedroom. With difficulty, I dragged myself from the floor to sit on the beige couch, reaching for the coffee he had left for me. I needed the warmth of it to thaw at least the frigidness of my hands. I knew the frozen depths of my heart and mind would take far more than one cup of coffee.

When Nick returned a few minutes later, I was still sipping the hot beverage slowly, having noticed instantly the generous amount of liquor he had added to it. I did not typically drink, but tonight? Oh, hell did I need the alcohol to numb the crushing pain I felt that threatened to send me into oblivion.

"Had to make it Irish, huh?" I murmured as he sat beside me.

"I figured you could use it."

We sat in silence for a few moments, his head in his hands.

"Ren," he whispered, his dark blue eyes peering up at me through his lashes, "I am so sorry I didn't make it in time tonight. I swear, I will do everything in my power to keep you and Dylan safe."

Setting my mug down, I allowed Nick to enfold me in his arms, both of us dissolving into tears once more. Apart from Max, Nicholas Spencer was one of the only other men in my life I trusted without question. I knew he meant every word. Without Max here to protect us now, I had to put my faith in Nick, and believe that when the time came, this time, we would triumph over Corey and his diabolical schemes.

CHAPTER EIGHTY-THREE

"**I**nto your hands, O, merciful God, we commit the spirit of your servant," the priest intoned, his voice grating on my nerves. "Though he was taken from his family too soon, we rest assured that Maxwell left a legacy of goodness and virtue behind, that will give strength to them in the days to come."

'Taken too soon'? He was not taken; he was fucking murdered, I wanted to scream at him. Tuning him out, I retreated inside my mind, thinking back over the past week. In the five days since Max had been killed, I had cried until I feared dehydration was sure to overtake me, nearly beaten a pillow to death, raged at the police during my statement, and felt like my heart had been skewered from my own chest...leaving a gaping hole just like what was on my husband's body.

Now, as I stood at Max's gravesite in my black dress, I felt numb. I was surrounded by family and friends who had been nothing but supportive for the past five days, but I may as well have been standing alone. The words the priest had been speaking did not register in my mind, my eyes focused on the casket containing his body. Nick gave my hand a little squeeze, snapping me out of my trance.

"Ren, it's over," he murmured, Dylan clinging to his neck.

One of his well-muscled arms supported my son's weight effortlessly while the other reached for my hand. He gently led me away from the grave, toward the limo waiting to drive us back to the funeral home. It was like walking through gelatin, each step heavy and made with effort with my mind so disconnected to the world around me.

Dr. Prajesh had taken the time to come to the funeral, for which I was immensely grateful, as had both of our bosses. I could not even fathom dealing with work currently, but I knew I would have to think about it soon enough since my job would never pay the bills. I slipped back into my silent, depressive state as we entered the back hall of the funeral home, lunch spread out and waiting for us.

A couple of hours later, the meal generously provided by the church was done and Nick was driving Dylan and I back to our apartment to pick up a change of clothes. My parents, along with Annie, had been helping me pack the place up, since there was no way in hell I could live there any longer. Even going inside for the half hour for our clothes felt like I was being stabbed through the heart repeatedly knowing Max would never again walk through the front door.

Nick had taken Dylan into his room to help him change and gather his clothes, leaving me alone in our bedroom. My eyes fell upon the bed, the same one where Max had patiently made love to me for the first time all those years ago, and the tears I thought I had finished crying sprang into my eyes once more. The blue bedspread was smooth and neatly made up to the pillows, just as it had been before we had left it the last time we were here.

Sinking onto the mattress, his cologne drifted to my nose, tugging at my heart painfully. I curled up on my right side, my arms wrapping around the pillow he used as the tears streamed down my face. Using the pillow to muffle my sobs, I lay there, the agony washing over me like a tidal wave of never-ending grief.

I could hear Dylan in the living room and knew I needed to snap myself out of my unrelenting sadness and change. Swallowing down the rest of my tears, I rolled over on the bed toward the bathroom, dislodging a small gift box from within the pillows as I went. It was the type of box that usually would contain a velvet jewelry box, and I closed my eyes in regret, wishing Max had been able to give it to me himself.

Carefully, I opened the box, revealing the expected navy-blue velvet jewelry box within. A small card fluttered out from the lid, its message giving me pause.

One for you and one for Dylan.

My mind was reeling. *What would Max have gotten for Dylan and me?* Confusion still written on my face, I opened the velvet lid, the blood in my veins turning to ice as I looked inside.

"Nick!" I yelled, the fear lacing my tone.

He came barreling through my door, concern plainly evident in his eyes as he saw me sitting on the bed, the box in my shaking hand.

"Ren," he asked slowly, "what's wrong?"

I handed him the note, seeing the concern morph into puzzlement.

"I don't understand."

My hand still shaking, I offered him the jewelry box. His cobalt eyes went wide when he saw the contents. And then his jaw snapped, clenching until I feared he would break his teeth with how firmly he was grinding them together. Anger flashed in his eyes like lightning flashing across the sky.

"Where did this come from?"

"I found it tucked in the pillows on the bed just now," I answered weakly.

The muscles in his jaw ticked again as the rage built within him. He closed the velvet box with a swift snap, holding it within his locked fist.

"I'm calling this in, Ren," he said, each word carefully enunciated with the barely contained ire he was feeling. "And I promise, he won't get to follow through on this threat, okay?"

I nodded, listening but not truly hearing. My mind was riveted on the contents of the box clenched in his hand, the contents that could easily destroy our lives. Corey had done it once already this week when he had used them to take Max from me. I knew the threat was not something we could brush under the rug.

Who would have guessed that small pieces of lead could have such power over an individual? With one, Corey had caused Max's heart to essentially explode in his chest, killing him almost instantly. Now, he was taunting me with two more…bullets he was designating for me and for my son. I had already lost more than I could afford to lose because of the first one…I would be damned if I lost anymore.

CHAPTER EIGHTY-FOUR

I was convinced Nick was going to embark upon a murderous rampage of his own after I found the box of bullets in my bed with how he ripped into the officers who responded. To say he was pissed that Corey had managed to gain access to my apartment a second time was an understatement. Livid did not even come close to describing his mood as he glowered at the other officers.

After I had given my statement, he called Zane and Annie to pick up Dylan and me, with the plan to take us to his place while he remained on-site. As he helped buckle my son into the car, he confiscated my cell phone, tucking it into his pocket with a grimace. I reached out, intent on taking it back, but Nick just shook his head.

"Not a chance, Ren." His eyes met Zane's, his fierceness returning. "Do me a favor and do not leave their sides when you get to my place."

"You got it," Zane answered. "I'll have my phone if you need to reach us."

"Renee, look at me," he whispered, drawing my gaze. "I need you to go back and pack up some of your things, okay? I think it would be best if you and Dylan got out of town for a while."

I gulped, realizing what he meant. *He wants me to run.* I knew running meant we might survive this war, but it also meant taking Dylan away from everyone and everything he knew. Looking at my son's wide brown eyes, I knew it did not matter. I would do anything to keep him safe and found myself nodding slowly in agreement.

Nick slammed the car door, allowing Zane to peel out of the parking lot. Twenty minutes later we arrived at Nick's, Zane and Annie practically rushing us inside from the car. Annie helped me throw clothes and toiletries in our bags while Zane stood watch at the front windows. Dylan sat on the floor in the bedroom, his little face full of confusion.

I hated this for him most of all. As a little boy, he did not understand any of this situation. Honestly, even I didn't understand it.

The front door opened with a bang, marshaling in an out-of-breath Nick, his blue eyes dark as a storm-tossed sea as they met mine. He rushed into the bedroom, grabbing his duffle from the closet as he went and haphazardly threw his own clothes inside. His hands worked frantically, tossing around necessities and within five minutes so he was ready to leave.

"Nick?" I murmured. "What happened?"

"We're leaving, and we're leaving now, Ren," he answered. "As soon as Officer Thompson gets here with the burner phones, we are out that door and on the road, okay?"

Burner phones? I couldn't help but wonder.

"Annie, as soon as we leave, I need you to head to the Westhaven's house and tell them I'm taking Ren and Dylan to a safehouse," he instructed my friend, grabbing our coats from inside the closet and tossing them onto the bed. "And then I want you to call Max's parents and tell them the same thing."

"Okay…" she said, her golden eyes filled with worry.

"We'll call from the burner phones when we make it to safety, but we won't call often so no one can get a location on us," he continued, marching into the kitchen to grab some snacks. "I'm going to leave you my keys, that way you and Zane can come over here to empty out my fridge later but try to not come by alone. The precinct will know you have keys and can assign an officer to come with you if you would like."

"Spencer?" called a man from the front door.

"Ren, you ready?" he asked me, grabbing the bags.

I nodded, quickly getting our coats and the food while Annie picked up Dylan from the couch. Officer Thompson met us at the door, a couple of phones in a plastic bag awaiting us. I glanced over my shoulder and noticed both my phone, as well as Nick's, were sitting on the kitchen table. With barely any time to think, Nick was escorting us to an SUV I had never seen, throwing our things into the back while I buckled Dylan into the seat.

"We'll talk to you all soon," he promised, tossing a wave to our friends as he settled behind the wheel.

And then we were speeding down the highway, weaving in and out of traffic as we headed north. The look on Nick's face kept me quiet until Dylan had fallen asleep in his booster seat, but I was desperate to know what the hell was going on.

"Okay, Nicholas," I said with a hiss. "Start talking. Why are we running?"

"Him killing Max and leaving a pair of bullets isn't enough of a reason for you?" he scoffed.

"No, it is, but I get the distinct impression something else happened after you sent us off with Zane and Annie. What was it?"

He sighed, his hands gripping the steering wheel so hard his knuckles began turning white.

"That bastard called your phone after you left," came his soft vehement reply. "He was not thrilled that I was answering your phone because he would have much rather tormented you with his venomous bullshit."

"Language, Nick," I scolded.

"He's asleep, Ren, and besides, I am too fucking mad to watch my tongue right now."

Rolling my eyes as I sighed, I rested my hand lightly on his arm, hoping to calm him enough to get an explanation.

"He was very explicit on what he wants to do to you, and to Dylan, and there is no way in hell I am sticking around to watch him make an attempt on either of your lives. I made you both a promise, and Max too," he breathed. "I plan to keep it, and that means I get you and Dylan the hell out of Amarillo before that psychotic ass takes anymore people I love away from me."

CHAPTER EIGHTY-FIVE

We headed northwest for more than ten hours, stopping briefly for Nick to pull cash from his accounts and to grab some extra clothes and food along the way. The farther into Colorado we went, the snowier the roads became, even though it was only late fall. Winding along the mountainous highways, we entered a dark forested area that was home to Nick's family cabin.

"Not many people even know we own this place," he explained as he drove, the headlights cutting through the darkness, "so it should make for a good bolt-hole for us. We cannot tell anyone where we are, Ren."

His warning was unnecessary, but I understood his desperation. This was our last attempt to get Corey off our trail. If we let it slip where we were, out here in the middle of nowhere we would be cut off from any assistance and be nothing more than sitting ducks. Our best bet was to ride out the storm for a few weeks and pray Corey lost interest.

The cabin was out past Aspen and was a charming four-bedroom affair in a small clearing in the woods, complete with a fully functional kitchen and hot tub in the back sunroom. Had we not been literally running for our lives, it was exactly the type of place I would have thoroughly enjoyed relaxing at for a week or two.

"How much further is it?"

"Maybe another half hour," he answered, glancing at the map on his phone. "Why?"

I offered him a thin-lipped smile. "Because I have been sitting in this car for the past four hours and I am long past stiff, Nick. I'm very ready to get out of here."

"Me too," chimed Dylan from the back seat.

"We'll be there soon, buddy," Nick assured him.

"Nick, how are things going to work with your job?" I asked softly.

He remained quiet for a few minutes, and I worried something more had happened before we had fled Amarillo than he had originally told me. Finally, he released a heavy sigh and glanced sideways at me.

"Both the chief and Thompson were standing beside me when he called your phone," he began. "They know he's threatening to come after you two. I had already filled them in on the entire situation a couple of weeks ago, when it became apparent he was back, so they knew I was going to remain involved no matter what.

"When they heard his call, they agreed you both needed to be out of town immediately, but there was no time to try and get you in witness protection, or anything similar. I managed to pull some strings with the chief and volunteered to be your security detail and get you both to safety."

I sat there, stunned by his words.

"They were wanting to put us in witness protection?"

"It's the typical choice in situations like this, but we did not think we would have enough time to get you into the program with the way Corey was acting. Next best thing was me getting you both out of the way."

"But…you still have a job to go back to, right?"

"Yeah, they aren't dumb enough to fire me over this," he replied. "And thankfully, because of my dad's law position and smart investing throughout the years, I'm pretty-well off, so we should be able to stay off the radar by using the cash I yanked on the way out of town."

"I can pay you back you know—"

"Ren shut up. I'm not taking your money." His hand reached over to lightly grip my knee. "I left instructions for them to finish packing up your apartment while we're gone, so you won't have to worry about that when we get back."

"You talk like we'll be going back to Amarillo," I said nervously.

"At some point, yes, we will. Us running…it's just temporary, Renee. You'll see."

We lapsed into silence once more, Nick focusing on the twisting roads in the dark. It was in the middle of the night when we finally pulled up in front of the cabin, and after he had checked to ensure it was clear, we stumbled exhaustedly inside, desperate to find the respite of sleep.

Over the next couple of days we slipped into a familiar routine, eating meals together like a family, Nick playing with Dylan to distract him from the pain of losing his dad, me writing in my journal in the afternoons since going to therapy was currently out of the question. Nick would go to the store for our groceries, and often would help me cook, and Dylan helped me with chores around the cabin.

Nick brought back stacks of books the first outing he made, some for Dylan, some for himself, and others for me. Since there was no television or internet, the books offered a much-needed escape from the day-to-day monotony that threatened us. And since Dylan was missing school, it allowed him to keep up with some of his reading assignments.

Once a week, we called our families for five minutes. The calls were never long enough to ease the building ache and loneliness we felt from being so secluded in the woods, but it helped them know we were still safe and surviving. It was something small, but it was a tangible thread of optimism in the sea of hopelessness we found ourselves in.

But I soon realized that even though we had fled Amarillo with the intent of escaping Corey's wrath, to avoid dealing with the inevitable backlash of what he had done years before…all we had done was replace the locale. We were still waiting, knowing that sooner or later, Corey would come for me, come for Dylan, and this time, we might not be as lucky with our escape. Our waiting might prove in vain.

And that thought fucking terrified me.

CHAPTER EIGHTY-SIX

One Month Later...

I sighed as I watched the lightly swirling snow outside the windows of the cabin, thinking of its purity in contrast to the fucked-up world I lived in. We had been hiding in Nick's cabin for a month now, and so far, the Amarillo police had not found Corey Foster anywhere. So...we had to keep twiddling our thumbs and waiting for a break in the case.

It wasn't that I hated being there with Nick and Dylan. It was that Max's killer was still out there, walking around free as a bird while my husband was gone. And there was not a damn thing I could do about that fact. It was slowly driving me insane.

My heart still ached with his loss, but day-by-day I found myself crying a little less, able to hear his name without completely falling to pieces. I missed him—and I always would. Max was my first love, the one who had stuck by my side when everyone else had run. Aside from Dylan and Nick, he was my everything—even if he didn't get to be my first time.

I could hear him in my dreams, telling me I was going to be okay. Telling me that it was okay to move on with my life and not feel the oppressive guilt of surviving when Corey had taken aim at us, even though Max had not been so lucky. I knew that if he were there, that was exactly what he would have told me, but that didn't mean it came easily.

Corey had taken—correction, stolen—so much from me through the years. My virginity, my confidence, my husband…

And now, he was stealing time from me as well. Time where Dylan and I could be healing from Max's death while surrounded by our family. Time where I wasn't fearing for my life. Time where I was at peace. I wanted it to end.

I wrapped my arms around my knees, leaning my cheek against my thigh as I sat on the window seat in the living room. My grey sweater felt cozy in the cool room, a fire crackling cheerfully in the fireplace behind me. Dylan had gone to bed over an hour ago, and Nick was working on some paperwork in the den, leaving me to watch the silvery flakes drift down from the heavens alone.

The silence thundered around me, a stark contrast to the constant barrage of thoughts rushing through my head. The only sound was the crackle from the flames as they licked at the logs in the hearth, and an occasional hoot from a nearby owl in the trees. It should have been peaceful. I found it anything but.

"Penny for your thoughts."

I turned to find Nick leaning against the doorframe of the den, his deep blue eyes glued to my face. His muscled arms were folded across his chest as he watched me, waiting for my answer. He looked so casual, so effortlessly confident standing there, earning a shy smile from me.

"Only a penny?" I teased.

"I am certain your thoughts are worth far more than a mere penny," he assured me, sauntering closer, "but that is the typical saying, you know."

I chuckled. "True enough, Nick. I'm just thinking about how much Corey has stolen from me, and how much I wish I could do something about it."

He dropped down on the window seat beside me, rubbing a hand over the stubble on his jaw. A sigh whistled past his lips as his hands dropped into his lap, his eyes peering into the darkness outside the window.

"I promise you, Ren, we are doing everything possible to find him and to keep him from hurting you again," came his ardent reply.

When his eyes met mine, the pain in their depths broke my heart.

Just like with Max, I had never doubted Nick's dedication or respect. I had never doubted he would do anything I asked of him in order to keep me safe. I knew Nick would go through the fires of hell for me, if that were required, and that he would do so without a second thought. That was simply the type of man he was and had always been.

Nick reminded me often of a bygone era, one of knights with chivalry, morals, and above all else, a sense of honor. The old feelings of physical and emotional attraction had begun to bombard me in the past several days, making me feel uncertain. And when I was already feeling so topsy-turvy from everything else in my life, the last thing I needed was uncertainty creeping in regarding an old friend who was currently trying to keep me alive.

I gave myself a little mental shake, tamping down the swirling vortex of emotions threatening to overtake my mouth, and gently squeezed his bicep. His eyes lit with surprise at my touch, along with another brief flicker of something indistinguishable before he forced himself to rise from the seat.

"I should probably let you get to bed," he stated, his eyes unable to meet mine.

Swallowing, I stood as well, trying my best to smile up at him. Before I can get another word out, Nick turns on his heel and strides from the room, shutting the door to the den once more. Slightly flabbergasted, I stare at the wood paneling through which he disappeared for a solid minute, feeling rooted to the spot.

Finally, I square my shoulders and march to my room down the hall, having to use every bit of restraint I possess to not slam the door shut in frustration. I could not even begin to describe why his actions annoyed me, but I was seething as I changed for bed.

This is ridiculous, Ren, I scolded myself as I stared at the ceiling from my place in the bed. *Clearly you have been locked away in the cabin for too long. Just go to sleep, and deal with whatever wayward emotions remain in the morning. Everything will be better in the morning after a good night's sleep.*

Too bad my dreams decided to not take a night off that night, but if they had, the revelations of the night might never have occurred. And since they were six years in coming, I'd say they had waited long enough.

CHAPTER EIGHTY-SEVEN

"*R*en, wake up," I heard his voice call through the haze of sleep.
I could feel his hands wrapping firmly around my shoulders, then running into my hair and stroking my cheeks. His gravelly voice repeating my name as he tried desperately to get me to awaken.

"Renee, you're safe. You're with me. Open your eyes now."

Finally, I was able to crack open my eyelids, my lashes fluttering upward to reveal the dimly lit room. Nick's deep blue eyes sparkled like sapphires in the lamplight as he hovered over me, concern making their color darker than usual. He was sitting on the side of my bed, his naked chest heaving like he had run into the room in a panic.

His large hands were cupping my cheeks, the thumbs gently caressing me in calming strokes as he stared deeply into my eyes. I could feel my lip trembling and the tears coursing down my face, the fear and adrenaline still pumping through my veins.

"You scared the shit out of me," he whispered, his eyes never leaving mine.

I frowned, scrambling to sit up higher in the bed, my cotton nightgown shifting with my motions. His gun was on the bedside table, the dull metal gleaming next to the softly glowing lamp. My eyes went wide as I looked at the firearm, and Nick was quick to turn my face back to his.

"I heard you cry out, Ren, and all I could think was somehow Corey had gotten to you. I grabbed my gun and ran in here, hearing you cry 'no' over and over. I can't even tell you how relieved I was to burst into this room to find you alone."

Realization dawned on me in that moment. I had been having a nightmare, and Nick had come to my rescue. Gratitude flooded my mind and I found myself launching into his arms, throwing my hands around his neck to hug him close. I could feel my breasts pressing against his chest through my nightgown but found I did not care as he crushed my body in his powerful embrace.

His face nuzzled into my neck while his hands slowly explored my back in soothing touches that seemed to ignite a fire within me. My fingers toyed with the dark brown hair at his nape, earning me a hiss from his lips. Slowly, his hands moved to tangle in my hair before lightly cupping my cheeks again, his eyes locking onto mine. Shivering, I licked my lips, the movement followed intently by Nick.

A sound like a strangled growl erupted from his throat, and his fingers tightened almost imperceptibly on my face. "Screw it; I'm done being virtuous tonight," he said with a hiss.

His lips crashed onto mine with a frenzy, sending my eyelids fluttering closed again as waves of insane pleasure streaked through me. Despite the fact Max had only been gone a month and Nick was his best friend, this felt right. The intense friction of his soft lips molding to my own did not feel weird in the slightest…instead, it had me moaning in delight.

Using that brief moment of opportunity, Nick slipped his tongue between my lips, running it sensually along mine. His hands and body gently pushed me backward, lightly caging me on the bed as his mouth continued to ravage my own. I was lost in a sea of passion and had no intentions of being found anytime soon. His hands roughly stroked my curves through my cotton nightgown, while still seeming to respect the invisible boundaries that lay between us.

Moments passed with us fighting for dominance over the kiss, our hands lost in each other's hair, tongues flicking and playing with one another, and the temperature rising unbearably in the room. When at last we broke apart, we both were gasping for air, our bodies reaching for each other in need. He rested his forehead against mine, his eyes shimmering as he met my gaze.

◇   ◇   ◇

"Ren," he breathed, gently shaking my shoulders.

Slowly, I forced my eyes to open to see the dimly lit room, surprise in my eyes I'm certain to find that steamy moment had all been nothing but my imagination. I could feel the blush climbing up my neck to my cheeks as embarrassment flooded my entire system while Nick's cobalt eyes studied me.

"Are you okay? You were crying in your sleep," Nick whispered, as he attempted to pull me in for a hug.

Mortified from the path my mind had taken on its own, I sat rigidly in his arms. Unfortunately, that did not go unnoticed by Detective Spencer.

"What gives, Ren?"

"You would only make fun of me, so let's not talk about it," I rush to say, keeping my eyes scrunched closed.

"Must be serious for you to react this strongly. Please tell me?"

I sighed heavily. "Fine, but don't...don't look at me." I swivel on the bed to face away from him and quickly describe the first half of my dream, how I had been having a nightmare and he had run in to wake me because he thought Corey was after me and then the moment turned surprisingly intimate. "You said you were done being virtuous and you kissed me."

I heard his swift intake of air and gulped, worried I had overstepped once more, but he simply placed one gentle finger beneath my chin to make me face him.

"You know, I have been waiting six years to do that."

I raised an eyebrow at him in question. He grinned at my puzzled face, but I was not about to let him off the hook that easily.

"What do you mean by that, Nick?"

He sighed. "Truth is, if Max hadn't decided to grow a pair and ask you out that summer while I was at the training camp, I was planning on making a move on you myself that fall." I felt my eyes go wide at his admission. "Both of us had a thing for you, Ren; Max just acted on it first."

Nick closed his eyes briefly before glancing back at me, a look of regret awash in their blue depths. "Plus, I assumed you liked him more anyway thanks to my own playboy ways back then, and that if I asked you out you would turn me down."

"Oh Nick," I sighed.

I reached out my hand and gently caressed his stubbled cheek. In college, I had liked them both at the start. I had assumed Nick was not interested in me because he was always surrounded by other girls who were so much prettier. Shaking my head in disbelief, I offered him a small smile.

"I never knew, but I'm glad I do now," I whispered. "So...where do we go from here?"

We both were silent for another minute. "Ren, as much as I would love to kiss you for real tonight, it has only been a month since Max died," he stated sadly. "I know he would not mind one bit if we got together, but out of respect for him, and for you, the brakes have to be applied."

"And then there's the other flaw in the system," I added, feeling my frustration return.

"Yeah. I promise, once Corey has been dealt with and we have waited a respectable amount of time, then we will have this talk again, say in a year, okay?"

"I can live with that," I assured him with a smile.

I just hope Corey lets me...

CHAPTER EIGHTY-EIGHT

Nick had just clasped my hand in his as we lay side by side on the bed, his thumb trailing softly along the back of my hand when all hell broke loose. My heart rate and breathing had finally returned to normal, his touch calming me…until my burner phone began ringing shrilly beside the bed. I frowned, rolling over to look at the screen, surprised to see my mom's name flashing.

"Hello?"

"Ren?" she rasped, her voice strained and full of anxiety, evident through the phone.

"Mom, what's wrong?"

"Oh, God, honey, I am so sorry to call, but there's a problem."

I felt Nick ease up on my back, his hands lightly gripping my shoulders to keep me steady and offer his silent support. It seemed like my heart had just dropped into my stomach, sending shivers down my spine as I waited for my mother to continue her disjointed narrative. Nick's warm breath tickled the back of my neck as he leaned closer, trying to listen with me.

"Your dad and I ran an errand this evening," she was saying now, "and when we got home, it was already dark. But Ren, the house…"

Her voice trailed off as she bit back a sob, the events of the night taking their toll on her. My grip tightened on the phone as I sat on the edge of the mattress, feeling my knuckles locking into place along with my jaw.

"What happened to the house, mom?" I asked through my clenched teeth.

"We came home to find the windows smashed in, the flower beds completely destroyed, and that's just what the police and us have found so far."

What the fuck? My mind is racing as fury builds within me. My parents have zero enemies. The only person who would have gone to such lengths to vandalize their home like this, is Corey Foster. My eyes close as my teeth sink into my lower lip, flooding my mouth with the coppery taste of blood.

"I'm so sorry, mom," I whisper, knowing my words can in no way make up to them what Corey destroyed tonight.

"Ren, this is hardly your fault, and I hate to even call you about it, but…" she paused, and I hear a loud gulp through the phone. "The police discovered a brick that had clearly been thrown through one of the windows, and it had a note tied to it. A note for you."

My heart stops beating for a second as I realize what she means. Destroying their home was not enough for that son of a bitch, he had to leave a bomb of sorts for them to find as well. Nick bristles behind me, and I try to tune out his soft, yet vehement, cursing.

"What did it say, mom?"

"Are you sure you want—"

"No, of course I don't want to know, but damn it all to hell, I have to know what that bastard wants!" I snap. "This has to end before he does any more damage."

My mother sighs heavily into the phone, the sound like a waterfall rushing over the edge. "I guess he's been trying to call your old phone and not been getting through and it's angered him," she begins. "He wants you to call him, Ren. He said that if you do not call him within twenty-four hours, this will just be the beginning."

"That motherfucker!" Nick says with a hiss as he leaps from the bed to pace my room.

I agree with him, but right now all I can think about is ensuring my parents are safe for the night, and then stopping anyone else I love from being hurt. As much as I absolutely do not want to do this, I know I must talk to Corey. The thought makes me nauseated beyond belief, but I know he is not going to stop until I do.

"What's his number?" I whisper, shakily picking up a pen and notepad from my bedside table.

Nick turns to me, his blue eyes wide and full of incredulity. Taking a deep breath, I write down the number my mother tells me, closing my eyes once I'm done and sitting back from the paper like it's a serpent ready to strike.

"Okay, got it. Are you and dad going to be okay for the night?"

"Yes, the chief is arranging for us to stay at a nearby hotel and have a couple of officers on standby," she replies. "Please, be careful, Ren."

"I will. I love you."

"We love you too."

She hangs up the phone, leaving me to stare numbly at the one in my hand. I grit my teeth and feel my blood pressure rise as I think about the amount of time and love my mother poured into her flowerbeds, into the house I had spent my whole life in, and how, in a single night, Corey Foster had managed to trash those memories and hard work for a single act of vengeance.

One he had no reason to be after, my mind screamed. My rage possessing me, I dialed the number on the notepad, waiting while that bastard's phone rang. Nick takes a step closer to me, but I hold up my hand to keep him at bay, not wanting to fight with him just yet. I can taste the bile rising at the back of my throat, threatening to overwhelm me with each technological ring.

Finally, I hear the telltale sound of the phone being answered, his raspy breathing coming through the line, sending my heartrate to a staccato. I stay silent, hating the fact he got me to do exactly what he wanted me to, all by terrorizing those I love.

"Well, well, well…" he says at last, breaking the silence. "I take it mommy-dearest passed along my message?"

"Of course, you son of a bitch," I hissed. "Now, what the hell do you want with me, Corey?"

"I thought you would never ask, Ren."

CHAPTER EIGHTY-NINE

"So, here's the deal," he spoke gleefully. "I think it's about time you and I had a little heart-to-heart, face-to-face, whatever you want to call it, don't you?"

"You are even more delusional than I thought if you think I ever want to see you again, Corey," I sneered. "But fine, you have my attention now, and I will meet you if it means we end this bullshit."

He clucks his tongue reprovingly. "What happened to the innocent little girl I first met, Ren? She rarely spoke to me like this, with fire and passion in her words, cursing at me. Almost seems like I was good for you."

I feel myself recoil at his words, my eyes narrowing to slits even though he cannot see me. My fist clenches the quilt on the bed as the rage cycles upward within me, and from six feet away I know Nick is seething as well. His arms are crossed over his chest, and he is struggling to not grab the phone from my hand…I can tell he's waging a war with himself by the way he's eying the device.

"You are good for absolutely nothing, you miserable asshole, and as far as I am concerned, you are nothing more than a waste of oxygen. As for the innocent part, you know very well you are responsible for ripping that away from me, and if I were not so anxious to get you out of my life, and the lives of the people I love, I would be more than happy to tell you repeatedly to go to hell!"

"I would watch yourself, Ren," Corey says, his words turning velvety soft and dangerous. "You know very well what happens when I get angry, and right now, you're pushing me to the edge. Now, I suggest you get that cute little ass of yours back to where this all began, because that is where we are going to finish it, babe."

Lubbock, I realize dimly. *He wants me to come to Lubbock.*

"Where exactly and when?" I ask resignedly.

"Good girl," he praises, like I am some sort of fucking lapdog. "I was going to give you twenty-four hours to get to Lubbock, but since today is Wednesday, I'll be nice and say be here by Friday at eleven o'clock at night. As to the question of where, we will meet out at the South Plains Gun Center. They will be closed at that time, but we won't be going inside.

"Do not be late or stand me up, Ren. You will not like the consequences. Oh, and bring my son, why don't you? I would love to get him to help me break you," he laughed sadistically before hanging up the phone.

I let out a strangled sob as I tossed the phone away from me, my hands clamping over my mouth to muffle the sound of my terror. Nick rushed to pull me into his arms, his fingers tracing lazy circles on my back as he tried to calm me. My hands dig through my hair, tousling it more than it was before while the tears streamed down my face, Corey's taunting words feeling like a punch to the gut.

"He will not get within one hundred miles of Dylan," Nick assured me. "I swear I'll make sure you are both safe, Ren."

"How?"

"Well, for starters, you sure as hell are not going to that meeting—"

"Nick, you heard him!" I cried. "If I don't, he's going to keep hurting everyone I love! I cannot and will not live with that on my conscience. I already lost Max because of this maniac; I will not lose anyone else!"

"And I can't lose you and Dylan either, Ren!"

We stare at each other, at an awkward stalemate. I know Nick just wants to keep us safe, but I cannot keep running. It isn't fair to Dylan, and it sure isn't fair to me. I am not getting the closure I so desperately need by continuing to run in the opposite direction. I have a chance to put an end to the terror, to the trauma, to the nightmare I have been locked in for the past six years.

I need to take that chance.

"Nick, this is something I have to do," I whisper, praying he will understand.

"We know where he's going to be now, Ren," he groans, "we can send the cops for him."

"You and I both know what will happen if the cops get ahold of him."

He sighs. "I don't agree with this, for the record, but fine. We will go in, but I am going to call for police back-up." His hand pops up, cutting off my complaint. "I'll give us a twenty-minute head start with him though. And Dylan is not going to be in Lubbock at all."

I nod, finally agreeing to his terms. Nick stands, preparing to walk away, but I grasp his hand to stop him. His eyes fall on my face, his brows quirking upward in confusion.

"Please," I murmur, meeting his gaze. "Please stay with me tonight...as my friend, not my lover. I just need to have you close."

His smile is soft and warm, as is his hand that cups my cheek tenderly and he soon nods his head. He crawls into the bed with me, pulling me into his arms and holding me throughout the remainder of the night.

Friday rolled around faster than I could have ever imagined. Nick had arranged for a Lubbock officer to take Dylan from me that morning, ensuring he would be far away from the proposed danger. Something at the back of my mind nagged at me all day, telling me it would never be that simple. Again, I wish I could say I listened to that little voice of intuition, but of course I did not.

I would realize my error all too soon, when Nick and I drove to the deserted location Corey had chosen for our meet-up. Nick waited around the corner of the building, ready to help me at a moment's notice, as I walked out to face the monster who had destroyed my life.

Only to find him with one arm around my son's shoulders, the other clutching a switchblade dangerously close to Dylan's neck. History was repeating itself...and like a fly caught in a spider's web, I was trapped.

CHAPTER NINETY

Dylan's eyes were so wide and full of fear—not that I blamed him one bit—and for a split-second, I was paralyzed by the terror that was turning my blood to ice. Even in the moonlight I could see his green shirt was splattered with blood and tears had stained his cheeks, and I knew with certainty that Corey had done something tragic to the officer who had been guarding my son today. I could only hope that Dylan had not seen whatever he had done.

"Mommy," he whispered, his timid voice breaking through the haze that clouded every part of my mind.

I slowly raised my eyes to meet Corey's, finding them already on me and gloating. He hadn't changed much it seemed in the six years since I had last seen him. His light brown hair was messy, and he may have tacked on a good twenty pounds to his frame, but he still looked like he could overpower me in an instant. His black jeans and red polo gave off the impression he was harmless.

The blade in his hand at my child's throat, and the menacing scowl etched on his face said otherwise. Swallowing thickly, forcing myself to take another step closer, I kept my hands in plain sight, indicating I was no threat. Corey's hands tightened on Dylan and the knife, stopping me dead in my tracks.

"Do you want to explain to me why you thought double-crossing me was a good idea, Ren?" he asked, his voice lowered to a sinister timbre.

"I am very confident I told you to bring him with you tonight, and you decided to drop him off with a stranger instead. That was not a smart move, babe."

"I'm here now, Corey," I stated, trying desperately to keep his focus on me. "Please, just let him go. You can have me. That's what you always wanted, right?"

I despised the pleading in my tone, but at the end of the day, if I was able to get my son away from the sadistic fiend who fathered him, it would be worth it. I was certain that Nick was probably debating how long to let me take Corey on by myself—especially in light of Dylan being here rather than somewhere safe—and hoped he would stay put long enough to get my baby boy to safety.

"You're forgetting something," jeered Corey, drawing my attention once more. "I already *had* you, Renee. Hence this little guy's entire existence, right? But I will grant you that I would far rather have you than him right now. Think we should let him head out into the desert? Maybe he'll run into a pack of coyotes."

As if on cue, a plaintive howl echoed through the darkness, with others soon joining the din. He laughed, the sound chilling in the stillness of the night. I had never been more convinced he was a madman than in that moment. And the fact that Dylan was still clutched in his slimy hands made my stomach churn. Despite the warm coffee-colored sweater I am wearing with my blue jeans, I shiver as wave after wave of terror continues to assault me.

"Let…him…go," I grind out through my clenched jaw.

Corey shrugged, loosening his grip on Dylan before shoving him forward. I hurry to catch him, snatching him away from the monster who would end his life without a second thought.

"Run around the building, baby," I whisper into his ear. "Nick is there. Do it now!"

He hugs onto my neck tighter, like he's afraid to let me go. I disengage his little arms and look intently into his saucer-like eyes, praying he will understand what I'm trying to convey. *Please Dylan*, I think, terrified he won't obey me for the first time in his life, and that it will cost him his future.

I manage to give him a gentle push in the direction of Nicholas, and mercifully, he sets out at a sprint. Corey is caught off-guard briefly by his sudden movement, and I take advantage of his distraction to whip out the pistol I had tucked in the back of my jeans. Taking aim at his midsection, I do everything in my power to not let my nerves show, knowing to do so allows him to gain the upper hand.

"Oh, aren't you cute?" he scoffs, tossing the switchblade into the dirt by his feet. "But do us both a favor and put that away, Ren. You and I know you won't be able to pull the trigger."

His hands slowly slip to his sides, and I struggle to keep my aim steady. I'm biting my lip as the anxiety continues to build like a raging hurricane, his words delving into my mind like a burrowing mole—intent on my demise. Suddenly, I find myself staring down the barrel of his own gun, his aim unwavering as he smiles maliciously.

"I came prepared for a gun fight too. And I think we are aware of how the last one ended..."

His implication is enough to cause the tears to spring to my eyes as I recall the sound of the gun going off, the jarring impact as my body went crashing to the ground, the gaping hole that was left in Max's torso by the bullet ripping through his body. My heart squeezes painfully, my breathing becoming labored, my hand shaking like a leaf on the wind.

"And while I may have been aiming for you last time, I admit I got a rush seeing Max bleed out like that."

Oh...hell, no.

"Why me?" I ask, meeting his gaze at last.

"What kind of question is that?"

"It is the only question I want you to answer right now," I snap. "Why the fuck did you rape me six years ago? Was it solely because I rejected you? Were you just that desperate to have sex with someone? Why did you do it?"

"I have a fucking gun aimed at you, and that's what you want to know?"

"Answer the damn question, you son of a bitch!"

"Because your innocent little pussy was supposed to belong to me, but you wouldn't get over your damn morals and just let me fuck you!" he roared. "I did it because I wanted to, and I knew you would not be strong enough to fight me off. That is why I fucking did it!"

I gasped; from shock, from disgust, from pain, from the crippling sense of hatred I felt bubbling within me. For a moment, my arm slackened, the gun lowering reflexively. His laugh reached the fearful hollow of my ear just before the sound of the gunshot.

CHAPTER NINETY-ONE

The pain almost did not register in my mind as I dropped to the ground with a thud. Then came the searing sensation and warm trickling of blood running down my side, letting me know I had been shot. From the distance, I heard Dylan cry out—Nick as well—and I knew they had seen me get hit. I kept quiet and still, hoping if I played like he had killed me I could turn the tables on him.

His shoes crunched on the hard ground, helping me know exactly where he was in relation to me. I pushed aside the burning pain and encroaching weakness, determined to finish this…once and for all.

"You son of a bitch!" I hear Nick rage. "Why don't you fight someone your own size, you fucking coward!"

"Do you think I'm afraid of you, Spencer?" Corey laughed.

He was maybe ten feet to my left now. I carefully peeked through my lashes, getting a better idea of what my next move needed to be as I laid there bleeding onto the ground. I still had the gun in my hand, and thankfully, the way I had fallen had allowed me to partially conceal the weapon. If I played my cards right, I had the advantage.

"If you aren't, you're an even bigger fool than I originally thought," fired back Nick.

Ever so slowly, I maneuvered the arm with the gun into position, readying myself. Corey had made a critical error after he had shot me: in his cockiness, he had turned his back to me. He believed me to be dead, dying, or unconscious. I was about to prove him wrong.

Doing my best to stay silent, I got to my feet. Nick had seen me move and engaged Corey further to distract him, which I both appreciated and feared. One misstep could lead to Corey taking aim at him instead, but so far, he was relaxing with his gun at his hip. I had tuned them out, trying to ensure I could do what needed to be done next…

The moment I cocked the gun, Corey's body went rigid.

"How in the hell…?" he began, turning to face me.

"Sheer force of will," I answered. "Something you will never understand. And I am going to tell you right now, Corey, although you thought you were breaking me that night—and you almost succeeded—and you put me through hell, you made one very significant mistake."

"And I suppose you plan to enlighten me as to what my mistake was?" he purred; his voice velvety, low…dangerous.

"Damn straight. Yes, you made me go through hell with everything that you did to me. Surviving what you forced on me that night has not been an easy task, and I may always hate you for that. You brutalized me, victimized me, stole my virginity, scarred me when it came to intimate matters, and let's not forget the fact that you got me pregnant.

"I have dealt with depression, anxiety, nightmares and night terrors… and that is just to name a few! But here is a news flash for you, dumbass," I said with a hiss. "I *did* survive, and Max *did* stay with me. Yes, I went through hell to get to where I am at today. I burned in the flames until there was nothing left of the girl I once was but a pile of ashes.

"But I did not stay in the ashes, Corey. I managed to rise like the proverbial phoenix, so messing with me—messing with my son—was the dumbest thing you could have done. Because now…you are going to burn right along with me."

I looked him dead in the eyes, my own narrowing. Nick was looking on, amazement in his eyes. It was easy to tell in that moment how proud he was of me, and of how far I had come in the years he had known me. Without him, I might not have made it though.

"So, looking at me now, gun aimed at where you should have a heart, I want to know one more thing," I said calmly.

"Just one?" he sneered.

"Yes. Still think it was worth it?"

I see his eyes widen and he starts to lift his hand holding his own gun.

But I don't give him a chance to get off another shot. I empty the clip into him, riddling him with holes until he falls in a bloody heap on the ground. The gun clicks as the chamber runs out of bullets, but I still squeeze the trigger another couple of times before my hand drops to my side.

At this point, I can hear the approaching sirens, and know that help is finally on its way. I drop the gun onto the ground, the adrenaline beginning to wear off and my strength feeling completely zapped. Dylan comes hurtling through the field to throw his arms around my neck, my arms going around him automatically, despite the pain returning to cloud my mind.

"It's okay, Dylan," I whisper to my son. "It's over now."

I'm angling his body away from the gruesome scene, letting his little face nuzzle into my neck as he sobs. Doors slam, and soon police and paramedics are rushing out among us. I'm stroking Dylan's head, trying to console him, trying to keep him from slipping farther into the trauma-induced nightmare he's being ensnared within.

Nick has flashed his badge at the arriving officers and is now striding over to where I'm huddled on the ground cradling my son. His hand lightly strokes my cheek before he helps lift us from the cold, hard ground, leading us back to the SUV we had driven out here. Keeping Dylan from looking at Corey's body is one thing, but my eyes continue to drift back to his bloody corpse.

And I realize I told my son the truth moments ago…it *is* over now. Max may be dead, but now, so is Corey. He cannot hurt us ever again. For the first time in nearly seven years, I can take a deep breath. I am finally free.

CHAPTER NINETY-TWO

Amidst my mewling protests, Nick gently takes Dylan from my arms, setting him carefully on the ground beside the SUV. I can see the worry filling his blue eyes as he takes in my sudden slouch, the blood pouring from where the bullet met my body. At this point, my strength has completely abandoned me, and my eyelids are beginning to feel heavy.

"Can I get a medic over here?" Nick yells, standing back up and facing the crowd behind us.

He pulls my son back, allowing the paramedics to rush to my side, but after that, things become a blur. I'm loaded onto a stretcher and hauled away to the ambulance, black spots dancing on my sight. I feel the slightest prick in my arm, and the warm sensation of medication rushing through my veins before I fade into oblivion.

When I come to, everything aches, and my mouth feels like it has been stuffed with cotton. I groan, wishing I could return to the comforting embrace of unconsciousness. The sound of pleather creaking draws my attention and I force myself to turn my head to the right, finding Nick easing off the couch, being careful to not wake up Dylan.

"Thank God," he breathes, coming to the side of the bed to grip my hand softly. "I have been worried sick waiting for you to wake up, Ren."

I offer him a sleepy and pained smile. "Sorry."

His lips brush lightly against my forehead, his eyes closed as tears of relief slip beneath his long lashes. The feeling of his fingers caressing my face is intoxicating and distracts me from the burning ache I feel in my side.

"I'm just glad the doctors said you were going to be alright and this whole mess is soon to be behind us. I already gave the police my statement, and since you were shot, they were pretty convinced it was self-defense."

I stared up into his eyes, the surprise drawing my lips into an "o" and knitting my brows together. The intensity of his gaze had me nodding in silent agreement, and I felt relief wash over me. I had not even considered what would happen in the aftermath of the showdown with Corey, but I was suddenly hit with the realization I had killed him.

It *had* been self-defense, since he was threatening my life, my son's life, even Nick's life to a degree, and he did shoot me prior to me emptying the gun into his worthless body. But I had taken the gun with me knowing I might need the protection, that he would stop at nothing until I was lying in a ditch somewhere. A part of me had known the only way this was going to end was for Corey to die.

"Ren, they raided his apartment here in town and found—fuck, this is hard to say—but they found a notebook I guess he had kept since college," Nick said slowly. "He wrote about everything."

"Everything?"

"Yeah. He talked about how you turned him down, how he wanted to take you to bed, teaming up with Mira, the person he got the chloroform from, coercing Roy to help…all the way down to what he did to you that night," he answered. "He even confessed to giving Roy the heroin to shut him up when he realized he was going to turn himself and them in. He wrote every dirty little detail in that book, according to the police. They even found a memory card in the book with your name on it."

I paled. "What do you mean a memory card with my name on it?"

He swallowed thickly; his blue eyes filled with regret. "He…oh God—he recorded raping you, Ren."

A shiver ran through my body, and I felt sick. My lower lip began to tremble as the tears flooded my eyes, blurring my vision. I thought Corey couldn't get any more despicable than I already knew, but Nick's words proved me wrong. As the sobs began to choke me, he pressed the button on the bed to page the nurse, knowing I could not handle anything else at that moment.

When she entered the room, compassion filled her eyes, and she quickly injected my IV with something strong enough to numb me almost instantly. Nick held me until I drifted off to sleep once more, his soothing touch tethering me to my sanity.

With the morning sun came mine and Max's parents, Annie and Zane, and a slew of officers from Lubbock's police department. Once my statement had been taken, they assured me that Mira was being taken into custody, charges of conspiracy, attempted murder, and assault being levied against her for her part in my rape, and for giving Corey information on my whereabouts years later. The notebook and memory card had been enough to incriminate her, and the District Attorney was confident he would get her convicted.

Nick and I were being cleared of our involvement in Corey's demise, namely because it was being ruled as self-defense, so we were free to return to Amarillo once the doctor released me. Three days after I had been admitted, I was being wheeled out to the SUV, my family more than ready for Dylan and me to be back home. The two-hour trip was grueling—despite the pain meds the doctor had given me—but soon enough we were pulling up outside of Nick's apartment once more.

It seemed strange that it had been a month since we had last been here, and things were so very different now than when we had fled to Colorado. But I held onto the hope that now that this nightmare was finally over and dealt with, I might have a chance at a normal life. I was certain it would still be a long journey until we all healed fully from the deep wounds Corey had inflicted upon us, but together, we could do anything we set our minds to.

For the first time in years, I was looking forward to the future without a black cloud hanging ominously over my head. I could now breathe without the crushing weight of fear suffocating me. I had finally found my escape from the prison the memories in my mind had created. And God, was it liberating to cast the chains that had bound me aside, reaching for the freedom I had fought for and won.

CHAPTER NINETY-THREE

Two Weeks Later...

"Well, Renee, it is certainly wonderful to see you again, and looking so relaxed," Dr. Prajesh said as I sat on the couch in her office.

Her chocolate-brown eyes smiled warmly at me; a gesture I returned easily. My gunshot wound was healing nicely, meaning the pain had been reduced significantly, allowing me to get around by myself easier these past few days. The only lingering side effect of this entire ordeal were the nightmares that still plagued Dylan and me, causing some minor exhaustion. But considering the other optional outcomes, nightmares and fatigue I could handle.

"I am certainly glad to be back," I replied, lacing my fingers together in my lap. "This past month and a half have been hell on wheels, but it seems to finally be over."

"Let's discuss that, shall we? I know things could not have been easy for you in the wake of Max's death—especially knowing what a crucial part he played in your earlier recovery from the initial trauma of the rape—to have to go on the run, and then come face-to-face with the man who stole so much from you."

I nodded in agreement. "You are correct with that assumption. I still find myself seeing something or doing something and thinking I should tell Max about it, only to remember with a crushing pain that he's gone.

Luckily, those moments are becoming rarer the farther out from his death we get, but when they do still hit, I'm fortunate that Nick has been so understanding of my emotions."

"Are you still living at his apartment?"

"Yes, for now at least. My parents are staying elsewhere while their home is being remodeled due to Corey's vandalism, and the apartment that Max and I lived at was emptied and rented to someone else already. I didn't exactly have many places to go," I said with a small shrug.

"I'm pleased you have had him around to help you during this time. Has Dylan responded well to being around him?"

"Nick has been in Dylan's life since the beginning, so they already had an amazing bond. Dylan sees him as a second father. He always has in fact. Not much has changed between them other than we spend so much time together, meaning they maybe are a bit closer than before. And Nick has been incredible with Dylan, making sure that he's okay, playing with him, stepping up to fill Max's shoes and covering for me while I finish recovering from my injury.

"I honestly don't know that I would have survived the past couple of months if not for Nick, so I am insanely grateful for his presence," I admitted. "He has protected us, soothed us both when the nightmares have disturbed our sleep, and just been there for us in general."

Dr. Prajesh smiled at my description of him, her hand holding her pen gesturing as she spoke. "Talk to me about how you feel knowing that Corey cannot harm you or Dylan ever again. There must be a great deal of relief in that knowledge."

"It's like the last six years I have been held under the water, struggling to break free, struggling to breathe…struggling to *live*. I hate the fact that Corey stole my virginity—my innocence—and so violently at that, then went on to steal Max from me, but the knowledge that he is dead, brings me so much closure. The answers I obtained that night when I stood up to him, while hearing them cut me deeper than any knife, finally having them was like hoisting a weight off me.

"Seeing him realize the moment that I was no longer cowering from what he did to me, and that I was strong enough to overcome the trauma he put me through, and then seeing his body hit the ground… I know it may sound horrible of me, but it was so fucking cathartic. I don't think I will ever be able to accurately articulate what that felt like."

She nodded, jotting a couple of notes in her files. Her eyes were thoughtful as they met mine again.

"That makes perfect sense, and while I completely understand your revulsion at the notion of seeing him die, the closure that his death brought to you probably will continue to unravel over the next several years. It took moments for him to bring your world crashing down around you, and even when you had rebuilt much of it, he managed to do it again. So, although his death brought immense relief initially, you will continue to heal and recover from everything that has been locked away within you for the past six years.

"Now, I am curious about one more thing," she said, a twinkle in her dark eyes. "How do you imagine things will turn out between you and Nick now that this is over and you both have admitted to having romantic interest in one another?"

I chuckled. "That is a good question, Dr. Prajesh. Honestly, I'm not sure just yet. I know he said we would discuss it once this matter with Corey was resolved, so I feel certain that conversation is looming in the near future. As for my own expectations, I agree we probably should wait a bit longer out of respect for Max, although I know his parents would not mind because they adore Nick as well.

"But I cannot deny that my emotions are leading me toward him. I know that Max would want me to be happy and for Dylan to have a father-figure in his life. Max and Nick were like brothers, and us getting together at some point in the coming months or years would not bother him at all."

"I am glad to hear you speaking so positively about all this, Renee. You know, when I first met you, you were this scared girl whose confidence had been ripped away from her so cruelly. And now, the aura you present is one of empowerment, of strength, of determination and hope. Never forget everything that you have overcome. It has certainly not been the easiest path for you, but it has made you the strong woman you are today."

I met her warm gaze and smiled in return, feeling in that moment, every bit as strong as she made me out to be. There was one last thing I needed to do to fully move forward with my life though. Squaring my shoulders, I knew I was ready to tackle anything else life threw at me.

CHAPTER NINETY-FOUR

One Year Later...

"Is there a reason you wanted to meet at Max's gravesite, over say, a restaurant, Ren?" Nick asked as he walked across the lawn to meet me. His tone was light despite the seriousness of what we were here to discuss.

I smirked from my spot on the ground, cocking my head to one side as he eyed the grass distastefully. He had just gotten off work and was still wearing his nice black slacks and blue button-up dress shirt while I was in a pair of jeans and a cold-shoulder peach blouse with my favorite sandals. Nick eased himself onto the lush grass beside me and waited for my answer.

"Well, I figured we should include Max in this conversation," I replied timidly, offering him a small smile. "This was something we put off for a year out of respect to his passing, and now, seeing as the two of you were such close friends, I thought it only right to talk this out 'with him,'" I finished in quotes.

Nick smiled warmly at me before nodding. His long legs were stretched out in front of him as he leaned back on his arms, his blue eyes locked on the words carved into the headstone. He looked so at peace in that moment.

"You know, as enamored by you as I have been since the day you literally fell into our arms," he said, eyes still focused on the carved marble, "I have both been dreading and elated to have this talk with you since that night in the cabin."

I cast him a sidelong look, puzzlement on my face. "And why is that, Detective?"

"I guess because I just figured that there was too much history between us for you and I to work. You were married to my best friend, Renee, and God knows how much Max loved you and vice versa. I can't, and never will try to compete with what the two of you had. And then there is the shit that you and I went through in the aftermath of Max's murder."

"Yeah," I breathe out, knowing it is taking everything in him to be admitting all this to me.

His hand reached over to lightly entwine itself with mine on the ground, drawing my gaze into the stormy blue of his eyes. "But I know that there is not another woman in the world that I respect more, or would be more willing to lay down my life to protect than you."

"And what about going out for dates or sharing the last piece of cheesecake?" I asked, a hopeful glimmer in my voice.

Nick grinned and cupped my cheeks as he leaned over me, his face shining with love and sincerity. "I would love nothing more than to take you out for dates, babygirl. And as for the cheesecake," he whispered, sending me a panty-dropping smirk, "for you, I would gladly give up the last slice."

I felt the tears prick in my eyes as his nose brushed lightly against mine, his thumbs stroking my cheeks. My teeth had sunk into my lip, something he noticed with those sharp eyes of his. One of his thumbs gently worked my lip out from my teeth, tsking me as he did.

"Easy there; we wouldn't want you to damage that sweet little lip now, would we?" he asked, his voice husky.

Looking up at him through my lashes, I couldn't help but prod him. "Are you going to volunteer to bite it for me?"

A strangled noise—sounding very much like a growl—erupted from the back of his throat as he stared at me with lust-filled eyes, and I knew he was trying desperately to keep himself in check.

"We need to make a decision about us and we need to make it right fucking now," he moaned, closing his eyes.

"Nick...you have been there for Dylan and for me so much during this past year," I whispered, stroking his whisker-roughened cheek. "You have always stood by us, even when Max was still in the picture. A part of us will always love him, but I also know that he would want me to be happy; to move on with my life. You are always going to be a part of our future, but I would much rather call you my partner or lover, rather than just a frie—"

My words were cut off as his lips met mine passionately. His hands were tangled in my hair, keeping me close as his tongue slid along my lower lip, entreating me for entry. With the first flick of his tongue against mine, I realized how much the dream paled in comparison to reality. The kiss I had imagined a year ago in the cabin was nothing compared to this.

Fireworks were exploding within my entire body as he tenderly held me, his lips molding perfectly to mine. When we both finally broke apart, we were breathing heavily, hands clutching wildly to each other as we came down from our high. Nick rested his forehead against mine, chuckling lightly.

"What is so damn funny, Spencer?"

"I am just so fucking happy, Ren," he told me, a broad smile showing off his straight white teeth. "And I cannot wait to tell my sister that you and I are dating because I can guarantee Allison will hit the roof with excitement."

I giggled, knowing full-well he was right. "Yes, she will. And so will a certain little boy."

"Dylan is going to be happy about this?" he asked, his eyes widening slightly.

Nodding, I gave him a small smile. "He has been a little unsure what all was going on between us since we all moved in together after Max died and we came back to Amarillo," I explained. "He didn't want to say anything to you about it because you had been so great with him, but he mentioned it a few times to me that he was worried you were getting tired of him being around, or if you and I were ever going to get married like Max and I were."

"How could Dylan ever think I would be tired of him being around?" Nick sadly asked.

"He's six. He can be loud, you know. And we uprooted you from your new apartment...twice. He had some justifiable concerns but I set him straight. He loves you, so for him to know that we are together I think will give him a sense of stability."

After thinking about it for a moment, Nick nodded in agreement. "I suppose that makes sense. And I am not going anywhere, babygirl," he said, wrapping his arms around my waist.

"Promise?"

"I promise."

"Care to seal it with a kiss?" I teased.

He chuckled. "Come here you minx."

And seal it with a kiss we did.

EPILOGUE

Three Years Later...

"Mom, Rhett and Adisyn are crying again," Dylan whined.

"I can hear that, Dylan. Will you go get out their bottles while I change them please?"

He bobbed his nine-year-old head and moved to the kitchen while I headed for the nursery in our house. *So much for starting dinner early tonight,* I thought with a sigh. I smiled tiredly at my seven-week-old twins, still on their backs in their cribs as they wailed.

"Mommy's here guys," I crooned, scooping up Rhett first.

Adisyn heard my voice and her little face searched for me in the room, along with her twin brother. I had barely finished changing Rhett's diaper and redressing him when I felt a presence behind me, a large hand cupping my hip.

"And how is my lovely wife this evening?"

I turned to Nick and smiled, handing him our son so I could pick up Adisyn next. He snuggled Rhett in his arms before leaning down to kiss my cheek.

"Eww! Do you guys have to do that?" Dylan gagged as he entered the room and handed Nick a bottle for Rhett.

We rolled our eyes at his theatrics, knowing it was not all that long ago he was encouraging us to be lovey-dovey with one another. It gave him a sense of normalcy after Max had died. I finished changing Adisyn and took the bottle Dylan had made for her, popping it into her mouth as I cradled her tiny body in my arms.

Nick and I had been married for almost eighteen months now, and things were going smoothly for us as a family. Dylan had three official sets of grandparents who loved and cherished him, and now younger siblings to love as well. Finding out we were expecting twins with our first pregnancy had floored us both, but my new husband was over the moon to not only have the opportunity to be a father to Dylan, but to two children of his own.

We had flirted with the notion of naming our son after Max, but Brenda had requested we not. While she was fine with Nick and I being married and having children of our own, the pain of losing her only child was still too agonizing for her to hear his name. We understood and respected her wishes, naming him Rhett James instead, and our baby girl Adisyn Faith.

Dylan has mercifully had few issues of late regarding what Corey did to him or us. I am sure at some point we will need to have an in-depth discussion about who Corey was for him and what that means for my son, but for now, we are simply living in the present. My nightmares have mostly stopped as well, for which I am immeasurably thankful.

Corey Foster may have stolen my innocence, my first husband, and robbed me of so many other firsts, leaving me covered in literal and figurative scars. I am so glad that scars do not indicate the direction our lives are forced to travel. That I did not have to be held down by the weight of their significance for the rest of my life.

The scars he imprinted on me will never vanish, always acting as a reminder of where I have been, of what I have overcome. But they also show that I am stronger than people ever believed possible. So much in life can be stolen from us. It is our responsibility to take back what we can, ensuring that our story will endure.

My innocence was stolen, but in the embers of my life that remained, I discovered myself.

ACKNOWLEDGMENTS

Thank you to my family for supporting me in writing this story.

ABOUT THE AUTHOR

While originally planning to pursue work as a zoologist, author Emberlyn Grace has always been captivated by literature. Some of her earliest, and favorite, childhood memories included reading with her mother and older sister. Emberlyn has been married to her college sweetheart, Mark, for more than a decade, happily homeschools her three children, and has a wide range of animals under her care. In her spare time, she enjoys reading, cooking and baking, and spending time with her busy family.

RESOURCES

End Rape on Campus (https://endrapeoncampus.org)

National Sexual Assault Resource Center (https://nsvrc.org)

National Mental Health Hotline (https://mentalhealthhotline.org or 866-903-3787)